CW01426151

JUNKYARD VETERANS

JAMIE MCFARLANE

PREFACE

FREE DOWNLOAD

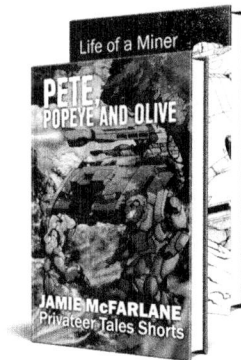

Sign up for my newsletter and receive a free Jamie McFarlane starter library.

To get started, please visit:

http://www.fickledragon.com

ONE

BAYOU

Muddy water dripped down Albert Jenkins' face as he breached the bayou's surface. A waxing moon spread little light onto the shoreline. His target, a dilapidated wooden cabin, had a single bare yellow light-bulb spreading a murky glow toward the water's edge. Next to him, Darnell Jackson slowly emerged from the water.

A plastic toy boat putted silently across the water's smooth surface. A tiny woman, no taller than six inches, sat behind the helm. She turned a wooden wheel and drove up next to them. AJ closed his eyes and shook his head. Beverly, his Beltigersk symbiotic guest, was not really in the small boat she was projecting, but had taken up residence inside his body and was interfacing with his visual cortex – and other things he preferred not to think about. The boat was, in fact, just a very convincing hallucination.

"Any sign?" AJ articulated subvocally.

"There is no sign of Cheell within the vicinity, Captain," Beverly reported, standing up from behind the boat's helm and saluting smartly. She wore a navy blue, mid-thigh dress with a white-trimmed hem and large white lapels. Her sailor-girl outfit was completed by a white cap. He smiled despite the circumstances. There seemed to be no end to Beverly's creativity with exploring the pop culture of different eras.

"Lefty isn't gonna love us sneaking up on him," Darnell said, utilizing subvocal communications with his own new Beltigersk rider, Petey.

A green dot appeared on the water in front of AJ, its reflected echo drawing a dot on his forehead. At the same moment, an overinflated, yellow inner tube appeared connected to Beverly's boat with a towrope. Atop the innertube sat a six-inch tall woman wearing Daisy Dukes and a tied-off halter top, her long dark hair trailing behind as if in a strong wind.

"Lefty wants to know if he should take the shot or if you boys are just looking for a couple of brews," Rebel asked. Rebel was Lefty Johnson's Beltigersk symbiote.

"When'd he make us?" AJ asked.

"Don't tell him I said it, but we got lucky and one of our neighbors called and said there was a rental car sitting at the south ramp," Rebel said. "We've been out all night looking for you fellas."

"South?" AJ asked.

Rebel pointed across the open water to a location opposite where AJ and Darnell had parked. "Tell him to take cover and stay away from his house."

"He wants to know why."

The unmistakable sound of propellant igniting drew AJ's attention back in the direction Rebel pointed. A bright contrail from an RPG silhouetted the pair of aliens. "Take cover, Lefty!" AJ yelled, jamming his feet into the mud beneath him. He fought to balance as he brought his M4 out of the water and to his shoulder. Next to him, Darnell did the same.

Lefty's cabin exploded brilliantly, lighting up the cove and momentarily exposing the two men who stood in the water. It didn't matter as they opened fire on the pair of aliens too awestruck by the explosion they'd caused to realize their danger. Looking like quintessential aliens from vintage TV shows and movies, the gray-skinned

Cheell stood only five feet tall and wore no clothing. Darnell and AJ's bullets lifted them from their feet and tossed them backward, killing them instantly.

AJ scanned the darkened shore but even with Beverly's light amplification, he was unable to see any movement until a finger of electrical energy reached across the water and struck his chest. "Gaaah!" His scream was pulled from his throat as thousands of pinpricks seemed to explode across his skin.

A single, loud pop from the swamp sounded and the attack paused. With a fix on the new attackers, Beverly artificially illuminated the last Cheell who, instead of standing tough, was now running. A small green dot followed the alien's progress until they heard a final loud pop and the Cheell went tumbling.

"Jenkins, are you up?" Lefty called.

"Waba." AJ felt strong arms brace him as he started to sink into the water.

"I got you, big fella," Darnell said. "Petey, make sure those Cheell don't get up to any shenanigans."

It had only been a few weeks since Pete and Darnell had been introduced to each other. Originally believed to have been vaccinated and immune to symbiotes or parasitical aliens, Darnell had recently learned the vaccine was reversible and that he could accept another Beltigersk.

Like his Beltigersk predecessor, 2F, Petey wasn't a big talker. However, like Beverly, he had a penchant for human culture, especially video games. To answer Darnell's question, Petey displayed an old scoreboard that looked like it'd been taken directly from a high-school football field. The score read: US – 4, THEM – 0 and TIME REMAINING – 0:00.

"Naja waba," AJ said, turning to Darnell.

Darnell dragged AJ toward shore. By the time they arrived at the bank, Lefty was there and helped drag AJ onto dry ground.

"Might have gone easier if you'd called ahead," Lefty said. "He gonna be okay?"

Rebel appeared on Lefty's shoulder and leaned back against his neck. "Beverly will take good care of him," she said. "He just got a lil short-circuited, that's all."

"You promised beer," AJ rasped, finally finding his voice.

Lefty raised an eyebrow and coughed out a laugh. "You come down here, blow up my house, and now you want a beer?"

AJ shrugged. "You offered."

"We need to get those Cheell cleared," Darnell said. "That blast is bound to draw attention."

"What's going on, Big D?" Lefty asked.

"Cheell have been targeting everyone with a Belti rider," Darnell said. "Queenie barely got off-planet. We lost two of the guys you recruited to help in the first invasion. The three of us and Doc are all that's left."

"We'll take the pontoon over," Lefty said. "Are you mobile, Jenkins? Or am I carrying your sorry ass out again?"

"Asshole," AJ said, standing with Darnell's help.

"I get that a lot," Lefty said, leading them to an old wooden dock. "Not sure why."

AJ slumped into a cushioned boat chair. Most of the pain was gone, but his muscles were shaky. The pontoon boat sputtered to life while Darnell jumped off and tossed lines onto the deck.

"You getting anything, Lefty?" Darnell asked, quietly, scanning the horizon with his weapon firmly pushed against his shoulder.

"That last Cheell is flopping around a bit," Lefty answered. "Otherwise, it looks like you boys took out the first wave with prejudice. Don't suppose you know what this is all about?"

"Our best guess is reprisal," Darnell said. "The attacks were targeted."

"If they wanted to make a statement, seems they had their shit-list upside down. They shoulda made a run over to hit you guys in Arizona first."

"They did," Darnell said. "You must have taught Humpty

Dumpty there a good lesson back in 'Nam because he saw 'em comin' a mile off."

"Shit, really?" AJ said. "I got shot, I'm not deaf."

"Shh, adults are talking," Darnell said.

"You get 'em in Arizona?"

"Negative," Darnell said. "We tossed a couple of rounds their way and they ran off. Cheell aren't exactly known for their bravery."

"Sparky shouldn't have fired on me then if that's his philosophy," Lefty said, slowing the motor as they approached the opposite bank. "He painted a target on his forehead and he wasn't outrunning my new Creedmore."

Darnell whistled. "That was a hell of a shot. Had to be at least six hundred."

"Six hundred eighteen yards and moving fast," Rebel said, appearing on Lefty's shoulder. "My boy was steady as a rock."

"You're kind of bloodthirsty for a Belti," Darnell said, grinning approvingly.

"I've got tattoos, too," she answered, standing on Lefty's shoulder and turning away. "Wanna see 'em?"

AJ coughed as he breathed in spit.

"Whoa there, not me! Maybe you haven't met the missus but that's a castration-level event, right there," Darnell said.

"You boys are about as stealthy as a herd of elephants," Lefty chastised, jumping off the front of the boat with a bowline in hand. "You able to walk, Jenkins?"

"Yeah."

The trio walked to the first pair of Cheell who looked even smaller in death. Lefty picked up the RPG launcher and turned it over in his hands. "Chinese made. Where the hell'd they get this?"

"That's all we need is China making friends with Cheell," Darnell said, picking up an energy weapon that had been made for the much smaller Cheell hands. "Did you ever get a response from Major Baird?"

"She said she'd have someone look into all the alien attacks. Apparently, everyone's getting diplomatic visits from the different alien governments and it's sounding more and more like we're starting a damn arms race. She's up to her armpits in security issues," AJ said. "She told me we were on our own unless I had a national security angle."

"Which attacking a bunch of old war dogs doesn't qualify as," Lefty said, turning over the third Cheell body. "These boys sure travel light."

"What were you looking for?" AJ asked.

"Something I could sell," Lefty said. "They blew up my house and that government pension barely keeps me in beer. How am I gonna rebuild my house?"

"Insurance?" AJ said, grabbing the Cheell Lefty had winged. The wounded Cheell had stopped moving by the time they'd found him. It was no surprise that the fragile alien had bled out.

"Can't afford insurance."

"What are we going to do with these guys?" AJ asked, unsympathetically.

"We should figure out how many Cheell are in the area," Darnell said. "Command has to know our location. Be nice to know if someone's gonna come looking for them with a few dozen friends or not."

"I say we let the swamp have 'em," Lefty said. "I've got a place."

"You've got a place ... that's not creepy," AJ said. " Maybe you could be more specific. You've got a place where you regularly dump bodies, or you've got a place you think nobody will find them?"

"Are you sure you want to know the answer to that?" Lefty asked, growing still. Then a smile broke out on his face. "I'm just messing with you. I figure we give the gators a shot at cleaning up the mess. Unless you want to call your girlfriend, Baird."

"She's not my girlfriend," AJ said.

"Oh, right, you're diddlin' that good-looking surgeon," Lefty said. "What was her name? Jayne?"

"Have a little respect," AJ said. "You know, she could be listening in."

"Aw, crap," Lefty said, abashed. "But hey, I said she was good lookin'."

AJ shook his head. "What about the weapons? Same place?"

"Yeah, there are mangroves all over the place. Nobody will ever find anything where I have in mind."

"How about you two dump and I'll go look for their vehicle," AJ said. "I think Rebel said someone reported a rental parked on the road. Probably need to move it."

Lefty waved them off. "You boys head along without me. I'll take the trash out. I'd kind of prefer not to give away all my secrets."

"Where do you want to meet?"

"It'll be morning in a few hours," Lefty said. "How about we meet up in Greensboro. There's a diner where 44 meets 278. You can dump their vehicle along the way. How'd you get down here if that rental wasn't yours?"

"You got your secrets, we got ours," AJ said.

"Fair enough."

"That's bull. We dumped our gear and walked in from the Super 8," Darnell said.

"Somebody's grumpy," Lefty said.

"Low blood sugar," AJ quipped before Darnell could respond.

"Maybe because I've been trudging around a swamp all night trying to save your worthless hide," Darnell growled.

"They said you flyboys were sensitive," Lefty needled.

"Jackass."

"Seems to be the consensus," Lefty agreed, affably.

"It's not worth it, Big D," AJ said. "He'll never bite."

Darnell dropped the last Cheell corpse onto Lefty's boat and grumbled to himself.

Without saying anything further, Lefty restarted the small motor and pulled away from the bank.

"You need a better class of friends," Darnell said, following the path identified by Petey.

"Won't get an argument from me," AJ said.

"So, let's say this is the end of the attacks. What now?" Darnell asked, pointing at the only vehicle in the parking area, a minivan.

"How are you and Lisa doing?" AJ asked, testing the driver's door, not surprised it was unlocked. A warning bell dinged prompting AJ to check the ignition where he found the vehicle keys.

"We're great," Darnell said. "She's pissed that your insurance company won't pay to complete your house, but that's about as far as things go."

AJ placed his M4 on the floor of the van along with his backpack and started the vehicle. "BB, could you get me a map back to the Super 8?" Instead of answering, Beverly projected a dim map onto the dash and a smoky arrow along the highway, showing the way. "Thanks. No, I mean financially. This whole thing has about ruined me. I'm gonna struggle to pay taxes on the junkyard this year because we trashed my savings, you know, saving the world."

"I'm surprised the good old US of A didn't step in here," Darnell said. "We *did* save humanity and all. We should be revered or celebrated or something."

"Didn't get in this for accolades," AJ said. "After 'Nam, I'd have thought you understood that."

"But we're supposed to be better than that now."

"Right. Tell that to the Iraq vets," AJ said. "VA is still messed up."

"A guy can dream, can't he?" Darnell said. "But to answer your question, things have been better. Most of my retirement was wrapped up in our company. When the Korgul took over, they pretty much tanked it. What they didn't tank, Lisa burned when that Korgul got ahold of her."

"How's Lisa taking that?" AJ asked.

"About how you'd think," Darnell said. "She's glad I'm all fixed up. Pissed that we might lose the house. Mostly, we don't talk about it. How's Jayne doing?"

"Same. And look, it isn't our first time through this," AJ said. "After 'Nam, you and I had to figure out what to do with ourselves.

We got our degrees, started that company, and built something. We just need to do that again."

"I just don't feel like starting over," Darnell said. "I know I have to, but fifty-hour weeks at the office, sitting behind a desk ... it's not who I want to be anymore."

"That's how I feel, too, buddy. Honestly, when I retired from Pacific Aerodyn and started working for myself in the junkyard, I was about as happy as I've been. It was tough losing Pam, but I never missed going to the office."

"No, I understand," Darnell said as they pulled into the Super 8. "How do you want to dump this van?"

"I say we wipe it down and leave it here," AJ said. "BB can take care of the hotel's video storage."

"Works."

The pair transferred their equipment to the nondescript blue sedan and were soon back on the road.

"I feel like you've got an idea," Darnell said.

"It's a little far-fetched."

"You're talking to the first human to pilot a spacecraft to a new solar system," Darnell said. "My threshold for *far-fetched* is pretty high."

"Funny you should mention that," AJ said. "And for the record, I'm not sure you were first. Do we know for a fact that Loveit didn't beat us into space?"

"I said pilot," Darnell said. "And I won't speak ill of the dead, but Loveit rode along with a Cheell crew."

"Got me there," AJ said.

"What's this big idea you have?"

"Well, I know this might not work too well for you and Lisa, but Jayne and I are talking about relocating."

"You're kidding? You'd leave the junkyard?" Darnell asked.

AJ nodded. "I might. But only because there's another opportunity."

Darnell chuckled. "Oh my Lord. Spill it."

"You sure you're ready for this?"

"Out with it."

"You remember that crazy Xandarj who ran the docking bay, Mads Bazer?" AJ asked.

"Sure, the one in love with Greybeard?"

"The same," AJ said. "Well, turns out she's got an option on a pile of junk that's in orbit over Xandarj, not far from Dralli Station."

"An option?"

"Means what you think," AJ said. "For a hundred thousand credits, she'll lease it to me for the next fifty years, with an option for fifty more if we're still game."

"One hundred thousand credits for fifty years or for one?"

"One year," AJ answered.

"And Jayne's okay with this?"

AJ shook his head. "No ... well, sort of. Jayne's okay with the idea of living on Dralli station, not on a pile of junk."

"Even after what happened to her there?"

"I should start at the beginning. Jayne got the offer first," AJ said.

"To lease a pile of junk?"

"Not exactly," AJ said. "Jayne got an offer from the Dralli Academic Society. It's our equivalent of a university."

"To do what?"

"Teach medicine and take classes."

"Why would she do that?"

"She'd be teaching a sort of history class – going over human medicine. Dralli Academic Society, DAS for short, is well known galactically and they have a lot of visiting scholars."

"What's her hesitation?" Darnell asked. "Sounds like that would be right up her alley."

"She thought it was a big ask to get me to go back to Xandarj."

"Is it?"

"No ... well, sort of. I wouldn't have anything to do," AJ said. "Someone must have figured out that was an issue for Jayne because that's when Mads Bazer's offer rolled in."

"Beverly, is this true? Is DAS a big deal?" Darnell asked.

Beverly appeared on the car's dash wearing a cap and gown complete with a blue tassel on top. "Yes, but most Beltigersk would never recognize DAS because of the history between our people. To be fair, the Xandarj allow researchers a lot of free rein. They can explore whatever science they want. As a result, positions at DAS are highly sought after. A proper analogy is *Field of Dreams*," Beverly said, switching to a baseball uniform. "If you build it, they will come."

"Never gets old, Beverly," Darnell said, appreciatively.

Beverly bowed deeply. "An actor only requires an audience of one to be fulfilled."

"How do you see me and Lisa fitting in?" Darnell asked.

"Well, that's a bit more sensitive," AJ said. "I know you have your daughter and her family, but I was thinking maybe you'd like to come along and help me make a go of things."

"So, in response to going broke, you want to sign a five million credit deal. What happens if you miss an annual payment? How much do they want on the front end? There are a million questions you need to ask on a long-term deal like this."

AJ took in a deep breath. "That's why I'm talking to you. You know I'm not great with all those details. I need someone to keep me out of trouble."

"What do you do with the junk? How would you make money?"

"Ah, that's the right question," AJ said. "Bazer said she can get us some contracts to haul junk. There are a lot of folks who will pay to have their old stuff removed, just like around here. We're talking old spaceships, reactors, earth-moving machines, and heavy equipment. Most of these folks would rather pay to have it moved than try to figure out how to recycle it."

"Pay enough to cover your annual nut?"

"Maybe ... not sure actually," AJ said. "But how long before someone lets the cat out of the bag about aliens?"

"It's happening right now," Darnell said. "Why, just about every day I see speculation on new fringe sites. Ask me, our governments are working together as they've never done before to figure out how to roll this out without causing pandemonium. That and trying to figure out how to get a leg up on the next guy."

"Ask me, that's why these Cheell came for us," AJ said. "With Belti riders, we're a threat."

"How?"

"We have access to the truth and we've already shown we can build the technology."

"But why not just send a CIA hit squad?"

"I'm pretty sure they tried that," AJ said.

"I'm still not seeing it," Darnell said.

"It's so simple it's staring you in the face," AJ said. "We repurpose alien technology for when the doors are finally opened. We'll have a stockpile of used alien gadgets that'll be worth millions."

"And what if this takes twenty years?"

"We'll have a really big stockpile?"

"No, you're missing the bigger question. Where did we come up with the money for your new floating junkyard?"

"It's not floating," AJ said. "It's in orbit."

"Answer the question."

"I was trying to buy time."

"Didn't work. Answer me."

"I haven't got that far. Although, I was thinking if we could get a ride, this time we could bring a bunch of barrels of whiskey. I bet we could get top dollar. Easily enough to get us off the ground."

"At least you don't dream small."

"So, you're in?"

"I'll talk to Lisa."

TWO

DINE AND DASH

"BB, would you send a text message to Major Baird and let her know we got Lefty out?" AJ said.

Beverly appeared on the dash, this time wearing what AJ considered her standard uniform, which was a pair of old blue jeans, a white blouse, and comfortable sneakers. "Sent," Beverly answered. "Oh, hold on. She's initiating a call. Would you like me to take a message?"

"She's up early," Darnell said, looking at an old watch on his wrist. "It's gotta be like 2 AM mountain."

"Patch her through," AJ said.

Beverly stood and a desk and chair appeared in front of her. She sat on the chair and slid a tiny speaker phone toward AJ. Stuffing a pencil behind her ear, she managed to look harried. "Major Baird on line one, Mr. Jenkins."

"Morning, Major," AJ said, grinning at Beverly's antics.

"I just got off a conference call with the US ambassador to the Cheell nation," she said.

"Uh oh," Darnell said.

"We have diplomatic relations with Cheell? You do know that not so long ago they were looking for a full-scale invasion of Earth, right?"

"Well, as Ambassador Dumnick informed me, the point of diplomacy is to keep us from going to war," she answered.

"He's not very good at his job," AJ said.

"That might not be fair. He didn't start until after things settled down on Beltigersk," Baird said. "And that's not the point of the call. Where are you right now?"

"Somewhere in Georgia, I think," AJ said. "What's going on? You knew we were going after Lefty."

"The Cheell ambassador has lost contact with a team of diplomats who were last seen in Georgia."

"That's interesting," AJ said. "Did the ambassador say what this team was doing? How secure is this line?" He looked at Beverly who nodded confidently and gave him a thumbs up.

"As secure as we can make it."

"How much do you want to know?"

"Shit. Tell me they started it and that you have video."

AJ glanced at Beverly who once again nodded. "They started it and we've got video."

"Is that the truth? Give me some details but don't send video yet. I need to figure out how to spin this."

"The spin is pretty easy, Major. Cheell assassins tried to take out an old war hero and managed to blow up his house with an RPG. The response, as provided for by the Second Amendment of our glorious constitution, was proportionate and final."

"How final?"

"Times four," AJ said. "If you want the bodies, you better hurry because nature's a bitch in these parts."

"Are you sure they're gone?"

"I believe that falls within Lefty's area of expertise," AJ said. "Have you figured out why we're being targeted? Seems like a lot of effort for reprisals after the fact."

"There aren't that many people who know the truth about Cheell involvement in the Beltigersk affair," Baird said. "That's our best guess as to why your old team is being targeted."

"Some of the GIs they killed only got the vaccine," AJ said. "They weren't involved with the Beltigersk coup d'etat."

"I wish I had more, AJ," Baird said. "Good job getting to Lefty in time. I'm sure I don't need to tell you that this is top secret."

"Never happened," AJ said.

"Good night, AJ."

"Stay safe, Major." Beverly made a show of hanging up the phone when AJ nodded to her.

"Why do I feel like this thing isn't over?" Darnell said.

"This *thing* is not over," AJ agreed. "I wish I knew why, though. Why are they attacking the vets who helped defend against the Korgul?"

"Any reason to think we'd be safer on Xandarj than we would be around here?" Darnell asked.

"Can't get a lot worse. I hate sitting around, waiting for the shooting to start," AJ said. "But that's not it. Fact is, I'm broke. We're broke. I see an opportunity on Xandarj and it'd let Doc do what she wants."

"I can see that," Darnell said.

It was dark and the drive up to Greensboro was quiet. A couple of hours later, just as the sun was streaming over the horizon, they found the diner Lefty specified and parked in front.

"I'm starving," AJ admitted as they exited their rental and walked around to a side entrance.

"You took some damage when that Cheell shot you," Beverly said, hovering in front of him with a rocket pack strapped to her back. "Make sure you get plenty of calcium."

"I could go for some ice cream," AJ said.

"Milk would be better," Beverly said. "But you could go heavy on the protein and it wouldn't hurt. A little citrus too."

"You say the sexiest things," AJ said, patting his stomach. "I'd marry you if I could."

"Our relationship is not that much different," Beverly said. "Thank you. I quite enjoy our time together as well. I don't completely understand your suggestion that I've made a sexual reference. I'm trying for minimal flirtiness without coming across as boring."

"You guys are too much," Darnell said, nodding at a waitress as they entered the side door of the diner.

"Anywhere you like, honey," the woman said. "Two coffees?"

"We're expecting a third, but he could be a while," Darnell said, leading AJ to a central booth that looked onto the parking lot through large plate-glass windows.

"I've got you, hon," she called over her back, pulling the coffee pot from its burner and bringing it to the table. AJ flipped a coffee cup right-side-up and slid into the booth. "Our breakfast special is cheese grits and bacon with three eggs any way you like 'em. There's a menu at the end of the table."

"How's your sausage gravy?" AJ asked.

"People seem to like it," she said. "I prefer the chicken gravy, myself. You boys from out of town?"

"Just passing through," Darnell said. "I'd take your special. Mind if I substitute links for the bacon? And over-easy on the eggs."

"For you, honey, I sure can," she said, winking at Darnell and turning to AJ. "Do you need some time, dear?"

"Nope. I'd take your biggest steak – medium – three eggs scrambled on top of hash browns and covered with that chicken gravy. A big glass of milk," AJ said. "Oh, and an OJ."

The waitress's eyes widened as she memorized the order. "That's a lot of food, hon. Are you sure?"

"We just got done working," AJ said. "I could eat a horse."

"I'll get it in."

Darnell checked his watch. "I'm going to step out and call Lisa."

"Bubba, I don't mean to tell you your business, but it's three in the morning in Tucson," AJ said.

"Petey said she just texted me. She's having trouble sleeping."

"You could use the time to talk with Amanda Jayne," Beverly said. "Nit says she's up, reading."

"Okay," AJ said. Almost immediately, his cell phone started buzzing in his pocket. "Heya, Doc."

"Nit says you're all safe," Jayne said. "Was there a lot of trouble?"

"Not more than we could handle," AJ said. "Kind of hard to talk here."

"Did you get any clue as to why they're coming after us?"

"We didn't have much of a chance to talk," AJ said, glancing around to make sure he wouldn't be overheard and whispering the next part. "They took out Lefty's house with an RPG."

"That's terrible. Can't Baird stop this? Cheell can't just attack US citizens," Jayne said, angrily.

"She's trying. It's just new territory for everyone. We don't have any way to respond to *that kind* of aggression," AJ said cryptically. "Tell me you're being safe."

"Baird's men are still in the hallway and I've got Greybeard on the bed with me," she said, referring to the thick bulldog – and Seamus, his Beltigersk rider – who often accompanied them on their adventures. "I was just reading. I don't sleep that well when you're away. When are you coming back?"

"We're meeting Lefty for breakfast and then catching the first flight home," AJ said. "I've been thinking about your DAS opportunity. I'd like you to go for it, but you need to ask about security."

"I already asked," Jayne said. "Security is something they've thought about. There are forty nations and eighteen species represented on campus. Some of these nations are at war with each other but they keep things safe. They take security very seriously. The entire campus is a weapon-free zone."

"Isn't that the opposite of secure?" AJ asked.

"I know. I think they have active weapon scanners," Jayne said. "Besides, I thought I'd keep Greybeard with me."

"Is Seamus okay with that?"

"I think Nit and Seamus are friendly," Jayne said. "Oh, I made her blush."

Like most Beltigersk, Nit, Jayne's third try at a symbiote, rarely spoke. Beverly was an exception although Nit had adopted a few of Beverly's quirks, occasionally manifesting herself as a doll-sized human.

The waitress smiled as she slid AJ's milk and orange juice onto the table. "Just a couple of minutes on your order, hon," she said and disappeared.

AJ was a little surprised when he looked out the window and saw Lefty pull in, seated behind the wheel of an old pickup truck. "Hey, Lefty just got here. Call you back later?"

"I'll try to get some sleep now that I know you're okay," Jayne said. "I'll call you in the morning."

He hung up the phone and waited for Lefty to find him, which didn't take long.

Flipping over another coffee cup, Lefty sat opposite AJ. "Time to spill, son," he said, equal parts agitated and irritated. "What in the hell happened back there? Why are those spindly-legged meat bags comin' after me already?"

AJ smiled at the waitress as she approached and poured coffee for Lefty. "Anything to eat, hon?"

"Whatever he's having," Lefty said, impatiently.

The waitress seemed to recognize Lefty's mood and got on her way without her normal cheery response.

"Hope you're hungry," AJ said. "And I don't know much more than what I told you in the swamp. Cheell have been coming for the boys involved in the first dustup with the Korgul when we got that vaccination. We lost some good men."

"How'd you know they'd come lookin' for me?"

"Major Baird got wind of something. She told us we didn't have much time," AJ said.

"You trust her?"

"I do," AJ said. "She's been there when I needed her."

Lefty nodded and acknowledged Darnell as he joined the two men.

"Any trouble?" Darnell asked.

"No. Never seen those gators quite so interested before," he said. "They were going crazy. Had 'em tryin' to get in the boat. Rebel says Cheell almost wiped out all reptilian species on their home planet. What do you bet that's why?"

"Because they taste good?" Darnell asked.

"Sure. Imagine if dogs thought we all tasted like pork chops in gravy? We'd have to put 'em down," Lefty said.

"Cooked right, we might," AJ said, chuckling.

"Where are we goin' next?" Lefty asked. "Who's the next target? I'm ready."

"You were the last target," AJ said. "We didn't hear about who Cheell was targeting until it was almost too late. I got the impression Baird broke some rule letting us know about you. Glad she did. Those little bastards weren't playing around."

"Here we go," the waitress announced from halfway across the room. To AJ, it seemed like she understood the men might not like their conversation being overheard. He decided she'd be getting that tip she'd been working so hard for. After setting down several plates, she looked at Lefty and smiled broadly. "I'll have yours up in just a couple of minutes, hon."

"I'd ask if you were eating for two, but I already know the answer," Lefty said, sitting back in his chair. "I probably should have made my own order."

AJ had already torn into the steak by the time the waitress left. "Nah, I'll finish whatever you don't," he said between bites. "I took a pretty good hit in the water."

"Oh, right," Lefty said. "You're lucky Rebel recognized you. I was about to squeeze one off."

"Your aim was short," AJ said. "You had your laser on the water. The dot was a reflection."

"I had it aimed just where I wanted. That Creedmore ammo

wouldn't have skipped. I'd have put it center mass, just like I planned," Lefty said.

"If you say so," AJ said, hungrily scooping up food.

"You expecting company?" Darnell asked, setting his coffee on the table.

"Oh, shit." AJ kicked off the diner's outside wall. A pair of Cheell stood outside the diner, making no attempt to disguise their gray alien bodies nor the fact that one of them held a grenade launcher. "Get down!!" AJ screamed, getting his feet under him and tackling the older waitress to the floor. When the grenade didn't immediately break the glass, he dragged her back under a booth, only to feel the shockwave of an explosion and the sound of plate glass imploding.

"Don't move!" he ordered the waitress. "BB, how bad am I?"

"I've blocked the pain receptor on the back of your left leg; you've got a large piece of shrapnel embedded there. I don't believe that leg will move. You have more shrapnel embedded in your dermis but it is not as life-threatening. You need to apply a tourniquet until I repair enough damage on your leg or you'll likely bleed out."

"We have hostiles, BB. I need to move." In the back of his mind, AJ could feel the shape of the object embedded in his leg but no pain.

"Pull the shrapnel out the back," she said. "It's big enough for you to grab. Use the waitress's apron to tie the wound off. That should buy you a minute, give or take. It's a risk, though. You need that tourniquet."

"Sorry about this," AJ said, tugging at the strings that held the woman's apron on.

With a calm he knew to be chemically induced, AJ pulled a shard of glass from the back of his leg and tied the apron around the wound. The amount of blood flowing freely was a problem and he questioned whether he had a minute.

Suddenly, another view from within the diner was displayed in front of him. It wasn't uncommon for Beverly to provide a HUD, but that meant either Darnell or Lefty had popped up to assess their situation – not good news. The second Cheell aimed an energy weapon and fired, causing the HUD's view to shake.

AJ pulled the pistol from his side and gingerly stood. The first Cheell was reloading the grenade launcher while the second was unloading on Darnell. The choice wasn't hard. AJ fired three shots into the small alien who was firing at Darnell. He didn't miss. The grenade-loading Cheell squeaked and dropped his grenade.

Bullets ricocheted off the ground at the Cheell's feet. AJ turned in time to find a bloodied Lefty firing shot after shot at the skittering grenade. On his fourth shot, he hit gold. The Cheell looked up for a moment as the grenades he was holding all exploded at once, tossing AJ and Lefty off their feet.

AJ's consciousness faded and he struggled to stay awake.

"I got you, buddy," Darnell said.

Pain lanced through his leg as strong hands tightened a belt above where the blood was pouring out. The sound of distant sirens cut through the fog of his consciousness.

"We gotta move, soldier," Lefty's ragged voice said. With help, AJ stood.

"Dammit, those were aliens you blew up." A heavy man wearing an open flannel shirt over a white t-shirt approached the three. "I saw the whole damn thing."

"Help the waitress," AJ said. "She's under the booth."

"Mags, you okay?" the man asked, distracted by AJ's redirection.

"Get him in the truck," Lefty said.

Darnell groaned as he climbed into the back row of the four-door full-sized pickup. With Lefty's help, they were able to drag AJ in and close the door.

"Where are you go ..." someone called, but their question was cut short when Lefty stumbled up and into the driver's seat, slamming the door. The truck fired to life and was put into gear.

"How bad are you hit, flyboy?" Lefty asked.

"I'll live," Darnell answered. "I took a pretty good jolt but Petey's got my head clear, at least for the moment. How are you doing?"

"Might have trouble staying awake," Lefty said. "Rebel's workin' overtime on a concussion. Got the old noodle a bit scrambled back there. What the hell'd we do to get 'em this fired up?"

"I'd like to know how they knew where we were," Darnell said.

"You boys tell anyone where we were meeting?"

"Jayne." AJ struggled to sit up, but Darnell held him down.

"You got nowhere to go. If they made our rental, it probably had a tracker," Darnell said. "There's a million ways for them to find us. Especially if they had help."

THE NEXT TIME AJ woke up, he found that Lefty had parked the truck off the road in a stand of trees. "What time is it?" he asked.

Beverly appeared, wearing a white nurse's uniform that fit tightly. He smiled, despite the pain he felt. "It's one in the afternoon. Rebel and Petey report that Lefty and Darnell are doing well. It's imperative that we stop at the quick mart two point four miles to the north of our position and purchase four liters of an electrolyte-based sports drink."

AJ winced as he moved his leg. The tourniquet had been removed. The bottom of his pantleg was soaked in blood and upon further inspection, he realized he was in no shape to be purchasing anything unless he wanted to draw attention.

Sliding off the seat and out the door, he limped to the back of Lucky's truck and opened the tailgate and topper. Not unexpectedly, he found Darnell asleep on a make-shift bed with boxes of supplies and several rucksacks pushed off to the side. He hit paydirt on the first duffle and pulled out an old pair of jeans that looked like they could use a couple of cycles in a washing machine. It took some effort, but he finally managed to don Lefty's jeans, which fit reasonably well, if not a couple of inches short in the legs. He pulled out an old t-shirt and his clothing change was complete.

He found Lefty's truck keys over the visor on the driver's side and backed onto the road, careful not to wake Lefty who was slumped in the reclined passenger seat. "BB, any messages from Doc or Baird?"

"Yes, both," Beverly said, sitting on the dash with one leg crossed over the other, still in her nurse's uniform.

"Let's hear what Doc has to say."

"She is awake and you will appreciate knowing she is having an uneventful morning. I have refrained from sharing recent events with Nit and Seamus. I did not wish to further distress Amanda Jayne."

"Thank you," AJ said. "What's Baird got to say?"

"I'm afraid you will find this either irritating or humorous."

"Hit me."

"At 06:30 this morning, seven minutes after the attack at the diner, Major Baird sent a message warning of further Cheell activity in the area and that we should take precautions."

AJ chuckled humorously. "Anything else?"

"That we were to avoid violent confrontation at all costs."

AJ shrugged. "Someone should have told the Cheell the same thing or at least stop handing them RPG launchers."

THREE

TRAVEL SUPPLIES

If AJ hadn't seen the weather-worn road sign announcing *Dan's Hidey Hole*, he'd never have seen the small gas station that emerged from the thick tree-lined road. Like the road sign, the small building with only a single gas pump in front needed a paint job. AJ smiled. It wasn't the sort of place where he'd have to worry about someone asking a lot of questions.

Stopping in front of the pump, he was surprised when an older man walked out to greet him. "Looking for a fill? Just got the eighty-five here," he said. AJ's eyes were drawn to the man's baseball cap that proudly announced he was a Naval retiree, having served on the *USS Hornet*.

"Yeah, we'll be driving a piece. Can you give her a fill?" AJ said. "Any snacks inside?"

"Small selection," the man answered. "Discount for cash, too."

AJ nodded and headed inside the small building to find a single-shelf unit with chips, candy bars, and various automotive supplies.

"Gonna need a couple of quarts of ten-forty," Lefty said, silently appearing behind AJ.

AJ nodded, adding oil to a growing pile next to the old cash register. "Figured I'd let you boys sleep it off," AJ said.

"I'm awake now," Lefty said. "I guess I got my answer."

"To what question?"

"If I'd be tagging along or heading back to the swamp."

"What was the answer?" AJ asked.

"Man, can you be dense," Lefty said. "If they're gunnin' for us this bad, we need to stick together."

"We're not sticking around," AJ said.

"Pretty good drive to Arizona from here," Lefty said. "You thinking about flying commercial? Might not be the best move given recent events."

The bell over the door jangled as the old vet limped back inside, holding a small notepad in one hand. "Restroom in the back if you need," he said, glancing at the tattoo on Lefty's forearm. "You earn that ink, son?"

"Three tours," Lefty said.

"Different war nowadays," the old man said. "Glad you made it back."

"You too, my friend," Lefty said with an uncharacteristic smile on his face.

"Can't see how you young'uns survive on all this crap," the man said, looking at the pile of junk food and bottles of sugared water.

AJ peeled off several twenties to cover the bill and nodded. He carried the bags back to the truck and unloaded them onto the front seat, opening a large sports drink and downing it in one go. Feeling refreshed, he opened the truck's hood and searched for the dipstick.

"She's probably down half a quart," Lefty said, handing AJ a small scrap of cloth to wipe off the oil. "What did you mean about not stickin' around?"

"I think we'll be headed out," he answered. "I'd have a place for you if you want."

"How far out?"

"Xandarj. I got a line on a pile of junk. There's a business opportunity I'd like to check out," AJ said.

"You and your junk," Lefty said. "I could tag along. Pay good?"

"Can't promise much more than room and board," AJ said. "I'll do better if I can."

"You're a horrible salesman."

"He's a worse manager," Darnell said as he came around from the back of the truck. "Bathroom in there?"

"In back," Lefty said. "Not sure I'm looking for a boss."

"Make it easier not to pay you," AJ said, shrugging.

"Damn, but you're an asshole."

"You in?"

"Hell, why not," Lefty said. "You thinking about driving all the way back to Arizona? This old girl might not have it in her."

"Never met a machine I couldn't keep running," AJ said. "Call it an adventure."

"I'm gonna need to eat better than pop and chips."

AJ chuckled and poured half a quart of oil into the old engine. "We'll stop whenever you want," AJ said. "BB just needed some raw materials to replace that blood I lost."

"Figured."

Beverly appeared on the hood of the old truck. "Lefty, how would you feel about us moving around some of the material in the back of your vehicle?" she asked.

"I suppose if there was a good reason, I wouldn't object too much," he said.

"What's up, BB?" AJ asked.

"I've got a line on those whiskey casks you were asking about," she said. "If you're driving back, it will only add eighty miles to your trip."

"Whiskey?" Lefty asked. "What's that got to do with a junk heap?"

"A junker never looks past opportunity," AJ said. "I'm gambling I can sell good old fashion Tennessee rye whiskey to aliens."

"You've got a market?"

"We'll find out," AJ said. "Now, we just need to make enough room for five casks. Think we can manage that?"

"How much is that gonna weigh?" Lefty asked.

"A ton, give or take."

"Son, you put a ton in the back and we're gonna be draggin' some serious ass out to Arizona. Isn't there a mountain range in our way? You'd best be one hell of a mechanic."

"You're in?"

Lefty shook his head. "Heck, sounds about as entertaining as anything I've seen."

"Tell 'em we'll be there by mid-afternoon," AJ said, looking at BB.

"Be where?" Darnell asked, joining them.

"Feel like doing some tag-team driving, Big D?"

"I wouldn't mind putting this place in the rear-view if that's what you're asking."

"Careful, flyboy, some of us call hearabouts home," Lefty said.

"And some of us been shot at every time we've come around here," Darnell said.

AJ put his hands up to stop them. "Gentlemen, no need to get snippy. Lefty, it's your truck, I guess you get to decide who's driving first."

"I'll drive."

AFTER UNLOADING Lefty's truck and pulling off his old topper, the casks were loaded into the back of the big pickup. Getting Lefty's junk stowed turned out to be more of a challenge but in the end, it all went back in. As for how the truck performed on the trip, she required babying through the southern Rocky Mountains but performed better than any of them expected. What had been a few hours of airline flights turned into almost two days of round-the-clock driving.

AJ pulled the truck to a stop in front of the tall chain-link fence that surrounded his junkyard. "Never gets old comin' home." Though it was after midnight, both Darnell and Lefty were awake, prepared for anything, given the proximity to their destination.

On the other side of the fence, lights turned on and the barking of a dog could be heard. AJ left the truck running and slid out, unlocking the gate in time for his chubby bulldog to jump on him.

"AJ!" Amanda Jayne followed close behind Greybeard. Younger in appearance than her mid-sixties age would suggest, Jayne had recovered the beauty of her youth, thanks to Nit.

"I'm not sure I smell too good," AJ said, enjoying a welcome-home hug. "Three guys in a truck for a couple of days isn't the best."

"You've got a little funk going," she replied with a smile. "But I'm glad you're back. Nit said you're loaded up with whiskey. Does that mean you're thinking about Mads Bazer's offer?"

"Things got a little dicey out at Lefty's," AJ said. "I figure you commit to DAS for a year and I'll bump around and see what I can get going."

"I've been talking to Lisa. Did you know she never finished her degree?" Jayne asked.

"Degree in what?"

"Are you sure you want to have this conversation in the driveway? I've got cots in the living room. Nit told me you were getting close."

He gave her a smarmy grin. "I was hoping we could head back to your condo."

"Hold that thought," Jayne said, hugging Darnell as he got out. "Lisa's inside, Darnell. She made dinner if you boys are hungry."

"I'm starving," Darnell said. "Did she make the good meatloaf or the bad?"

"I've been on more of a vegetarian diet lately," Jayne said, shrugging.

"I could go for some meatloaf," Lefty said, his face lighting up. AJ and Darnell exchanged a look and laughed. Lefty knit his eyebrows in confusion. "What?"

"Lisa's got a knack for meatloaf," AJ said and then turned to Jayne. "I'll pull the truck in. You can catch me up when we're inside."

"I'll ride along," Jayne offered, sliding into the driver's seat and across to the middle.

"Sure is good to see you," AJ said, hopping in and patting her thigh. "You and Nit getting along all right? Any issues with the vaccine reversing agent?"

"No, it's been a big success so far. Darnell say anything about problems with Petey?"

"Not one," AJ said, rolling the truck forward. "What's going on with your condo?"

"I just sold it and put the money into investments," she said. "I also traded my car in for a junker. I'm a free woman AJ. It feels so strange. I've always had all these commitments and places I've needed to be. Suddenly, I have nothing but a job offer."

AJ chuckled. "A job offer on an alien planet."

Jayne held one of AJ's hands between hers. "I know I'm moving fast, AJ. I'm glad you decided to come. I'm not sure what I'd have done if you'd said no. It's just ... I never knew what I wanted long-term, but now that I do, I can't think of anything else."

Loud voices drew their attention to AJ's unfinished house. The structure was dried-in, thankfully, but was missing just about every-thing else. At first, AJ worried that the voices were upset, but then he realized the sounds were actually excitement.

AJ turned back to Jayne. "Doc, I'd follow you anywhere. You know that."

"Do you mean it?"

"Isn't that what people who care about each other do?" AJ asked. "I don't have much going on and you've got this amazing opportunity. I'd be a fool if I asked you to decide between me and your happiness. What kind of friend would do that?"

"It's a mistake to underestimate you, Albert Jenkins," Jayne said. "Thank you. I've been worried ... well, up to the point when Nit told me you bought five barrels of whiskey."

"Think we can get 'em into space? I didn't think to check with you on transport," AJ said, hopping out of the truck.

"The transport is already inbound. Someone at the Dralli Academic Society must have pulled some strings because we're approved for a night take-off in six days from a private airstrip out by Three Points," Jayne said. "They told me I could bring as much stuff as I wanted. I guess we'll see how serious they were about that."

"I don't suppose there's a lot of traffic between Xandarj and the US," AJ said.

"The transport has been making a few stops around Earth dropping off emissaries to different countries. They don't have many who are ready to go back yet, so it's convenient to take us to Xandarj. Otherwise, it was six months until the next transport," she said, walking up the steps to AJ's house and pulling open the front door.

"Sounds perfect. We'll button things up around ..."

AJ stopped dead in his tracks as his eyes fell on Lisa Jackson. Only it wasn't the sixty-year-old Lisa he was used to seeing. Lisa looked like she was twenty-four years old and every bit the knockout his buddy Darnell had fallen in love with so many years ago.

"Cat got your tongue?" Lisa asked, hands on her hips and head tipped to the side. Her hair had grown out considerably and she'd fuzzed it into an afro.

"Dag-gone," AJ said, tongue-tied. "Wow."

Lisa's sassy confrontational style melted into a smile. "Well, it's nice to know I've still got it. Come here; show me a little lovin'."

AJ felt awkward as Lisa drew him into a warm hug. "How? Did you get a symbiote?"

"Nope," Lisa said, pushing him back. "Turns out, Doctor Jayne and her little buddy have been working on a therapy to reverse some effects of aging. I've never felt so good in my life." Lisa spun in place, giving AJ more than an eyeful in her tight clothing.

"Um, wow. Can you imagine what people would pay for this?"

"I don't do pictures, sweetie," Lisa said, smiling.

"You know what I mean," AJ said.

"I do, but give an old girl a few minutes to enjoy the center stage again," Lisa said. "It's been a while since I've turned a head."

"Not true," Darnell said, handing an open beer bottle to AJ. "You've always turned my head, hot stuff."

"And that's why you get the private shows," Lisa said, her eyes half-lidded and suggestive.

AJ chuckled. "Sounds like you guys need to get home and catch up."

"About that," Lisa said. "There might be some issues with that."

"Issues?" Darnell asked. "Lisa, what'd you do?"

"Don't you start with me, Darnell Jackson," Lisa said.

"Tell me," Darnell said.

"Fine. I sold the house," she said. "Got a darn good price for it too."

"How much?"

"Twenty over market," she said. "I put half into a new IRA and invested the other half in portable trade goods."

"You what?"

"Careful," Lisa said, warning in her voice. "If you want to go over it, I'd be happy to. I talked with Jayne about Xandarj culture. According to her, Xandarj seem to have something of a crush on humans."

"True," Darnell agreed warily.

"It stands to reason that beauty items like jewelry, perfume and clothing would be interesting to Xandarj who are into looking more like us," she said.

"You spent a couple hundred thousand on jewelry and perfume?" Darnell asked. "What if it doesn't sell?"

Lisa shrugged. "We're young again, Darnell. We've got our whole lives ahead of us. We need to take risks and live a little."

"Or have a heart attack," Darnell said, scratching the back of his scalp.

"I also bought a bunch of DVDs of cheap movies," she said. "I don't know how copyright law will extend, but I figured I couldn't go wrong with that. Nit says it won't be hard for Xandarj to translate the CDs to something they can play."

"Old movies?"

"Cultural exchange," Lisa said. "Seriously, man, you need to sack up. We're in for the ride of our lives here."

"Damn, girl," AJ said, looking at Lisa with newfound respect. "Get 'em!"

"Thank you, AJ," Lisa said, looking defiantly back to Darnell. "I'm glad someone gets me."

Darnell shook his head. "We don't even know if this Mads Bazer thing can make money."

"Bubba," AJ grabbed Darnell by the shoulders. "I need you to look at the woman in front of you. Can you do that?"

"Yes."

"Tell me, is she about the hottest thing you've seen in the last decade or not?" AJ asked.

"Sure." His word caused Lisa to *hmmm* unappreciatively. "I mean, yes. She looks amazing. She's a damn supermodel."

AJ patted his chest. "There you go. Now you're thinking. She's also the woman who kept you guys afloat in those early days of our first company. You remember when we were eating peanut butter sandwiches just to survive?"

"What are you saying?"

"I'm saying you're lacking perspective," AJ said. "Lisa sure as hell knows what's at stake and your arguing will end up with you sleeping in separate cots. Ask me, I might be thinking about backing her play on this. Sounds like she put some thought into it."

"Come on, AJ," Jayne said, pulling on his arm. "I think Lisa and Darnell need time to talk."

"Go easy on him, Lisa, it's been a tough couple of days," AJ said and then followed Jayne into the unfinished kitchen where Lefty was seated at a card table, happily working on a large slab of meatloaf.

JUST UNDER FIVE FEET TALL, a fine-blue-furred, hominoid alien opened the hatch to his boxy transport ship and extended the long ramp down to the cooling cement runway in the Arizona desert. Due to the fur, the alien's body resembled a monkey except for the refined, furless facial features. Stepping out in a pale green jumpsuit with worn black boots, he tested the atmosphere before opening his suit's visor. Like his other stops, Earth's atmosphere was a bit lean of oxygen, but it was the extremely low humidity he found dramatic because it was something he'd not previously experienced.

A pair of unusual vehicles approached the transport and a thrill of anxiety passed through his system. While he'd seen the vehicles that rolled on wheels at his other stops, there had been considerably more activity to welcome his vessel and greet the arriving Xandarj emissaries. His anxiety quickly passed when a view on his HUD zoomed in on one of the vehicle drivers and showed the familiar face of his old friend, Albert Jenkins.

"Crewman Chok, lower the aft cargo elevator," he called.

"Yes, Blue Tork," the smaller, white-furred engineer answered quickly. "Is it Albert Jenkins and Darnell Jackson?"

"I have seen Albert Jenkins. I do not have a good view of all passengers. Our only required passenger is Amanda Jayne, although she has considerable latitude to modify the shipping manifest," Tork said, walking down the ramp.

When the vehicles stopped and the doors opened, a familiar grey ball of fur raced across the tarmac and bounced against the blue alien. Greybeard barked happily in greeting and received a quick ear scrubbing as a reward.

"Tork, you old pirate!" AJ called, jogging over to the much smaller alien. "I can't say how great it is to see you again."

"Why would you avoid this?" Tork asked. "I find it is very enjoyable to see you. I am concerned that perhaps you did not think to bring sufficient supplies for the considerably larger group than we originally contracted for."

"Lots of food, my friend," AJ said. "Jayne even packed an assortment of Earth fruits for you and Chok to try out. I don't suppose you brought along one of those anti-grav pallet jacks, did you?"

"It will not be difficult to lift your vessels into the cargo hold," Tork said. "I will retrieve our large lifter."

"The vehicles aren't coming, just the cargo," AJ said, looking back at the two pickups they'd brought along. "Unless you think Red Fairs could sell them. I guess I figured they'd have too much mass."

"I was under the impression you were allowed to supply Fantastium for the return trip," Tork said, referring to the precious element that fueled most space travel and was still available on Earth.

"The government auditor calculated that we were allowed to harvest eighty milligrams," AJ said. "We might have brought a hundred twenty just to be on the safe side."

Blue Tork looked up to the left, a signal AJ had learned meant the small alien was accessing a translation program. "Oh, yes, that will be quite sufficient. I will extract only what is necessary for the trip. I do believe that Red Fairs would enjoy the challenge of consigning actual Earth vehicles. You have more than enough Fantastium to cover this mass. It is up to you, though."

"I'll talk to Lefty to see if he wants to sell his truck too," AJ said. "How big is your ramp?"

Blue Tork pointed at the underside of the large transport from which a twenty-foot-wide, thirty-foot-long rectangle was slowly descending. "I believe both of your vessels will fit on that platform."

"Blue Tork," Jayne said by way of greeting as she hugged the small alien.

"Ahh, Amanda Jayne. You bring joy to my heart," Tork said. "Is it true that you have brought Tork and Chok fruits of the Earth to try?"

"It is true," Amanda said. "I also brought a large variety of vegetables and the seeds that produce them."

"Ohh, you are a naughty one," he said, smiling conspiratorially.

"Naughty?" Jayne asked. "Dried seeds are just a convenience. Most of the fruits and vegetables have fertile seeds within them."

"That is sensible, given your life experiences," Tork said. "Your government has not yet traded with other kingdoms. It is important to protect your world's resources by sterilizing your produce. I will ask you to leave the seeds behind and we will sterilize what you have brought. Humanity has given up enough to greedy aliens and we will not be part of that."

"You are so thoughtful," Jayne said, hugging the little alien again.

AJ chuckled as Tork's face seemed thoroughly enraptured by the close contact.

FOUR

BIG BOYS

"We might have company," Lefty said, as AJ approached his old pickup. AJ scanned the horizon but saw nothing of importance. "I caught a flash of gear about four hundred meters to my nine o'clock."

"Crap," AJ said. "I was coming back to see if you wanted to sell your old rig."

"My truck?"

"That's right," AJ said. "Tork thinks his wife, Red Fairs, could get a decent price for it if we brought it back. Kind of an Earth collector's item type of thing."

Lefty knit his eyebrows. "What kind of price?"

"No idea," AJ said. "We sold some handguns last time though and made enough to pay for supplies for all that sailing around we did. I imagine it depends on the market."

A bolt of electricity arced across the dry sands and tagged the back of AJ's old Ford, setting the rear quarter on fire. "Aw, hell. Looks like I'm not gonna have a choice," Lefty said, goosing the old truck and driving toward the lowered cargo elevator.

AJ ran around his truck, barely dodging a second long-range shot from a Cheell weapon. Jumping into the cab, he fired up the engine and raced after Lefty.

"AJ, they're aiming a rocket-propelled grenade at our vehicle," Beverly said, displaying the silhouette of a Cheell standing a hundred yards back. "I've calculated the trajectory and if you successfully dodge, there is a sixty percent chance Lefty's vehicle will be struck, which could be catastrophic with Darnell, Lisa, Greybeard, and Jayne still standing on the platform."

"Dammit. Raise the platform!" he yelled, skidding to a halt and pushing the gearstick into park. Without hesitation, he jumped from the vehicle and grabbed his old M4 from the seat next to him. "Raise the platform!"

As he took off running for the ship, thankfully, the platform started rising.

"Run, you old shit!" Lefty encouraged, jumping out of his pickup and flattening out onto the elevator's deck.

For a moment, AJ thought about trying to reclaim his old truck which was loaded with items he and Jayne thought would sell on Xandarj. Even before he turned, however, a bright fireball and a wave of pressure knocked him to the ground.

"You are not badly wounded," Beverly immediately appeared in front of him. "You must get up."

The ringing in AJ's head was overwhelming and he tried to shake off his disorientation. It wasn't his first concussion, but it never got easier. Stumbling on shaky legs, he pushed forward only to feel hands pulling on his arms. Through the fog, he saw Jayne and Darnell guiding and painfully lifting him onto the elevator platform that was already five feet in the air. With preternatural agility, the pair jumped up beside him. Several loud pops of gunfire startled AJ and he turned to find Lefty firing out into the desert.

"We will slowly evacuate this location." Tork's voice sounded like it was next to AJ, but when the transport ship slid sideways and lifted, AJ knew it was Beverly bridging their communications. "I advise staying low on the platform until it has seated well into the vessel."

"Were they having a damn sale on RPGs somewhere?" Lefty cursed, firing a few more shots at increasingly longer range.

Rebel appeared on the deck. "Settle down there, big fella. We're out of range and you're wasting ammo."

Lefty grunted. "We don't even know why they're firing at us."

"I find it interesting those weapons also bore the signature of a Chinese manufacturer," Rebel said, sitting cross-legged next to where Lefty lay prone. "I believe your enemies might well be domestic instead of galactic."

"You have a funny description of domestic," Lefty growled.

"Gotta put on your big boy pants, Lefty," she said. "The propellant-fired grenades are useful for only one thing."

"Blowing us up?" Lefty said, perturbed.

"Well, that, yes, but they also mask the use of the more sophisticated Cheell weapons," Rebel said. "That suggests they're trying to hide their direct involvement."

"And trying to take us out," AJ said. "How would they even know about this place and why didn't they try to hit us at home?"

"There is a lot of attention focused on your junkyard home, AJ," Rebel said. "I believe there are satellites from at least three different nations focused on your property at any given moment. The Cheell activity would have been exposed by this."

"So Cheell want us dead but don't want people to know they did it," Lefty surmised.

Air whistled through the constricting opening and made it impossible for anyone to hear for a moment. The noise cut off as the deck seated into place.

"Well, that was exciting," Darnell said, wrapping a big arm around Lisa, who'd lost most of her generally sassy attitude.

"They were trying to kill us," she said.

"Blue Tork, is there a medical bay in this vessel?" Jayne asked. "AJ took shrapnel to his back."

"I'm transmitting the public ship layout," Tork's disembodied voice said. "You'll find the medical station twenty yards forward on the portside. I'm afraid it's just an alcove. This transport is minimally equipped. Darnell Jackson, if you would join me in the cockpit, I could use your assistance."

"Duty calls," Darnell said, helping AJ to his feet.

"Wait a damn minute," Lefty demanded, stomping his foot on the deck. "I've put up with about as much as I can take. Aren't any of you concerned about the fact that Cheell are attacking us? We're just going to move on like nothing happened?"

"I'm with Lefty on this," Lisa said, folding her arms over her chest. "What the hell is happening?"

"You all know as much as we do," Jayne said, irritated. "Except for us, everyone involved in stopping the original Korgul invasion has been killed. Someone is trying to clean up and they're using Cheell to do it. The fact that our government is unwilling to protect us tells me everything I need to know. Now, AJ is bleeding and I'm going to get him patched up. If anyone wants off this ship, you'll need to figure that out in the next couple of minutes. And Lefty, if you want to act like a child and stomp your feet, then expect to be treated like a child.

AJ's eyes were wide as saucers as he and Lefty exchanged glances before Jayne pulled him through a hatch and into the main portion of the ship.

"If you have anything to say, I'd think about keeping it to yourself," she continued once they were in the hallway.

"Nope," AJ said. "I'm just trying to figure out what kind of problems we're going to run into on Dralli Station."

"Do you regret your decision to go?" Jayne asked, pulling at a panel in the wall that folded down into a seat. "Sit."

He sat. "No regrets. I figure with Beverly, I've got a better than average chance of seeing them coming. Far as I know there's no love lost between Xandarj and Cheell. They'll have to cool it. Heck, who knows, maybe they were just trying to get us to leave."

"Thank you, AJ," Beverly said, appearing between them, wearing a shiny Jetsons-styled spacesuit and a rocket pack. "Is Nit familiarizing you with the medical station controls, Doctor?"

Jayne sighed. "Yes. Sorry. I guess I came on a little strong back there."

"It was a lot to process. We lost a lot of the goods we purchased in that truck," AJ said. "I'm sorry."

For a few minutes, Jayne was lost to the process of cleaning the fresh wounds on AJ's body. "This burn cream is pretty remarkable," she said as cool relief spread across AJ's shoulder. "Humanity is in for some big changes. If Cheell are trying to hide their involvement in the first attacks against Earth, I can't imagine why. Very soon, none of the alien species will need to work hard for good press. Can you imagine the headline when they announce that cancer and heart disease have been cured in the space of a week? How much attention will anyone pay to the fact that we repelled an invasion and that the aliens were ransacking our planet?"

"I have a theory," Beverly said.

AJ and Jayne both turned to the tiny, shared hallucination. "Well, let's hear it then," Jayne said.

"The first targets were misdirection," Beverly said. "Cheell aren't known for military prowess. They're significantly more strategic than that."

"Misdirection from what?" AJ asked.

"What if they wanted to stop someone on this ship from going to Xandarj?" Beverly asked.

"Then they sure went about it the hard way," AJ said. "They gave away their advantage of surprise."

"What if Cheell didn't want your government to know who the actual target was?" Beverly asked. "This level of misdirection is not beyond Cheell strategists. It's maybe even a little rudimentary for a species who is content to allow plans to develop over decades."

"Kids, we're going to need you to all get strapped in," Darnel said over the ship's public address. "Chok has taken the liberty of manufacturing space suits for each of you and is standing by in the main cabin."

"What's going on, Big D?" AJ asked.

"There's a Cheell frigate about a hundred thousand miles out," he answered. "We'll overtake them in forty minutes. They're not paying us too much attention just now but if recent events are any guide, we could be in for some trouble."

"Do we need to turn back?" Jayne asked.

"No, Amanda Jayne," Blue Tork answered. "This vessel is sailing with a Dralli diplomatic transponder. If the Cheell vessel were to attack, no Cheell vessel would be allowed in Dralli controlled space until reparations were achieved."

"What if they've got credits to burn?" she asked.

"If burn means spend, then that would mean we need to outrun them," Blue Tork answered. "The fines for attacking a diplomatic transponder would be significant, even for a nation as wealthy as Cheell. Also, I might have failed to mention that there is a second frigate between us and Earth."

"I've got a bad feeling about this," Lisa said, startling AJ as she and Lefty approached.

"You get used to it," AJ said. "We better get strapped in. Has anyone seen Greybeard?"

"He's up here with me and Blue Tork," Darnell answered.

As a group the four moved forward through the wide passageway, passing an engineering bay, private sleeping quarters, and the galley before opening into a wide compartment AJ assumed was the main cabin.

"Welcome aboard, Albert Jenkins and Amanda Jayne," Cariste Chok, the small white-furred Xandarj said. "I do not believe I've met this beautiful new human male and female."

"I'm sorry," Jayne said. "Lefty Johnson and Lisa Jackson, meet Cariste Chok, engineer of considerable skill."

"It is now clear why Darnell Jackson refused to share my sleeping quarters," Chok said. "Lisa Jackson is even more beautiful than I could imagine."

Lisa looked equal parts irritated and confused at Chok's bald-faced comment. "He better not have!"

"Lisa, no, Darnell was a perfect gentleman," Jayne said. "Don't be offended, Xandarj aren't quite as monogamous as humans, so Chok wasn't trying to make trouble."

Chok's ears flattened against her head as she peered up at Lisa, who stood almost a head taller. The small Xandarj grasped Lisa's hand with her own. "Do not be mad at Chok," she said, stroking the back of Lisa's arm. "Darnell Jackson was very insistent about sleeping alone. And I cannot get past how soft your skin is with those tiny, little hairs."

"Is she okay?" Lisa asked, looking at Jayne.

"Xandarj females are often physically affectionate in social settings," Jayne said, taking Chok's free hand and pulling her away from Lisa. "If it's too much, you can rebuff her, but it'll take a few times before she understands." Chok let go of Lisa and wrapped her thin white tail around Jayne's leg as she transferred to Jayne's arm.

"That'll take some getting used to," Lisa said.

"I find it endearing," Jayne said. "Generally, most Xandarj have little guile. Chok is just happy to see us and meet new people. Right, Chok?"

"Yes, Amanda Jayne," Chok said, with a slightly confused look on her face. "Why would I not be happy to see my friends?"

"I hate to break up the xenobiology lessons, but we should probably get into these suits," AJ said, picking up a folded suit that Beverly had placed a virtual glowing nametag on. "They're thin enough that you can wear them under your clothes if you want, but that ends up getting old after a while. Sometimes I just throw on pants because they're a little snug around the middle."

"This passenger compartment is a lot nicer than the rest of the ship, what gives?" Lefty asked, picking up his suit and turning toward one of the adjacent heads.

"Earth is not a high-priority diplomatic destination," Chok said, unwrapping herself from Jayne. "The diplomats were not powerful enough to request the luxury transports. I am sorry if it is not to your liking, Lefty Johnson. I assure you it is quite well maintained and will serve us well."

"Fair enough."

"How about weapons?" AJ asked. "Does it have any offense?"

"No, Albert Jenkins, diplomatic vessels are unarmed. The armor, however, is very sturdy," Chok said, picking up a suit. "Lisa Jackson, I will help you dress. It is sometimes difficult the first few times. Please remove your clothing."

"I will not," Lisa said, taking the folded suit from Chok. "I've been pulling tight clothing over these old bones for decades. I'm certain I can figure it out." Anticipating her next move, Jayne quickly intercepted and showed Lisa how the latches worked on the hatches.

AJ changed into his suit once Lisa was gone, leaving his shirt crumpled on a chair before heading forward to the bridge.

"Have they changed their bearing?" he asked, placing a hand on Greybeard's back to pet the dog, who had his face in a display.

"We could get around the frigate that's tailing us from Earth. We have a bunch of fuel and this little diplomatic transport is pretty sporty – if we're willing to lean into it," Darnell said.

"It would delay our trip," Blue Tork said. "But I would enjoy an opportunity to explore Earth."

"Kind of feels like they're trying to lead us down that path," Darnell said.

"You think they want us to go back?"

"It's just a feeling," Darnell said. "They've drifted away from the primary navigation line. Why introduce that inefficiency? It's not like Cheell don't have decent computers."

"What happened to Earth being on lockdown?" AJ asked. "I thought Galactic Congress had us on quarantine."

"That was recently lifted for diplomatic missions," Tork said.

"The Cheell risk penalties from the Galactic Congress in addition to reprisals from Dralli if their actions are hostile."

"Let me guess, it would take Galactic Congress a long time to make that sort of decision," AJ said.

"That is true. Often the penalties for actions are not outweighed by the rewards. I hope this is not such a case," Tork said.

"I feel like going back to Earth is a trap," AJ said. "Galactic Congress might not be much of a threat, but wouldn't getting cut off from Xandarj be immediate?"

"Yes. Inbound trade would be cut off and contracts would be shifted to non-Cheell carriers. It would be a boon for crews such as mine."

"You're kind of hoping they come after us, aren't you?" AJ asked.

"Oh, no," Tork said. "A Cheell frigate is not to be underestimated. Even with our enhanced diplomatic armor, if the frigate were to stay in weapon's range for even one minute, we would be destroyed."

"Got it. So why not just accelerate hard at them? You said we're faster, right?"

"It is a matter of cost. Such acceleration would run past even your generous reserve of Fantastium," Tork said. AJ's smile drew the Xandarj's attention. "Unless you have even more Fantastium. Albert Jenkins, have you sand sacked me?"

"Term is sandbagged," AJ said. "How much do you need?"

"An additional forty milligrams would allow us to accelerate maximally," he said.

"I was saving it for a rainy day," AJ said, pulling out a small vial.

"I thought the auditors were all over that," Darnell said. "How'd you bring so much extra?"

"Like they have any idea how to track this stuff," AJ said.

"Right, but if the government is watching – like we know they are – they'll be able to calculate our usage," Darnell said.

"I think you give them too much credit," AJ said. "And besides, at this point, I think the goal is to make it to Dralli station in one piece.

If the US government wants to send a pencil pusher after us to make some accounting entries, I say, let 'em."

"It might make going back home harder," Darnell said. "You need to be sure, AJ. Those government boys aren't screwing around."

"I say we worry about today and let tomorrow take care of itself."

Darnell heaved a sigh. "I'm in. Tork, the man says light her up and I say we give him a show."

"Crewman Chok, please join us on the bridge," Tork called.

A couple of moments later, Chok appeared. "Yes, Captain?"

Tork handed her the vial of Fantastium to her and smiled as her smile turned feral. "Now we're getting somewhere," she growled throatily, snatching it from his fingers. "I'll instruct our passengers to take their seats and get this loaded."

"AJ, you should probably go back with her," Darnell said. "This little ship has darn big engines for her mass."

AJ followed Chok and exchanged a glance with Jayne.

"What's up, AJ?" she asked.

"We're going to make a run for it," he said. "There's a frigate on our tail and one ahead of us. We think they're trying to box us in or at least drive us back to Earth. We need to get into the center seats and strap in. The inertial systems will work more effectively if we're not out toward the ship's edges."

"What about the truck? Did anyone even think to strap it down?" Lefty asked.

"Oh, you are a cute one, too," Chok said, smiling at him. "I would not be much of a crewman if I allowed cargo to bang around unsecured."

Lefty sat in a chair and started fumbling with the straps. Even with Rebel's instruction, he struggled. Chok pulled his hands away and snapped him in, and then scampered from the compartment, singing happily as she did.

"I can't get a read on her," Lefty said. "Is she simple in the head?"

"Xandarj intelligence scores are roughly equivalent to human," Jayne said, chuckling. "What you're getting confused by is their society's dislike of pretense. As humans, we judge people we meet on external factors and make decisions about how we'll interact with them. Xandarj are more social and seek physical contact. For whatever reason, that leaves much of the pretense behind. If you give it time, you'll find it refreshing."

Suddenly, the four humans in the passenger compartment were pressed into their chairs as if a big hand had grabbed them and was trying to smash them like bugs. A moment later, when the inertial systems adjusted to the changing environment, much of that pressure was reduced.

"What was that?" Lisa asked, reaching for her neck.

"Are you feeling nauseous, Lisa?" Jayne asked, concerned.

"I don't normally get motion sick, but yes, I might be ill."

"Nit tells me there's a panel in the top of the arm of your chair," Jayne said. "Push your finger into the leftmost well. It might be a little tight since it is designed for Xandarj."

"Ow," Lisa said.

"Sorry, I should have warned you. That was a small injection. It should help."

"Thank you, Nit," Lisa said.

On the forward bulkhead of the passenger compartment, a starfield appeared. Earth, the Moon, and Mars appeared on opposite ends of the projection. The view zoomed in, eliminating Mars off the right edge and Earth off the left edge until only the moon could be seen. As the moon continued to expand, suddenly three vessels appeared, two bulky frigates bracketing a much smaller, sleeker vessel that was easily identified as the Xandarj diplomatic transport.

"That's us," Lisa pointed out unnecessarily.

"Holy cow, look at the speed we're putting on," Lefty said.

"We'll never get around that frigate in front of us," Lisa said. "We're headed right at it."

"Beverly, at current acceleration, for what duration will we be within range of that frigate's weapons?" AJ asked.

"No more than fifteen seconds."

"That's bad, right?" Lefty asked. "Fifteen seconds is a long time to be under fire. Tell me we have some way to fire back or that we'll drop a kinetic load and jam 'em up, good."

"This ship is heavily armored," AJ said. "It's designed to withstand at least four times what that frigate can throw at us in that much time."

"And you're going to hang your hat on that? There's a freaking busted faucet in the head. Who knows what else is busted?"

"Lefty, are you claustrophobic by chance?" Jayne asked.

"Let me guess, you've got a shot for that."

"There is a shot for just that," Jayne said. "You should try it."

"This sucks. I better not get some new disease from a dirty needle," Lefty said, nervously exploring a similar opening in the top of his chair that Lisa had utilized. A moment later his head sagged onto his chest.

"What was that?" AJ asked, chuckling. "Did you solve his issue by knocking him out?"

"Seems to have worked," Lisa said. "Are we safe?"

AJ looked at the display nervously as their ship pulled into the area Beverly had shaded to represent the Cheell ship's weapons range. Tension filled the cabin as their smaller ship passed the larger one in complete silence and slipped out the other side of the shaded area without any exchange of hostilities.

A whoop of excitement carried through the hallway from the cockpit. A moment later, Darnell appeared in the cabin and wrapped up his still strapped-in wife with his big arms, kissing her fully on the lips.

"Now that's how the big boys do it," he said when he finally released her.

FIVE

PIRATE TREASURE

"You know, nobody prepares you for how boring spaceflight is. I'm all in," Lisa said, pushing a stack of candies and pretzels into the center of the table.

"You will not win again, pretty lady," Chok said, pushing her stack of snacks into the center. "This might be a new game to me, but I have very good cards this time."

"It hasn't gotten old to be called *pretty*," Lisa said. "But it won't change the cards. Doc, I think it's to you."

"I value my snacks too much to chase this hand," Jayne said, munching on pretzels.

"AJ?" Lisa tilted her head at him in challenge.

"Too rich for my blood," he said with a shrug.

Lisa grinned and flipped her hand over, exposing a pair of jacks.

"Aww, you are the winner again," Chok said, placing her hand right side up with a pair of twos and a pair of fours.

Lisa shook her head and slid the snacks in Chok's direction. "Two pair beats any single pair in poker."

Chok grinned as she swept the snacks into a plastic bag. "We will exit jumpspace in thirty minutes. I have tasks that must be accomplished. Would Lisa Jackson like to help Chok? I can pay quite well with snacks."

Lisa wiped the tabletop with a damp rag and dropped it in the ship's recycler. "I don't even need to be paid," Lisa said. "Ship maintenance beats sitting around and staring at the walls."

"More than two pair beats a single pair? Will you tell me of your children while we work? I want to hear more about this football your son plays. Why do they wear pads?" Chock asked, the volume of her voice diminishing as she walked aft to the engineering bay.

"Grandson," Lisa said, hurrying to catch up.

AJ looked at Jayne and smiled as he sat back in his chair. "Anxious about what lies ahead? It's been a while since you had a first day of school."

"I don't think I'd do it if Nit wasn't along," she said. "I didn't think I'd ever be okay with a Beltigersk rider after Jack but Nit is so curious about everything."

"Not sure I'd like to have someone with a constant stream of questions hammering away at me," AJ said.

"She's not like that," she said. "We do have extended conversations sometimes, but mostly, I just get a feeling about her moods and interests. She's a lot less animated than Beverly."

"Hope you still have room for this old vet when I come scratching around."

Jayne leaned over and picked up his hand. "It's going to be a challenge for us with you off-station messing with your junk pile, and me all wrapped up in academics. We need to be careful so we make time for each other. I'm committed to making that time, AJ. I hope you are too."

"You know I am," he said, leaning over to kiss her cheek. She turned and met his lips with her own.

"Okay, you two, break it up," Darnell said, appearing from the forward cockpit he and Blue Tork had been sharing. "We're not sure what we'll run into once we drop into Xandarj space. Probably best if we get everyone strapped in."

It was a conversation they'd beaten to death over the last few days in jumpspace.

"Go time?" AJ asked. "Anyone seen Lefty?"

"I'm coming," Lefty grumped from the open hatch to his private bunk. Having been at sail for the better part of twenty days, the confinement of a small ship had been especially hard on him.

"BB, would you mind projecting a forward display once we drop from jumpspace?" AJ asked. "I think Lefty would appreciate seeing something other than stars and all that."

"That's an understatement," Lefty said. "I'll tell you, I miss the swamp something fierce."

"Maye we should get you over to hang out with Queenie," AJ said. "There's a darn fine bog on Halfnium-8."

"Wouldn't be the same," Lefty said, sitting heavily in a chair with a quickly drawn cup of water. "You're not trying to kick me out of your junkyard, are you?"

"Nope. Just spitballing."

"I've been talkin' with Rebel," Lefty said. "She's been tellin' me about zero-g and gettin' around in space. Did you know they've got a thruster suit that makes a man into a spaceship for all intents and purposes?"

"You mean we don't need to use handguns for thrust?" AJ asked.

"No. I didn't like that one bit," Lefty said. "These thrust suits use a propellant. She says they're good enough to get us between Dralli Station and that old heap Mads Bazer sold you on."

"There's a lot of small ship traffic around Dralli Station," AJ said. "Wouldn't that be like walking on an interstate?"

"Thank you, AJ," Rebel said, appearing on Lefty's shoulder. "Just because you can do something doesn't mean it's a good idea. I told him about those suit enhancements and that's all he can talk about, now."

"Lefty, we'll get a small craft that can get us around," AJ said. "No need to be risking life and limb."

"I don't know. I like to wander. You know how it is."

"I do," AJ said. "We'll get it worked out."

"You are very good at ship maintenance." Chok could be heard saying as she and Lisa came forward.

"Time to get strapped in, ladies," Darnell said, addressing Chok and Lisa as they joined the others in the passenger compartment.

Lisa pecked him on the cheek and when he smiled and started forward, she slapped his butt before taking her seat.

Darnell had no more disappeared into the cockpit than Beverly started a projection onto the forward bulkhead. At first, the display showed an all too familiar scene of faraway stars moving across the viewing area, sometimes jittering and other times simply resetting with what looked like a fresh set of stars.

"Twenty seconds, guys," Darnell warned.

Beverly added a count-down timer. At the end of the countdown, the display suddenly changed. In place of sparse fields of distant stars, a green and blue planet appeared, about the same size as the Earth appeared when seen from the moon. In near space, a Dralli patrol ship steamed slowly toward the diplomatic vessel on a perfect line from Xandarj.

"Tork, is that patrol going to be a problem?" Darnell's voice filtered into the passenger compartment.

"Patrol Twelve, this is Dralli Diplo Fourteen," Blue Tork said. "Patrol Twelve, response requested."

For an uncomfortable minute, the two ships continued moving toward each other.

"Dralli Fourteen, this is Captain Longbur with Dralli Defense. Welcome home," the answer finally came.

"Darnell, the patrol will not be a problem. Captain Longbur is a friend of Chok's. He would not desire to make her angry."

"Tell Longbur that I will buy him a drink after his shift," Chok said.

"Patrol Twelve, we've had some trouble with Cheell warships in Sol. Can you inform as to any Cheell activity?"

"Negative Cheell activity," the disembodied voice added. "Mads Bazer has requested we escort you to Dralli Station, do you accept?"

"We do. Also, Chok would like to pass along a message that she invites you to drinks," Tork said.

"I had wondered if she might be aboard. I will message her privately," Longbur answered. "Patrol Twelve ends communication."

"Chok, why'd you invite him to drinks?" Lisa asked.

"Blue Tork spoke correctly. Longbur has an interest in Cariste Chok," she said. "I do not find him attractive, but I enjoy his company, especially when I have been locked into a vessel with beautiful monogamous humans for many days."

"Booty call," AJ said, laughing.

"AJ, you don't need to be crass," Lisa said.

"Beverly, can you highlight Mads Bazer's junk pile so I can get an idea of where it's at in relationship to the Dralli Station? And maybe highlight that Illaden station also," AJ requested.

Three faint blue circles appeared atop planet Xandarj. Even though the planet was about the size of a dinner plate on the projection, the circles were difficult to separate. "Could you zoom in so the stations fit?"

"Yes, AJ," Beverly said. The green planet seemed to sail toward them as it grew in size, its northern and southern poles just touching the ceiling and deck, respectively. Center right, the fat white tire shape of Dralli Station appeared with small crafts zipping all around it like bees on a hot day. Almost halfway across the Xandarj globe, an almost indistinguishable smudge sat centered within a second blue circle. The third blue circle sat only a bit to the left of that.

"What's with the left two?" Lefty asked.

AJ walked up to the projection. He'd worked enough with Beverly that they'd developed common hand signals for manipulating three-dimensional projections. Grabbing the smudge in the center of the circle, he pulled it near and pushed his left hand away, expanding as it grew closer, effectively zooming in.

"I've seen a couple of renderings of this pile," AJ said. "At the center of the heap is an old Pertaf spaceliner that got busted up when it collided with a freighter."

"Spaceliner?" Lefty asked.

"BB, drop the planet and other stations," AJ said.

The green planet blinked out from behind the junk heap. "Add ambient light so we're not working so hard to see things." The details jumped to life as hidden surfaces became visible. What quickly became evident was that through the center of a morass of unrecognizably twisted ship hulks, ran a two-mile-long and three-hundred-yard-tall ship. As his eyes followed the line of the once-majestic ship, AJ noticed that large portions looked like they'd just left the shipyard on its maiden voyage. About a third of the way forward from the aft, however, an entire section of the ship was missing, like a giant shark had taken a big bite.

"That's a lot to take in," Lisa said. "And you've got control of that whole junkheap for fifty years? I'd think others would have already salvaged everything valuable."

"More like we have control," AJ said. "I was thinking I'd make a company. Xandarj law isn't that much different than ours for incorporation. We might be able to declare ourselves an independent territory if we want."

"Make your own laws?" Lefty asked.

"Taxes are more likely," Lisa said. "Don't you want Dralli Station to provide protection? If those Cheell are still coming, separating from one of the big boys on the block might not be a good idea."

"It's the Wild West out here," AJ said. "Dralli patrols won't break up most fights unless it spills over to damaging Dralli property."

"If the fight lasts, sometimes we're ordered to intervene," Blue Tork added from his hidden position in the cockpit. He and Chok accepted diplomatic mission contracts but more often fulfilled patrol contracts much like Longbur. "Many times, a Dralli boss will reach out to one party or the other to offer protection in the middle of the fight. That almost always puts an end to it. And you are right, Lefty Johnson, that junk heap has been well picked, at least on the edges.

I've heard rumors that there are treasures deep in the Pertaf liner that no one has ever gotten to. There's even a story about how the captain of the freighter was paid to hit 'em right where she did so it would open up that liner's belly."

"Hidden treasure? Are we pirates now?" Lefty asked, chuckling for the first time in many days.

"Yar!" Darnell called from the cockpit.

AJ continued to virtually spin the junk heap. As he did, the surfaces that pointed away from their ship showed up as less distinct and even fuzzy in places as Beverly's uncertainty grew.

"Hey, hold on," Lefty said. "Is someone living there? Look at that flat space. Who'd do that if they were just dropping off junk?"

"There have been six owners of this heap," AJ said. "Mads Bazer is just the latest. According to her, at least two of them lived out there – like I plan to do. That's part of the reason I'm interested. I need a place to stay while I do my junkyard thing."

"Is the space liner livable? Can we even walk around in it?" Lisa asked. "What if it was built by a race of midget goats?"

"BB, want to show her a Pertaf next to a human?" AJ asked.

The screen suddenly switched to show examples of the two humanoids side by side. The human was Darnell, wearing a pair of tight shorts but otherwise naked. Next to him stood an alien with a slightly protruding, muted yellow beak in place of its mouth, bright blue eyes slightly set back into its skull and short, wide feathers in place of hair on its head. The Pertaf body was similar to a human's: muscles in roughly all the same places. Identical shorts to Darnell's were also required. One noticeable difference was the claws protruding from the ends of each finger and toe.

"Well, hello there," Lisa said, when the Pertaf slowly turned, exposing tufts of feathers covering its shoulder blades. "Can they fly?"

"The Pertaf cannot form an airfoil and is not capable of flight," Beverly said. "Not visible is the fact that their skeletal material is stronger than a human's but is porous. They are fifty percent less dense per volume than humans and Xandarj. They are also twenty-five percent taller than average humans."

"So, there should be plenty of room to get around if we end up getting into that liner," Lisa said.

"Why, Lisa Jackson, you sound like you've got some interest in this here venture," AJ said.

Lisa poked up a single eyebrow and grinned at AJ. "Nobody told me about buried gold," she said. "I was in when we were talking about scrapping, but this just took a real interesting turn."

"HEY KIDS, we're closing in on the station," Darnell said. "Might want to look out front for a while."

"Go ahead, BB," AJ said.

For the several hours it had taken them to sail in from the jump-space terminus, Lisa had quizzed AJ on his vision for setting up a business to take advantage of the orbital junkyard over Xandarj-3. Lefty had seemed mostly interested and tossed in a question or two. Jayne, on the other hand, had grown quieter and more withdrawn as they approached.

On the forward display, gaped the large mouth of a hanger. A blue film of energy was the only thing holding atmosphere from escaping, while allowing ships to pass, unhindered. Blue Tork slowed the diplomatic vessel and slid through, barely occupying a fifth of the opening with an expert's touch and directed the ship to its assigned berth.

"Place looks abandoned," AJ quipped, noting an occupancy that probably didn't exceed a third.

"Shift change for patrols," Blue Tork explained. "Although, I've heard business through Bazer's hangar has been down. Probably some seasonal thing."

"You have seasons in space?" Darnell asked.

"No, but planetside needs labor when it's fruit picking time," he said. "Lots of festivities at the end of the season, so there's always a lot of vacationers on the downside."

"That sounds fun," Lisa said, picking up on the conversation.

"Hey, are you okay?" AJ asked, nudging Jayne.

"I'm a little nervous," she said. "What if I don't like it. It's a big opportunity. I don't want to mess it up."

"You'll finally get to hang out with your people," he said.

"My people? I'm pretty sure I'm going to be the only human around," she said.

"Eggheads," AJ said. "You've been slumming it long enough with us grunts. Time to see if you can get that pinkie to rise back up when you drink your tea."

"I prefer coffee, now," she said.

AJ grinned. "Look Doc, I'm not looking forward to splitting up. But if I know one thing, it's that you need to hang out with a better class of people."

"Hey!" Lisa objected.

"I'm sure he doesn't mean you, Lisa," Jayne said. "By the way, whatever happened to you taking classes?"

"Oh, that's still on the table," Lisa said. "This DAS is so fired up about their diversity that they're offering to pay me to attend. And, Albert Jenkins, I don't want any of your lip about school bussing and integration."

"I'm just glad you addressed the elephant in the room," AJ replied with a laugh.

"Ship is secure," Darnell said. "Nice landing, Captain Tork."

"I'm receiving a communication request from my DAS coordinator," Jayne said, involuntarily touching her ear and standing so she could walk to the head where she could get some privacy. "Sorry guys, I need to take this."

"Get it," AJ said. "It'll take us a little doing to get settled."

Greybeard's barking started in the cockpit and announced his travel to the passenger compartment.

"Would someone shut that dog up?" Lefty complained.

"Lefty Johnson, I have started lowering the rear cargo elevator," Chok said. "Perhaps you would like to accompany me so we might offload your pack-up vehicle."

"Pickup truck," Lefty corrected.

Chok smiled. "Have you talked with Red Fairs yet about commissioning it for sale?"

"No. I was thinking Blue Tork would set me up."

Their voices faded as they walked aft, even though Greybeard continued his excitement. Blue Tork slipped down the outer edge of the passenger compartment where, once at the midpoint, he punched in a code on an antiquated numerical keyboard lock. The side of the ship popped outward, releasing cabin pressure and allowing thin beams of exterior light to intrude. As the door opened wider, clean station air replaced the slightly funky ship's air.

"I thought we were starting to develop a smell," Lisa said. "Chok said the ship needed new filter media but Dralli Diplomatic Core was too cheap to pop for it."

With the door fully open, a long staircase extended from the side of the small ship. Unexpectedly, Greybeard bolted for the stairs and raced down them, his muscular bulldog body barely clearing the edge of the treads which made him look like he was sliding down.

"Greybeard!" AJ called after him concerned that the barking dog was about to cause no end of trouble. Jumping onto the stairs, AJ raced down, taking them two at a time. He was no match, however, for the dog's speed. AJ watched as Greybeard hit the bottom of the stairs and tried to turn, his paws losing traction on the hangar's metallic decking. "Shit, Greybeard, get back here."

Greybeard regained his footing and with a clatter of nails on steel, raced forward, dodging behind a stack of crates. AJ sprinted after him, sliding around the stack of boxes. He saw Greybeard's target. A fat, old gray-furred Xandarj with oversized, aviator-styled glasses stood, looking at the bulldog missile headed her way.

"Mads, take cover!" AJ called, but to no avail. The old Xandarj stood her ground, watching as Greybeard left the ground, launching himself into her. For a moment, the noise was horrifying, a mix of screeches from the old woman and barking from the dog. AJ finally reached the two and pulled Greybeard off, terrified of what he'd find.

He was surprised to find Mads Bazer grinning broadly up at him as she wiped a grey-furred arm across her mouth. "Help an old woman up, you scrubbed hiney-ended simpleton."

AJ had to set Greybeard down to help the old Xandarj woman up. Greybeard, having expressed his joy at their meeting, was now wiggling almost uncontrollably as he bumped his forehead repeatedly into the short woman's body for attention.

Bazer pushed her gnarled fingers beneath Greybeard's collar and scrubbed his neck, accepting the dog's big pink tongue across her gnarled face. "Oh, you're a good boy."

SIX

HUMBLE BEGINNINGS

"Albert Jenkins, if you believe this animal will soften my negotiation, you have eaten too much fermented orangetag."

Mads Bazer – all three and a half foot of her – stood with her grey-furred arms planted defiantly on her hips, struggling to avoid a smile at Greybeard's continuing antics.

"We just landed and this guy decided to make a break for it," AJ said. "Although, if you want me to lease a junk heap that's been picked over for four decades, you're going to need to sharpen your pencil quite a bit."

"I do not know this idiom," Bazer said. "The price is very good. Many would take this deal."

"If that were true, you wouldn't have been trying to entice an earthling in an entirely different solar system ... but now's not the time. We just landed and we need to stow our supplies. I'd love to get on your calendar, though."

"You speak like an idiot," Bazer said, shaking her head. "I will make time for you tomorrow. You had better not waste it. I already find you distasteful."

"Be nice, Mads," AJ said, placing his hands over Greybeard's ears. "Kids are listening."

Mads' face transformed from anger to something more maternal, although still terrifying. "This beautiful animal is the only reason I speak to you at all."

"Tomorrow, then."

AJ went back to the ship where a small crowd of aliens had assembled. At first, he wasn't sure what the interest was, but then he saw that the cargo elevator had been lowered. On display was Lefty's old pickup truck, still holding five barrels of whiskey beneath its ratty old topper.

"What is it?" AJ felt a tug on his arm and found a younger Xandarj dressed in an oil-stained jumpsuit.

"Earth doesn't have anti-grav," AJ explained. "A good portion of our transportation is wheeled. We call that a pickup truck."

The adolescent Xandarj's eyes widened. "But it has so much corrosion. Is that part of the design?"

"It is," AJ said. "When the truck falls apart, they figure we'll buy a new one. Now, old Lefty there, he doesn't go by that and likes to keep 'em even after they start looking crappy. Still works. No reason to get a new one."

"Albert Jenkins."

AJ found the speaker. With fine red hair atop her head and virtually no visible fur on her face or neck, Red Fairs, Blue Tork's wife, was easy to pick out in a crowd. That she was flanked by a pair of helpers wearing the stylized, gray robes of her business didn't hurt, either.

"Red Fairs," AJ said, moving through the crowd to greet her.

"I was hopeful that Blue Tork would return with you," she said. "I hope you are pleased with how well our business was concluded."

"Damn, that's right, you were selling a bunch of stuff for me," he said. While he hadn't specifically forgotten, he'd also not checked in on his Galactic Empire financial account, either. "Did you already deposit the proceeds?"

When Red Fairs smiled, it broke the illusion that she was mostly human as her front canines were pronounced like most Xandarj. "I have included a detailed accounting for the items that were sold. We were quite fortunate as a Pertaf collector took significant interest in your rudimentary space vessel."

"BB, would you show account highlights?" AJ asked.

Beverly appeared, standing on a stack of crates from their vessel. She wore a conservative dark blue woolen skirt complete with a white blouse and suit jacket. "Of course. Red Fairs was quite success-ful," she said, holding out a piece of virtual paper to AJ. When he reached for the paper, it grew from the tiny size appropriate for Beverly to a full sheet of paper.

"Damn, one hundred forty thousand for that piece of crap? I think I paid six thousand," AJ mused. "Twelve thousand each for the weapons. Looks like we got killed on those Vred engines, though."

Red Fairs nodded. "It is easier to produce new engines that are specifically designed for an application than to refit. I was pleased that we were able to sell them at all."

"And this is after your cut?" AJ asked. He had one-hundred-sixty-two thousand galactic credits in his account.

"Yes, our books are settled."

"Does anyone else know how much we earned?" AJ asked.

"I suspect Mads Bazer is watching this conversation," Red Fairs said.

"Right. Darn it," AJ said. "Rookie mistake."

"Will you consider joining us for our mid-morning meal?" When she saw he wasn't understanding the invitation, she added. "Which is in four hours."

"We'll try to make it. There are a lot of things going on," AJ said. "Any chance I could request a favor?"

"Asking is always free," she said.

"We need a place to store that," he said, pointing at Lefty's truck.

"Ah, yes, the pick it truck," she said, carefully repeating what he hadn't thought she'd overheard. "The principal of wheels is not unfamiliar. What motivates it to move forward? An electric motor is contained within?"

"We call it the internal combustion engine," AJ said. "Don't suppose you've heard of that."

"It sounds dangerous."

"Can be," AJ said. "But that depends on who's behind the wheel."

"Is it operational?"

"Yeah. Probably looking at ten thousand pounds, give or take, though," AJ said, knowing his measurements would be translated.

"It is quite dense," Red Fairs said. "I hope you brought more trading goods. I have been receiving inquires as to your return."

"That's a different conversation," AJ said. "Any chance you can help stash the pickup?"

"You trying to sell my truck already?" Lefty asked, joining them.

"Just looking for storage, Lefty," AJ said. "I'm not sure you've met Blue Tork's wife, Red Fairs. She's a local trader down in The Trailer."

"I'll pretend I know what you just said," Lefty said. "Nice to meet you and don't lose my truck, okay?"

"It will be quite safe," Red Fairs said. "Enion, you will take this *pick it truck* to the green bay in our warehouse. Lefty Johnson, please instruct my helper as to the operation."

"I don't think so," Lefty said.

"I do not understand," Red Fairs said. "How will we move this internal combustion vessel?"

"Lefty, you'll be fined for atmospheric pollution if that truck is turned on here," Rebel said, appearing on the truck's hood, leaning against the cracked windshield. "Have them bring a tow spider. They'll know what I'm talking about."

"Well, apparently, we need a tow spider because of pollution," Lefty said. "But I'm still driving. I'm not gonna lose value because some idiot runs her into a post or something."

"Make sure you're packing, Lefty," AJ said. "We've had run-ins with Cheell on Dralli Station before."

"Most Xandarj do not care for Cheell, but caution is always

reasonable," Red Fairs said. "Enion, alert the staff that Cheell are about."

"As you say, Red Fairs," Enion answered, speaking for the first time. "Lefty Johnson, the tow spider approaches. Let us make haste."

"Fine, don't get your panties in a bunch."

"AJ, I'm glad I caught you," Jayne said, grabbing AJ's arm.

"Caught me?" AJ followed Jayne's eyes to a pair of well-scrubbed, neatly dressed, unassuming Xandarj. "Holy cow, are nerd types the same everywhere?"

"Be nice. My colleagues are quite distinguished in their respective fields," Jayne said.

"Which are?"

A tiny smile played over Jayne's face. "I have no earthly idea," she said. "They tried to explain. I think something like anthropology and xenobiology."

"I was hoping I could walk you over," AJ said. "You know, help you get checked in?"

Jayne's smile was warm. "I appreciate that AJ, I do," she said. "But I need to put on my big girl pants and do this on my own."

AJ swallowed, a lump forming in his throat. On numerous occasions, Jayne had seemed like she wanted them to be more than close friends. This was not one of those days. For most of the trip from Earth, she'd grown increasingly distant, not unlike his high school girlfriend who'd drifted away, going to college after AJ had been drafted.

"I gotcha, Doc," AJ said. "Kind of took me by surprise. That's all."

"Hey, we're still good, AJ. You're always going to be a big deal for me," she said and leaned in to kiss him. "I'll call you when I get settled. Okay?"

"Do you need help with your gear?" he asked, managing a smile.

"Nope, it's all loaded. Can't help but love those grav pallets," Jayne said and seemed to recognize his struggle. "Hey, bubba, nothing changes. We're all good."

"Knock 'em dead, Doc," he said.

Recognizing that the conversation was becoming awkward, Jayne smiled, turned toward her waiting colleagues, and set off.

"If you love her, let her go." The faint smell of Lisa's perfume reached AJ before her words.

"It's not just me, is it?" he asked, not turning to acknowledge her, wanting to keep his eye on Jayne as she departed.

"Relationships are strange business," Lisa said, wrapping an arm around his waist. "That woman has lived an entire life on her own. You're doing the right thing by not smothering her. I'll never admit I said this, but you're a pretty great guy. Maybe she just needs to know you'll stand by her."

"You don't think she's trying to brush me off?"

"Nah, she's more honest than that," Lisa said. "Don't get clingy. She'll let you know what she's feeling soon enough."

"I'm not sure if you're wise or you just suck," he said.

"Just 'cause I'm right, don't mean it don't suck." Lisa's voice shifted to a southern drawl.

"Well, shit. I suppose we should think about what's next," AJ said. "Enough moping for one day."

"There ya go," Lisa said. "Did you get that junk heap all worked out with that Mads Bazer?"

"I asked her if we could finish negotiations tomorrow."

"No need to be standing around," Darnell said, joining the pair. "I've got us a locker rented for our gear, but it isn't gonna move itself."

As they sailed for Xandarj, the group had manufactured standard shipping crates and repacked the remaining gear that hadn't been blown up by the Cheell. As almost all of AJ's gear had been in his truck, he had the least amount. Only one small soft-sided suitcase survived, containing a single change of clothing, five 750ml bottles of his favorite scotch and one bottle of the same rye whiskey Lefty had in the back of his truck.

"Hey, Tork," AJ called, getting Blue Tork's attention. "How hard to rent a runabout that's got enough juice to get over to Bazer's junk pile?"

"Due to your status as visiting aliens, Mads Bazer will want a significant deposit," he answered, pushing a stack of crates containing his gear over to them on an anti-grav pallet. "You could hire me to pilot you to your destination for a better price."

"How much?"

"Three hundred twenty credits."

"When can you leave?"

"I STILL CAN'T BELIEVE Lefty didn't want to come along," Lisa said, as the now-familiar junk heap grew in front of them.

"He needed to let his hair down," AJ said. "I'm not sure locking him back up in an even smaller ship made a lot of sense."

"It sounded like Chok wanted to go with him," Darnell said. "I didn't think those two got along all that well."

"Funny," Lisa said.

"Funny how?" AJ asked. "Funny that Chok would like Lefty or funny that a Xandarj and a human got together?"

"Funny that you didn't think they got along," Lisa said.

"No," AJ said, scandalized. "They completely ignored each other every time I was around."

"I don't think they know I know," Lisa said. "One late shift, I heard something odd. Someone had left a trap door open in Engineering. I would have just closed it, but I thought they might have gotten hurt. Let's just say, we don't need to question compatibility of the species."

AJ chuckled. "That dirty dog, playing off like he didn't have a care in the world."

"It is offensive to speak of pairings that occur in private on voyages," Blue Tork said.

"Are you saying Xandarj don't gossip?" Lisa asked.

"If it is gossip, it is okay," Blue Tork said. "It should not be mentioned to those who might take offense. Red Fairs knows that

Chok and I are often cozy on long trips just as she finds warmth from Enion when I am gone. It is not discussed, though."

"And that works for you?" Lisa asked. "If I found out my man was steppin' out on me, the last thing he'd hear would be me reloading my pistol."

"Ah, well that would explain Darnell's insistence on locking his bunk each time he slept," Blue Tork said. "Where is it you would like to visit on this heap, Albert Jenkins?"

"Let's see what kind of facilities the previous tenants built," AJ said, pointing to a makeshift scaffold of steel beams atop which sat a heavily weathered, stubby old spaceship. "Tell me that's not the tow vessel Mads Bazer was talking about."

"Looks like an old tugboat," Darnell said. "You know, except for not being in water and all."

Beverly appeared, wearing coveralls and a rocket pack. "That is a Veneri Class V extra-atmospheric hauler. Your analogy to a tugboat is accurate, AJ. It has multiple lift systems and was originally designed by Veneri Corporation for moving ground-built space habitats into orbit. Later on, these same ships were retrofitted with significantly oversized engines to help with moving orbiting hulks into position. Historically speaking, Dralli Station couldn't have been built without the Veneri EAH ships."

"So only good for in-close trips then?" AJ asked.

"Not exactly," Beverly said. "Nothing is preventing the Veneri EAH from long-haul trips aside from the cost of fuel."

"Veneri EAH. Doesn't exactly roll off the tongue," Darnell said.

"VEAH," Lisa said. "Like *yeah*, but with a *V*. Geez guys, get a little creative once."

"I believe Mads Bazer's EAH is in poor repair," Beverly said. "Although, if it is a consolation, I have located at least seven other partial EAH hulls in the heap."

AJ scanned the quickly approaching junk pile and took note of the highlighted tugboat wrecks in varying degrees of disintegration.

"Well, we'll need something that can move stuff. It doesn't need to be pretty."

Blue Tork set the small cargo vessel onto the scaffolding and deployed three mooring cables to stabilize its purchase. In front of an exposed forty-yard-wide, thirty-yard-tall portion of the Pertaf space liner sat a narrow porch that someone had welded onto the structure, just beneath a series of three rectangular hatches that looked like tall garage doors.

"I believe this was the previous occupant's base of operation," Blue Tork said.

"Any idea what they were doing?"

"The same as all previous occupants," Blue Tork said. "Looking for the treasure of the Pertaf liner."

"That's a pretty believable rumor if people are willing to pay so much to be out here," AJ said.

"It has become something of a joke amongst the Xandarj people," Blue Tork said. "If someone wishes to talk about a venture not likely to be successful, it is referred to as a Pertaf treasure hunt."

"Do you think Mads Bazer is making fun of me?"

"That is unavoidable," Blue Tork said. "Do you intend to go inside? Mads Bazer has asked that I ensure you do not remove any items."

"Did she pay you?" AJ asked.

"Forty credits," Blue Tork said, looking sheepish.

"Well played," Darnell said.

"It is the nature of Xandarj – please do not be offended. I would not have taken the credits if I believed you intended to remove property."

"You're good, my friend. She's got a right to her stuff," AJ said. "At least until it's my stuff."

"Are we going to do a spacewalk?" Lisa asked. "I've been pretty quiet about all this alien stuff so far, but I don't know how a space-walk is going to work. I don't want to be floating off or anything."

"We'll run a line from Tork's ship over to the door," AJ said. "Zero-g isn't that bad if you can keep your cookies down. Just get that face mask down and we'll take it nice and slow."

Blue Tork bled the small vessel's interior atmosphere and opened the wide side door. True to AJ's promise, he shot a magnetically anchored cable over to the Pertaf space liner, cinching it tight. With a short run of cable from their belts to a carabiner on the cable, he hoped the idea of a spacewalk would seem less intimidating.

"I will stay with the vessel so that I can respond to any failures," Blue Tork said.

AJ nodded and pushed away from the cargo vessel, appreciating the tug of the safety line when he veered from his intended destination. When he finally reached the space liner, he transferred his line to a waiting ring next to a man-sized hatch. "Come on across, Lisa," he called.

To her credit, Lisa jumped away without additional complaint. Her jump was aggressive, causing a hard yank when she reached the end of her short leash. "Dammit!" she exclaimed, cursing for the first time in AJ's memory. She tumbled as she continued toward him but managed to snag the taut cable with a flailing arm. The contact looked painful, but she used her grip to adjust her flight, this time, sailing with legs behind her and her hands pulling her along.

"Nice job, Lisa," Darnell encouraged and followed her out, having similar troubles on the way across.

"I'm getting one of those propulsion suits Lefty was talking about," she said. "I'm not doing that again. That was stupid."

AJ manipulated the simple handle and pushed open the door. "No atmosphere, not even an airlock," he observed, floating through the hatch. "Big D, see if you and Petey can find some lights."

"On it."

The room they entered was a hundred yards across and sixty yards deep with a soaring ceiling. Piles of junk were scattered all around. Scanning the area with powerful headlamps, AJ paused to assess the sleek curves of a civilian passenger vessel covered in dust. He had no idea of the ship's actual condition, but his junker's interest was piqued. He continued scanning and found a deep workbench, covered with tools, parts, and discarded food wrappings. Without gravity, some of the items were floating, but others retained their connection to the metal bench.

"I located a power plant, but it's going to take work to get it back online, AJ," Darnell said. "We're missing what amounts to a big fuse. Petey says they have plenty of 'em back on Dralli Station."

"Does that workbench seem off to you?" AJ said. "Who leaves their tools behind?"

"Someone expecting to come back," Darnell agreed. "We might have wanted to circle and investigate this heap a little more before we stopped. We don't know for a fact this place is abandoned."

"You know, good chance we get back to Tork's runabout and someone's got a gun on him," AJ said. "Seriously, how many times we gotta play this game?"

Lisa leaned out through the man-sized door. "Nobody out there aside from Blue Tork," she said. "AJ, what's on your mind? What are you looking for?"

"In here, I just wanted to see what kind of facilities were available. Big D, you said they have a power plant. Is it big enough to power gravity and life support systems?"

"That and quite a bit more," he said. "Petey says it's an artifact from the Pertaf liner. Power for days and then some. It's also multi-fueled and we can even use solar arrays ... which it looks like we don't have."

"Cool," AJ said. "I've seen enough in here. I'd like to check out the VEAH, though."

SEVEN

THAT'S A BIG PILE

"Man, that's a big sucker," AJ said, whistling through his teeth.

"Doesn't look that big until you get up on it," Darnell agreed.

"When first produced, the Veneri EAH was capable of lofting twenty thousand tons from the surface of Xandarj," Beverly said, appearing in her sparkly Jetsons suit in front of AJ as he pulled himself along the line connecting them to the sleeping workhorse. "Those boxy, external engines can rotate two hundred and seventy degrees and produce lift with gravity-repulsive technology as well as directed thrust."

"Twenty thousand tons?" AJ asked as he impacted a heavily rusted hatch and clipped over to a welded ring. Holding the line back to Tork's vessel, he tugged on his safety line to ensure the corrosion on the ring attached to the VEAH was solid. "That's almost a damn Naval cruiser. Can you imagine putting lines on one of those suckers and lifting it into space?"

"A little-known fact is the EAH vessels were designed to operate in groups. I read that the biggest recorded lift in Xandarj history was of a team of eight EAH lifters working on Dralli Station's central core. Once in orbit, the core was added onto for two decades until the station started manufacturing its own components," Beverly said.

"And then they didn't need these old girls anymore," AJ said, banging on a cover over the hatch controls.

Lisa bumped into the back of AJ as she arrived and switched over her safety line. "Why is there so much rust? I didn't think that was possible in space."

"This isn't that bad," AJ said, brushing off the exposed panel. "This ship is – what – maybe a couple centuries-old?"

"Very close. Two hundred forty years," Beverly filled in.

"We're maybe five hundred kilometers up," AJ said. "There's a little oxygen around, so oxidation still happens, but it's a slow process. The International Space Station has the same problem back home."

AJ tapped out a code he'd gotten from Mads Bazer and was gratified when the panel flashed green. A clank from within the ship warned that the ship's systems were waking up. The ten-foot-tall, six-foot-wide hatch hinged open, throwing a plume of red dust out from the ship.

"That rust doesn't seem like nothing," Lisa said.

"If this relic holds atmosphere, we've got nothing to worry about," AJ said. "If it doesn't, we'll add some steel. I have the same trouble with my old pickup back home."

"Trouble with atmosphere?" Lisa said.

"Kind of," AJ answered, pulling himself into an airlock big enough to hold six people. "If it rains too hard, I get wet. That's why I like living in Arizona. Doesn't happen often."

"Want me to add gravity?" Darnell asked, pulling a keyboard from the wall that was sized for the shorter Xandarj.

"How can you read that keyboard?" Lisa asked.

"Pretty common interface remap," Darnell said. "Most technology is designed to facilitate different species. Petey just uploads QWERTY and renames the commands. Look at the screen, you should be able to read it."

"Son of a gun," Lisa said. "Does that mean I'm gonna need to get a Petey?"

Darnell chuckled. "No. Petey says we can manufacture a simple interface translator for you to carry, just in case we get separated."

"I'm not sure I'm ready for that," Lisa said.

"I could pressurize too," Darnell said. "This old girl has full O_2 tanks. She's pretty good at recovering ambient gasses."

"Let's not," AJ said, his feet settling to the deck as gravity systems were energized. "We have no idea if she leaks. I'd hate to start her up with no way to make repairs. BB, could you give me a floorplan?"

"EAH vessels were designed for a semi-permanent crew of eight," Beverly said, displaying a single passageway, running the length of the vessel. "We will take the elevator on the other side of this airlock to the only deck."

"Deck? That looks like a hallway to me," AJ said, pushing open the unlocked airlock door. Unlike the exterior of the ship, the interior showed no corrosion, although there was considerable evidence of the many salvagers who'd come before them.

"It might be easier to see it in person," Beverly said, as the elevator moved upward. AJ pulled at Beverly's projection. Beneath the passage were boxy rooms, all in a row but with no hallway joining them, aside from the overhead passageway.

Lights blinked on as the steel cage of the elevator rose upward. AJ took interest in hatches both aft and forward as they passed them without stopping. "Maintenance hatches?" AJ finally asked.

"There are five maintenance decks," Beverly said as the wobbly, steel elevator suddenly stopped, its floor a few inches below the height of a long, wide passageway leading forward. Dim green lights popped on, sequencing from aft to forward in recognition of their presence. "The maintenance decks are just passages that lead to ship systems."

"They didn't exactly go all out on interior finishes, did they?" Lisa asked, gingerly stepping up and out of the elevator after swinging open the expanded steel door to the elevator car. For emphasis, she wiped her glove along the wall, blackening the material and leaving a swipe mark.

"Utilitarian is probably the keyword here," AJ said, jumping up next to her.

Instead of being perfectly rectangular, the passageway was more of an irregular octagon. The flat surface under their feet was six feet wide and then the floor angled up at a twenty-degree angle for another three feet on each side. He noticed the same angled detail above his head near the ceiling.

"What's with the squat octagon?" Darnell asked, joining Lisa and AJ.

"I think that's how you get into the crew quarters," AJ said, pointing forward to the rows of hatches on both the port and starboard angled walls.

"The EAH is too narrow for normal crew accommodations," Beverly said. "This design allows for rooms to utilize minimal horizontal space."

AJ walked up to the first hatch and pulled it open. "It's like looking into the top of an orange juice box," he said. "There's a reason people don't have hallways on top of rooms. Nobody wants to fall in."

"Room gravity is adjusted to .4g," Beverly said. "If you were to jump in, your fall would not likely cause damage. There are direct gravity systems for the bunks so occupants do not suffer calcium loss."

Lisa scowled in disgust. "Looks like they used this one for storing trash."

"It is unlikely this vehicle has been used recently," Beverly said. "There would be no reason for expending effort for upkeep."

"We need some ball gloves," Darnell said. "This is a great space."

"Or tennis rackets," Lisa said. "The slanty floor would be interesting, though."

"Frisbee?" AJ offered, earning him an appreciative nod as the trio walked forward.

"More cockpit than I was expecting," Darnell said, sliding into one of the five available seats. Glass windows wrapped around three sides, overhead and even on a portion of the floor, although the floor windows were covered with gunk. When he started flipping switches and moving levers, the cockpit display jumped to life. "We've even got some gas. That was thoughtful. Should I fire up the engines?"

"I'd say so," AJ said. "If I'm gonna drop my life's savings on this, I'd like to know we've at least got some wheels."

"Blue Tork, this is Darnell, do you read?" Darnell said, adopting his calm pilot's voice.

"Darnell Jackson, I am looking at your position in the Veneri vessel. Do you think it will meet Albert Jenkins' needs?"

"We were just thinking about taking it out for a spin," Darnell said. "Would you mind detaching the safety line?"

"A spin? I do not believe the Veneri EAH is suitable for acrobatic maneuvers," Tork said.

"Sorry, buddy, it's a figure of speech," Darnell said. "We just want to see if it flies."

"Yes, I am detaching and I will follow so that I might provide aid if it is needed."

"You mean you want to make sure you can tell Mads Bazer what we were doing, right?" AJ said, unable to resist pointing out the obvious.

"Yes. Darnell Jackson, the safety line is detached. You are free, but please be aware of my position. The EAH vessels are notoriously difficult to navigate due to their substantial bulk."

"Wouldn't be fun if it was easy," Darnell said. "Petey, you ready?"

In AJ's peripheral vision, a red exclamation point appeared over the top of a grime-encrusted video display. "Is that a problem, Petey?" AJ asked, settling into a seat farthest from Darnell.

If not for Beverly's overlay, AJ might have had trouble making out the information scrolling on the screen. Two of the four main engines were having trouble maintaining requisite pressure in a subsystem he didn't recognize the name of. From the damage they'd seen on the outside of the ship, he wasn't surprised to find systems not working.

"BB, can we turn these two off?" AJ asked, dragging at a virtual fuel intake lever.

"I believe so," she answered, appearing on the bulkhead that held the display, wearing coveralls and a red polka dot scarf. "But not all the way. That will shut all systems off."

Without full understanding but a lifetime of working with complex mechanical systems, AJ feathered the valves, adjusting the flow of fuel and oxygen so that minimal amounts were lost and Darnell still received a portion of the available power. "Big D, I think that's about as good as it's gonna get for now," he said. The red exclamation point above his panel turned into a green checkmark and disappeared. "Looks like Petey's in agreement, too."

"Hold onto your butts," Darnell said, his fingers flying across a panel. A low vibration rattled through the old ship. "That doesn't sound good."

"Kind of like a chicken bone caught in a garbage disposal," AJ said. "I think I see something, give me a second." With visual suggestions from Beverly, he adjusted the control surfaces of the four massive engines and did what any good mechanic does – listened to the changes. After several failed attempts, the engine noise evened out. "Not sure if this should sound like an old Ram diesel, but I think that's about as good as it's gonna get for today."

"We're moving," Darnell said. "Darnit. Tork, move out of the way."

"You need to turn or you will hit the junk pile," Tork answered. "I will not be in your way, however."

"I see it," Darnell said as the large vessel continued to slide dangerously toward the old space liner and surrounding junk.

"Big D, you have this?" AJ asked, nervously watching their progress.

"It's gonna be close," Darnell answered, chuckling. "I've got two engines on the starboard and just about nothing on the port. Not sure how anyone ever used this thing."

"Bubba, I'm pretty sure we're gonna hit on the bottom," AJ said.

Darnell was making progress at turning the ship, but that

progress was evenly matched by how quickly they were approaching the topside of the junk heap.

"Yeah, I see your point," Darnell said, working to keep the strain from his voice. At the last second, he spun the starboard engine to twist the ship clockwise, lifting the belly up and over the tallest piece of junk. "That's a good girl." He leaned forward and patted the ship. "Any chance we could put some work into getting at least one of those port engines working? It'd make this whole flying thing a lot easier."

"Sure," AJ said. "I'm not sure how you made it work at all, though. Kind of defies physics, at least the way I see it."

"I was using the gravity repulsor to balance things," Darnell said. "Doesn't work real well, but it should get us around the block a couple of times."

"I'll get those engines on the list," AJ said. "Feels like it's gonna be a big list."

"Do you see that light?" Lisa asked, interrupting the conversation and pointing. Both AJ and Darnell tried to follow her finger, but they couldn't see what she saw.

"What kind of light?" AJ asked. "Big one, like maybe a reflection, or more like a flashlight?"

"More like a flashlight, but it did come and go fast," she said. "I suppose it could have been a reflection."

"BB, mark the general area," AJ said. "We can come back and poke around later if things work out."

"You crack me up with all that," Lisa said.

"All what?"

"Saying, *if things work out*," Lisa said. "No way you're walkin' away from this."

"Not sure how I'd make money here," AJ said. "You know why you never see a junkyard get sold?"

"They have to get sold," Lisa said.

"Not very often," AJ said. "It's because nobody sees the real value in it. Owners see all the possibilities. Buyers see a pile of junk."

"It is a pile of junk," Lisa said. "And you made money back in Arizona."

"Barely enough to survive," AJ said. "If I didn't have my retirement account from the company, I'd have likely starved."

"You're admitting that rebuilding those Subarus wasn't a money maker?" Darnell asked.

"No," AJ said defensively. "I made damn good money fixing them up."

"Could have worked at Wally World and come out better," Darnell said.

"Hardly," AJ said. "I've seen two dozen halfway decent-looking runabouts since we've been sailing. I bet I could put a few of those back together and turn a decent profit. Besides, I think the real money is in long haul recoveries."

"Say what?" Darnell asked.

"Look at this Pertaf liner," AJ said. "The ship got its ass broke off and someone turned it into a permanent orbital feature, but most wouldn't go to that much trouble. What if we came along and offered to haul derelict craft off? We'd add to the pile and get paid for doing it."

"I don't think even this EAH could bring back a broken-down space liner," Darnell said.

"Maybe not in one piece," AJ said. "Imagine getting a salvage contract on a space liner. These Xandarj lack imagination. They are so darn used to everything getting printed in dumb little manufacturies. Junkers are all about repurpose and reuse."

"Still on the fence, then?" Lisa said, grinning.

"You've got me there," AJ agreed. "What I need are partners. This here is on a new scale. I was kind of hoping you'd join me, Big D."

"What about me?" Lisa asked. "Or am I just a weak woman that you need to drop back at the station?"

"Don't answer that, bubba," Darnell said. "That there is a trick question."

"You're the one who said she wanted to get a degree at DAS," AJ said. "You want in?"

"What are the terms?" Lisa asked.

"Credits invested are shares," AJ said. "We share based on a percentage of ownership. If you go off on your own and use company resources, you gotta cut us in on the revenue. We can draw something up, but I'd think we could play it fairly loose as long as we're talking."

"Who's in charge?" Lisa asked.

"I am," AJ said. "It's my idea, but I don't need to run everything. We could come up with roles. Like I'd be in charge of long-haul recoveries. And you could be in charge of cleaning hallways."

Lisa was out of her chair and had taken two quick steps before AJ even saw her move. The punch he saw coming, and he knew better than to dodge it. A meaty thwack sounded when she made contact. "You're an asshole!"

"I've never heard you cuss in my life and now, twice in an hour. Are you sure you want to be part of this?"

"I'm not cleaning your damn hallways."

"I wasn't serious," AJ said. "We'll make Big D do it."

"Don't drag me into this," Darnell said.

"I want to work the markets," Lisa said.

"How?" AJ asked.

"I want to find buyers for stuff we get working or I want to buy stuff people need," she said. "I've always had a good eye for quality. I made out on eBay until it got crazy."

"Yeah, those online auctions turned into commodity markets awful fast," AJ said. "If you want to run marketing and sales, I say, you're in. I know I don't love selling. We might need to get you a commission, though. Most salesmen don't do well without a structured payout."

"If I own part of the company, I'm not sure why that'd matter," Lisa said.

"Motivation for when you're having a crappy day. Let's say you've struck out ten times in a row, commission is one of those reasons why you'll make that eleventh call," AJ said.

"He's right, Lisa," Darnell said. "Sales are tougher than it sounds – take the commish."

"Let's set it at ten percent. If you don't think that's fair after you've done it a while, we can adjust."

They sailed quietly as Darnell circled the junk pile.

"Can you imagine what NASA could do with just one of these EAH vessels?" AJ asked. "They'd pay hundreds of millions, possibly billions, for something that could comfortably lift fourteen thousand tons."

"What happens to Earth's economy once all this alien stuff gets out?" Lisa asked. "Just about everything we've seen would wreck some part of the economy."

"Crap," AJ said as Darnell slowed his approach to where the Veneri vessel had been moored.

"What?" Lisa asked.

"What if that's it?" AJ asked.

"What if *what's* it?"

"The attacks on the vets who helped us run off Korgul," AJ said. "We all saw technology that was revolutionary and besides, the simplest answer is generally the truth. If the government and big business can slow the release of technology to Earth, they make bank on every big new idea. If technology is just free to everyone, those in charge don't make nearly as much money."

As a group, they walked down the passageway and into the rickety elevator, taking it back down to the airlock.

"You know, it should be obvious if that's the case," Darnell said.

"How?" AJ asked.

"If they think we're all distracted trying to make a go here in Xandarj space and we don't make a move to capitalize on bringing tech back home, they should just leave us alone, right?" Darnell said.

"Yeah, but that kind of makes it seem like we're rolling over," AJ said, grinning.

"Oh, come on already," Darnell said. "I know what it means when you get that look in your eye. We don't always have to be troublemakers, you know."

"But how will the information get back to humanity?" Lisa asked. "What? We're going to trust government officials to make sure any tech we send will be fairly and equitably distributed?"

"Oh, man," Darnell said. "There's no putting that cork back in its bottle."

"Don't you sass me, Darnell," Lisa said. "Time and time again, we've seen our highest elected officials making backroom deals to line their own pockets. This isn't getting rich on foreign energy contracts. We're talking about technology that would save people's lives – medicines to cure cancer, Parkinson's, and ... everything. The treatment I was given, for example. Did you know I had colon cancer?"

"What?" Darnell asked, his face suddenly ashen.

"Yeah. Gone now," Lisa said. "All because of what Nit and Amanda Jayne did for me. Should I be treated differently than the woman down the street?"

"We gotta be careful, Lisa," Darnell said. "Yes. I agree. It's important that medical technology – heck, technology in general – gets distributed fairly, but that's a tall order. I'm not sure it's something we can do."

"I'm not letting this go," Lisa said, opening the airlock door and clipping her line to the reattached safety line.

Darnell looked to AJ for support but found his friend just smiling back at him. "You're no help."

"Nope," AJ said, sliding along the safety line.

EIGHT

TRADES ON THE TABLE

"If you believe leaving this gray monster behind will soften my negotiation, you are incorrect," Mads Bazer said, peering up at AJ from behind her immense round spectacles.

"Honestly, we didn't have a good suit for him," AJ said. "He seems to enjoy being with you. The current plan is that he's going to live with Doc Jayne over at DAS."

"Is that still the plan? Have you talked to Amanda?" Lisa asked. Greybeard turned to each speaker in turn and then barked at Lisa's question. "What is it, boy? Did Timmy get stuck in the well?" Greybeard's tail wagged furiously and he bumped his head against her leg.

"Who is Timmy?" Mads asked.

"Inside joke," AJ said. "And no, no bribe with Greybeard. However, I do have something else." AJ withdrew a 750ml bottle of ten-year-old Rye Whiskey. "I brought this bottle to facilitate our negotiations."

"Is that your fire drink?" Mads asked, greedily eyeing the bottle.

"Having time to prepare, I selected this bottle especially for our meeting, Mads," he said, accepting glasses Mads pushed onto the table in her office where she sat with him and Lisa. "I also brought a few chunks of ice to temper this Rye Whiskey from Tennessee. Just so you know, this is a one hundred and twenty dollar bottle. It's expensive."

Lisa dropped two ice cubes into each glass and waited for AJ to pour.

"Where is the pretty, dark man?" Mads asked.

"Shopping in the Trailer," AJ said, referring to the large market-place that sprawled across an entire level of the massive space station. "Blue Tork is helping him find parts we need."

Mads tipped the glass back and allowed a small amount of whiskey into her mouth. Like before, her face registered discomfort, but she soldiered through. "Humans are indeed different than Xandarj. This drink is stronger by three times than anything available at any Dralli bar."

"Long ago it was called the devil's water. It was said to make a man go crazy with desire for it," AJ said, dramatically.

"Yes." Mads eyed AJ as he took a long pull from his glass. To her satisfaction, he exhaled a choking breath, having taken in too much.

"Tell me why you've set the price you have on the orbital junk pile," AJ said. "One hundred thousand credits annual lease seems high."

"Haven't you heard? There's treasure buried within the wrecked liner."

"I'm not interested in buried treasure," AJ said, shaking his head. "I've been contemplating opening my own trading/salvage company. That's my interest in the junk pile. I'm not sure I can extract a hundred thousand in value from it, though. Seems like I could talk to the Dralli governor and just lease another orbital position and start a pile."

"I don't think she'd be interested," Mads said, sitting back in her chair. "You say you have no interest in the treasure, but I have heard this before. Words come easy to many peoples. What would prevent you from searching for and discovering this long-lost treasure?"

"Pertaf treasure is fool's gold," AJ said and then waited for Mads' translation to catch up. "How about I agree to give you fifty percent of whatever treasure is discovered on the Pertaf space liner. What would your price be then?"

"Why only fifty percent if you are convinced the treasure isn't there? Why not ninety percent or a hundred?"

"Indeed, why not?" AJ asked. "You know you have squatters out there, right?"

"Squatters?" Mads asked. "No – I think not. I have surveillance as well as regular patrols."

"We found evidence," AJ said, projecting a small video of the tools in the primary habitat. "I'd guess they're bringing in their own power source. We also saw a light, but didn't have time to investigate."

"I own all treasure and you pay seventy thousand each year," Mads said.

AJ poured her another finger of whiskey. "That's hardly negotiation in good faith," he said. "According to you, the rate was set based on my interest in the treasure. If you take that from the table, seventy thousand is hardly a concession. I need the right to trade or sell any piece of junk or equipment on that pile. I take direct ownership of any vessel I repair sufficiently to sail and any piece of equipment that isn't used to support the habitat. I'd pay forty thousand a year for this privilege."

"The currently operating Veneri vessel is worth three hundred thousand," Mads said. "And I won't take less than sixty thousand for a lease where you're allowed to strip my junk pile clean."

"Hold on, you're suggesting that pile hasn't been stripped by vultures for decades? Let's not pretend we're talking about a virgin pile, here."

"Virgin," Mads chuckled, slurping a drink down.

"I don't want to be insulting, Mads," AJ said. "We're not that far apart. Tell me how much you would value this bottle of Tennessee Rye for?"

"Not enough to sway my negotiation," she responded.

"It's a serious question. Place a value on it. Let's say it was yours and you wanted to sell it."

Mads nodded and her fingers flew across an invisible keyboard. Finally, she looked up. "I would sell it for perhaps seven hundred credits. Of course, I would not buy it for that."

"No, of course not," AJ said, pushing the bottle to her. "It is my gift to you."

"Pretty and sugar-tongued," Mads said. "You humans have so many advantages in negotiation. It is unfair when you are also generous."

"I think of us as friends, Mads," AJ said. "I'd like to be business partners. What would you like to buy a bottle like this for?"

"Three fifty," she answered immediately.

"I will trade you three barrels of Tennessee Rye that holds two-hundred-eighty bottles for your Veneri EAH in its current condition," AJ said. "By my calculation, that's an even trade."

"You seek a deal for this vessel outside of our negotiation for the junk pile lease?"

"Yes."

"I accept," she said. "I will trade the Veneri vessel you operated for three barrels of Tennessee Rye as long as truth has been spoken."

"You saw the barrels," AJ said. "To your junk pile and the Pertaf treasure. I will further trade two barrels of this Tennessee Rye for a five-year lease."

"That is unacceptable. Valued at one hundred thousand, that would only provide forty thousand for each year," Mads said, slamming her hand onto the table.

"Hold on, Mads," AJ said. "If during this period any Pertaf treasure is recovered, you and I will split evenly the owner's portion. Which is to say, if we allow a treasure hunter a fifty-fifty split, you and I would each receive twenty-five percent."

"That does not make up for the poor price," Mads said, angrily shaking her head.

"You're lowballing me on the whiskey."

"You accepted this price for the Veneri vehicle," she said.

"Would you prefer that I make inquiries across the station to find buyers for it?" AJ asked. "Imagine what would happen to the price of your Tennessee Rye if I allowed competitors to each have their own barrel."

"That is good negotiation," Mads said. "Human thinks fast. Three years, sixty-forty split on treasure that favors me."

"Four years, Mads, and an even split. *And* I won't import more whiskey in that same timeframe unless it is to be sold to you at fifty percent current retail value," AJ said.

"Oh, a delightful little barb at the end," Mads said, gleefully rubbing her hands together. "You would flood my market with whiskey and reduce its value. I should cancel this negotiation. You are very clever and I might have missed something."

"I prefer you as a friend rather than an enemy," AJ said. "I'm hoping to bring deals to you from time to time. While I want you to respect my negotiation, I want you to be open to my approach."

"Pretty mouth, pretty words, too much alcohol," she said. "I will accept four years and an even split for two barrels of Tennessee Rye. You may strip this pile of anything you find valuable other than a list of precious items I will present to you tomorrow. This list will be what we consider treasure, Pertaf or otherwise."

"Let me guess, Fantastium and Blastorium will be at the top of the list," AJ said. "Can you at least leave out what's left in the Veneri vessel?"

"It is adorable that you believe there is Fantastium to be found within the Veneri vessel," she said. "I will review this deal in twelve hours when I have not had so much to drink. If it is acceptable when I am sober, I will reach out to you."

"Lisa, what do you think?" AJ asked. "You'll be a partner."

"I'm not sure where Darnell and I fit in," she said. "You have your junk pile and a big hauler. What do you need us for?"

"Startup capital," he said.

"Lisa Jackson, did you also bring Tennessee Rye?" Mads asked, leaning back in her chair, glassy-eyed.

"No. Although hearing the price you're willing to pay, I wish I had," Lisa said. "I made a different sort of gamble – one I have yet to determine will pay off."

"We'll talk with Red Fairs," AJ said. "Lisa has small, crafted items of significant value from Earth. Most made from precious and semi-precious metals."

"What sort of metals?" Mads Bazer said.

"Silver, gold, platinum. Different kinds of gems also: sapphire, ruby, diamond," Lisa said. "Of course, there's more silver than platinum and not much diamond or ruby."

"Do you have an accounting for the volumes of these metals?" Mads asked. "Perhaps you are not aware, but Xandarj governments made it illegal to export precious metals. When we were first allowed into the Galactic Empire, Xandarj was plundered by immoral, hostile species. Our tradable metals and exotic elements were traded for technology we would later learn was easily accessed."

"See!" Lisa said, smacking the back of her hand across AJ's arm. "I told you that would be what happened on Earth!"

"And I told you I saw it, too," AJ said. "I just don't know what we can do about it."

"We gotta tell folks," Lisa said.

"We do," AJ said. "But it's not like we need to tell 'em today. What we need to do is come up with a plan that doesn't get us shot."

"It is enjoyable to watch the pretty humans talk," Mads said, rocking back and forth, humming to herself.

"Is she going to be okay?" Lisa asked.

"They have a hangover pill that removes alcohol from your system," AJ said. "She wants to be drunk."

"Who does not want this?" Mads asked. "Would you mind if I squeezed your cheeks?"

"I'm ... uh, no. We need to be somewhere," AJ said, standing.

"Greybeard, maybe give Mads a goodbye lick or something and we'll be on our way."

Mads waved lazily as Greybeard, Lisa and AJ excused themselves from her office.

AJ was already familiar with how to locate the open market locally referred to as The Trailer. The quickest path was to move to the station's central hub where elevator shafts, both public and private joined the twenty-eight levels of the station.

Spanning sixteen square miles, the Trailer occupied the entirety of Dralli Station's lowest level. The Trailer was so open that if one were to stand high enough and position themselves just right, they could look across all of it, something not possible on any other level of the aging station.

"Whoa, that's a lot of smells," Lisa said, upon exiting the elevator. "I smell fried food. Is that right?"

"They aren't big on proteins," AJ said. "And some of their cheese has fruit in it. If you're hungry, I've got a couple of go-to favorites."

"I was a vegetarian for three years," Lisa said, approaching a small food-vendor cart where dried fruits had been tied into flower arrangements. "How much?" she asked, nodding at a stick holding pale yellow leaves with shrunken dark red berries.

"I am honored by your presence, beautiful human, Lisa of Earth," a young Xandarj stuttered, picking one of the items Lisa was interested in and handing it to her. "It is Bandar's gift to you."

"Oh, aren't you cute," Lisa said, touching the back of the adolescent's hand. "Thank you, Bandar."

"Careful, Lisa," AJ said. "You're catnip to these guys. Notice you didn't have to introduce yourself."

Lisa shot AJ a funny look and took the offered fruit stick. "I pay for the next one, okay, Bandar?"

"So very glad to meet, Lisa."

AJ placed his hand in the middle of Lisa's back, noticing that they were starting to draw a crowd of onlookers. "Bye, Bandar."

"Why is everyone staring?" Lisa asked. "I thought it was weird that Mads Bazer kept making references to our looks, but will everyone be doing that too? Blue Tork and Chok seemed so normal, well except for Chok's thing about sex. That was weird."

"You have a grandson, so maybe this analogy will work. Think of yourself as a Dallas Cowboy cheerleader at an all-boys junior high school," AJ said.

"I'm a sixty-seven-year-old grandmother," Lisa said.

AJ laughed. "You don't look like any grandma I know of."

"I know I shouldn't like this, but it's hard to stop smiling," Lisa said, unable to hide her amusement.

"I don't think cheerleaders wear those skimpy uniforms because they help keep their butts warm," AJ said. "Everybody likes to be interesting, but we'll need to get some robes from Red Fairs and cover up so we don't get bogged down in the crowds."

"This is delicious," Lisa said, biting into the fruit. "I was expecting something like a raisin, but this fruit is still juicy, kind of like a tart blueberry. Want a bite?"

"No, you earned that one. It's all yours."

"Oh, you stop it. I didn't know," she said.

"There's Red Fairs' headquarters," AJ said. "You met her when we landed."

"She stored my crates," Lisa said. "She seemed very businesslike."

"She is. You've probably noticed more female Xandarj in business roles – not like it's a hundred percent or anything – but a larger percentage of the shopkeepers are female," AJ said.

"Albert Jenkins, welcome!" Red Fairs said, pushing through a knot of customers. "And, Lisa Jackson. Are you here to visit or negotiate? I saw Darnell Jackson and Blue Tork earlier. I think they have retired to our home after making several purchases."

"I wouldn't mind a little negotiation," Lisa said. "Have you had a chance ..."

Red Fairs held up her hand and closed her eyes, effectively cutting Lisa off mid-sentence. When Red Fairs recognized that Lisa had stopped talking, she opened her eyes. "Private negotiation, perhaps?"

"Sure," Lisa said, allowing Red Fairs to pull her along.

"Want me to come?" AJ asked as Lisa looked back at him before being pulled through a slit in the fabric wall.

"Yes," Lisa said, her normal confidence momentarily fading.

AJ followed and found himself in a private room with several comfortable chairs. Stacked in the middle of the room were the crates containing Lisa's trade goods. The seal on the side had not been broken and additional black bands had been added.

"Do you consent to these crates being opened?" Red Fairs asked.

"Did you add those black bands?" AJ asked.

"I did," Red Fairs said. "The metal rods used to hold these wooden boxes together can be defeated. My bands are not easily removed and require special equipment."

"Thank you, Red Fairs," AJ said.

Red Fairs smiled, which was unusual for the normally reserved businesswoman. "I will admit to excitement at the prospect of the treasures contained within."

"I hope you're not disappointed," Lisa said. "I don't have a lot of experience with interspecies trading."

"Before we open them ..." Red Fairs reached over to a side table that held a thick carafe and three opaque glasses. She poured a steaming amber liquid into each and handed one to Lisa and then to AJ. "What were the criteria you established in selecting your trade goods?"

"It was something AJ said."

"Which was?"

"Xandarj see humans as physically attractive. Pretty even," Lisa said.

"This is true," Red Fairs said. "All humans I have seen are quite attractive and everything about you is discussed in electronic communications. You are, in fact, celebrities on Dralli Station. I imagine you experienced this celebrity while coming here?"

"I did," Lisa said. "It's flattering. We don't get that kind of attention at home."

"I see. How did our view of humans affect your choices?" Red Fairs said, sipping her hot drink thoughtfully.

"I decided to go with what we think makes us pretty," Lisa said. "Or what things human men and women wear to feel pretty."

"Risky," Red Fairs said. "Our sense of aesthetic could be significantly different."

"I've been worrying about that since I purchased the items," Lisa said.

"Let us remove the suspense," Red Fairs said, producing a small device that slipped through the black bands as if they were spaghetti noodles. "I assume you have a mechanism for removing the iron rods used to knit the top to the sides."

"Well, kind of thinking you'd have a crowbar," AJ said.

"Would a long-handled knife work?"

"That'd do." Red Fairs disappeared and then reappeared with a knife. "Are you sure I won't break it?" AJ asked.

"It will not break."

AJ struggled to remove the top, and in the end, his youthful strength and determination got him through. As soon as the box was open, Lisa carefully removed the lightweight packing and withdrew the first small item. "This is a good example," she said, extracting a necklace and holding it between her fingers. "May I?"

Red Fairs nodded curiously and watched with anticipation as Lisa spread the necklace out and slipped it over her head.

"This is human jewelry?" Red Fairs asked, gently lifting the gem at the end of the necklace.

"Gold necklace with a sapphire setting," Lisa said.

The description caused Red Fairs' eyebrows to lift. She made no effort to hide a small scanner that she waved over the necklace. "A necklace is uncommon as jewelry," Red Fairs said, causing Lisa to frown. "I do not know the effect of it being of human origin. The materials are valuable and the workmanship is simple, but not offensively so. If I offered this for sale, I would request eighteen hundred credits."

"How expensive of an item was that on Earth, Lisa?"

"Five hundred forty dollars. Have you figured any sort of exchange rate?"

"Yes. The exchange for commodity items like clothing and food isn't far off one dollar for one credit," AJ said. "All bets are off for unique items."

"Red Fairs, is there much of a market for jewelry?" Lisa asked.

"There is interest in jewelry. It sometimes takes time, but with the valuable metals and gems, items like this will sell easily. Are you considering consignment or selling to me wholesale?" Red Fairs asked.

"You offer both?"

"Yes. And there is a third alternative. You could barter directly for needed goods. I have a considerable inventory of items you will need," Red Fairs said. "I would give you an even trade for the value I assess."

"What about consignment?" Lisa asked.

"I will take a thirty percent commission and you will be paid when the item is sold. Generally, my wholesale rate is fifty percent of assessed value."

"Maybe we should keep looking through what I have," Lisa said. "There are more items. I'm a little worried about the perfumes. I haven't smelled anything like that on aliens here."

"You have scents? For what purpose?"

"We use them on our bodies. To make us smell good," Lisa said.

Red Fairs pursed her lips. "I hope you did not invest considerably in your perfumes. Xandarj people have sensitive noses. To me, these boxes are quite unpleasant."

Lisa blew out a hot breath. "I considered that. I've got maybe ten grand in perfume. How about rings for fingers?"

"Show me ..."

NINE

DIVERGING PATHS

"What kind of buy-in are you looking for?" Lefty asked, rocking his chair back and balancing as he drank from a colorful plastic bottle.

Red Fairs, Blue Tork, Chok, Lefty, Lisa, Darnell, and AJ had gathered around Red Fairs and Blue Tork's family table, taking advantage of the friendly aliens' hospitality for an evening meal. The kids had been put to bed and Lefty had handed out his recent acquisition of a local Xandarj beer.

"What do you think of Xandarj beer?" AJ asked, warily eyeing the bottle in front of him.

"Tends to be too sweet for my taste," he said. "I'd have made a killing if I'd thought to bring some cinnamon-flavored whiskey. You didn't answer my question."

"I've got half a million credits already in. Lisa and Darnell are in for a hundred eighty thousand," AJ said. "One share costs you one credit."

"What if I'm not looking to buy in? You got any place for me?"

"Nothing's changed, Lefty," AJ said. "You've got a place if you want it. I'll need folks I can trust."

"I'm too old to be somebody's employee."

"How about you tag along and take time to figure out where you fit in," AJ said. "I'll cover room and board. Maybe you could cover personal items like weapons and a spacesuit. I've got credits I could lend you if you haven't cashed in on your truck yet."

"How much were you thinking of paying if I did sign on?" Lefty asked.

AJ considered pointing out that Lefty had already said he wasn't interested in employment but decided not to push the man. "I'd cover living expenses, a decent space suit, and access to our armory," AJ said. "I'd probably add five hundred credits a week on top of that."

"My job would be security then?"

"And other things," AJ said. "Don't know enough to get specific, but security is high on the list."

"Maybe we start that way. I was wantin' to hold onto the truck until I know what it's worth, so I'm a bit strapped for cash," he said. "Rebel said she'd get me some, but I don't like how that feels. A man needs to earn his way."

"Five hundred a week work for you?" AJ asked.

"I need four days off every second week and a ride back to town," he said, sitting forward in his chair and holding his hand out to shake.

AJ shook his hand. "BB, would you give Lefty his first two months upfront? Could you also create a separate account and move twenty thousand credits from my account. Give Lefty access to the account so he can get started on the armory."

Beverly appeared, wearing cuffed woolen pants and a white button-down shirt with a red striped tie. "Got it, boss," she said, pushing her sleeves up to her elbows.

"Guns and armor. I feel like I'm probably the right guy for that," Lefty said.

"How about you, Red Fairs?" AJ said. "You lookin' to invest in a fixer-upper?"

"Friendships often suffer when business is involved," Red Fairs said. "Consider me a friendly advisor."

"Big D, did you find the power transfer coupling we needed for the habitat?" AJ asked.

"You mean the big fuse thingy?" Darnell asked. "Yeah, good thing I had Petey along. You can't believe how many different patterns they have for those things. Those old Pertaf motors are old, but that's the thing about the manufactory technology, once you find the right plans, they can make any old part."

"How expensive was it to make?"

"Materials were the expensive thing," Darnell said. "The pattern was only a hundred fifty credits. We're in six grand for materials."

AJ whistled. "That's some cheddar. When will it be done?"

Darnell glanced away for a moment, obviously looking at a virtual display. "We're fourteen hours out."

"Ask Petey how often those break down," AJ said. "Maybe we need a spare."

"Petey says that since you're an engineer you'd understand MTBF of seventy-thousand hours," Darnell said.

"Yup. That's about eight years," AJ said. "We'll worry about a spare part later."

"I was looking into getting one of those food printers," Lisa said. "Since we'll be coming back to Dralli Station at least every other week, we could supplement with fresh items on those trips."

"How much?" AJ asked.

"There are three models I was looking at. Maybe Blue Tork or Red Fairs would have an opinion," she said. When she gestured, a video panel on the wall switched from a serene jungle scene to a display of three boxy items.

"We should consult Tonka," Red Fairs said, referring to her brother who was also their live-in housekeeper.

"I'll get him," Blue Fairs said, taking advantage of the need to get up to grab another of Lefty's sweetened beers.

"We might need two," AJ said. "That VEAH isn't likely to be fast, so we'll need something for long trips."

"I'm curious as to your business plan, Albert Jenkins," Red Fairs said. "What advantage do you plan to create in leasing Mads Bazer's junk pile and owning a Veneri EAH?"

"Promise this doesn't leave this table?" AJ asked.

"I will not share your business secrets," Red Fairs said. "Do you believe you can find this Pertaf treasure?"

"No," AJ said.

"Hold on a minute," Lefty said. "Let's not get too hasty with that."

"Are you looking to turn into a treasure hunter?" AJ asked.

"I might. You got an issue with that?"

"No. Matter of fact, I'll sign a contract with you so you keep thirty percent of whatever you find," AJ said.

"Remember, I'm the guy who rescued you from that mud pit back in 'Nam."

"Forty percent?" AJ asked.

"I keep fifty, you get the other half."

"Which I have to share with Mads Bazer," AJ said. "Besides, you're gonna be looking for treasure while I'm paying you. That doesn't seem real fair."

"Good point. Forty works for me."

"Did you check on those powered spacesuits you were so interested in?" AJ asked.

Lisa put her hand up. "Hey, I want one of those too."

"Fourteen grand with armor. Two grand if you don't mind being squishy," Darnell said.

AJ looked at his rapidly diminishing personal funds, which were sitting just a little north of sixty thousand.

"Don't even think about going cheap, Albert Jenkins," Darnell said. "Me and Leese can get by on squishy suits, but you and Lefty need to get armored as long as you can move around in them."

"Why do you say that?"

"Because ever since you met Beverly, you've barely gone a week without getting shot at," Darnell said.

"That's not true," AJ said. "It's been at least four months since I got shot at. Well, if you don't count getting plinked at in the swamp."

"That was no plinking. That was an RPG," Darnell said. "And what do you call the airstrip in Arizona?"

"I'm gonna be doing a lot of repairs on the VEAH, I can't afford to be tied up with armor blocking my movements," AJ said.

"Nobody throws slugs around here," Lefty said. "The armor is a woven polycarbonate matrix with a ground wrapped around the fibers and tied to something like a whole-house lightning arrestor. Or at least that's what Petey explained."

"BB, toss another twenty thousand from my account into the armory account," AJ said.

"This is your business plan?" Red Fairs asked. "I do not understand how you will receive credits."

"No, that's not the plan," AJ said, laughing. "That's basic Maslow's Hierarchy stuff. We need shelter, food, and security. Something I've had the good fortune to learn is that people don't see the value in junk. Seems to me that the good peoples of the Galactic Empire have that same problem. The idea hit me back on that moon over Halfnium-8. An entire moon was dedicated as a junkyard. Perfectly good ships had been left in the dust because the Halfnies thought they might be leaking contaminants. I guarantee there are others not quite so concerned about microscopic contaminants who would pay good money for those ships."

"The Vred take the pollution of their ecosystem very seriously," Red Fairs said.

"Sure, and that's good for us," AJ said. "They've got money to burn if they're dumping perfectly usable ships. Fact is, they're contaminating that moon. So, they're not completely against the idea or they'd have run those ships into their sun."

"An interesting perspective," Red Fairs said. "Will you attempt to make contract with the Vred to buy their moon ships?"

"Maybe, but that's just an example," AJ said. "First rule of owning a junkyard is to not pay for anything. In the short run, we'll look for hauling contracts – find people who need big items moved."

"What kind of large items?" Red Fairs asked.

"Doesn't matter," AJ said. "As long as it's not illegal and they're willing to pay to have it both moved and stored. Of course, that'll require I get the VEAH up and running."

"You need a better name than VEAH," Darnell said, wincing as he took a drink of the overly sweet beer.

"Suggestions?" AJ asked.

"Sweet Lisa?" Darnell asked.

"You're not naming some big-butted old hauler after me," Lisa immediately objected.

"Feels like the sweet was probably wrong, too," AJ added, earning him a backhanded slap on the arm.

"Try to score points and it gets me nowhere," Darnell said.

"Today's patrol reported a Cheell vessel arriving at Dralli Station, Bay 6," Blue Tork said, either unaware of AJ's emotion or in response to it.

"Any idea what they're doing here?" Lefty asked, sitting forward in his chair.

"Trade was listed in their official registration," Tork said. "Dralli Station doesn't require more information than that."

"I might check it out and see what they're up to," Lefty said.

"A human will stand out," Lisa said.

"Nah, Red Fairs has me set up with one of those robes the traders all seem to wear and Rebel can do the actual spying. I just need to be nearby," he said.

"What's the rule about weapons on Dralli, Tork? If a Cheell started shooting without provocation, is that enough cause for Lefty to fire back?" AJ asked.

"Yes, but don't shoot good people," he said. "If you get close, you can shoot, no problems."

"What Blue Tork is saying is that it is allowable to surveil someone if you keep ten yards separation," Red Fairs explained. "If you cause damage to non-involved structures or sentients, you are liable for damages."

"That is what Tork says," Tork said, mildly irritated.

"I'm gonna need some rack time before I get on that," Lefty said. "Hopefully, I can find the Cheell in The Trailer so I can see about getting us outfitted with armor and such while I watch."

"I have a hammock prepared, Lefty Johnson," Tonka said, appearing in the doorway.

"You're a good man, Tonka," Lefty said, standing. "Lead the way."

"You mentioned short-term and long-term plans," Red Fairs said. "Do you mind sharing your long-term objectives?"

"I've got this, AJ," Lisa said, glancing at AJ who was more than happy to sit back and let her do the talking. "Trade with Earth is our long-term objective. What you all see as a big pile of junk would be considered the richest treasures back home. Unlike these Cheell and whoever else they've dragged along, we're just looking to make our fair share and do some good in the process."

"Earth is quarantined by Galactic Empire," Blue Tork said. "No go."

"That's one problem," AJ said. "Does that apply to humans?"

Beverly, who'd been sitting quietly behind a virtual desk she'd constructed on the table, took that moment to speak up. "The Galactic Empire cannot make laws that apply to humans as they still refuse to recognize their full sentience," she said. "That Earth governments have not publicly recognized the existence of aliens, however, is significant."

"That's why it's part of our long-term plan," Lisa said. "Even though I don't like how things stand, we can at least let folks back on Earth get their feet under them, so they aren't taken advantage of. Fact is, the cat's out of the bag and there isn't much the government can do to stuff the existence of aliens back in."

"That is an unfamiliar idiom," Red Fairs said.

"I'm just saying that even before we left Earth last month, there were reports in major news publications about alien sightings," Lisa said. "You can't just roll that back. Our biggest problem is that sooner than not, we'll be competing with the big boys and they don't play fair."

"Who are these *big boys?*" Red Fairs pushed.

"Multinational companies with huge piles of capital," Lisa said. "They'll want to tie up interstellar trade and make it impossible for the little guys to succeed. I'd bet they've already paid off their favorite politicians and bills are already getting crafted. They'll hit the big-ticket items first like curing cancer and heart disease. Gotta get the FDA involved in that though to make sure it's safe. Then they'll trickle out new drugs at ridiculous prices ..."

"Lisa, we get it," Darnell said, recognizing she was spinning herself up. "Greedy people making money on the backs of hard-working folks. We're all in agreement."

"Sort of," AJ said.

"Come again?" Lisa said, turning toward AJ, her expression showing that she was ready to argue.

"We can't go shooting our mouths off at every opportunity," AJ said, returning Lisa's glare. "If those Cheell were after us because they just *think* we might be doing something, imagine how hard they'd try after hearing this conversation. We can't paint targets on our backs. No, we need to convince them we're just looking to get into the salvage business and the best way to do that is to do exactly that."

"Don't you get soft on me, Albert Jenkins," Lisa said. "People's lives are at stake."

"Tell me what I don't already know," AJ said. "If Pam had survived long enough to meet BB, she'd be alive right now. I get what we're fighting for. My point is that we need to stay alive long enough to make a difference."

"We're basing a lot on our theory about why those Cheell were trying to take us out," Darnell said. "No question they were coming for us, but we haven't answered the question as to why."

"You boys need to understand that I'm not gonna sit on my hands forever," Lisa said. "Between Nit and Amanda, I have years back that I wasn't counting on. Instead of a good dozen more, I might as well be a young woman. I'm gonna make that worth something. You read me?"

"Loud and clear, Lisa," AJ said.

"Jus' sayin'" she grumbled.

"I'M okay with gold and platinum being listed as treasure, as long as they're in raw form," AJ said. "If they're a component in a piece of machinery, I'm gonna need a carveout. Same with any other rare element, aside from Fantastium and Blastorium. I sent you an updated list to approve."

"I have it," Mads said, leaning against one of the five barrels of whiskey. She made a flourish as she signed the agreement. A virtual contract appeared on AJ's HUD, showing her signature.

AJ held his hand out to Mads Bazer, who readily accepted it. "You do know that I got the better of you today? Five barrels of Tennessee Rye whiskey and I'm the only person in the entire Galactic Empire who has a drop. You have made me wealthy today, Albert Jenkins. You would have been smarter to sell the contents of these barrels instead of leasing that old pile of junk."

"Humans have a saying that goes something like this – one man's trash is another man's treasure."

Mads cocked a furry eyebrow and looked up at AJ. "Be straight with old Mads. Are you after the Pertaf treasure? You are, aren't you."

"Truthfully, no," AJ said. "I did however make a sixty-forty arrangement with one of my crew who wants to see what he can find."

"There is always a dreamer. That is how I see you and that junk pile. When I was approached with the suggestion to offer it, I told the DAS academic that it was a foolish endeavor. No sane person would lease a pile of space junk," Mads said.

"Sanity is an elusive concept," AJ said.

She laughed and reached down for one last scrub of Greybeard's back.

"Let's go, Greybeard." AJ walked off, leaving Mads cackling.

"Where are we headed, AJ?" Beverly appeared in her sparkly Jetsons suit, putting along next to him.

"Thought I could check in with Jayne and drop Greybeard off," AJ said. "Mind pinging her for me?"

"Of course," Beverly said, pulling out an old-fashioned rotary phone.

"Hi, AJ," Jayne said, her face appearing on a screen on his HUD. "What's up?"

He was encouraged by her upbeat mood. "We're getting ready to head out to the junkyard. Thought I'd drop Greybeard off like we talked."

"That might be a problem," she said. "The dorm where they have me staying isn't friendly for pets."

"Are you sure? We wanted him with you as kind of a security thing," AJ said.

"Pretty sure," she said. "Will you be okay with him?"

"I've got it. You up for a visitor today?"

A guilty look passed over her face. "They have me pretty busy," she said. "Could we try again in a couple of weeks?"

"No problem, Doc."

"Are you doing okay?" Jayne asked. "If you're headed to the junk-yard it sounds like things are all right."

"Doc, I kind of feel like you're moving on without me," AJ said. "Am I reading this wrong?"

Jayne pursed her lips and tipped her head. "It's complicated, AJ," she said. "I've just got so much going on. I'm not sure I have enough room in my life to be fair to a relationship. It hasn't changed how I feel about you, though."

"Okay, Doc," AJ said, trying to keep from sighing. "Can't say I'm not disappointed, but I get where you're coming from. It's a big oppor-tunity and they're lucky to have you."

"Now who sounds like they're breaking up?" Jayne asked.

"Can't break up what we never really got going," AJ said. "I can be good with friends, Doc. You let me know if that changes for you, okay?"

"It kind of feels bad saying it out loud," Jayne said. "Friends, okay?" AJ heard muted voices behind Jayne, clearly trying to get her attention. She turned away, said something, and then turned back. "I don't want to lose you as a friend, AJ."

"Not sure that's possible, Doc," AJ said, hearing the same, but now more urgent voices behind her. "Sounds like you need to get going. Look me up if you get some free time. I shouldn't be too hard to find."

"Okay. We'll talk later," she said. "I promise."

And with that, she turned. AJ caught a glimpse of a diverse group of younger-looking aliens, laughing and talking excitedly in a café setting. Mercifully, the display terminated.

"I don't suppose Nit has anything to add to that," AJ asked Beverly, his heart in his throat.

"No," Beverly said. "She'd never share personal information with me any more than I would with her. I'm sorry you're feeling bad."

"Yeah, thanks."

"AJ, where are you?" Lefty's whispered voice got AJ's attention.

"Near the elevator banks on four," AJ said.

"I've got a problem," he said. "Show him, Rebel."

A video screen popped up on AJ's HUD and he appeared to be in some sort of closet or vestibule. On the ground in front of him lay two gray-skinned Cheell. Neither were moving.

"Send location. I'm on my way," AJ said.

TEN

BUMBLING BOUNTY

"How'd you find this place?" AJ asked softly, drawing Greybeard around a partition into a secluded seating space on the outer rim of the eighth level of Dralli Station. The floor-to-ceiling view was currently that of planet Xandarj, which was mostly dark except for a small crescent of light that showed the approaching horizon.

"Rebel found it," Lefty said. "These two yahoos got on my ass and I led them back here."

"You trapped yourself in a dead-end? That doesn't seem safe," AJ said.

"Depends on if you're a badger or a mouse," Lefty said.

"I assume you're the badger in this story?" AJ asked, kneeling next to the two bodies. The Cheell averaged a few inches above four feet and were dead ringers for the alien images popularized by 1950s pop culture. "They dead?"

Beverly appeared, wearing a stark white WWI ward nurse's uniform, complete with a boxy hat. Placing an old-fashioned stethoscope onto the first alien, she looked up at AJ. He needed to physically place his hand on the alien for her analysis to work. He obliged.

"They're alive," Beverly said. "This one has a pair of fractured ribs

and the other will need a reconstructive procedure on his alar cartilage." When she got a raised eyebrow from AJ, she continued.
"Broken nose."

"I barely got 'em," Lefty said. "I clocked Mr. Chatty there on the
right when they came around and had to tackle the coward there on
the left."

"Any way to wake 'em?" AJ asked.

"How should I know?" Lefty asked.

"Not talking to you. BB?"

"Mr. Chatty is conscious," Beverly said.

"Oh, playin' possum, are yah?" Lefty asked, roughly grabbing the
alien's loose-fitting suit.

"Please, leave me. I mean you no harm," Mr. Chatty said, his
black, kiwi-sized eyes fluttering open and three-digit fingers splaying
defensively.

"Any weapons on them?" AJ asked.

Lefty palmed a small energy weapon that was well suited to the
alien's long fingers. AJ knew from experience the weapon would be
uncomfortable for a human. "They each had one. They came cruising
around that corner loaded for bear."

"They shoot?" AJ asked.

"Didn't give 'em a chance."

AJ turned to Mr. Chatty who was staring at him, unblinking. "I
bet you know who I am, don't you," AJ said.

"No, we do not know you," Mr. Chatty said.

"Odd that you'd follow my friend here down a dead-end hallway."

"We are new to Dralli Station and our maps were not sufficiently
updated. This is just a misfortune. If you allow us to separate, no
complaint will be made."

"I'd like to see that complaint – you know – how you followed my
friend here with your guns out into a dead end. Nah, that's not how
this is going. Tell me you don't know who I am again," AJ said,
plucking one of the small weapons from Lefty's hand. "I seem to

recall getting shot by one of these not so long ago. I also seem to remember it hurt like the dickens."

"You cannot shoot me. The station warning will bring security," Mr. Chatty said.

"I was just thinking that," Lefty said, pulling off his shirt and handing it to AJ. "Wrap the gun with that. It'll probably block enough noise or whatever the sensors are scanning for."

Mr. Chatty blinked once. "That is untrue."

"You have a horrible tell," AJ said, wrapping Lefty's shirt around the gun and pressing the mass into Mr. Chatty's stomach.

"*Tell*? This is confusing. I do not understand."

"Tough. Why were you following Lefty? Before you make up an excuse, you should know that I'm going to shoot you if you lie."

"A human on Dralli Station is easy to locate," Mr. Chatty said. "We were going to take his valuables."

AJ shook his head. "You just had to push it. You need to see if I'm willing to do what I said," AJ said, shaking his head. "You do know who I am, right? I'm the guy who boarded one of your ships while in jumpspace and took it over."

"I do not know this," Mr. Chatty said. "We have difficulty distinguishing humans from one another."

"Shit, did he just say we all look alike?" Lefty asked.

"He should be glad Big D isn't here," AJ said, pulling the weapon back so he could see the controls. "He'd probably cave his skull in for that." The weapon was dialed up to full power and a tight beam. The Cheell wasn't looking to disable, it had been looking to kill. AJ dialed it back and spread the beam wider.

"Please, do not shoot me. I have done nothing wrong."

AJ wrapped the barrel again with Lefty's shirt and set the tip on the alien's chest. "Was that your final answer? You do know, if you die, we'll just get the info out of your buddy? I imagine he'll be all kinds of talkative when he sees how you fared."

"Stop. I will converse," Mr. Chatty said. AJ pressed the weapon harder into the Cheell's chest. "There is a bounty on the human called Lefty Johnson."

"Well, hell," Lefty said. "Just me? What'd I do?"

"Darnell Jackson, Lefty Johnson, Ernesto Ruiz, Roland LeBeau," Mr. Chatty said.

"Ruiz and LeBeau were from my old squad," AJ said. "I didn't even know Frenchy was still alive and Ruiz, last I heard, was living in Mexico. Is that the whole list?"

"It was longer. Many names were removed," Mr. Chatty said. He then seemed to understand how his statement could be taken. "We were lucky and already in transport when news of your presence on Dralli Station was marketed."

"How much is the bounty and what are the terms?" AJ asked.

"Each name listed is worth two hundred thousand credits if captured. One hundred thousand for certified death," Mr. Chatty said. "Two have an increased payout of four hundred thousand for capture or certified death. We did not want to target them as we are not qualified for missions that exceed two hundred thousand credits."

The Cheell next to Mr. Chatty groaned and tried to sit up. Lefty was on him instantly knocking him back to the deck. "You are a horrible liar," the second Cheell complained. "We are qualified sixty thousand, but you said this would be a good way to increase our rating. Now, we will die and it is your fault."

"Quiet," Lefty said, increasing pressure on the prone Cheell's chest. The Cheell squeaked but stopped talking.

"Who are these increased payouts for?" AJ asked.

"Albert Jenkins and Amanda Jayne."

"You really can't tell us apart, can you?"

"YOU JUST LEFT THEM THERE, ALIVE?" Darnell asked.

AJ had found his friend standing next to a stack of banded crates in bay-4 next to a small runabout leased for the day.

"Put this on," Lefty said, handing Darnell a sleek pistol-gripped weapon and a holster. Once Darnell concealed the weapon, Lefty tossed a bag onto the crates next to him. "Put that on, too."

Darnell opened the bag and found a spacesuit. "At least I got one of the lightweight ones," he said. "Answer my question."

"Yes. We left them there," AJ said. "What were we supposed to do? Gun 'em down?"

"Well, that was kind of their plan," Darnell said. "Maybe call station security?"

"Nah, we did one better," Lefty said. "Took their clothes and left 'em their guns."

"You should have taken their guns."

"You should have heard 'em, it was great. Mr. Chatty –the one who wouldn't stop talking –was bawling about how word was gonna get out that they got pantsed on their first big job," Lefty said. "I told 'em if they came around again, we'd mess 'em up for real. It's not like finding a gun is hard on Dralli and besides, those little pea shooters they had were about as usable as a two-handed spoon."

"We're on a hit list, Darnell," AJ said. "That's a full-armor suit. Everybody's getting one. I even got one for Jayne and I don't give a crap what she thinks about it."

"You have any money left?"

"Some. I'm getting a little light, but it'll work out."

"Sounds like there's friction between you and Doc," Darnell said. "Want me to run it over?"

"Do you think you can get her to wear it?" AJ asked.

"She's always listened to me," Darnell said. "That wasn't a denial on the friction thing."

"I don't know what's going on," AJ said. "It's the same old Doc. One day the sun rises and sets because of me and the next I'm about as interesting as an old sock. It's kind of tough. She said she wanted to cool things, that she has a lot going on and needs space. Not exactly her words but that's the gist. Put the suit on. The boys Lefty ran into weren't exactly superstars, but that kind of money is gonna draw some real hitters sooner or later."

"What are we gonna do about Ruiz and LeBeau? And why the heck do Cheell care about them? They're old men now. They're not even part of this," Darnell said.

"I suppose someone's worried we might recruit them," AJ said. "I've got BB sending a message to Major Baird. I'm hoping she'll send someone out to warn 'em about the threat. Otherwise, we might need to make a trip home. No fair letting those boys twist in the wind."

"'That's right," Lefty said. "We don't leave our boys behind. No matter what."

Darnell handed his robe to AJ. He stooped to pull off his shoes and the thin spacesuit covering his body. "Damn son, you been working out?" AJ asked, holding the robe up to block as many eyes as possible. In that the bay was filled with spaceships and cargo, there weren't that many who could easily see him. Although, those who could, stopped what they were doing for a moment.

"Knock it off," Darnell said, shaking out the new spacesuit and stepping into it. "Are you sure this is armored? Feels like sweatshirt material."

"Best against energy weapons," Lefty said. "But a blade won't cut it. Trust me, I tried. Haven't had the guts to test it against bullets, though."

"Maybe we shouldn't field test that," AJ said, handing Darnell his robe back.

"Did I miss you boys givin' a show?" Lisa asked, approaching with a bundle of dried fruit bouquets.

"Nothin' like the show we're in for," AJ said, raising an eyebrow. "We need you to change into this armored suit."

"You're gonna need to work harder than that, AJ," Lisa said, grinning. "This here girl already has her man."

"All seriousness, there's been a development," AJ said. "A couple of Cheell went after Lefty. There are some Cheell bounty hunters with a list and Darnell's on it. Don't want you getting caught in the crossfire. You need to put this new suit on asap."

"I can't always tell when you're joking, but you sound serious. You do know there's a restroom twenty feet from your position, though, right?" She pointed across the bay to the outside wall.

"How? It's barely marked," AJ said.

"It's a *woman thing*," Lisa said, taking the offered package from Lefty.

"Is this mine?" Lefty asked, patting three long crates.

"Yup and I'll be right back," Darnell said, following Lisa to the restroom.

"We're going to need to think about security out at the junkyard," Left said, turning to AJ. "Once they figure out where we are, they'll have an easier shot at us."

"Good luck shooting at a pile of junk," AJ said. "Although we might consider moving the habitat."

"What? Create a fake front?"

"Something like that. At least for where we sleep," AJ said. "We should get proximity alarms or tracking so we know someone's coming up on us."

"Talkin' my language now," Lefty said. "Rebel and I have been discussing the value of all that junk. We figure some of those old ships in the pile have their radar still in 'em. We could cut out the sensors and create some sort of mesh."

"We need more defense. I can think of scenarios where those hunters might try to come at us and collect their bounties," AJ said. "We're gonna need something bigger than hand weapons when someone rolls up on us with ship-to-ship."

"Sounds expensive," Lefty said.

"I wonder if it has to be," AJ said.

"Are you thinking about getting creative?" Lefty asked.

"I am."

"You and Doc havin' trouble?" Lefty asked out of the blue.

"Not from my side of things, but she's kind of giving me the cold shoulder," AJ said. "I think it's exactly what she said; that she's just excited about this DAS thing."

"That sucks."

AJ nodded. "Were you going to get something to help us move around in space? It doesn't seem like these suits have anything like that."

"I went another way," Lefty said. "We can still get what you're talking about, but they're pretty expensive add-ons. Instead, I got everyone a zero-g sled. Think of it like you're using one of those creepers that helps you slide under a car, only this works in space."

"What if you fall off?" AJ asked.

"Way it was explained to me was that you strap it on when you're going out. Doesn't exactly come off," Lefty said. "It's got a recall feature if you become separated and are floating apart. Seriously though, it dropped the suit price by two grand and the sleds only cost four hundred. Figured it was worth a try."

"With our current burn rate, that kind of thinking is appreciated."

Movement through the translucent energy screen that kept atmosphere inside the docking bay drew AJ's attention. A boxy vessel entered their side of the bay and traveled directly toward them. Through the windshield of the craft, AJ recognized Blue Tork and was surprised to see that Cariste Chok sat next to him.

"Looks like our ride's here," Lefty said. "Can't say I'll miss this place."

"You're the one who negotiated four days off and a ride back every other week," AJ said, pushing a gravity-assisted palette jack under the first stack of crates.

"A guy needs his recreation."

AJ slid the crates to the back of a vessel roughly the size and shape of a twenty-foot moving truck. Fiddling unsuccessfully with the locking mechanism, he was relieved when one of the two wide doors swung open.

"Albert Jenkins, I heard a rumor you require comforting," Chok said, jumping off the back. The cargo hauler was a simple vehicle and inexpensively built. There was no separation between the cargo section and the pair of chairs that made up the cockpit at the front, requiring that occupants and cargo share the same atmospheric pressure, necessitating spacesuits by occupants.

"Damn, word sure gets around fast," Lefty said, sliding his stack of crates over the vessel's tailgate.

"No, Chok," AJ grumbled.

"Where is Darnell Jackson?" Tork asked, jumping onto the deck and joining them.

"He and Lisa are delivering an armor suit to Jayne," AJ said. "They should be back in a few. We might be waiting on some groceries, too."

"That is no problem, we are allowed to dock for two hours," Tork said. "The commissary transport is making rounds. I will wave him over so he stops here first."

"Lefty, why don't you leave the loading to me so you can keep an eye out," AJ said. "We've already had trouble today."

"Copy that." Lefty pulled his robe's hood up and quietly walked away from the cargo vessel.

"What kind of trouble?" Chok asked looking up at AJ.

He couldn't help but notice she'd change the dyed pink ends of her hair to neon green. He felt a momentary temptation, then pushed the thought away, knowing his actions would be more about retaliation for Jayne's earlier rejection.

"Cheell bounty hunters went after Lefty," he said.

"Did he kill them? The chat feeds did not talk of this," she said.

"No, we took their clothes and left them with their guns," AJ said. "Figured they'd have trouble following us that way."

Chok's laugh was high and melodic. "You did what? Did you remove their clothing? Please, I beg Albert Jenkins, send me a video clip, I will be most popular chatter of day."

"BB, think that'd be a problem?" AJ asked.

"Your goal was humiliation," Beverly said, not appearing. "A video clip would further that goal. I will strip all reference to you and Lefty and send to Cariste Chok."

"Thanks," AJ said. "You should get it shortly, Chok."

Chok's eyes grew wide and unfocused as she watched the short clip. She chortled again and then snorted as her laughing become uncontrollable. "They would have preferred to have been shot," she said when she could finally breathe. "They will never live down this embarrassment."

"Tork, what's up with Cheell bounty hunters?" AJ asked. "My experience is that they're cowards and aren't that good in a fight."

"Cheell is not a wealthy planet," Tork said. "They have rigid laws that have restricted many freedoms a Xandarj or human would not allow. Cheell bounty hunters are allowed the freedom to move throughout the galaxy in search of an approved quarry. It is also well known that they are not often successful. The video clip will cause those two to be recalled and punished. Are you certain they were following a bounty?"

"They admitted to two hundred thousand for Lefty," AJ said. "Four hundred for me and Doc."

"That is bad news, Albert Jenkins," Tork said. "If your price continues to rise, they will publish this bounty widely. More hunters will come and they will not be as weak as those you embarrassed."

"I figured as much," AJ said. "I understand if you need to put distance between us and your family."

"I will talk to Red Fairs," Tork said. "Perhaps it is not wise to have you at our dinner table, but I will not stop as your friend. We have bled together and our bond is complete."

"Is DAS a safe place for Jayne?" AJ asked. "She's got a huge bounty on her."

"DAS is secure," Tork said. "They might decide she is too much risk and send her away, though."

AJ had mixed feelings on that. While it was appealing to have the woman he'd invested so much emotion into getting pushed back into his arms, it wasn't what she wanted. "Let's hope it doesn't come to that."

"I will be back with the commissary delivery truck. It is important for us to leave quickly," Tork said.

Chok giggled as she gestured wildly, updating her virtual displays. "What's going on, Chok?" AJ asked.

"My chat is very popular today," she said. "Many readers are sharing and making funny comments. I would not like to be those *booby hunters* as they have been nicknamed."

"And I thought I left all that crap back on Earth."

"You should join this chat. Pretty humans would be popular," she said. "Many would watch you sleep. You could have credits for doing nothing."

"Not likely," AJ laughed, sliding the last of the crates into the now full cargo vessel. "Why'd you come along, anyway?"

"I have nothing to do for three days," Chok said. "I wanted to offer my services for two hundred credits."

"Services?" AJ asked, concerned at what she might be hinting at. "Chok, I've got a relationship I'm still working on. I can't do that."

Chok's green highlighted eyebrows rose and she laughed. "Silly. I would be naked with you any time you request. I am an excellent mechanic and I have heard you wish to repair a VEAH. You will need my help."

"Do you have tools?" AJ asked.

"Some," she said. "I could bring them. Do you have no tools?"

"There are tools at the habitat," AJ said. "I'm not exactly sure what I'll need, so I'm expecting to come back to Dralli in a few days for more supplies."

A shout drew AJ's attention. When searching for the source, he found Darnell and Lisa weaving through stacks of cargo and around parked ships, stress on their faces. At first, AJ couldn't tell who they were fleeing from but soon located a trio of Cheell enter the docking bay from the same entrance.

"Chok, take cover," AJ said, drawing his weapon. His HUD

popped up an overlay, bright dots tracing Lisa and Darnell as well as their three pursuers.

"Flanking," Lefty whispered. AJ forced himself not to look at Lefty as the man slid along the outside wall of the docking bay, unseen by the pursuers.

"D, Lisa, down!" AJ ordered as one of the trio pulled up short and leveled a long-barreled weapon at his fleeing friends.

Darnell dodged left and dragged Lisa to the deck, the pair scrabbling behind a stack of crates only forty yards from AJ's position. AJ aimed at the pursuers, his range of uncertainty too much for him to feel good about pulling the trigger.

"Shooter has you in their sights, AJ," Beverly warned.

AJ ducked in time for the rifle shot to miss, but he caught a ricochet. The reflected shot burned but was damped by his armor. Three shots in quick succession sounded and AJ's HUD updated. Lefty was standing at the position where the Cheell sniper had been. Instantly, the advancing pair turned hard and raced away, giving up their fight.

"Shooter down," Lefty said, quietly. "Dammit."

"Lisa, Big D, are you up?" AJ called, keeping his weapon handy.

"We're okay," Darnell answered.

"We are most certainly *not* okay!" Lisa sputtered. "They were shooting at us!"

ELEVEN
STOWED

"Your shots caused no damage and it is recorded that you were fired upon first," Mads Bazer said. "I will report to the Dralli government and you will not be encumbered further."

"That's it?" Lefty asked.

"The translation is poor," Mads said. "What are you asking?"

"No police?"

"There is no reason for government involvement. There was a conflict and algorithms decided you are not liable," Mads Bazer said. "The Cheell are marked as aggressive and will be asked to leave."

"That's it?"

"Dralli government does not make judgments regarding alien conflicts," she said. "If the offending parties wish to resolve this, they may attempt to do so. It is expensive and the evidence is considerable against them."

"That's crazy," Lisa said.

"I have explained poorly, but this system works for Dralli," Mads said. "The Cheell have exposed themselves as first shooters. Tell me, how is this different on Earth?"

"The government would find those Cheell and punish them," Lisa said.

"Except they didn't," AJ said. "We were attacked back home and our government was more concerned about their relationship with the Cheell government."

"It's like the wild west!" Lisa said.

"Which is why we're wearing high-tech armor," Darnell said. "Now, before anyone else gets a bright idea, we need to get moving."

"What should I do with the body?" Lefty asked. Over one shoulder he carried the Cheell and in his opposite hand, held the long-barreled weapon.

"For eighty credits, I will have it disposed of," Mads Bazer said.

"What about the rifle?" Lefty asked. "Not exactly usable by humans."

Mads shrugged. "It is worth twice that. But if you do not care, I will take it in trade."

"All yours," Lefty said and dropped both on the deck. "Jenkins was right. We need to clear out of here."

Without further conversation, Lisa allowed Darnell to push her into the cramped quarters of the cargo transporter. They were joined by the rest of the crew, including Greybeard.

"Everyone ready?" Blue Tork asked cheerily, jumping into the cockpit next to Chok who sat in the sole passenger's seat.

"Yes. Go," Lisa grumped.

For several minutes, the group traveled in silence, each processing their own thoughts. AJ finally broke that silence. "How'd Doc look when you talked to her?" he asked, looking hopefully at Lisa.

"Busy," Lisa said. "She said she appreciated the armor but thought DAS would keep her safe."

"Shit, did she take it?" AJ asked.

Lisa nodded. "I made her promise to put it on at least for a couple of weeks."

AJ nodded. "She say anything else?"

"Not really."

"That's a cop-out," AJ said. "Tell me."

"I think Amanda is trying to figure things out, AJ," Lisa said. "She doesn't want to hurt you or ruin what you have together."

"I'm not even sure what that was," AJ said.

"I get that," Lisa said.

Greybeard pushed himself onto AJ's lap and bashed his thick head into his chest. AJ gave the dog the attention he was looking for.

"Think we're done?" he asked.

"That's not for me to say, AJ," Lisa said. "You've got to figure that out for yourself. Amanda's being emotionally distant. Most men don't deal with that well and most women understand."

"Like women are okay with it?" AJ asked.

"More than men."

"Well, not like there are options out on the junk pile," AJ said.

Lisa smiled. "I suppose that depends on if Darnell pisses me off."

"Hey!" Darnell complained.

"Just seein' if you were listenin', big boy," Lisa said, patting his leg.

"I apologize, Albert Jenkins," Chok said. "I have made comfort arrangements with Lefty Johnson."

"That's okay, Chok," AJ said, looking for any reason to change the subject. He opened his planner and looked at the long list of tasks he wanted to accomplish. "After we get unloaded, Lisa's gonna take charge of finding a place to set up our home office. Lefty will do a quick security sweep and then start on a security plan. I figured that Big D, Chok, and I could work on getting power and atmo up and going."

"I'd like to have Darnell if you could spare him," Lisa said. "I've got a few things I need moved around."

AJ shrugged as he exchanged a look between Darnell and Lisa, who had clearly already talked. "I imagine Chok and I can handle power and atmo systems."

"I have been excited to work with these great Pertaf systems," Chok said. "It is said they are inefficient but extremely reliable."

"Sounds perfect for a junkyard," AJ said. "We don't need the best; we only need it to work."

"I've been thinking about our bounty problem," Lefty said.

"Oh?" AJ asked.

"I don't like that there are a couple of boys left back home who are still under the gun," he said. "What would you feel about me making a trip?"

"When?" AJ asked.

"Soon as I can find a ride," he said. "Don't suppose you have any of that go-go juice left? I've got a buyer for the truck, but I need another eighty grand to buy Fantastium."

"You're just full of surprises." AJ pulled a small vial of Fantastium from a pouch on his belt and handed it to Lefty. "This is all I have left. I wish I had more. You should know I was thinking about makin' the same trip."

"I figured," Lefty said. "Thing is, I don't think Earth is gonna be safe. If up to me, I'd prefer it if you stayed here and got this place up and running. I'd like to have somewhere to come back to – if you know what I mean. If they'll go for it, I'll bring Ruiz and LeBeau back. At a minimum, I'll leave them with a warning."

"Hope you get there before those damn assassins," AJ said. "Think we should reach out to Baird? She might know something."

"Hasn't been helpful yet," Lefty said. "And I'd hate to announce our plans, just in case her security isn't that strong."

"I hope that's not a thing."

"You gonna be able to hold down the fort without me?"

"I can't imagine getting in your way on this, Lefty," AJ said. "Those boys don't deserve what's comin' their way. I'm glad you're takin' the mission."

"Well, you don't need to go getting all mushy," Lefty said. "I'll take a quick security sweep when we get out to the heap. Make sure you don't have an infestation problem before I leave."

"That'd be appreciated," AJ said.

Twenty minutes later, Blue Tork spun the rented cargo vessel around and executed a flawless landing, leaving the back end only a few yards from the old Pertaf liner's converted cargo bay doors. First out was Lefty, who, with the help of his new thrust board, jetted over to the man-sized entrance.

"Someone's been here," he announced.

"Are you sure?" AJ asked, unholstering his blaster.

"I tied a string across the bottom of the door. Old spy trick," he said. "It's gone. Strap on one of those thrust boards."

From the crate where Lefty had taken his, AJ pulled out what looked like a slim x-shaped boogie board. On his HUD, Beverly projected a video of a person setting a thrust board on their back. AJ did as instructed and felt a satisfying clunk as the sled clamped onto his suit.

"I don't know how to fly this thing," he said.

"Use the same motions you used for the rocket pack," Beverly said, appearing next to him, wearing her Jetsons suit and rocket pack. AJ nodded and leaned forward, jetting out of the back of the cargo vessel. His short flight was inelegant, but he crossed the few yards without incident.

"You get the door. I'll sweep," Lefty ordered. AJ knew the drill well and stacked up on the door, taking hold of the handle. Soon, Lefty tapped his shoulder, indicating he was ready. AJ pulled the door open and waited for Lefty to sweep the interior. Together, they flowed into the large space, racing for the cover of junk that had been left behind.

"I'm not getting anything," AJ said.

"I'm coming in," Darnell said.

"We're on the right," AJ answered.

The pair adjusted to a third person and worked as a team to clear the large hangar space. In the end, they didn't find anyone, although the fact that there were several unlocked hatches left AJ feeling insecure.

"We're going to need to lock down all ingress points," Lefty said. "You have a welder handy?"

"I do," AJ said. "We need power first, though."

"Copy. Where's that?"

"You boys hold the fort," AJ said. "I'll be back with that power regulator."

He half jetted, half stumbled across the deck as he struggled to gain control of the thrust board strapped to his back. In the beginning, using a rocket pack had given him the same problems. It was only a matter of time before he gained the needed expertise. By the time he arrived at the cargo vessel, Chok already had the part unpacked and loaded onto a zero-g pallet jack.

"You stay here, Chok," AJ said, noticing that Chok had picked up his newly acquired toolbox. "We don't know if our visitor poses a danger yet."

"No," Chok said simply. "I will stay safe next to Albert Jenkins."

"I don't have time for this," he grumbled, pushing the equipment from the cargo vessel toward the man-sized door. At first, he was concerned the regulator wouldn't fit and he'd have to figure how to open one of the bay doors. Once he realized the crate could be turned on its side, he slipped it through.

"Still good?" AJ asked, pushing off toward a second-level landing that bordered one side of the cargo bay. It was on this landing where previous inhabitants had set aside a galley, waste facilities, and sleeping quarters. At the far end of the block of rooms was the entrance to the mechanicals, which was their destination.

"Hold on. We need to clear mechanicals," Lefty said.

AJ set the pallet jack aside and joined Lefty and Darnell in working through the gymnasium-sized room that hosted a semi-truck-size powerplant. The walls of the massive room were covered by both manual and electronic controls and status displays.

"Man, some of this stuff is seriously old-school," Darnell said, getting distracted as it became clear there was no one unexpected within the large room. "Can you say *steampunk?*"

"I don't even know what you're saying." AJ was surprised when

Beverly's outfit changed and she wore a leather vest with tools in the pockets, a leather cap, and a pair of oversized goggles on her forehead.

"No?" she asked.

"No idea." AJ shook his head as he jetted back to where he'd dropped the oversized replacement part that would hopefully get the powerplant up and running again.

"I told you it would be safe," Chok said, dragging the toolbox to the center of the room.

Maneuvering the heavy regulator took some doing, but AJ finally set it next to the large panel in the powerplant where its non-working twin had sat for many years. Before AJ could request anything, Chok had the toolbox magnetically clamped to a nearby shelf and was extracting the large wrench she would need to extract the old regulator.

Having spent a good deal of time researching the ancient Pertaf powerplant, AJ knew its function was both simple and elegant. Multi-fueled like the Veneri EAH ship engines, the powerplant's primary energy came from gravitational fields found in a planet's orbit, which was where this space liner would have spent a majority of its time when operational.

AJ became concerned as the force exerted on the old nuts spun well past three hundred pounds. He'd suspected there would be corrosion and had bought a few replacements. If he continued, the bolts were likely to break, but he had little choice. In the end, however, the nuts freed and he and Chok slipped the old part out.

"Looks like it'll fit," AJ said, visually comparing new and old parts. "That's always a good sign."

"I do not understand your surprise," Chok said. "This part was specifically manufactured for this purpose."

"Oh boy, but I've heard that before!" he said, ducking into the alcove created by the missing part. Using a special compound and a brush, he wiped down the massive contacts, removing a black film of corrosion.

"I have seen parts that were manufactured to the wrong specification. It is not common, though," Chok said, taking the brush from him. "Are the contacts smooth?"

Chok had read the same maintenance instructions, but AJ didn't mind the question. If the material that made up the contacts was damaged, it would have been better to manufacture replacements than further damage the machine with destructive energy arcs.

"Folks, if you're not near a deck, you should probably make your way down," AJ said. "Once I fire this up, there's no telling what the default settings will be for gravity. I'll adjust it to Earth norms soon enough, but we don't need any broken limbs."

"This is a magnificent machine," Chok said. "I am grateful you have allowed me to work with you."

AJ smiled as the two worked the dresser-sized regulator into position. As desired – but not necessarily expected – nothing bad happened when the part finally seated, touching the contacts exactly. With the efficiency of people who'd worked together before, Chok and AJ cleaned and replaced the bolts, tightening them to specifications.

"I'm not feeling anything," Darnell called.

"Me either," Lisa said.

"Hold onto your butts," AJ said. "Honor is yours, Cariste Chok."

"Ooh, yes!" Chok said, wasting no time as she flipped the wide manual switch on the side of the newly installed piece. A green light blinked, slowly at first but increasing in speed. When the light became solid, a heavy vibration transmitted from the machine as if something heavy within had moved.

At first, AJ wasn't sure if he was feeling things right, but when several previously lofted pieces of debris fell to the deck, he was certain gravity was being restored. "Are you feeling that out there, Lisa?" he called, wondering if the entire ship was experiencing the same effects.

"Yes. It's kind of weird – lots of junk settling to the deck. We're going to have to get something out here to clean this up."

"Said every junkyard owner ever," AJ said, chuckling.

"I'm reading about .2g and rising," Darnell said. "I'm looking for a control panel so I can see what the target is."

"I've got one right here, Big D," AJ said, dusting off a screen that he couldn't have read if not for Beverly's overlay. "Presets are going for .87g. I think that's Xandarj sea level. I'll dial up to Earth normal. No sense backtracking."

"Have you seen any sign of the intruder?" Lisa asked.

"Negative," Lefty said. "I didn't think to leave more traps. I brought a hundred video dots this time, though. I've got a surveillance plan. Maybe you could get someone to put 'em up since I'm gonna take off."

"That works," Lisa said. "Did we get one of those energy thingies on the door that keeps atmosphere inside?"

"It's in the plan," AJ said. "I don't know if it's operational. I'm going to turn off the atmo generator until we figure that out. I'd hate to vent too much while we're getting settled."

"Okay. Darnell, Lefty, why don't you get your butts back here so we can get these crates offloaded. I don't want to be sitting around all night twiddling our thumbs," Lisa said.

"Coming, dear," Darnell said.

"I'm on the photonic pressure barrier," AJ said, jogging up steel stairs to the second level and then back down to the deck of the large bay, unable to identify a hatch or door that would allow him a direct passthrough.

"These are huge barrier projectors," Chok said, crouching next to the main entry door, trying to stay out of the way of crates as they were pulled through.

"And they're turned off," AJ said, fishing in the toolbox for a probe Beverly was prompting him for. With the probe in hand, he carefully removed an access panel and touched the indicated spots.

"It is missing an inexpensive control," Beverly said. "Perhaps one of the larger doors has a working circuit we could take."

"Are you sure you weren't a junker in a past life?" AJ asked, walking over to the farthest entry door that was designed for large machines because it was twenty feet wide and forty high. He removed an access panel and inserted the probe.

"It is common sense," Beverly said. "And this is a working item."

AJ followed her instructions for removing the small part and returned it to Chok, who had already removed the broken piece on the man-sized door. No sooner had she replaced the control mechanism than a blue film of photonic particles appeared across the opening. "That is a thick field," she observed.

"Does it matter?" AJ asked.

"I do not believe so. The Pertaf are known for building machines well past specifications," she said.

"If it's keeping the O2 inside, it's hard to feel bad about that."

"Should we try pressurizing the hold?" Chok asked.

"Absolutely," AJ said as the two traipsed back to the machine room. They had to adjust manual valves to allow oxygen captured from Xandarj's atmosphere to mix with the remnant gasses.

"Do you see the filtration system warning?" Chok asked.

AJ searched his HUD and found it immediately. "You just love your filters," AJ grumbled as he followed Chok to another section of the room.

"Are you looking for filter media?" Darnell called, appearing on the second level with a six-foot-tall bundle that looked like a roll of carpet.

"Probably, bring it down," AJ said, turning to the first indicated panel. He accepted a wrench from Chok but when he looked for the bolts that held the panel in place, he didn't find anything.

"It's super light. Catch," Darnell said, tossing the large roll over a steel railing.

AJ was already in motion trying to pull open the panel. Before he could turn to look back up at Darnell, he froze. A gun barrel was pointed directly at his face. Unable to process the events unfolding, AJ stood there as the filter bundle struck him, knocking him to the side. A loud squawk from the person holding the gun startled him almost as much as the gun's discharge. He realized instinctively that the round had sailed harmlessly above his head.

"Intruder!" Chok screamed. Before AJ could right himself, she threw her shoulder into his body, finishing the job started by Darnell's filter, knocking him to the ground.

Knowing time was critical, AJ twisted and pulled Chok to the side as he scrabbled against the unwieldy filter roll. Expecting at any moment to be on the receiving end of a fatal weapon's discharge, he struggled to find his footing. When he finally popped to his knees to face his attacker, he was surprised at what he saw in front of him.

An unusually feminine face was visible behind the clear face shield. The girl's nose was tapered to a point and her narrow lips followed the same lines, almost giving the appearance of a beak. She was talking rapidly which allowed AJ to see that she didn't have an inflexible beak specifically. She had skin, just like any human or Xandarj, just oddly shaped and instead of fur or hair, her eyebrows and head were covered in brilliant blue and white feathers.

"Weapon down!" Lefty ordered, landing next to AJ before he could gain his footing.

"Where'd you come from?" AJ asked Lefty.

"Video dots," Lefty said. "Weren't you listening to me at all?"

The woman, who was a little taller than AJ, held her hands up defensively. "Please, don't shoot," she said. "I will not prosecute you for your trespass."

TWELVE

CONSPIRACY

AJ considered the woman in front of him. Once he got past her beak-like nose and her feathers, he realized she wasn't unattractive. More importantly, she seemed to have a keen intelligence behind sharp blue eyes that darted between the quickly gathering crew.

"That's a funny greeting for someone hiding in the air ducts," AJ said.

"I thought you were bandits," she said, shifting her attention to him. "I see nothing to dissuade me of this."

"Where I come from, you'd be called a stowaway. For the record, I've got salvage rights on this old junkheap, so you're the one who's trespassing."

Anger crossed through the Pertaf woman's face as a blue blush filled her otherwise pale cheeks. "You dare speak such insolence while standing aboard my family's vessel? How did you know the power modulator was in such disrepair?"

AJ made a quick move to grab the woman's arm as she lowered her weapon. She yowled with pain as he twisted her wrist and disarmed her. Something struck his chest and when he released her and gained some distance, he realized she'd kneed him.

"You're a feisty one," he said, stuffing her pistol into his belt. "You can knock off the theatrics of how we're stealing your ship."

The woman rubbed her wrist, looking from it to AJ. "You're a brute. What kind of man are you that you would attack me so?"

"Look, lady, I just needed to secure the gun," AJ said, holding his hands up defensively. "Now, maybe you can tell me why you're running around my junk pile threatening to shoot me and my crew."

The woman blinked several times, still holding her arm.

"AJ," Beverly said, appearing between the two. "I've scanned this woman's biosignatures. Her name is Faramor Poecile. She's been listed as missing and presumed dead."

"Faramor?" AJ asked.

"Ah, now the truth of the situation becomes clear," Faramor said.

"AJ," Beverly continued. "She was listed as missing sixty-two years ago when the Poecile family's space liner was damaged beyond repair."

"She's not dead," AJ said.

"Who?" Faramor asked.

"Her bio-signs show that she's been in some sort of suspension," Beverly continued. "AJ, she is confused. The Poecile family all perished on that day sixty-two years ago. It's been long speculated that the accident was anything but that. They were effectively royalty and she was a princess. Her family was completely wiped out."

"You're not dead," AJ said again.

"AJ, be gentle," Beverly warned. "She doesn't know."

Faramor blinked a couple of times and then responded, irritation clear in her voice. "Of course, I'm not dead!"

"What's the last thing you remember?" AJ asked. "How'd you get in that air duct?"

Faramor blinked. "I, uh ... I don't answer to you," she finally added, angrily.

"Lisa, could you come down here," AJ called.

"I'm here," Lisa answered, coming up behind AJ.

"Who is this?" Faramor asked.

"Farah, please go with Lisa," AJ said. "She'll run you up to the galley and find you a nice place to rest while you gather yourself. We're in the process of repairing the atmospheric systems and I need to make sure we're not venting too much atmo into space."

"Why would *Poecile Aerie* be venting?"

"That's the ship's name, *Poecile Aerie*?" AJ asked.

"Yes, you ridiculous man. You are strange looking. You talk strangely, you act strangely and you do not belong on *Poecile Aerie!*"

"Look here, princess," AJ said. "While I'd love to stand around discussing how strange I am, I've got a crew who'd like to get settled in and we can't do that if we're not airtight. So, go with Lisa – the nice lady behind me – and get out of my hair for a bit. I'll come and talk to you once I know we're not all gonna suffocate. You okay with that?"

"You cannot talk to me like that!" She sputtered the words at AJ, but she wasn't resisting Lisa's guiding hand.

"It's okay, dear," Lisa said, soothingly. "You must be hungry. Why don't you come with me? We'll find you something to eat and I'll look at that arm. AJ seems like a brute, but he's not that bad once you get past the bluster."

"Are you kidding me?" AJ asked. "How exactly do I turn into the bad guy in this?"

"Don't listen to him," Lisa said, wrapping an arm around the Pertaf woman's back and directing her around AJ. "He's all bark and no bite."

"Albert Jenkins, you might find this interesting," Chok said, stepping into the air vent.

AJ grumbled, not loving Lisa's depiction of him, but he knew better than to push that conversation. The unexpected stowaway was calm and Lisa was getting her out of his way. Stepping in behind Chok, the lights on the side of his helmet illuminated a hidden compartment that had dozens of dangling wires and a few tubes. Along the bottom of the compartment was a cushion indented in the shape of a humanoid.

"Suspension chamber?" AJ asked, pushing the hanging cables

aside and inspecting a control surface that blinked with a low energy warning.

Beverly appeared, standing atop the cushion. "I believe the mystery of the missing Faramor Poecile, heir to the Poecile legacy, is resolved."

"What do you have in there?" Darnell asked, ducking his head into the opening.

"Check it out for yourself," AJ said, stepping out.

"Holy cow," he said. "Think it's a coincidence that she woke up when we came aboard?"

"Low energy on her pod there," AJ said. "I bet when we started the power plant, it caused the pod to kick her out."

"That's messed up," Darnell said. "She must be tripping."

AJ slid closed the panel that had for so long hidden the suspension chamber and extracted the empty screen that would hold the filter media they'd brought along. "Not much we can do about it at the moment," AJ said. "We need to get this habitat sealed up and pumping out some good air or we're not going to have enough atmo to stay out here."

"Yeah, copy that," Darnell said. "Did you get a look at her, though? I always figured those Pertaf would be kinda gawky looking, what with the pointy nose and those long legs. Kind of a looker, though, if you ask me."

"And here I thought I was supposed to be the dirty old man," AJ said, chuckling. "You gonna tell Lisa all that?"

"Uh, no," Darnell said. "I was just sayin'."

AJ and Chok struggled with reloading the filter media for a few moments and then slid the assembly back into place. "Maybe you should grab the welder," AJ said. "I'll map out the repairs."

"I've never done much welding," Darnell said. "You know that."

"Yup. Figured you could carry the welder for me. I was thinkin' that'd buy my silence," AJ said.

"I have no idea why we're friends."

"AM I YOUR PRISONER?" Faramor asked when AJ and Darnell returned to the galley. It had taken four and a half hours to seal up the largest leaks and they were in for a long couple of days finding the remaining non-critical pinholes.

"Do you have somewhere you want to go?" AJ asked.

Faramor blinked, apparently a habit when she was thinking.

Lisa jumped in before Faramor could continue. "I assume Lefty and Blue Tork got off all right? Did Chok decide to stick around?"

"All three took off. Chok said she'd come back in a week. I identified a bunch of parts we need manufactured. She'll bring them back with her," AJ said.

Faramor adjusted her shoulders uneasily, drawing their attention. "I want to go home," she said. "Lisa Jackson has been polite. You do not seem to be bandits, but she has disallowed access to the ship's communication systems."

"How old are you?" AJ asked.

As Faramor turned her head, AJ realized what had been bothering him about her motions. Pertaf seemed to have limited eye movement and were forced to move their heads when focusing on someone. "I am thirty-two years. I assume your communication property translated that."

AJ sighed. "Lisa hasn't denied you access to ship communications. This is a derelict ship. Virtually none of its systems are operating. Didn't you notice how cold it is aboard and that there's no atmosphere?"

"You have misstated," Faramor said. "This word, *derelict*, it is incorrect."

"Maybe, but I wouldn't bet on it," AJ said. "Farah, you're not thirty-two years old. You're ninety-four. *Poecile Aerie* was wrecked in Xandarj's orbit sixty-two years ago. Someone who wanted to keep you alive stashed you in that air vent compartment."

"Ninety-four?" she asked, visibly shaken. "But ... my family."

"Nice going, AJ," Lisa said, annoyed. She led Faramor over to a chair and helped her sit.

"What? This was never going to be a great conversation," AJ said. "Trust me, there's no easy way to hear this. If I was her, I'd want it straight."

"Yes, honesty is preferable."

"Look, Farah. If you want a ride to Dralli Station so you can contact people on Pertaf, I'll get you there in a couple of days, but a lot has changed during the years you were hidden on this ship. Whoever attacked your family won't love to see you suddenly show up. Then again, you might have family that's waiting for you. I have no idea. Right now, there aren't many who know you're alive. Might be best to keep it that way until you get your bearings."

Faramor nodded, pushing Lisa's hand away as she stood. "Show me, Albert Jenkins. Show me that *Poecile Aerie* is ruined. I will see this with my own eyes. Until then, I will only believe you to be common bandits who deserve punishment."

"Are you sure you're up for that?" AJ asked. "I mean, you did just wake up from the longest nap in history. Shouldn't you take it easy for a couple of days?"

Faramor waved her hand dismissively. "Your delays only confirm what I already know. You are holding me, probably for ransom. It is an intricate lie you tell, but a lie nonetheless."

"Good lord, woman," AJ growled. "And you call me ridiculous. Fine, we've got a stack of thrust boards by the front door. We'll get you a look from the outside."

"You *are* ridiculous."

AJ shook his head and could only manage to grumble as he led the Pertaf from the galley and down the metal stairs to the external hatch. Considering how *Poecile Aerie's* auxiliary generator was now pumping out excessive amounts of energy, they'd decided to keep the photonic pressure barrier powered even when the hatch was closed.

"Are you ready to give in yet?" Faramor asked.

AJ picked up a thrust board as sympathy filled his face. "Look,

Farah, this will be disturbing," he said. "I shouldn't have pushed you so hard. Are you sure you want to do this? Look around, this cargo bay should tell you everything you need to know. Do you think we could make all this up? The rust. The junk. Look at everything."

Faramor's expression also softened. "What would you do, Albert Jenkins? Would you not want to know for certain?"

"Have you used one of these before?" AJ asked, handing her a thrust board. "It'll clip to your back."

Faramor inspected the board for a moment and then positioned it in place. "The concept is obvious enough."

AJ attached his board and then pulled on the latch, swinging the hatch inward. Through the door, Xandarj filled their view and for a moment, AJ could imagine a time when *Poecile Aerie* sailed proudly. Of course, the piles of junk and the rusty hull of the Veneri EAH came into focus and popped the momentary fantasy.

"How could this be?" Faramor asked, stepping through the barrier. "Who would leave all of this mess next to *Poecile Aerie*?" Without warning, she leaped from the deck and, utilizing the thrust board, jetted away.

"Follow her, BB," AJ said, coiling his leg muscles and jumping as hard as he could and at the same time willing the thrust board to its highest setting. Unlike Faramor, he barely escaped the landing pad's gravity. When he looked for her, she was difficult to find and without Beverly's tracking, he'd have lost her. Pushing hard, he still could not gain on her as she sped along the length of the ancient wreck. "Farah, slow down," he called.

AJ raced after Farah but had to decide between safety and speed. Where the willowy Pertaf was graceful as she sailed through the veritable minefield of floating junk, AJ was a plodder with no natural grace to his path. Several times, he had to bank away suddenly to avoid larger pieces of junk. He ended up ramming into smaller pieces that if not for the armor he wore, might have caused irreparable damage.

When Faramor finally made it to the fore of the ship, she

slowed and gracefully floated around the bow and up the centerline until she rested in front of the ship's once majestic bridge. Time and scavengers had not been kind to the ship's technological hub. Strands of cabling had been pulled through long-ago broken windows.

"Be careful, Albert Jenkins," Faramor said. "It would appear your power generator has circuits that are connected. There are a few live wires that carry significant voltage."

"How can you tell?" AJ asked, finally catching up with her.

"I see evidence of the electrical charge," she said. "It is well known that a Pertaf's eyesight is the greatest of all species."

"For what it's worth, Farah, I'm sorry," AJ said.

"Why is it you call me Farah?"

"I tend to shorten names," AJ said. "It's probably a human thing. You know like you have good eyesight. We make names shorter."

Farah squawked and as she did, brought her hand up to her face shield. "You are very odd, Albert Jenkins. Very odd and humorous. Short names are not a racial benefit like good eyesight."

"Humor," AJ said, floating through a huge opening that had once held a massive piece of glass. He landed next to Farah, who was scanning the room. "I'm good at that too."

"My grandfather built *Poecile Aerie*. It was his dream and took much of his wealth and all his strength. He never sailed her, dying only a year before we set off for Xandarj. I always felt sad for him to have missed his dream."

"That is sad," AJ agreed.

"I don't remember any accident or attack," Farah said. "But I was on the maiden voyage. Our entire family was aboard. Mother was so proud to stand at the helm of grandfather's legacy. Perhaps others survived as I did."

"Greetings Faramor Poecile," Beverly said, choosing that moment to appear between them, wearing formal black robes. I am 49231125-0-B of Beltigersk. I extend sympathy to you in the moment of your personal tragedy."

"Thank you. I'm sorry, I didn't catch your entire name," Farah said.

"We call her Beverly. Actually, I call her BB," AJ said.

Farah looked momentarily confused. "Is it true? Do you have a special skill at shortening names? I believed you to be joking."

"Humans, like most species, find numeric designations tedious," Beverly said. "I am comfortable being addressed as Albert Jenkins suggests. Indeed, most humans call him AJ, although you would need to understand humanity's English alphabet to understand how that came to be."

"I am unfamiliar with the human species, but I am of course knowledgeable of the great peoples of Beltigersk. I am honored by your attention, Beverly," Farah said. "If I knew Albert Jenkins had a symbiotic rider, I would have addressed you more formally upon our meeting. I have not intended offense."

"I did not expose my presence to you as I felt it would be easier if you discovered for yourself the truth of that which has happened," Beverly said.

"You feared that I would have acted improperly under the stress that I was feeling," Farah summarized.

"I thought it possible. You should know, I am not acting in an official capacity for Beltigersk," Beverly said. "I separated from my mother's leadership so that I might travel with Albert Jenkins."

"He is indeed lucky for your presence," Farah said.

"I created a conduit so that you can make communications and research what happened in your absence," Beverly said. "The remains of all your family except for you were recovered from *Poecile Aerie's* wreckage. Your mother was not physically damaged by the impact of the vessel which struck this one. It is believed she was assassinated by Poecile rivals who were punished by your government."

"Kalibaster," Farah spat.

"Kalibaster Corporation was disbanded and their leaders imprisoned," Beverly said. "There was justice, but it did not undo the tragedy."

"Thank you again, Beverly," Farah said, bowing slightly. "Albert Jenkins, would you continue to accompany me as I circuit my once proud home? I would see the damage and observe the ravages only time is capable of delivering."

"Sure," AJ said as a message appeared on his HUD.

Lisa: How is it going?

AJ: We're on the bridge. She just met Beverly.

Lisa: Poor kid. Is she still in denial?

AJ: Nah. She pretty much had it figured out once we were out of the hatch.

Lisa: Is she okay?

AJ: She's tough. Seems sad, but she's working through it.

Lisa: I have food. Will you be back soon?

AJ: Not sure. Maybe half an hour.

Lisa: It'll hold.

Wordlessly, AJ followed Farah from the bridge and down the opposite side of the ship. Since the ship was two miles long, it took a while for them to make their way along the length. Farah stopped when they got to the point where the collision had occurred. It was as if a massive fist had punched the side of the ship and pulled out a forty-yard-diameter chunk of the hull. Surprisingly, there was little in the way of buckling near where the chunk had been removed.

"Whatever hit, had to be moving fast," AJ observed. "That kind of damage is hard to imagine."

"My brothers were in the starboard engine room," Farah said. "There is video of the moment of impact. One moment they are alive and joking with each other. The next they are simply gone. My father was not so lucky. He was only ten yards away. Molten debris struck him where he stood, watching with horror as his sons were carried away. There was anguish in his face."

AJ placed a hand on her shoulder. "Gosh, that's hard, Farah. I'm sorry you had to see that."

"Mother survived three hours, working tirelessly to evacuate the crew. Nine hundred thirty died in those first hours," Farah said.

"Authorities didn't immediately know that she'd been murdered. It wasn't until twelve days later when she didn't show up in any of the refugee camps that an investigation was launched. They originally suggested she'd committed suicide. Anyone who knew her would have known that was a lie."

"How'd they figure out what happened?" AJ asked.

"I don't know," Farah said.

"If you would allow, I can fill this in," Beverly said. "It is part of the public record, so you will find it soon enough."

"Of course, honored Beverly," Farah said.

"Careful, you'll give her a big head," AJ said.

"I do not see how that is possible," Farah said.

AJ winced at the fact that he'd chosen a poor time to try to inject humor. "Ask me later," he said. "Sorry for interrupting."

"Thank you, AJ," Beverly said. "Unusual for the time, *Poecile Aerie*'s video recordings were constantly transmitted to Pertaf. It was at extraordinary expense, but it turned out to be quite valuable. When poison was found in your mother's body, a team of investigators discovered the perpetrator to be one of her assistants. According to news reports, this assistant was relentlessly interrogated until he gave information on the Kalibaster conspiracy."

"My best friend was from the Kalibaster family," Farah said. "There was competition and jealousy between our parents' generation, but we had promised to end it. It is hard to believe her family would do such a thing."

"You have the news accounts," Beverly said.

"Please, can we return to the vessel? I feel I might be sick," Farah said.

"Of course."

THIRTEEN

HUNTERS

"I got a message from Baird last night," AJ said, accepting a cup of a bitter, caffeinated drink resembling coffee from Lisa. "Where's Darnell?"

"He was in the garage clearing off that runabout," Lisa said. They'd taken to calling the primary cargo bay area *the garage*, mostly because of the tall doors which resembled garage doors.

"Is he going to try to get it running?" AJ asked. "That'd be handy."

"It's pretty messed up," Darnell said, entering the kitchen and making his way to the pot of alien coffee.

"AJ got a message from Baird," Lisa said, short-circuiting the conversation.

"Now that's news! Only took her what, eight days to respond?" Darnell asked.

"Not that bad considering distance and all," AJ said. "BB, would you mind reading it out loud for all of us?"

Albert Jenkins, et. al.:

Per your timely warning re: Private LeBeau and Corporal Hernandez, United States Army Intelligence successfully interdicted hostile actions already in progress. I am pleased to report our actions were successful. You are to be commended for raising this issue using proper channels. As a result, no human nor alien lives were needlessly forfeit.

To the subject of potential additional hostile actions by as yet unidentified actors, I strongly urge you, Darnell Jackson, Lisa Jackson, Amanda Jayne, and Marion 'Lefty' Johnson to return to Earth where protective services can be extended.

As I believe it is unlikely you will return, I ask that you consider how your future actions might further complicate US interactions with alien governments. POTUS has received direct assurances from the Cheell ambassador to the US that the terminal actions of Cheell citizens were not sanctioned or approved by the Cheell nation.

If you act outside of the interests of the United States, it will be our position that you should be subject to Galactic Empire law. In plain language, we will not attempt to negotiate for your release in the event you are captured in the commission of illegal acts. I say this to reinforce my strong request that you and those who have traveled with you to Xandarj return to Earth, where you will receive the full protection of the United States Army.

With Respect,

Major Jacqueline Baird

"At least they got LeBeau and Hernandez out," Darnell said.

"Has Lefty already taken off?" Lisa asked.

"He transitioned to jump space eighteen hours ago," AJ said. "I wonder if they'll take him into custody or if they'll let him turn around?"

"If I forward this message to Rebel, they will receive it upon exiting jump space," BB said. "It would give Lefty the most flexibility in making a decision."

"Let's do that. Send a copy to Jayne," AJ said. "She should know what's going on."

"You all seem quite engaged this morning," Farah said, joining them in the kitchen. "Has something important occurred?"

"Letter from home," AJ said. "Nothing that impacts you, I wouldn't think."

"Are you still expecting a visit from Cariste Chok today?" Farah asked. "I would very much like to visit Dralli Station."

"This is it?" AJ asked. "Your big coming out? Have you decided to let people know you are alive?"

Farah shook her head as she poured hot water into a small cup. "No. I will take Lisa Jackson's counsel and remain anonymous. I do not wish to further endanger my life. I have also been thinking about your predicament."

"Oh?" AJ asked. "Which predicament? The one where we're burning money and still don't have a workable ship or the one where we're on someone's hit list?"

"Perhaps both," she said. "Given my position in a wealthy family, I am not completely unfamiliar with the issues associated with paid bounties. Concern for one's security was a way of life as a Poecile. Why do you think my grandfather built a massive vessel and placed his entire family aboard?"

"Girl has a point, AJ," Lisa said.

"Okay. So sixty-five years ago, you knew something about the bounty business," AJ said. "The universe has probably changed a bit since then."

"Undoubtedly," she said. "The Pertaf are fond of saying, however, that change is simply the journey of a circle. That is to say, change is often an illusion."

"Oh, don't go all Yoda on me," AJ said. "I imagine you have a point here?"

Farah nodded. "I made gentle inquires after constructing a false persona and discovered that the bounty originates from a powerful Cheell industrial family."

"No kidding?" AJ said, sitting forward. "BB's been trying to figure this out and hasn't gotten anywhere. How in the heck did you do that?"

"The bounty allows for live delivery," Farah said. "I merely stated that I had Albert Jenkins in custody and requested a transfer."

"Why would they believe you?" AJ asked.

"I supplied a short video and provided the location of *Poecile Aerie*," she said.

"You did what!?" Darnell gasped. "Are you crazy!?"

"I have been concerned for my sanity as well, Darnell Jackson," Farah said. "I am quite convinced that my mental facilities are operating well."

"You told the bounty holder to come here and pick up AJ?" Darnell said. "This was our hideout, Farah, a place of safety."

"You are naïve, Darnell Jackson. Do you believe that any competent hunter will not be capable of finding details of your move to *Poecile Aerie?* My actions allow us to set a time and place for an encounter with the transfer agents. They will, of course, be suspicious. It is why we must travel to Dralli Station today so that we might manufacture the necessary circuitry for the claws of my home."

AJ's head turned sharply at the word claws. "Talk to me about claws, Farah."

"Permanently mounted weapon systems are illegal in upper echelon systems of the Galactic Empire," she said. "My research has shown that this has not changed in the time in which I have been asleep."

"Upper echelon?"

"The old worlds," she said. "Pertaf, those of Tok Supremacy and Beltigersk, although Beltigersk aren't known for travel. There are too many others to list, but they are well known."

"Cheell? Korgul? Vred?" AJ asked.

"Vred are well respected," Farah said. "And no, Cheell and Korgul are despicable."

"Sounds like the same us-versus-them type thing we're still struggling with on Earth," Darnell said.

Farah looked at Darnell, blinked slowly, and then turned back to AJ. "I believe Darnell Jackson refers to a truth that is well known. To have wealth is to protect it from those who do not, regardless of stated morality. There are indeed moral Cheell and possibly the same is true of Korgul, although not in my experience. It is not my intent to be drawn into an argument. My only point is that *Poecile Aerie* was built with weapons that I believe to be easily restored to function. They are weapons that hide their function with a second purpose."

"Way to bury the lead," Lisa chuckled.

"What kind of weapons?" AJ asked.

"Escape capsules," Farah said. "An entertainment vessel such as *Poecile Aerie* is equipped with tens of thousands of launchers designed to fling small, habitable vessels safely away in the event of an emergency. The mechanism required to achieve quick separation is easily utilized to accelerate small, dense objects at great speeds upon predictable courses."

"How great of speed?" AJ asked.

Farah reached into a pocket and withdrew a round black object the size of a golf ball. From the way she moved her hand, AJ could tell it was heavier than he'd expected.

"A loaded habitat has the mass of eight thousand kilograms," she said, dropping the ball into AJ's hand.

"Crap, what is this? Tungsten?"

"You surprise me, Albert Jenkins," she said. "How would you know this by mere physical observation?"

"Gold, lead, tungsten, and uranium are about the only elements that could weigh this much in such a small package," he said. "Gold and lead were easy to eliminate and most people – Pertaf or otherwise – don't pick up uranium."

"Unless it is stabilized," Farah said. "But you are correct, it is tungsten."

"How many of these little balls do you have?" AJ asked. "On Earth, this stuff is expensive."

"How expensive?" Darnell asked.

"Well, not that bad if you buy in bulk," AJ said. "Maybe thirty bucks for this little ball."

"We set sail with a stock of one-hundred-thirty-thousand," Farah said. "In my exploration, I have recovered perhaps ten thousand."

"Four million bucks in hard little balls," Darnell said. "Did Mads put tungsten in her Pertaf treasure list?"

"Probably not," AJ said. "Kind of thinking that selling them isn't the smartest idea, though. Especially if we can get some of those launchers working."

"What is *Pertaf treasure?*" Farah asked.

"Hold on," Darnell interrupted her. "Explain exactly how this ejection system works. I've seen lifeboat deployments. You're not knocking down ships by flinging little balls at them. Most designs have the engines aft and you'd have to get a ridiculously lucky shot to clog one up with debris."

"Wrong-oh, bubba," AJ said. "I'd say this ball weighs maybe a pound. That's sixteen thousand times lighter than a lifeboat. Imagine that a typical lifeboat craft is launched at 5gs. I don't have my calculator handy, but it doesn't take a genius to realize that if the same force were used on a golf-ball-sized chunk of tungsten, that ball would be moving pretty damn fast."

"How fast?" Darnell asked.

"Maybe five thousand feet per second."

"AJ, I feel compelled to make a point," Beverly said, appearing in her black robe, which AJ knew meant she wanted to speak as a representative of Beltigersk.

"What's that, BB?" AJ asked. "Did you math that out for us?"

"Yes, your calculation is reasonable, although there is no reason to believe the launchers are limited to the force used to launch a lifeboat," she said. "No, my concern is this: mass weapons are highly illegal, especially in habited orbits. A weapon thrown from *Poecile Aerie* will not stop until it strikes either the atmosphere of Xandarj or another, more massive object capable of absorbing the kinetic energy."

"That's kind of the point," AJ said. "Someone comes knocking and we blow 'em up."

"If you miss and strike Dralli or Illaden Stations, or possibly a nearby vessel, you will be liable," she said.

"What happens when it hits atmosphere?" AJ asked. "Isn't there a little atmosphere right here?"

"There is not sufficient atmosphere to slow the type of weapon you are discussing," she said. "If it were to be thrown at Xandarj, the tungsten would not cause a problem."

"I don't see the big issue then," AJ said. "We only take shots that aim at Xandarj or off into deep space. It's not like we can't calculate the trajectories."

"It is a grave risk, Albert Jenkins," Beverly said. "I advise against it."

"Would you advise letting bounty hunters do their thing?"

"No, but this is not a binary choice," she said.

"Given our current resources, it is right now," AJ said. "We'll be careful, but I'm not going down without a fight."

"Pertaf treasure, Albert Jenkins?" Farah asked.

"Seems like something we could talk about while you show me how these launchers work," he said.

———

WITH GREYBEARD AT HIS SIDE, AJ approached the main administration building of the Dralli Academic Society. He looked through the long, floor-to-ceiling, curved-glass windows that showed an atrium almost entirely devoid of furniture or other appointments. On the opposite side of the space, a second similarly curved window afforded an expansive view of a brightly lit, grassy hill tall enough to block further view into the campus.

A few minutes after his arrival, a sole figure dressed in a light brown robe appeared at the top of the hill and walked toward the bank of windows. Amanda Jayne smiled cheerily as she made eye contact with AJ and waved. AJ mustered a smile and waved back.

A thin break in the far panel formed as she approached, sticking to the only sidewalk AJ could see on the grassy hill. Just a step or two before she reached the glass, a five-foot-wide panel shifted to the side and allowed her entry into the atrium. Without breaking stride, she continued toward AJ, earning her an excited woof from Greybeard.

"Be good, buddy, we don't want to get kicked out before we've even gotten inside," AJ said, watching as the door closed behind Jayne. As she got closer to his expanse of windows, Jayne pointed to the side and turned in the direction she'd indicated. AJ nodded and followed the curved glass until he arrived at a gray painted patch on the station floor.

"AJ, I'm so glad you messaged," Jayne said after a large glass panel had whooshed open and they were face to face. "Please step inside. There's a security monitor jabbering away in my ear right now and he doesn't like something."

AJ and Greybeard stepped through, barely clearing the threshold before the panel closed behind them. AJ turned and scanned the few passersby but didn't see any obvious threats. "Everything okay?" he asked.

"Uh, sure," she said, sounding less certain than he'd expected. "Could you place your energy weapon on that black pad over there?"

AJ followed her eyes. A small white cylinder with a padded black shelf had risen from the floor next to them. Wordlessly, he withdrew his weapon, placed it on the pad, and watched as the cylinder withdrew into the floor, disappearing from view like it'd never been there.

"That's fancy," he said.

Jayne wrapped her arms around him and hugged him tightly. "I'm so glad to see you," she said. "I've missed you so much."

AJ returned her hug. He was glad to see her, but the circumstances of their last parting still bothered him. Jayne, however, didn't seem to notice. She crouched and spent a few seconds vigorously rubbing Greybeard's neck, to the dog's great enjoyment.

"There's so much I want to show you," she said, standing back up but avoiding direct eye contact.

She took his hand and pulled him toward the opposite side of the atrium. Once through the second door, AJ felt a moment of vertigo as the sky seemed to soar above him. His disorientation persisted as they neared the top of the hill and he could see the grass extending out at least a mile before the first building.

"How is this possible?" AJ asked. "The station isn't this wide."

"Clever optics," Jayne said. "Although DAS does take over three entire levels, the campus is made to look even bigger. Isn't it amazing?"

"I don't see a lot of people," AJ said.

"Oh, they're around," she said. "Many prefer to be inside the halls, teaching or working out problems. For the aesthetic of quiet contemplation, there's a lot done to reduce sound and visual detail."

"Detail, like people are being hidden?"

"Yes. Again, clever optics, advanced audiology – that sort of thing," she said. "Would you care for a coffee, a scone, or something?"

"Whatever you'd like," AJ said. "Do you want to show me your digs?"

"Uh, no, there's not much to see," she said. This time, AJ had no trouble picking out her evasiveness.

"Whatever you like, Doc," AJ said. "Coffee and a scone sound nice."

Jayne brightened and pulled on his hand, leading him toward a building that approached more quickly than he'd have expected. "I got your messages about security and that whole bounty thing. I talked to the head of security. She says that bounties on students aren't a new thing and as long as I stay on the grounds and follow directions, I should be fine."

"Are you wearing the armor?"

"Well, I kind of can't," she said.

"Really? It doesn't feel that restrictive to me," AJ said.

"I'm part of a xeno-life study," she said. "The fabric interfered with observations."

AJ's eyebrows shot up and he bit back his first response. "Nit's okay with this?"

Jayne tipped her head to the side almost apologetically. "Nit is currently disabled. The researchers don't want interference from a symbiote while I'm on the study."

"What do you mean *disabled*?" AJ asked, allowing Jayne to direct him to an outdoor chair next to the warm bricks of a building that was in full sun.

"Kind of a suspension. She said she was okay with it," Jayne explained. AJ nodded, biting his tongue. "Their coffee is really great. I'll be right back."

"BB, are you there?" AJ asked. When she didn't answer after twenty seconds, he tried again but still got no response. Five minutes later, Jayne reappeared, this time carrying two coffee cups and two frosted scones, both of which could have been from any coffee shop on Earth. AJ hadn't seen such Earth-like food on Dralli Station or anywhere else in the Galactic Empire.

"They had to scan me to recreate this coffee and scone combination. Don't they look perfect?" Jayne asked.

"Looks pretty perfect," AJ agreed. "Nit's suspension ... do you think the same thing is happening with Beverly? I can't seem to contact her."

"Probably," Jayne said. "The founders of DAS are Xandarj. They're not really down with Beltigersk so much. But don't worry, I've been reassured they don't come to any harm."

"But you don't know for sure?"

"Well, no, not for sure," she said. "AJ, don't. We're having a nice time. Don't get all weird on me here."

"Doc, you're the scientist and humanitarian," AJ said. "How should I react when someone causes Beverly to become unconscious, suspended, or disabled – however you described it – especially without her permission."

"Surely she knew it was happening," Jayne said.

"I'm leaving, Jayne," AJ said, standing. "Beverly is my responsibility and someone has attacked her. I'm not okay with that. Honestly, I don't understand how you're okay with it. You know Beverly almost as well as I do and this is okay with you?"

"AJ, it's not like you're saying."

"The Amanda Jayne I know would never go for this," AJ said, attempting to retrace his steps back to the main entrance. For some reason, the path kept changing in front of him, the horizon subtly shifting so he soon felt disoriented.

"It's not like that, AJ," she said, grabbing the back of his arm.

"You can't fool me," AJ said. "You look like her and sound like her, but lady, whoever you are, you're not Amanda Jayne."

Jayne sighed. "Before this gets too crazy, what exactly was it that gave me away?"

"Oh, shit," AJ said, looking furtively around him. "What'd you do with Jayne?"

"Was it the face? They say humans spend a lot of time reviewing facial features," the woman in front of him said.

AJ jumped at her. There was a scuffle, but he brought his arm around her neck. "You've got about twenty seconds before you run out of oxygen."

"She said you'd be trouble," the woman replied.

He felt a sharp prick in his side and when he turned, he saw a furry arm floating in the air with something like a hypodermic needle.

"Aww, dammit," was about all he could manage before his arms turned to rubber and he collapsed onto a steel gray deck.

FOURTEEN

BIRDS OF A FEATHER

When AJ awoke, he wasn't a bit surprised to find himself in a steel paneled room, one side of which was a transparent panel. He'd been placed on a narrow bed with a minimal cushion.

"I wasn't sure they'd get you."

AJ slowly sat up. Whatever drug that had been used to disable him was still in his system. Turning, he found Jayne sitting on the steel deck, her knees pulled up to her chest.

"Fancy running into you here," AJ said, discovering that his back and legs hurt.

"I'm sorry, AJ."

"I don't suppose there's any water," AJ said. "My mouth feels like cotton."

"It's the drugs they used. Not very sophisticated, but effective," she said. "Did you hear me?"

"You said you're sorry," AJ said. "Sure. Me too. I don't think this is your fault, though."

"You scare me, AJ," she said.

AJ turned, confusion on his face. "I scare *you*? Doc, when have I been anything but gentle with you? I feel like I've given you space when you've asked for it. I'm not gonna lie and say I don't care for you, but you've made it clear you don't want to be with me. Now you say that I scare you. I don't know how I can be more hands-off without completely ignoring you."

Greybeard stood, walked over, and rested his big head against AJ's knee. AJ stroked the dog's head and tried to contact Beverly, but all he got was silence.

"Were you trying to contact Beverly just then?" Jayne asked.

AJ nodded.

"They're projecting some kind of high-powered magnetic field," she said, getting up from where she sat on the floor. "Do you mind if I sit next to you?"

"Sure," AJ said, shrugging. "Do you remember when we were coming back from Beltigersk after we defeated Alicia and the Cheell?"

Jayne nodded and sat next to him.

"You said you were all in – or something like that," he said. "It's been less than six months. What changed?"

"Would you believe nothing?"

AJ shook his head. "No."

"It's true," Jayne said. "Nothing except this self-destructive streak I have of pushing everyone who loves me away. AJ, there's a reason I lived in a condo by myself. I'm not good with people – even my sister calls me cold and distant."

"Younger or older?"

She smiled at the question. "Does that make a difference?" When AJ didn't answer she continued. "Younger. And before you ask, yes, she's got a family, she runs a small pharmaceutical business, and everyone in the universe loves her."

"Everyone?"

Jayne nodded. "I feel like a used napkin next to her. She's everything I'm not."

"That's a strange thing to say," AJ said. "I'll remind you that you're a respected surgeon who served in Viet Nam and dedicated her life to saving others. Oh, and you saved the world about a year ago."

Jayne sighed and bumped AJ's shoulder with her own. "This is why you terrify me."

"If I hadn't been married to Pam, I'd question if all women were as nutty as you and swear off them forever."

"See, I told you. I'm damaged goods."

"Like I'm not? Pam loved me even when I screamed at her after coming back from the war," AJ said. "She got me help when I needed it. Do you know what one of the last things she said to me before she died?"

"That she loved you?"

"Yes, but if you knew Pam, that was part of her, like breathing. No, she told me that once I was done grieving her, I was supposed to find a new partner – someone I could share my life with, someone who would love me like she did," AJ said, his voice catching.

"Gosh, how could anyone live up to that?" Jayne asked. "Seriously, it sounds like something my sister would say."

AJ chuckled. "If it's any consolation, her saying that really messed me up," AJ said. "How could I think about someone else when there was no way I would ever find someone as good and pure as Pam. I didn't deserve it the first time. It didn't matter though, because after she was gone, I found what I needed in a bottle."

"So you're saying, I'm what you deserve?" Jayne asked, looking at him thoughtfully.

"Only you could take that from what I just told you," AJ said. "No, Doc, that's just it, I don't deserve you. You're so far out of my league, it's like I'm a kid trying out for the Cardinals."

"I won't lie. Saving lives is a worthy cause. I feel good every time I've played a part in someone's recovery," Jayne said. "Is it selfish to want more than that?"

"Do you listen to yourself?" AJ asked. "You're complaining that you don't have any love in your life while I'm sitting right here in front of you."

"Pretty messed up for someone who's supposed to have their shit together, huh?"

"Did you just curse?" AJ asked.

Jayne rolled her eyes. "I cuss. Sometimes."

"Stop running away from me, Jayne."

"I don't deserve you. I've gotten you into this mess with DAS. We're probably being taken somewhere so they can do experiments on us."

"Probed," AJ agreed.

"Did you know that was a thing? Cheell really were abducting people and they absolutely used probes on various orifices," Jayne said. "Before I was captured, I found documentation in the DAS archives."

"Is DAS behind our capture?" AJ asked. "Seems like someone in DAS had to have helped to make this all work."

"Not the entire organization," Jayne said. "But someone in power, certainly. I think I was offered a fellowship at DAS just so they could capture me – or us, I suppose."

"Have you seen our captors?"

"Are we okay, AJ?" Jayne asked, ignoring the question.

"Depends on your definition of *okay*," AJ said. "As far as relationships go, you're a bit of a trip. Then again, I had a woman stand by me through almost ten years of violent PTSD episodes. I haven't told anyone this before, but I broke her nose once when I was freaking out."

"That's horrible."

"So, you deciding to go off to university and hang out with academics is hardly on par with the crap I put Pam through."

"But we're not together," Jayne said.

"Is that how you see it?" AJ asked. "Because from my perspective, we couldn't be more together."

Jayne rolled her eyes. "Sure. We're trapped in a tiny cell, probably on an alien spaceship that's headed to an alien world where horrible things will happen to us ... together."

"A guy takes what he can get," AJ said.

The flippant comment drew a smile to Jayne's face. "Do I really deserve you?"

"Oh geez, I hope not."

"WHEN DO THEY FEED US?" AJ asked, his stomach grumbling loud enough it caused Jayne to glance back at him.

"I haven't seen our captors, yet. Drink more water, it should help that hunger feeling," she said.

"I was hoping they'd eventually show themselves."

"They will when we get to where they're taking us," she said.

"Did you see anyone before you were captured?" AJ asked.

"No. I was just coming to let you onto campus when I was drugged."

"How were things going?" AJ asked. "Did they have things for you to do? Or was this whole thing some sort of sham?"

"I'm not sure," she said. "I was definitely participating in activities, but it felt a little off. I chalked that up to poor translations."

AJ nodded. Feeling *off* when surrounded by aliens was a normal enough state. "I think we've transitioned into jump space, so if we're getting out of this mess, it's probably time to start making some waves."

"What are you talking about?" she asked, suddenly interested.

"Think about it," AJ said. "How often have we been imprisoned since this whole thing started?"

"You mean from the moment you met Beverly?"

"Right."

"Three or four times?"

"Counting now, this makes four. Although we also broke into a prison," AJ said, pulling off the soft sandals provided by the still unseen aliens. "Not sure if you'd count that or not."

"What are you doing?"

"At some point, a person needs to acknowledge the likelihood that all these events are not a coincidence," he said, picking at the rough skin at the back of his heels.

"You're saying this imprisonment is related to the others? That doesn't make sense," Jayne said.

"Ahh, there it is," AJ said, pulling a thin strip of material embedded between layers of his skin. "And I can't tell you just how funny that feels."

"AJ?"

"Oh, right ... no. The relationship between our ... er, mishaps ... is actually us. We do things that cause aliens to want to put us in cages," he said, spreading his hands to encompass their current cell. "I guess I called it early on. Too many aliens see us as raccoons or wild animals that they need to cage."

AJ switched feet and picked at his other heel. "You know, I'd kind of expected that Beverly would be around when I did this and she'd make it feel less creepy."

"What is that?" Jayne asked, eyeing what looked like long, thin pieces of tape.

"This is very difficult to detect," he said, walking to the glassy wall that separated them from a narrow hallway. "Beverly grew it in my foot. It's a binary explosive, low yield but super flexible." He stretched the tape in a long arc next to a seam in the glass.

"AJ, they're gassing us," she said, pointing at a small plume being released from the ceiling.

"Hold your breath," AJ said, applying the second strip of material atop the first and rushing back to Jayne and Greybeard, covering them as best he could. Ten seconds later, a loud pop was followed by a sound like dominos falling on the floor. He turned back to the shattered door, picking up Greybeard and pulling Jayne behind him as he slipped through, wincing as he stepped on the shattered material.

Jayne exhaled and sucked in a deep breath. AJ took it as a good sign that she didn't pass out and followed suit. The short hallway led to an electronically locked metal door. He knelt and pulled a second pair of strands from his feet and repeated the process. Jayne drew another breath and slumped next to Greybeard, who already lay in a heap on the deck.

Still holding his breath, AJ waited for the binary agent to explode. Ten seconds seemed an eternity, but the explosion was just as effective as it had been before. With his lungs begging for relief, AJ pulled on the hatch and swung it open, lurching through. An electrical shock momentarily stunned him as the end of a weapon was placed against his shoulder.

"Pertaf?" AJ asked, coming face to face with a blue feathered male half-a-head taller than himself.

He slid down the wall, unable to support himself as his limbs jellied. Blessed relief spread through his body as he drew oxygen into his lungs. The relief was short-lived as a second shock caused his body to seize. The pain was momentarily bright and excruciating but it dissipated instantly.

With sudden clarity, AJ tracked the next, attempted strike of the Pertaf's long weapon. AJ rolled to the side and the weapon struck the deck, discharging harmlessly. He rolled back, trapping the weapon under his body and forcing it out of the tall birdman's clutches. Recharged by success and fueled by necessity, AJ twisted and kicked a bare foot into his assailant. Bones snapped beneath the vicious kick and the Pertaf squawked angrily, falling back into the passageway.

AJ pressed his advantage. He jumped onto his fallen adversary, scrabbling his way up the suited body even as the Pertaf fought back by scraping and clawing at AJ's face. Howling in agony, AJ knew no matter how much pain he was in, he couldn't relent. This was life or death and besides, giving up wasn't something he was particularly good at. He tried and missed a sloppy but powerful haymaker, hitting the Pertaf's cheek because the Pertaf's head turned more quickly than AJ could have imagined. Unfazed, AJ followed through, twisting his shoulder and driving his elbow into the bottom of the Pertaf's jaw, cracking and dislocating the bone. He felt the fight drain from his opponent.

"Grab the ident at his waist," Beverly ordered, popping into view, wearing jungle fatigues with warpaint covering her face. "Plug it into that socket before they lock me out!"

AJ didn't need to be told twice. He ripped the thick card from the Pertaf's waist and jammed it against the socket Beverly high-lighted.

"How many are there?" AJ asked, scrabbling back to where the spear-like energy weapon lay.

"Two," she said. "A pilot is watching us on video right now."

"Can he hear me?" AJ asked.

"She. Yes," Beverly said. "I've got her locked out for the moment, but she's fast. I'm not sure how long I can keep this up."

"Pilot, remove your hands from the console or I'll do to you what I did to your partner," AJ warned. "I'm immune to energy weapons. Humans have low conductivity. I'm also pissed off and don't mind ruffling some feathers if needed."

"Are you immune to blaster fire?" she asked, pulling a pistol from next to the chair in which she sat.

"Why do you suppose I waited for you to enter jump space, darling?" AJ asked, kicking open the three doors between him and what he imagined was the cockpit door. With Beverly projecting video, he could see that the pilot faced the cockpit hatch with a pistol in hand.

"You have hurt my mate," she said. "Why should I agree to anything you request? You will do the same to me."

"That's a real possibility," AJ said. "You've got it coming, that's for damn sure."

He felt the familiar brush of Greybeard's shoulder against his calf. "Seamus, are you up?" he asked. Greybeard barked in response. "Do you mind unlocking this cockpit door for me? BB's busy keeping our friend there from regaining control."

Greybeard barked again and jumped against the wall, stretching his back legs so his front paw rested near the security pad. A moment later, an electronic lock turned over.

"Last chance, bird brain," AJ said. "Weapon on the floor or I'm coming in hard. Trust me, I won't go easy on you because you're a chick."

The last comments drew a sidelong glance from Beverly. "Are you serious right now?" she asked.

"I'd say she's plucked," AJ said, earning him an exasperated look.

"I'm setting the weapon down," the Pertaf woman said.

He kicked open the door and closed the distance between them in a rush. The Pertaf squawked fearfully as he twisted her around and cranked her arms up behind her back. "Please, stop! You're hurting me," she begged.

"Back you go," AJ said, loosening his grip. He found Jayne kneeling over the male Pertaf, inspecting his wounds.

"You good, Doc?" AJ asked.

"Better than this guy," she said. "He's going to need more attention than I can give him to fix these broken bones. What is her name?"

"I am Hetra," the female Pertaf responded. "That is my mate, Kornat. Please, what are his injuries?"

"Blunt force trauma," Jayne said. "Broken bones in his jaw and the upper cartilage of his neck. I believe he also has a broken iliac crest on the right side – hip bone if that's not familiar."

"How is this possible? Are humans this strong that they cause so much destruction?" Hetra asked.

"Doesn't that seem like the sort of question someone should know the answer to before taking human prisoners?" AJ asked. "I mean, really. If I was going to haul around grizzly bears, I'd sure as heck be carrying something that could put 'em down if they got loose."

"There is no bear," Hetra said. "Our brig has not been breached before. How were you able to do this?"

"Stop," Jayne said. "This man ... Pertaf ... whatever! He's severely injured. Do you have advanced medical facilities aboard this ship?"

"Not sufficiently advanced, but it should give us time to reach our destination where he can receive proper care."

"Help me move him now," Jayne said, her eyes flashing irritation as AJ held Hetra tightly. "AJ, let her go. Hetra, trust me. We'll take you both to the medical bay unless you cause us trouble. Do you agree to act without aggression?"

"I will do what you say so that Kornat is not further harmed," she said.

AJ released the Pertaf woman and watched with interest as she and Jayne carried Kornat to a closet unit. Depressing a panel, the medical station slid into the narrow hallway leaving barely enough room to maneuver the male onto the examination chair. Snippily, Jayne swatted at Hetra's clawed hands as they sought to engage the medical system controls.

"I've got this, Hetra," Jayne said. "Tell AJ where you have the means to physically restrain yourself. I don't think you'd appreciate his first choice when it comes to keeping us safe from you or you trying to take this ship over again. Do we understand each other?"

"Who is this new Amanda Jayne?" AJ asked. "Large and in charge. I like it."

"I'm irritated to have been treated so poorly again," Jayne said. "Is there no sense of decency anywhere in the universe? I'm a doctor for crying out loud. My entire life has been dedicated to healing people. What do I get for that? I get placed on a hitman's list, drugged, kidnapped, and dumped in a cell. Need I mention the crazy, rogue CIA agent who locked me away on a black site interrogation ship? When does this all end?"

"We'll get answers, Doc," AJ said. "We've drawn some bad attention and someone definitely has it in for us. We'll track them down and the drama will all slow down. Remember, before Beverly showed up and started all this, I was lying under a pile of rubble and you were rotting away with cancer. As my dad always said, nothing worthwhile is easy."

"Did you know there's a galactic library of every known disease that's been cured? Every newly inducted species into the Galactic Empire have had virtually all disease irradicated within the first decade after contact."

"Well, that's fantastic," AJ said.

"AJ, the US government has been in contact with the Cheell for over seventy years," she said.

"No crap, " AJ said. "Lisa and I figured Earth hasn't been given those benefits because of our semi-sentient status."

"I thought that too, but the Galactic Empire doesn't restrict access to medical technology because of political status," Jayne said.

"You learned this at DAS?"

"Yes ... and there's more. Galactic Empire doesn't directly restrict trade with willing partners. Earth is listed as one of those partners. The only real hitch comes because humanity doesn't have representation in the Galactic Congress. And since humanity doesn't have representation, all trading must be initiated by human-owned entities, which is why only human-owned or diplomatic vessels are allowed into human space."

"Girl goes to school. Girl gets educated," AJ said, grinning.

FIFTEEN

END OF THE COASTER

"Hetra, how does this normally go once you've been captured?" AJ asked, sitting calmly across from his Pertaf abductor. He couldn't tell if she was unusually anxious or if her demeanor was natural for the bird-like species. They were stuck in jump space for at least four more days, so he had plenty of time to work through the questions he had.

"I do not understand this question," she said.

"I'll put a pin in that for a moment," AJ said. "Exactly what was your part in abducting Doctor Jayne and me?"

"Our contract requires that we do not attempt communication with cargo," she said.

"We're not exactly cargo now, are we?" AJ asked.

"I do not understand."

"The way I see it, you engaged in illegal activity by abducting and transporting us without our permission," AJ said. "Kidnapping is what we call it on Earth."

"Humans are not within the law of Galactic Empire," Hetra responded.

"You and I both know that's not exactly correct, don't we," Jayne said. "The Galactic Congress specifically states that unrecognized sentients are to be afforded basic civil rights. I'll shorten it up a bit for you. It is illegal to detain or transport semi-sentient species against their will. Do you believe you have our permission for transport?"

"You were not conscious when you were loaded onto our vessel," she said. "It was communicated to us that you had been informed of transport and were willing. Our legal obligations were fulfilled."

"You're actually in a bit of a pickle," Jayne said. "Four months ago, Xandarj recognized humanity as a fully-sentient species to start the process of normalizing trade. We both know that Xandarj law is lax when it comes to punishing offenders. One thing it isn't, however, is unclear on disputes. You've wronged us – provably so. If you were to die in the process of us defending ourselves, there would be no consequence to us. As it stands now, your lives are forfeit and so is your vessel."

"You will kill us?" Hetra asked, her already pale face draining of all color.

"No," Jayne said. "Turns out humans have this thing about killing in cold blood. Well, most of us do anyway. Although, we're really offended by kidnapping. I imagine we could work out some sort of deal that allows you and your mate to survive this ordeal."

"What do you want?"

"Turn over complete control of this ship to us," AJ said.

"It is not our ship," Hetra said. "We are only using it per our contract."

"I can have Greybeard over there break your codes and get in the hard way or you can turn it over and act like you care about what happens next," AJ said. "Otherwise, we'll let Doctor Jayne here discuss other options with you."

"I will do as you say," Hetra said. "Remove a portable terminal from the wall. I will need both hands free for a few moments."

"I assume you understand that if you do anything beyond what AJ has asked, there will be consequences?" Jayne asked.

"I understand this," Hetra answered, rubbing her wrists where they'd been bound.

In AJ's periphery, he found Beverly was sitting on his shoulder, interested in what Hetra was doing. That she could only see what AJ saw, he made sure to focus on the screen as well as the bird-woman's fingers as she clacked away on a keyboard.

"You have access, AJ," Beverly said. "Would you mind if I use you to drive for a minute?"

"You can do that?"

"I just did," Hetra answered, not understanding that AJ was talking to Beverly.

"Yes. You've not appreciated me taking control of your body in the past, but I do not yet have sufficient control of this vessel."

"Right, that's fine," AJ said, waggling his eyebrows at a confused Hetra as he pulled the keyboard away from her. Looking at the keys, he found an uncommon configuration and blank keys. Before he could ask, Beverly worked her magic and his hands flew across the tops of the keys. He felt a small amount of nausea at the motion he wasn't consciously controlling. The feeling passed almost as quickly when Beverly finished.

"Hetra and Kornat are corporate transport agents for a mid-sized Pertaf shipping company," Beverly said. "Their specialty is in moving small-volume, high-value cargos. They're very good at it as they've received numerous four and five-digit bonuses in the last year."

"Think they'll get a bonus this time?" he asked.

"I don't understand," Hetra said.

AJ shook his head. "You should ask about your cargo before you agree on a pickup. The people who captured us knew we had Beltigersk symbiotes aboard. You do know that you kidnapped Beltigersk as well as humans, right? Why else would you have a suppression field turned on in the back?"

Hetra's eyes grew wide. "This is not good."

"Nope."

"You'll understand why we'd like to know where you were planning to take us," AJ said. "And who hired you."

"You were destined for Manosh, the third orbital planet of the Cheell's origin," Hetra said. "We were to drop this vessel at a transfer warehouse on the outskirts of Nala Oompal."

"And then what? You walk home?" AJ asked.

"Nala Oompal is a large city with tens of millions of inhabitants," Hetra said. "Despite your experiences, Cheell culture is quite welcoming. Kornat and I planned to relax at a mountain retreat as we awaited a new assignment. I now have a similar question. Will we arrive at Nala Oompal and if we do, what will happen to us?"

"At a minimum, I'd hope you'd reconsider your career choices," Jayne said. "I doubt very much that you didn't know you were involved in illegal activities. Nobody is that naïve. Ignoring what's in your cargo bay so you don't have unpleasant thoughts will get you arrested, even killed."

"You speak as if you will not kill us," Hetra said.

"Right now, I'm trying to figure out what to do with you so I don't have to," AJ said.

"AJ, stop," Jayne said, noticing Hetra's flinch at AJ's words. "Hetra, as long as you don't threaten us, we'll not harm you."

"BB, what would it take to repair the damage we did to that holding cell?" AJ asked, gently reapplying Hetra's cuffs.

"I was not able to see the damage, AJ," Beverly said, flitting off his shoulder.

"Can you turn off that suppression field or whatever it was?"

"It is off."

"Doc, see what else our girl is willing to share," AJ said. "I'm gonna take a look."

"I was thinking about manufacturing some lunch. Roast beef sandwich sound okay?"

"Uh, right," he said.

"I learned how to replicate several items while at DAS," Jayne said. "They were very curious about our food."

"Until they decided to lock you in a box," AJ said. "You never saw any of this coming?"

"Yes and no," Jayne said. "So many at DAS were exactly what I expected. They were open-minded, curious, friendly – the best of the best."

"But ..."

"But ... there were those who were friendly to my face, though I felt they were acting against me," she said. "It was more of a feeling than anything."

"Pay attention to that feeling next time," AJ said. "You were right."

"How I'd left things with you didn't exactly help me focus."

"Do you want to have this conversation now?" he asked.

"Do you have somewhere to go?"

"No, I suppose repairing the brig can wait. I just have one question, Doc," AJ said. "Is this just another cycle on the roller coaster? I mean, I was cool about you headin' off for DAS, but then you wanted to cut me out of your life. That hurt, Doc. Call me crazy, but I'm starting to develop trust issues."

"I want to say *no* – that there's no more roller coaster," Jayne said. "The fact is, I'm terrified of our relationship. I've never had someone keep coming back after I do that thing I do."

"Squash 'em like a bug? That thing?"

"Yeah, that," she said. "I cried when I sent you away. I wanted to call and have you come with me, check out the school with me, have one last dinner."

"Damn, Doc," AJ said. "You need to work on that."

"Physician, heal thyself?"

"Or, maybe, just don't push me away," AJ said. "Next to Darnell and BB, you probably know me as well as anyone – or any being. Do you think I'd hurt you?"

Jayne shook her head as tears rolled down her cheeks. "Don't give up on me, AJ," she whispered.

AJ knelt in front of her and pulled her into a hug. "Men in my family aren't known to be good with subtle," AJ said. "If you're trying to get rid of me, you'll have to work a lot harder."

Jayne placed a hand beneath his chin and lifted it so she could kiss him. "I'm done running, AJ."

"Either way," AJ said, chuckling. "I'm not done chasing."

"YOUR EXPLOSIVE STRIPS did a number on this plexiglass," AJ said, sweeping the crumbled material to a vacuum port.

"The transparent security partition is not methyl methacrylate in composition, but similar in function to plexiglass," Beverly said. "Are you satisfied with the resolution to your issues with Doctor Jayne? I am noticing an increase in your heart rate and respiration that I am unable to attribute."

"Ah, I suppose she's got me a little off-balance," AJ said. "It's nice to have her back, but she's unpredictable. What if this whole kidnapping thing hadn't happened? Would she have come around or not?"

"Are not all relationships subject to external stimulus?"

AJ continued sweeping and pushed a final pile into the vacuum port. "People in a relationship should be able to count on each other," he said. "I thought we were good and she kind of went off the rails on me."

"Maybe it is she who needs reassurance," Beverly said. "Maybe she has never experienced someone as faithful as Pam."

"Whoa, now we're pulling out the big guns," AJ said. "Careful. This is a tricky subject for me."

"I will be careful, AJ," Beverly said. "Were you not a difficult man to be married to?"

"I can't disagree with that."

"As you were building your company with Darnell were there not times when you left Pam behind and gave her inadequate attention?"

"You know how to land a punch," AJ said. "BB, do you really want to bring this up? Yes, I was a crappy husband."

"But that's not the truth, is it?" Beverly asked, unusually persistent for such a personal topic.

"No. We worked it out."

"There is no fixing the broken security glass," Beverly said. "Fortunately, the hatch that provides access to the rest of the vessel is repairable. I should also say that I am surprised and impressed that the binary explosive strips were so useful. You were right to have me manufacture them."

"I hope you're working on replacing them," AJ said. "And it hurt when I pulled 'em out. Was that supposed to hurt so badly?"

"Part of making them undetectable," Beverly said.

"Are we done with the other conversation?"

"Do you need more advice?"

"Some days I sincerely doubt your intelligence score is so much higher than mine," AJ said. "But today isn't one of them."

"Aw, I'm feeling all warm and fuzzy, now," she said.

"Stop mocking me. For the record, your big advice was that Jayne and I *work it out?*"

"We won't be able to manufacture a new panel to cover the electronics and mechanicals," Beverly said. "I have, however, found parts in other locations on this vessel that are suitable replacements. There are tools in a compartment next to the medical bay."

"It's more of a closet, you know," AJ said.

"Medical closet doesn't have the right ring to it," Beverly said. "Captain Kirk would never beam someone down to the medical closet."

"You've been watching *Star Trek?*"

"It's amusing."

"I used to love that show! I watched it with my mom before I joined the Army," AJ admitted, allowing himself to be momentarily diverted from more serious issues. "Did you get a chance to send a comm to Lisa and Darnell? They're probably going crazy trying to find us."

"The message is sent, but it will take time before it arrives. Jump space is not conducive to facilitating message transfer." Beverly paused, a contemplative look on her face.

She finally continued, "is it a coincidence that the pair who came to transport you are Pertaf? Is there a relationship between us finding Farah Poecile and your abduction? Is there an actual treasure on *Poecile Aerie* or are those references referring to the long-lost wealthy heiress, Farah? Assuming someone wanted you and Doctor Jayne for a reason, who could have facilitated a position for her at DAS and then had enough resources in place to kidnap you both upon your first meeting?"

"That's a lot to think about," AJ said. "I can see why you're distracted."

"I am jealous of the distraction your relationship with Doctor Jayne causes," Beverly said. "For a short period, it consumed you almost entirely."

"Feel like we're getting on that warning track again, BB," AJ said. "Kind of on the edge of calling me simple again."

Beverly flashed him a broad smile and switched her outfit to a skimpy 1960s polka-dotted bikini. She leaned back languorously along a brightly colored surfboard. AJ chuckled at her not-so-subtle dig. He was indeed distracted by her outfit change.

"For the record, this is me calling you simple," Beverly said huskily, stretching like a cat and coming dangerously close to falling out of her top. Suddenly, she switched back to her Jetson's vac-suit. "Now are you going to work on that lockset or not?"

"Does it bother you that I'll solve this problem before you do and without doing all the head damage you're doing?" AJ asked. "By the way, don't forget that swimsuit. I'm gonna need you to make one of those for Jayne if we ever find a beach."

"Do you think she'll wear it?"

"Maybe. And see, that's the stuff I think about when I'm solving a problem," AJ said. "Can't get my brain all filled up on problems that I can't figure out. I like to think about fun things and just keep pulling on strings."

"Metaphorical strings?" Beverly asked.

"Sure. You know, a string that unravels the whole problem if it's pulled on hard enough."

"There has to be more going on in that head of yours," Beverly said.

"Don't count on it," AJ said, opening the cabinet she'd indicated and withdrawing a soft-sided tool bag. "Now where's that first lock you need me to dismantle?"

"SANDWICH?" Jayne asked, finding AJ in the brig wrenching a final bolt into position.

"I'm starving," AJ said, accepting what looked just like a roast beef sandwich. He took a good-sized bite and chewed on it. "Hey, that's not bad."

Jayne smiled at his praise. "Close, right? I love steak, but I'm not quite there with that recipe. Nit's been helping me with fine adjustments. I can manage hamburgers and sliced roast beef, but a big juicy steak doesn't work. The meat comes out with a ham-like texture and not enough juice trapped inside – kind of ruins the whole thing."

"BB says I need to be more forgiving," AJ said.

"Most men would run," Jayne said, quickly switching back to their previous conversation. "Correction. All men I've met have run by this point."

"Beverly reminded me that I put Pam through some stuff."

"You talk to her about Pam?"

AJ nodded. "Not very often, but it comes up once in a while."

"Good for you, AJ."

"Doesn't bother you?"

"No more than it should," Jayne said. "Hard to compete with a sainted wife who's passed. I bet she didn't give you the runaround like I do."

AJ smiled. "See, this right here, this is what relationships are.

Talking truth, admitting unflattering stuff. That's where it's at for me and why men have good relationships with other men. We're real about our crap. We also know everyone's screwed up in one way or another."

"Except sainted wives."

"Especially sainted wives." AJ chuckled. "Doc, there's no competition from Pam. I hope you believe that. If I ever make it seem another way, hit me upside the head. Pam had her share of crap. I just don't think about that now and only remember the good stuff."

"I'd like you to tell me about Pam, AJ."

"I'll have to take it slow," AJ responded. "It's still kinda painful."

"Do you have any idea how that makes me feel?" Jayne asked.

"Sorry, Doc."

"No. Don't be sorry, AJ. You loved Pam so much that even after all these years, you still feel the loss," Jayne said. "Nobody in the universe feels that way about me. I love that about you, AJ."

"I think you're selling yourself short, Doc."

"Probably not," Jayne said.

"I'm volunteering for that kind of relationship, Doc," AJ said. "I'm right here. And if you push me away again, I'm coming back. I'll be your stalker. You won't be able to shake me."

"That took kind of a weird turn."

"Too much?"

"No," Jayne said, shaking her head. "Not too much."

"What are you saying, Doc?"

"Don't let me go, AJ. Ever. Even after I said goodbye and was walking away from you toward DAS, I was praying you'd come after me. I knew I'd probably push you away again if you did turn back, but that didn't stop me from wanting it," she said. "There's this crazy voice in my head that says I need to do big things with my life, that I need to reach some pinnacle. I push everyone away when that voice is talking to me."

"Doc, there's nothing wrong with that voice," AJ said. "How many lives have you saved? Hundreds? Thousands? Heck, I know you've saved mine at least three times. Why would I get in the way of that? I'm just asking that you make a little room for me. Let me be your cheerleader."

"Really?"

"Unless you're really fond of junk," AJ said.

Jayne blinked as she considered the man in front of her with new understanding. "Well, recycling junk is noble," she said. "But it's kind of on the wrong end of technology for me."

"So, we contact DAS and find out if they caught the asshats who nabbed you," AJ said. "Don't tell me Nit and BB can't make a lot of trouble for DAS if they aided in the kidnapping of Beltigersk citizens."

"And then what?"

"You go back," AJ said. "But I'm serious about you taking Grey-beard this time. You need someone watching your back."

"I hadn't considered going back," she said. "I just figured that was a burned bridge."

"Well, you and Nit need to figure that out," AJ said. "I don't know how big a security problem they have. If DAS can't guarantee your safety, then we might need to make some different choices."

"We couldn't live together," Jayne said. "Not very often, at least. I mean I've got some private space in the dorm, but I still have a couple of roommates. I don't think ..."

"Stop," AJ said. "I'm all about sleepovers, but I'm not going to live at DAS. Jayne, we can make this work. You do your thing, I'll do mine. We'll make plans to be together as often as we can. If that needs to change, if you need to go somewhere else, we do that. Trust me, junkyards aren't that hard to find. I can move more easily than you think."

"So, what does this make us?" Jayne asked. "I mean, I'm okay if you're not into labels."

"Hold on," AJ said, turning to the scraps of what he'd been working on. He located a length of copper and gold braided wire. Blocking her view, he stripped the insulation and formed a loop.

"What are you doing."

"Hold on a sec." AJ struggled to clean the loop up so it was presentable.

When he turned around, he dropped to one knee and picked up her hand, causing her to gasp. "AJ, are you sure?"

"This is a promise ring, Doctor Amanda Jayne," AJ said, holding the loop of wire out so she could see it. "For as long as you wear this ring, I promise that I'll be faithful to you, that I'll always have your best interest at heart and that I fully intend to find you a better ring so you're not wearing a stupid piece of wire on your hand."

"Oh, AJ," Jayne said.

"And I want to marry you, Amanda Jayne," AJ said. "I'm placing you on notice. I'm going to find a ring and when I do, the next thing that'll happen is, I'll be taking a knee and asking for your commitment. So, you've got a little time to think about things. If you need to run, you better get those track shoes laced up."

"Yes, AJ," Jayne said. "One million times, yes! But there's one condition."

"Anything."

Jayne pushed her hand forward. *"That's* my ring."

"But ..."

"Not negotiable."

SIXTEEN

STRAINED ALLIANCE

"AJ, we will drop from jump space in four minutes," Beverly said.

"Finally," AJ complained. "Talk about a giant waste of time."

"You exposed a conspiracy at one of the leading academic institutions of the Galactic Empire," Beverly said. "Investigations have already begun. Bad actors were exposed. The ramifications of what has occurred will resonate for years. AJ, this action will raise questions as to why so much was expended to capture two humans. Further, that three Beltigersk were taken captive will allow my family to press this issue with the Galactic Congress."

"We've all seen how slowly your precious Galactic Congress acts," AJ said.

"It is a reasonable point," Beverly agreed. "But that does not change the significance of the moment."

"Are you sure I can't keep this shuttle?" AJ asked. "It was used in the commission of a crime."

"I believe you know the answer to this question."

"Fine," AJ said. "We'll be sure to contact the owners and let them know they can come pick it up after paying retrieval and storage fees."

"What is that?" Beverly asked.

"Hey, I recovered their property which was being used to commit a crime," AJ said. "I'm not running a charity."

"I am not sure there is legal precedence for this."

"There is on *Poecile Aerie*," AJ said. "If you want to run a successful junkyard, there's just one rule: nothing's free."

"Transition to normal space in ten seconds," Beverly announced.

Jayne grabbed AJ's hand as their small vessel transitioned from jump space, with a view of the now-familiar sight of their adopted home, Xandarj.

"AJ, you've received priority coded messages from Darnell Jackson, Lefty Johnson, and Strigo Corporation," Beverly said.

The influx of communications after exiting jump space was something AJ had come to expect. When they'd turned around in the Cheell system and re-entered jumpspace, he'd had a few moments to inform Darnell and Lisa of their situation. He'd also had a chance to receive and respond to a few messages from Blue Tork and Cariste Chok.

"I've got something from DAS," Jayne said. "Do you want to hear it?"

AJ nodded, setting aside his burning curiosity regarding Darnell and Lefty's messages. "Absolutely."

Addressing Doctor Amanda Jayne of Earth:

Dralli Academic Society wishes to convey its deepest apologies for its failure to adequately provide a protected environment. It is a primary principle of DAS that scholars be provided an environment for the free exchange of ideas without fear of political reprisal. In this, we failed.

After a careful review of the events leading to your forcible removal from DAS grounds, we found no action taken by yourself to be contributory. To that end, your invitation to study and share the experiences of humanity from your unique perspective has been reaffirmed. You will face no sanctions. Further, it is believed that all those involved have been identified and expelled with prejudice to their sponsors.

It is our great desire that you, Doctor Amanda Jayne of Earth, rejoin the Dralli Academic Society at your earliest convenience.

End of address.

"Could they be more full of themselves?" AJ asked.

"That's pretty mild for academic-speak, AJ," Jayne said. "I'm surprised they apologized at all."

"Did they at least sign it?"

"Nit says it was signed by each member of their governance council," Jayne said. "I guess that makes it kind of a big deal."

"Think you could stomach going back?" AJ asked. "I mean, sure, they're full of themselves, but can they really suck that bad at security?"

"Would you mind my opinion?" Beverly asked, appearing in the black robe that showed she meant business.

"Of course, Beverly," Jayne said.

"Dralli Academic Society published this letter on their public forum," she said. "They also published the names of the individuals identified as being involved in the attack. In addition to those names, they identified those governments and corporations that sponsored those individuals. To use an idiom common to Albert Jenkins: they're not fooling around. Being identified negatively by DAS is a significant embarrassment."

"I think the big question is about security," AJ said.

"Estimates are that the loss of reputation for those listed is in the tens of millions of credits," Beverly said. "Significantly, though, it continues to highlight humanity's bid for recognition and the steps being taken to deny this."

"And that means what about security?"

"If someone is willing to pay enough, no one is safe," Beverly said. "The cost for attacking Doctor Amanda Jayne while on DAS grounds has just become very expensive."

"See, I knew you had it in you. Short sentences, packed with information," AJ said. "Doc, I guess you've got a decision to make."

"Are you sure you'd be okay with me going back?" Jayne asked, fingering her wire ring subconsciously.

"We'll work it out," AJ said. "That's the thing about being us – no rules but those we make. If you want to be part of DAS, then I want that too."

"We really should have had this conversation before," she said.

"Seems like it worked out," AJ said. "Now, let's see what Lefty's got to say."

I made it to Mexico and found Ruiz. Damn, he's a cranky old bastard. Not only that but he's got a pile of Cheell and a couple of those bird folk stuck in an old mine shaft. I can't figure out if he needs help or if bringing him along will end up being a mercy to the aliens. Either way, we're headed for LeBeau back in Missouri. And for the record, Baird never reached out to Ruiz. Can't tell you more for op sec.

"Not a man of many words," Jayne observed.

"Said a lot, though," AJ agreed. "I wonder what Baird's deal is. She didn't seem like a bad egg before."

"There must be a lot of pressure on her," Beverly said. "The Cheell are certainly working through official and unofficial channels. They will be seeking to influence all of Earth's governments. The chaos she is experiencing is likely quite profound."

AJ nodded. It wasn't a new conversation and he wasn't sure how to resolve it. "Doc, any chance you'd be willing to help a couple of old vets regain their youthful vigor?"

"LeBeau and Ruiz? Of course," Jayne said. "How do you propose getting into contact with them?"

"Figure maybe I'll call in a favor," AJ said.

"With whom?"

"Let's see what Big D's got going first."

Damn son, we're glad you finally showed up. We've been beating the bushes hard, lookin' for you. We also ran afoul of a couple more Cheell bounty hunters. I'm starting to wonder if they'll eventually take us down by dumb luck because they sure the heck aren't gonna do it with the low-rent crews they've been sending. I've got a couple of updates on the VEAH but I imagine those'll wait until you get back.

"Jayne, you think you can get us back to *Poecile Aerie*?" AJ asked.

"Sure, what's going on?"

"I'd like to talk to our guests," AJ said. "I just had an idea."

"Feel like sharing?"

"I'll tell you when I get back," AJ said and pushed out of the comfortable cockpit seat. He set one of the Pertaf weapons in his seat, the other still locked in a cabinet. "If things get unruly, don't worry about zapping me. I'm a big boy and I've got the charge dialed down a bit."

"It doesn't seem like the Pertaf are particularly stout individuals," Jayne said. "Hopefully they won't cause too much trouble."

"Nah. I imagine we'll be friends soon enough."

He knocked on the hatch and held down the intercom, watching the viewscreen. Hetra and Kornat both sat against the opposite wall and stirred when they heard the knock. "I need you guys to keep cool," AJ said. "I'm coming in."

"We cannot change the temperature," Kornat said, subconsciously feeling his side where AJ had broken a rib.

AJ pushed open the hatch and stepped inside, tensing in anticipation of an attack that did not come. "Good choice," AJ said. "I imagine you felt our transition from jump space. We're back in Xandarj and I've been thinking about a way you could work off your debt."

"What debt are you referring to?" Hetra asked.

"The debt you incurred by kidnapping recognized sentients in Xandarj, not to mention the Beltigersk you brought along. Add on top of that the fact that I'm gonna charge whoever you rented this buggy from a retrieval and storage fee and I'd say you've got a rough few months ahead. Am I right?"

"Unquestionably, our capture will lead to significant unpleasantness for us," Hetra said.

"I can't do anything about the fact that you're not going to make your delivery," AJ said. "But I do have some ideas on how you might have a chance to return the ship and get us to forget about the whole kidnapping thing."

"Our employer will not be happy if we return without the cargo. They will accuse us of theft," Kornat said.

"I imagine incompetence," AJ said.

"That would be insignificant," Kornat replied.

"You must stop talking, Kornat," Hetra chimed in. "We will lose our bond for the loss of cargo and yes, our reputation will suffer, but it is not nearly so significant as kidnapping Beltigersk citizens. The Beltigersk are known for rigorous litigation. We should not have become involved in this transfer at such a low price."

"You do realize that regardless of the price, you'd still be in this predicament?" AJ said.

"Yes, it would not be so difficult to endure the humiliation because of the great possible reward," she said, hanging her head. "We are both foolish and incompetent."

"What if I had a deal for you?" AJ asked. "You'd get to keep the ship and we'll have the Beltigersk agree that they won't sue you."

"This deal sounds too risky," Kornat said.

"Let me be clear. You've chosen this moment to become picky about your deals? Now? After you've been captured and are up to your pinfeathers in legal trouble?"

"Kornat, Albert Jenkins has treated us well. Given the circumstances, should we not at least listen to his proposal?" Hetra asked.

"This human broke my bones," Kornat squawked.

"You gotta do something about that pride, bird boy," AJ said. "It's getting in the way of you making good decisions. But if that's how you want to play it, I have options."

"No, Kornat will remain quiet," Hetra said, turning her head quickly to focus on AJ. "What is your proposal, Albert Jenkins?"

"I need you to do what you're good at," AJ said. "I need you to make a quick trip to Earth and pick up a couple of boys for us. You bring them back in good condition to *Poecile Aerie* and we'll send you on your way like nothing happened."

"Earth is quarantined," Kornat added.

"Kidnapping is illegal," AJ said. "Look, you guys operate outside the law all the time. I know it, you know it. This is about risk and reward. The risk isn't that great. My guess is this little baby can get past a quarantine. Cheell have been doing it for decades. Think about it." AJ stood and walked to the hatch. "When we get home, we'll be getting in contact with the authorities. At that point, your fate will be out of our hands. You've got a couple of hours to talk it out."

"Wait," Hetra said. "A single journey to Earth?"

"AJ, you would send these two to pick up three who have outstanding bounties?" Beverly asked, hovering near his face.

AJ nodded. "Yes, that's right. They'll be armed, though, and they'll be warned about your proclivity for bounty transport."

"He is sending us into much danger," Kornat said. This time Hetra's response was physical. She lashed out with a clawed hand across Kornat's cheek, raising red welts but little blood.

"I would ask your symbiote to agree to your terms," she said. "Much of the value of this transaction depends on its agreement."

"*Her* agreement," AJ said.

"I see."

Beverly switched to her black robes and it was plain when Hetra and Kornat were both able to see her. "If the earthlings are returned safely to *Poecile Aerie,* then I will hold you harmless to the actions of my kidnapping."

"*And* of the other Beltigersk?" Hetra pushed.

"We agree," Beverly said. "Do not cause me to regret this concession, Hetra Paroquet."

"Family name is a nice touch," AJ subvocalized, grinning. "It's like you know who she is and could cause her trouble."

"Perhaps I too should work on being more subtle," Beverly said, grinning so only AJ could see her.

"Could you send a message to Lefty and see if he's amenable?"

"Of course. I will pass along all pertinent details to Rebel so she may handle future contact," Beverly said. "It appears this ship has sufficient fuel to travel to Earth and return. They may be short for their return to Cheell space, but that is an issue for another day."

"Okay, you guys sit tight. Like I said, we've got a couple of hours until we're home and you can be on your way," AJ said.

"I do not like it," Kornat grumbled.

"Hetra, you should explain what the other options are," AJ said. "I suspect he's not seeing the entire picture."

———

"YOU GOOD TO HANG OUT WITH us for a couple of days, Doc?" AJ asked as their shuttle approached *Poecile Aerie*.

"Of course, I'd love to see what you've done," she said.

"AJ, tell me that's you comin' in," Darnell's voice called over private comms.

AJ shifted the conversation to the cockpit. "That's right. Pertaf are just droppin' off me and Doc."

"Your description of the plan was a little light," Darnell said. "These Pertaf are going after Frenchy, Ruiz, and Lefty? Aren't these the guys who grabbed you?"

"They're mostly transportation," AJ said. "We've got things worked out. At least I hope we do."

"As long as you think so."

AJ noticed a pair of derelict cargo vessels resting next to *Poecile Aerie*'s primary entrance. Neither ship had been there when they'd left. "Mind explaining the two ships parked by the garage doors?"

"The bad news first. Word's out on our location and we've had a few bounty hunters show up. The good news is old-man Poecile's tungsten ball launcher is a big hit. And I mean that both figuratively and literally."

AJ chuckled. "I don't see holes ... oh, wait, there they are. Crap, I didn't expect tungsten to spread out that bad. That looks like a hollow point hit it."

"Petey says it'll be different against armored ships," Darnell said. "Cargo ships have thin hulls that barely hold the pressure. It's a little like hitting a balloon, you get help from the internal pressure."

"Any survivors?" AJ asked.

"A couple," he answered. "I had to manufacture a temporary brig. Fortunately, Farah's pretty handy with a welder."

"Hey, wait. I see welding sparks up on the VEAH," AJ said. "Is someone working up there?"

"Yeah, buddy, but don't ruin it by looking too hard. Get docked and come on in," Darnell said.

"Be there shortly," AJ said and turned to Jayne. "Doc, see that door on the side? That's where we go in. We've got gravity on that pad out front. I'd say just set it down there."

"Can do." Jayne adjusted a virtual reticle that showed an outline of the shuttle, worked the controls until the ship sat on the landing pad just how she wanted it to, and then allowed the automated systems to take over. "Are you going to let our guests out so they can visit the station, too?"

"Nah. No sense giving away any more information about our place," AJ said. "I'll let 'em out of their cell and have 'em be on their way."

"Can't say I'll miss Kornat," Jayne said.

"I think Hetra's the one you want to keep your eye on."

"I don't love that deal you struck with her," Jayne said. "Well ... I don't love that she might not honor the agreement. I do like getting Lefty and those other boys off Earth where they're in danger. Did you know LeBeau and Ruiz very well?"

"As well as you know anyone in your platoon," AJ said. "If someone was shooting at me, I'd like to have them in my corner."

"That's our life right now, isn't it?"

"Only until we get the princess back into the tower," AJ said.

"Now I kind of feel like I'm shirking my duty."

"You tell that to Frenchy and Ruiz after you get 'em all fixed up," AJ said. "I imagine they'll have a different take on things. I'll warn you now, Frenchy can get a little handsy."

"That'll be a new experience," Jayne deadpanned, causing AJ to bark out an unexpected laugh.

The end of the landing sequence was punctuated by a shudder as the shuttle contacted the gravity well and then the steel decking. "BB, you mind dealing with the handoff to Hetra?"

"Of course, AJ," Beverly said, appearing in an old-school law enforcement uniform and holding a black baton. "I'll catch up with you momentarily."

AJ and Jayne loaded into the airlock and found themselves walking down metal lattice stairs onto *Poecile Aerie's* hull next to where the two Cheell cargo vessels had been unceremoniously piled. "Is that the Veneri ship?" Jayne asked, pointing up at the massive VEAH lifter. "It's so bulky."

"Does it remind you of a tugboat?" AJ asked.

"Yeah, I mean, sure, in a functional kind of way. Certainly looks like it could push something around."

"Crazy amount of lift," AJ said, gesturing to the photonic pressure barrier. "Make sure you read about how they were used to build Dralli Station."

"Albert Jenkins, historian," Jayne said. "Maybe I'm having a positive effect on you after all."

AJ followed her through the hatch. "Oh, man, what happened here?" he asked, taking in the massive cargo bay, which had been completely rearranged. Either the walls had been painted or cleaned – maybe both.

"You like?" Lisa asked, jogging down the stairs and racing to hug Jayne. "Amanda, I was worried. I'm glad you're okay."

Jayne smiled, enjoying Lisa's attention. When they parted, Jayne held up her left hand, wiggling her fingers, showing off the copper and gold braided wire ring.

"Is that what I think it is?" Lisa asked.

"Is *what* what you think it is?" Darnell asked, following close behind and not waiting for an answer. He lifted Jayne in a big bear hug. "Don't ever do that again, Doc. You had us worried sick."

"What am I? Swiss cheese?" AJ asked.

"We figured you'd be okay," Lisa said, smiling. She relented and hugged him to her as she whispered, "Is that an engagement ring?"

"Promise," AJ whispered back. "Until I can get her a nicer ring."

"No," Jayne said. "This is not a promise ring. We're engaged, simple as that. How could any ring mean more to me than this one?"

"About time you two figured things out," Darnell said.

"So, what's the big secret in the VEAH, and who's out there working?" AJ asked.

"Chok had a crazy idea, although I think you got back faster than she was hoping."

"Not hardly," AJ said. "I'm about done sitting around in a shuttle."

"Did you know that shuttle just took off?" Darnell asked.

"That was the agreement," AJ said. "It should be fine."

"I'm gonna run up to command and make sure there's no funny business," Lisa said. "Glad you're back, AJ. Amanda, don't you be takin' off before we get a chance to talk."

"I'm here for a few days, Lisa," Jayne answered.

"That'll work."

"Doc, you have any experience with a thrust board?" Darnell asked. "We still don't have a great way of getting up into the VEAH. The low entry is about ten yards off the end of the dock."

"I'm not sure what a thrust board is," Jayne said.

AJ picked up one of the boards and settled it on his back. "How about you let me get you out there? After that – if you want – you can get some practice time in on one of the boards."

"That's fine," Jayne said, following AJ back out onto the dock.

"Are you coming along, Big D?" AJ asked.

"I'll be right behind you," Darnell said.

"Probably best if you wrap your arms around my waist and face me," AJ said.

"That's convenient," she said with a warm smile.

"You know, with these masks, there's no kissing." AJ grinned as he applied lift and jumped from the end of the dock. They sailed off into space.

"Ooooh, that'll get your stomach."

"It's easier if you're the one in control," AJ said, gently settling down next to a small pad beside the VEAH's airlock. The door, which had previously opened stubbornly, swung easily, exposing the airlock which no longer had debris in the corners. "Lisa's been in here."

"I'm not sure if she's cut out for life on a junk pile. She hates clutter," Darnell said, landing next to them.

"I can hear you, Darnell," Lisa said. "For the record, junk in its place is fine. What you're referring to is *trash*, which does not belong in spaces where we live. Tell me you understand the difference, dear."

Darnell raised his eyebrows comically and closed the airlock door behind them. "Yes, dear." Atmosphere flooded the compartment, equalizing within the vessel. Green lights illuminated the interior hatch and red lights flashed outside. "And ... we're good."

"Where are we going?" AJ asked.

"Third 'tween," Darnell said. "Chok and Farah are aft. It's a bit of a squeeze getting through, but they're just around the corner."

AJ and Jayne amiably followed Darnell to the portside. "This is promising," AJ said, orienting himself upright inside a large room the shape of which resembled a giant tire.

"Amanda Jayne!" Chok squealed in surprise, pressing a tool nearly the size of her entire chest against the wall where it stuck when she let go. With speed and agility common to the Xandarj people, she approached and greeted Jayne with a quick hug, running the backs of her fingers along Jayne's cheeks. "What a treat that you have visited."

Farah Poecile stood from behind a bulkhead where she'd been working and walked up to join the group. She seemed amused by

Chok's excitement. "Albert Jenkins, it is good to see you," Farah said. "Is this your mate?"

"Uh ..."

"Amanda Jayne," Jayne said, offering her hand.

"What's going on in here?" AJ asked. "If I've got my bearings right, we're looking at engines one and two on portside."

"Is that significant?" Jayne asked.

"Yeah, they don't work, so sailing is nearly impossible," AJ said. "I guess I'm curious about how you replaced the engine housing in such a short time. It has to weigh at least fifteen tons."

"Try sixty-two tons," Chok said, puffing her chest with pride. "But Farah told us about *Poecile Aerie's* cranes next to the big loading bay and that gave me an idea to swap out the engine mount. We've been working for almost eight days straight. The housing holds two engines, both of which were broken. Without the crane, we never could have removed them or affected a replacement."

"The engines are working?" AJ asked.

"Not really," Chok said. "We have at least four more days of work before we can test. Are you going to be here for a while?"

"Yup, we're back," AJ said. "I can't think of anything more important than getting those portside engines operational. This is great, Chok and Farah."

Chok puffed out her chest and gave a funny smile to Farah. "See, I told you he'd love it."

"Yes, you did," she said.

SEVENTEEN

WORD PICTURES

"You bought this ship for how much?" Jayne asked, plopping down in one of the large chairs on the VEAH's bridge.

"Would you believe a few barrels of Tennessee Rye?" AJ asked.

"That's crazy," Jayne said.

"I imagine I've about ruined that market, at least on Dralli Station. For a guy from Earth, it wasn't a bad trade," AJ said.

"Why are these seats so far from the viewing glass?" Jayne asked. "It's not a terrible view, but I'd want to be closer if I had to maneuver this big ship into a tight place."

AJ pushed out of his chair and stood next to the forward-most windows. "The seats are for deep space system monitoring," AJ explained. "If things are at all tricky, standing makes a lot more sense. That way, you can move to one side or another for a better view."

"If you're hauling anything big, how will you see enough from up here?" she asked.

He tapped a cracked glass screen on the forward bulkhead below the thick windows. "That's our job today," he said. "These broken panels are video screens. When operational, they allow the tug captain to look *around* their load. I've been researching the hook-up.

The installation of video sensors is an important part of getting everything to run smoothly."

"Seems like a lot could go wrong," Jayne said.

"Imagine how a tug operator feels in a congested channel back home," AJ said. "Get out of control for any period of time and the amount of damage you could cause to other vessels or even the docks could be extremely expensive."

"That's where Darnell comes in," she said.

"He's got a knack for flying things," AJ said. "I'm not sure if I have more experience with moving big loads or not ... either way, we'll figure it out."

"Show me the living spaces before we get to work?" Jayne asked.

"Why? Are you looking to mark some territory?"

Jayne smiled. When she'd awoken in a cell aboard the Pertaf shuttle and discovered AJ was with her, something changed. She realized she'd been subconsciously blaming him for how crazy her life had become. So many things changed since they'd reconnected, like how she was being forced to reinvent herself in an alien world. Even after she'd cruelly pushed him away, AJ came to visit her at DAS to make sure she was all right. As she'd sat staring at AJ, unconscious on the cell floor, she realized her actions had endangered him and that her previous perspective had been poorly considered. AJ wasn't the cause of the problems they were having with aliens, but he *was* the kind of man who would go to any length to solve those problems and protect his friends.

"You're a remarkable man, Albert Jenkins," she said, looking fondly at him. "Have I told you that lately?"

His look of surprise elicited a laugh from her. "Uh, is this a joke?"

"Am I that bad at saying nice things?" she asked, looping her arms around his neck to keep his attention. "Who in the world would ever think of rebuilding an old alien spaceship so he could have a junkyard in space? I only know of one such person."

"Most people don't think of junk like I do," AJ said. "I'm an equal opportunity junker. No distance is too great if there's a decent profit.

If we're saying nice things, do you mind if I mention how much I like how you look in the skin-tight vac suits?"

Jayne's cheeks flushed. She'd been hesitant to leave her DAS-approved robe behind, but the loose material didn't work well with the thrust board. Fortunately, the female armored suits looked more like a shirt dress with leggings. They were not as form-fitting on top and had an A-line mini skirt overlay which disrupted the eye a bit from the female form underneath. "I suppose it's all right you feel that way," she said.

"The mighty Doctor Amanda Jayne blushes," AJ said. "Could it be she's only human?"

"I take back all the nice things I was saying," she said, swatting at his chest.

AJ pushed a little further. "Have you looked at yourself in a mirror, Doc?"

"In passing."

"You can't tell me you don't see how amazing you are," AJ said. "And no, I'm not just interested in your body. I'm simply stating fact."

"If I want any pretense of modesty, there's no reasonable answer here," Jayne said. "But between Nit clearing up my skin and firming things up and this oh-so-comfortable-but-form-fitting suit, I can understand why your eye might be drawn. I suppose I should compliment you for holding the comments for so long."

A moment of sadness crossed AJ's face and he pushed it away, trying for a smile. "You know, that doesn't matter, right?" AJ asked.

Jayne didn't miss the micro expression. "What's wrong, AJ?"

"I was just thinking about Pam," he said. "In her day, she was a real looker. It used to make me mad how other men would look at her. She called me out on it once. Told me to knock it off, that what we had was worth a lot more than a cheap look. She was right. I'd take her sixty-five-year-old self back in a second."

Jayne nodded, holding his face with a hand on his cheek. "I'm glad you can tell me that," she said.

He blinked, suddenly realizing who he was talking to. "Oh, crap, Amanda. I didn't mean it like that. I wouldn't trade ... shit ...!"

"It's an impossible situation, AJ," Jayne said. "Pam isn't coming back. You will never have to make that choice. But you need to understand, I love that you loved her so deeply. As long as there's room for me, it's okay."

"Amanda, I know she's gone," AJ said. "I was just trying to describe why looks aren't everything. I went overboard. I wasn't thinking."

"Overboard would have been to tell me Pam was nicer looking than me," Jayne said, pressing a finger to his lips. "For the record, comparisons to a deceased and therefore sainted spouse is a big no-no."

"She'd have liked you, you know," AJ said. "You guys have a similar kind of humor."

"So, tour?" Jayne said.

AJ nodded. "There are two primary crew entrances," he said, switching into tour-guide mode. "We came in the aft crew-elevator. It's big enough to bring in equipment and supplies. Back here, on the starboard, just behind the bridge is a second smaller crew entrance. I imagine it gets used more than the aft, even though it only comfortably fits three."

"Why more?" Jayne asked.

"I can't imagine when you're docked that you want to back in, engines first," AJ said. "I might be wrong on this. We haven't tried her out yet."

"Fimil didn't even have actual docking bays if you remember," Jayne said. "You just stopped and hooked up to their mooring balls and they sent out transparent walking paths."

"I suppose it matters what the tech level is where you're visiting," AJ said. "I'd like to get that little shuttle back in *Poecile Aerie* working so we could park the VEAH further out and shuttle in. You know, use it like a tender."

"I fell out of a tender once," Jayne said. "I was visiting Gerald Firth and his yacht. He was so proud of that thing."

AJ chuckled, leading her aft into the hallway. He tapped on a control and opened the first angled portside hatch. "These are our quarters," he said, turning so he could use the metal rungs of the ladder to drop into the room below.

"That's not so hard. Did the gravity change on that ladder?" Jayne asked.

"It's configurable. I put it at .2g because I prefer some pressure against my boots." AJ explained. "So, this General Firth. How'd you fall out of his tender?"

"Gerald," she corrected. "Let's just say he was trying to impress me with his boat-handling skills and might have fallen a little short."

"Of the boat?"

"I was in the tender and he slipped while trying to join me. I tried to help him, but he pulled us both overboard."

"Where was this? The Caribbean?"

"Good guess. We were near Nassau," she said. "The water was warm but poor Gerald was humiliated. He was not a good sport on the way back to where we were staying."

"Did you sail all the way from Miami to Nassau?" AJ asked.

"We did. You learn a lot about people when you're in close quarters," Jayne said. "I learned that while Gerald was a brilliant surgeon, he was not good company."

AJ nodded, turning back to inspect the room. "I'll need at least a good mattress in here."

"Let me guess ... sleeping bags?"

"See, this is the point where I know there's a trap but I'm not smart enough to figure out how to escape it."

"They say you can't teach an old dog, but I see progress," Jayne said. "Ask yourself what I see when I stand in here."

He turned, looking at the twelve-by-twelve-foot space. "Well, I suppose the trash in the corners is troubling. Paint's pretty old, but it's got a nice porthole window."

"This is where you ask for help," Jayne said. "Remember, we're a team now."

"Would you be interested in figuring out how to make this livable?" AJ asked with real surprise in his voice.

"Why, yes, AJ. I would be honored to design the living space you and I might end up spending considerable time within," Jayne said, mockingly giving him a small curtsey. "Nit is already proposing several different plans. Have you considered renting one of Dralli Station's robots that will condition a space? It looks like you could do several of these rooms for four thousand credits."

"*Do?*" AJ asked. "Four grand is some pretty good cheese."

"The robot removes dirt and resurfaces the walls, ceiling, and floor to your specification," Jayne said.

"How do you know this?"

"Nit is displaying the information for me. She anticipated that I'd need our quarters to look nice. Let the remodel be my treat. It'll make me happier."

"Uh ..."

"Stop right there," Jayne said. "Accept a gift when it's offered. None of this *male-provider* noise."

"It's not entirely crap," AJ said. "It's kind of how I'm built."

"I can accept that, but you'll need to accept that I'm a strong, independent woman who needs her space to be a certain way."

"I can't argue," AJ said. "At least let me pay for furnishings. Lisa is working on the galley. Maybe you should talk to her about your robot."

"We've already talked and decisions have been made," Jayne said. "I'm just getting you up to speed. The robot and furnishings will be dropped off in three days."

AJ shook his head. "This will take some adjusting."

"Don't fight it, AJ," she said. "You need to focus on things outside of how your bedroom looks."

"There's a shared head through this hatch. We share it with the starboard berth which is Darnell and Lisa's," AJ said, leading her into a narrow space that consisted of a shower, restroom, and three hatches.

"Starboard hatch is Lisa and Darnell. What's aft?"

"Shortcut to the galley," AJ said. "We're right below the main hallway right now. There's a smaller, mirror berth configuration aft of the galley."

"What's opposite of the galley?"

"Storage or berth. It's just an empty room right now."

"That must have been the closet Lisa was describing to me. She said six rooms needed the cleaning robot."

"Do you think you'll come along sometimes?" AJ asked, sounding hopeful.

"On junking trips?"

"Yeah."

"I sure hope so," she said. "DAS has a schedule a lot like US colleges. The school year is divided into sessions and there are decent breaks in between."

The aft hatch opened, startling them. "I thought I heard voices," Lisa said. "I was just removing the last of the junk from the old galley. Whoever lived here before was a real slob. I hope that robot knows how to get stuff off the floor."

"Nit says the robot will take surfaces down to the metal if necessary," Jayne said.

"It's gonna need to in there," Lisa sighed. "Hey, I'm glad we have a little privacy."

"Oh?" AJ asked. "What's up?"

"Farah," Lisa said. "I don't know if it's a problem or not, but she's been disappearing quite a bit lately."

"What do you mean?" AJ asked.

"No one can find her for six hours and then she shows up like nothing's going on," Lisa said. "When I asked where she'd been, she was evasive and played the *it's-my-family's-ship* card."

"Any idea where she goes?"

"Definitely back into *Poecile Aerie*," Lisa said. "She's not wrong, you know. The ship belonged to her family. I feel bad for giving her trouble about what she's doing."

"Thing is, we have a contract with Mads," AJ said, sighing. "If she's looking for that treasure and finds it, we could have trouble."

"I didn't think about the treasure angle. I'll talk to her," Lisa said. "I'm a little surprised to see you down here. I figured you'd be helping Chok with the engines."

"I wanted to show the ship to Doc," AJ said.

"You mean before she heads back to Dralli Station?" Lisa asked. "What are your plans with that, Amanda?"

Jayne shook her head. "I don't exactly know," she said. "I told them I needed some time."

"Well, you're more than welcome to stay as long as you want," Lisa said, grabbing her arm companionably. "I know AJ enjoys it."

"Might be true, but right now I think he wants to get back to working on those engines. Don't you, AJ?" Jayne took pity on him. She was secretly very touched that he was trying to put her needs above the ship's.

"Not really," he said nonchalantly.

"You're not a very good liar," Lisa laughed. "You skedaddle. Amanda and I have girl things to discuss. I've got dinner planned for 2000. Set an alarm because I'm tossing your plate if you're late."

"Copy that, boss."

"Hey, did you see that message I sent this morning? I might have a job for us," Lisa said before he could turn to leave.

"Seriously?"

"That's right. I was talking with Blue Tork and he told me about several derelict hulks out by the jump space transition point," she said. "There's a group of shippers who've had trouble with 'em. They'd like us to bid on cleaning the area up."

"How many hulks?" he asked.

"Seventeen that are a higher priority," Lisa said. "They're drifting into the main sailing channel. There's another forty or so they'd consider if the price was right."

"Did they suggest a price?"

"No. Think about it," she said. "They'd like an answer in the next couple of days for the seventeen."

"It matters what shape the wrecks are in," AJ said. "We don't want to get into cleaning up debris."

"Right. Take a look at the message. It's got all the details."

"You good to hang out with Lisa?" AJ asked.

"Of course I am," Jayne said.

He leaned in for a kiss and excused himself, humming as he worked his way back to the engine room.

"Now you show up," Darnell said, looking up from a pile of multi-colored wires lying in his lap.

"Where are we at?" AJ asked, crouching next to him.

"No, no, no," Darnell said. "You find your own rat's nest. Whoever pulled that housing off snapped all these damn wires, and rebuilding them sucks."

Greybeard barked, pawing at another pile of wires nearby.

"What's up, boy? You need help over there?" AJ asked.

"Yeah, Seamus is the project boss," Darnell said. "I'm kind of surprised how much this is like our technology back home. I mean, some of it is kind of mystifying, but a lot is just soldering, wrenching bolts, screwing screws – that sort of thing."

As AJ approached Greybeard's pile, Beverly showed the tasks required to reestablish connections between the ship and the newly installed engine housing. At the edge of his display, a countdown timer showed the remaining man hours: ninety-two.

"I'm not sure I'm in love with this remaining-effort gauge," AJ grumbled, retrieving tools from the bucket and getting to work.

"DINNER BELL," Darnell announced several hours later.

AJ glanced at the countdown. He'd spent four hours working alongside Chok and Darnell, so he expected to see a reduction of twelve hours, however, fourteen had been subtracted. The timer showed seventy-eight work hours to go. They'd worked faster than estimated.

"I need ten more minutes," AJ said, not wanting to stop his current progress.

"Don't even think about it," Darnell said. "We show up for dinner with clean hands or we don't eat. I, for one, have no interest in skipping a meal, even if it's meatloaf."

"Is it meatloaf?" AJ asked.

Darnell chuckled. "I don't think so."

"Are you coming back after dinner?" AJ asked.

"Nah. If we can keep the three of us working the next couple of days, we'll make enough progress that Chok can take off and we can finish it by ourselves. The good news is, we're finally not missing any parts, as long as nothing busts, that is."

AJ set his work down and accepted a hand up. "I'd be lying if I said I wasn't excited to see this old girl sailing straight," AJ said. "I can't imagine having this kind of lift capacity back home. Imagine what NASA could do with something this big." AJ's voice trailed off as he spoke.

"AJ?" Darnell asked.

"Ah, nothing. Just thinkin'," AJ said and then changed gears. "BB, pull up that Xandarj contract from the shippers and see how it's worded."

Beverly appeared on a small, round, floating platform atop which sat a desk. She wore a tight fitting wool business suit and had her hair up in a bun. "What are we looking for?" she asked, floating along in front of them as they extricated themselves from the short 'tween deck and into the large crew elevator.

"Do they give any hints on what they think a reasonable hauling fee might be?"

"There is no language covering expected costs."

"How about debris fields? The VEAH isn't set up for cleaning up a section of space," AJ said.

"The RFP specifies the objects they consider making up the project," she said. "There is some debris, but nothing smaller than a pickup truck."

"Now, see what you did there?" AJ asked.

Beverly beamed at his praise. "Fewer words, more details?"

"That's it," AJ said. "Did it hurt?"

"It did not," she said. "It is a challenge to consider analogies that easily convey concepts. Human communication is full of this. Beltigersk rarely utilize analogies. I believe the human's visual cortex is so integral to thought, that large ideas are easily and quickly communicated with simple word pictures."

"We have a saying about that, you know," Darnell said.

"Henrik Ibsen receives credit for this concept although he was quoted as saying, *a thousand words leaves not the same deep impression as does a single deed*. It was Tess Flanders who related this to a picture," Beverly said.

"No points for searching Wikipedia," AJ said. "Okay, pickup trucks and bigger. How many objects are in their initial RFP?"

"The initial seventeen ships are within seventy-three total objects spread across a field of seventeen thousand miles with a depth of two thousand miles," she said.

"That's a big chunk of space," Darnell said. "Thirty-four million cubic miles."

"The location of each object is well known," Beverly said. "I have calculated the round-trip fuel cost to be eighteen hundred credits for the VEAH. Also, a one-way trip with economical fuel usage is six hours for the furthest point."

"How much total mass are we looking at?" AJ asked.

"Sixty-three thousand tons."

"That's a lot," AJ said.

"Seventy-three trips would cost a hundred thirty thousand in fuel and take thirty-seven days," Darnell said. "I'd say that's the upper boundary of your bid. Tell 'em you can get it done in sixty days and we'll need two hundred fifty-thousand credits with half that upfront to cover fuel."

"That's brutal," AJ said. "Where are you getting your math?"

"You know I was the CFO of our aerospace company, right?"

"Sure. Lay it out for me," AJ said.

"Assume worst case, which would be if we have to make an individual trip for each object. Pay three people five hundred credits each day for sixty. Give 'em three thousand tons storage for a credit. We're practically giving that away," Darnell said. "I'm telling you, they'll take the deal."

"We better make sure we get this old girl running first, don't you think?" AJ asked.

"Nah, I'll give us a five-day escape clause," Darnell said as the small group popped through the photonic pressure barrier. "Send me the RFP. I'll write up the bid and you can review it. Sound like a deal?"

"Does it smell like meatloaf to you?" AJ asked apprehensively.

"Certainly does. I didn't want to break your spirit."

EIGHTEEN

PROPOSAL ACCEPTED

"You're up and working early," Jayne said. "Coffee?"

AJ looked surprised as he popped his head above the panel he was working behind. Jayne had found him in the personal shuttle-craft that had been resting in the main bay, ignored for several weeks. "I was just seeing what this little craft might need to get running," he said, accepting the coffee.

"I'm surprised you aren't over at the VEAH. Wasn't Darnell saying today's the big day?" she asked.

"We have maybe ten hours of work left," he said. "If I know my salvage rebuilds though, there'll be a constant stream of issues that need to be worked through. I figured I'd get a run at this shuttlecraft so we could stop paying to run supplies back and forth to Dralli Station."

"What do you make of the fact that we haven't had any more visitors trying to cash in on our bounties?" Jayne asked.

"Didn't you hear? Lisa ran a shuttle off around three this morning," AJ said.

"She didn't mention it."

"I watched a vid replay," AJ said. "She ran a few tungsten slugs through the ship, right in front of their engines. Not enough to disable them, but enough to make her point. They took off like scalded dogs."

"When will it end, AJ?"

"We have to figure out the *why* behind everything that's been happening," AJ said. "Related to that, I got word from Lefty. He and Ruiz found Frenchy. They're holed up in Mexico, waiting for extraction."

"Are you still confident Hetra and Kornat will make good on their end of things and bring those three boys safely here?" Jayne asked.

"Lefty knows how to take care of business," AJ said. "Besides, BB sent Rebel override codes for Hetra's ship."

"I'm glad you're feeling okay about the plan. Trusting those two Pertaf makes me nervous."

"Those aren't mutually exclusive thoughts," AJ said. "Lefty made up his mind on going home. We're doing the best by him that we can. How hard would it be to help Ruiz and Frenchy with that therapy you developed and used on Lisa to reverse the aging process? Is that something you're willing to do?"

"With the medical resources available at DAS, it should be a relatively simple process," she said. "Their bodies will do most of the hard work. Takes a couple of months, but they'll feel immediate relief from any current medical conditions or normal advanced-age degeneration."

"I can't imagine the implications for humanity," AJ said. "You're getting rid of dying from old age."

"I don't think that's true," Jayne said. "All species I've studied end up passing at some point. We don't know what that magic threshold is for humans. On average, though, humanoids across the Galactic Empire live to roughly a hundred fifty years, give or take twenty years."

"What, so these perfectly healthy people just keel over when their time's up?"

"Not far off," she said. "Generally, they have some warning. Their systems start to shut down a few months before the end and virtually nothing can be done to reverse it. That's not to say some species don't live significantly longer. There's speculation about advanced technology being withheld by the older species."

"People in power always mess it up for the rest of us," AJ said, closing the panel on the small shuttle. "I'm glad I looked at this shuttle. It needs parts, but I'll have them delivered with that surfacing robot that's coming today."

"If you miss that load, Lisa and I have another delivery coming out tomorrow with interior furnishings. I hope you're still up for providing help with installation."

"Like what?"

"Carpets, beds, a couple of wardrobes, exercise equipment, and we ended up replacing that entire galley because, well, let's just say it was beyond disgusting," Jayne said.

"Whoa, how much did all that cost?"

"I'm not sure, but Lisa might have suggested that you better get off your duff and respond to that Xandarj Shippers Consortium RFP because otherwise we're gonna be eating beans and rice from this point forward."

"Ugh, I suppose it needed to be done," AJ said.

"I feel like you're not seeing the big picture, AJ," she said.

He chuckled without much humor in his voice. "How's that?"

Jayne raised her eyebrows at his obvious challenge. "How much time do you think you'll be spending in the VEAH, AJ?"

"Not sure."

"Take it from someone who's spent more than her fair share of space travel in cramped, poorly thought-out rooms, there's no way I'm going anywhere in that VEAH in its current shape," Jayne said.

"Ah, so you're saying if we make it nice, you'll come along more often?"

"If that makes it so you see the logic, sure," she said. "AJ, people are often the product of their environment. If you live in filth, you start to believe that's acceptable."

"Sounds pretty *new age* to me," AJ said, suppressing a grin.

"You just love to press my buttons," Jayne responded.

"I'll admit it. I kind of like to see you all spun up and passionate," AJ said. "You've gotta know, though, I'm worried about money. I have no idea if we can make enough to survive out here. I feel like I've sold you all a bill of goods that I have no idea if I can deliver on."

"What's holding you back on sending the RFP?" Jayne asked, her voice less confrontational.

"It requires penalty clauses for non-performance," he said. "We could be obliged to finish the work and forfeit the payday if we miss their targets and I have no idea if the VEAH is going to behave."

"From my side of things, it seems like you've got the VEAH under control," she said. "You've already replaced an entire engine housing. How much more complex could it be?"

"That's the question, isn't it?" AJ asked. "Back home, I knew every piece of equipment in the yard. I knew what would likely break, how much it took to fix it, and generally how to get along without it. This RFP will extend us."

"What if you didn't make seventy individual trips?" Jayne said. "You know, bring back several pieces at a time. Wouldn't that speed things up?"

AJ nodded. "Sure would. Big D and I have a process where we figure out a way to state a problem in its simplest form and cost it out with the most obvious solution. That's always our first proposal. If we get an agreement, then we feel really good about the project. A lot of times though, they reject that first proposal and want us to come in lower."

"You're not sure what kind of trouble we might run into out there." Jayne filled in the rest.

"Right. One thing I was thinking about was using this little shuttle to help us run lines out to those big debris chunks, or maybe some sort of big net. Who knows? I've been mulling it over while I was seeing what needed fixing."

"Are you upset that we spent money on the remodel?" Jayne asked.

"Took me by surprise is all," AJ said. "You and Lisa are smart. If you say we need stuff, I need to get on board. Hard to argue against having a nicer place to live. Besides, you're doing most of the work. I figured it'd be me scrubbing down decks with a wire brush. I'm all over having a robot do that work."

"How much will it cost to get this little shuttle working?" Jayne asked.

"If I've got it right, we're looking at thirty-eight hundred," AJ said.

"How are your cash reserves looking?"

"I'm runnin' on fumes," AJ said. "Fortunately, D and Lisa partnered in so there's some money left."

Jayne nodded, her curiosity sated. "Do you have time for breakfast? Darnell is making waffles."

"I'm done enough here."

"You know, being out here is more relaxing than I thought it'd be," Jayne said, as they climbed the stairs to *Poecile Aerie's* makeshift galley. "Don't get me wrong, I love the energy of a hospital surgery or the excitement of academia, but planning things out, making deals, building things ... I see the appeal."

"Boy, are you in for a treat," Darnell said, as soon as they entered the room where Darnell and Lisa were busy working.

"I am excited to see what a waffle is," Chok said, her eyes big as she held a cup of tea in her white-furred hands, her knees drawn up to her chest. "It doesn't have any meat in it, does it?"

"Nope, one hundred percent carbohydrates," Darnell said. "And just for you, Chok, I've added the closest thing I could find to blueberries, and Lisa made two different kinds of fruit syrup. Too bad Xandarj doesn't have maple trees."

"It sounds very good," Chok agreed.

"Anyone see Farah this morning?" AJ asked, settling next to Chok.

"Last I saw her was the day before yesterday," Darnell said. "Did you think about that RFP last night, buddy? I don't think we should hold onto it much longer."

"Think they'd give us two more days?"

"No. I've been getting pressure," Darnell said.

AJ nodded. "Committing to their timeframe is a risk, but I'm not sure what our alternative is."

"That's always been the risk, buddy," Darnell said. "I doubt we'll see this cherry of a deal in the future."

"Fine, fine, you're right," AJ said. "Just a lot of stuff going on with this whole bounty thing. Nice job, by the way, Lisa, on running those guys off this morning. Probably good if we're not stacking bodies any more than we need to."

"Baptist upbringin'," Lisa said. "But I don't have trouble pokin' a stick in their eye to run 'em off."

"There's stick poking in the Bible?" AJ asked. "Someone should have told me that a long time ago."

"Just shut up," Lisa said.

AJ chuckled, his stomach growling as Darnell slid a dinner-plate-sized waffle in front of Chok. "Pour as much syrup as you want over the top," he instructed, setting a bowl of fruit-laden syrup next to her.

"Big D, would you and Chok mind if I went looking for Farah this morning?" AJ asked. "She's either in trouble or she's treasure hunting. Either way, I need to talk to her."

"I'm sure that's fine," Darnell said. "We'll lose Chok this afternoon, but we'll have our hands full with that robot coming in. Tomorrow we've got a couple of bigger deliveries. Even so, I figure we should be good for a test run by tomorrow afternoon."

"Exciting times," Jayne said, accepting a plate of waffle from Lisa. "I'll help look for Farah, okay?"

"I don't see why not," AJ said, digging into his waffle. "This is fantastic!"

"Good enough that you'll stop complaining about spending enough money to get a decent galley in the VEAH?" Lisa asked.

"Yup," AJ said, knowing better than to further engage in the conversation.

"Anyone else think we need a better name than VEAH?" Darnell asked. "I was thinking *Big Max*."

"That's a good name," AJ said, remembering his old bulldog that had died the day he'd met Beverly.

"I like it," Lisa agreed. "Maxie was a good dog."

"Good, I'll see about registering it with Dralli Station then," Darnell said. "The ship's transponder was deregistered so if we want to fly a Dralli flag, we'll need to check in with them."

"Any clues on which direction Farah headed out last you saw her?" AJ asked.

"Not really," Darnell said. "Most of the time she heads off through the airlock at the back of the garage."

"When she went, did she take a board with her? I'm just trying to get an idea of how far she might have traveled."

"Or how high to set tripwires," Darnell said. "I think she took a board. Can't be sure. One's missing though."

"I'd like a few cameras to place," AJ said. "But I didn't think to have any manufactured."

"Probably not too late to add some in tomorrow's delivery," Lisa said. "What are you looking for?"

"Small, cheap, and stick-on," AJ said.

Lisa pulled a small pad from the galley counter and flipped through an interface. "I can get you a hundred for sixty credits. Three hundred sixty degrees and guaranteed to stick to any hard surface."

"What kind of radio range?" AJ asked.

"Coverage range twice the size of *Poecile Aerie*," Lisa said.

"What about using those when we've got tricky loads to deliver?" Darnell asked. "Any discount for a thousand?"

"No," Lisa said.

"Let's start with a hundred then," AJ said.

"That was fast," Darnell said, his eyes glazing over as he read a communication on his virtual screen.

"What's that?"

"Xandarj Shipping Consortium accepted our proposal at two hundred seventy-five thousand credits. They'll move half of the amount once a three-day cancelation period elapses. Are you sure you want to go dungeon diving for Farah?"

"Damn," AJ said. "No, you're right. This feels like an all-hands-on-deck moment. Chok, I don't suppose you've got any more room in your schedule?"

"Not for seven days," she said. "After that, though, I could get at least a five-day block. Why?"

"We need to get that shuttle in the garage running and to make a test run with *Big Max*," AJ said. "Call me a pessimist, but I'm betting we'll need an experienced spaceship mechanic."

"I don't know, Albert Jenkins, you are very talented for someone who has never seen our systems," Chok said.

"That's all BB," AJ said, pushing back from the table, his appetite suddenly disappearing. "If anyone needs me, I'll be in the portside engine room hookin' up spaghetti."

"You should eat more, AJ," Jayne said.

"Maybe, if you have antacids handy."

"You could put me to work," she offered, concerned with AJ's singular focus. "I don't have to spend all day working on the living spaces with Lisa."

"Nah, I'm not going to be very good company until *Big Max* is up and rolling. Sorry ...," AJ said, holding her gaze for a moment.

"No, you go," Jayne said.

AJ nodded and excused himself, making his way back to the engine bay on *Big Max*.

———

"AJ, would you two take a break and join us in the main hallway?" Beverly showed a doll-sized image of Jayne, standing only forty feet from his position in the hallway, just outside of the bridge.

He had exactly twenty minutes of work left to complete his current project, but he'd been short with Jayne at breakfast and didn't want to further aggravate things. "Yup, coming."

"Now that's what I'd call growth," Darnell chuckled.

"Don't push it, bubba," AJ said, mostly kidding.

"That darn robot's been making one heck of a racket all day," Darnell said. "I'll admit I'm curious what the hullabaloo was all about."

"Hullabaloo? Are you reverting?" AJ asked, straightening as he entered the large, aft elevator. To AJ's delight, the elevator floor had been painted light gray and had a new, nonstick surface applied. Further, the walls of the shaft were painted bright white, with vivid numerals and lined graphics showing each 'tween deck as they passed. "Damn, I didn't think the cleaning would include the elevator."

"Say only positive things, AJ," Darnell said, his voice holding a warning. "With the new contract, Lisa thought it would be good to extend the robot's work and get a few more areas cleaned up."

AJ lifted an eyebrow. He didn't love people making decisions without consulting him, but even with the slight irritation he felt, the shiny new surfaces were quite an upgrade. "It looks new."

"There you go," Darnell said, clasping a big hand onto AJ's shoulder. "Just keep sayin' things like that."

When the elevator stopped at the top, it opened to the long, open passageway leading directly to the bridge. Where before, the hatches along the sides were difficult to locate, they were now painted with a light gray offset by the dark green color of the deck and medium green of the walls. Even the ceiling had been painted a light blue. At the end of the hallway, Jayne and Lisa beamed with accomplishment.

"Tell me this doesn't make you think of a nice green space," Lisa said. "Blue is the sky, green is grass."

"I see," AJ said, not sure if he liked it as much as she did.

"Oh, don't get your panties in a wad," Lisa said. "Everything except for the deck is controlled by little projectors. Watch this."

The blue sky faded out and they would have been left in complete darkness if not for the strip lighting that ran the length of the hallway and outlined each hatch to the rooms below. Small points of light started appearing on the dark ceiling as it turned from pitch black to a starfield.

"Well, that's something. Wait, Is that Ursa Major?" AJ asked, pointing to a familiar star pattern.

"If you mean the *Big Dipper*, yes," Lisa said. "Jayne had Nit load Earth's star charts into the projectors. We couldn't afford any holography, but really, the effect isn't bad for low tech."

"Wait, can they show movies and baseball games?" AJ asked.

"Get your beer and hotdogs ready," Lisa said as the display on one of the walls transformed into a rectangular video screen. An Arizona Diamondbacks game appeared to be in progress.

"Wait, when is this game from?" AJ asked.

"Three weeks ago?" Lisa speculated.

"Turn it off! Turn it off! I haven't seen it yet," he said, shielding his eyes.

"I'll take that as praise," Lisa said, as the scene shifted back to normal daylight, only this time with realistic clouds floating high overhead.

"We also had time to remove all the broken video panels in the bridge," Jayne said. "There's some bad news, though. There were casualties on some of the control surfaces. We called over to get replacements made, but we're a couple of days out."

"How'd that happen?" AJ asked.

"Don't be mad. The robot has a fairly vigorous cleaning mechanism," Lisa said. "Some of the flight controls were so corroded that they snapped off."

"Do we need to take apart the bulkhead and see if more needs replacing?" AJ asked.

"Probably," Jayne said. "I'm sorry, AJ."

"Better if this happens at home," he said, shrugging. "I'd hate to lose control when we're swinging in with a big old pile of junk."

"You're not mad?"

"I'm irritated at the circumstance, but not at you," AJ said, placing a hand on her waist as he stepped around the pillar that blocked the view into the bridge from the hallway. "This looks great. That glass was clouded, now it's clean. Good surface to walk on. Antiskid and a little give is a good choice for tired people. I wish we could afford to replace all the vid screens, but we shouldn't need 'em for now." He looked at where four chairs had once adorned the center of the bridge. In their place were tan-painted mounting brackets, but no seats.

"Seats come tomorrow," Lisa said, looking a little sheepish. "We weren't originally going to replace them, but with all that money coming in, we'll be spending a lot of time on this bridge. It seemed like a necessary expense."

"Who ran the finances at your house, Lisa?" AJ asked. "You or Darnell?"

"What, you think because Darnell was a big-time CFO that I'm not capable of looking after money?" she asked, irritated. "I'll have you know, I kept him out of our household budget. And because of my thrift, we put a kid through college and left money for my grandbaby's college."

"*Too many cooks in the kitchen* is what I'm saying," AJ said.

"Pardon me?" Lisa said, growing angrier.

"AJ, you need to stop," Jayne said, more hurt than angry.

"Whoa, whoa, whoa there," AJ said. "You're misreading me. I was pretty sure Lisa ran the Jackson household budget. I remember Big D saying something about it years ago. I also seem to remember that you guys never seemed to struggle. What I'm saying is that maybe this should be Lisa's role in the company. Someone's got to watch our accounts. I know I don't want that job."

"Wouldn't that be Darnell's job?" Lisa said, still a little irritated.

"Ask him what Bob Simmons used to do for him," AJ said. "Big D's good with big numbers, but the day-to-day stuff drove him nuts.

Simmons was the guy you had to talk to if you wanted money for a project."

"You're telling me my Darnell was just a pretty face?"

"I'd never say that," AJ said, chuckling. "Did you ever notice how Big D takes complex numbers and spits calculations back almost immediately?"

"You mean like he did with the RFP?" Jayne asked.

"That's right. Aside from flying helicopters over the jungle, that's his superpower. He can look at a deal and tell you if it's good or bad in seconds. It's pure instinct and raw math horsepower. Lisa, the reason you had to run your household is because I'm pretty sure Darnell couldn't."

"Hey, now!" Darnell growled.

"You know, just when I think you're a complete idiot, you surprise me, Albert Jenkins."

NINETEEN

CONTROLLED CRASH

Jayne flopped onto the wide bed and closed her eyes. "Can I sleep now?" she begged.

AJ sat next to her and patted her leg. "We did good, kid," he said. "If *Big Max* decides to break down in the deep dark, we'll at least have a nice place to sleep."

Jayne looked up at him. "You know, most of the time, I can't tell if you're being sarcastic or not."

"Probably both," he said, lying back so his head rested on her stomach. "I'll admit, it sure looks a lot nicer in here. Are you gonna help me put those parts into the shuttlecraft, now?"

"Sure, but first I need a snack."

"I think Lisa left some granola in the galley," AJ said, making no effort to get off the bed. They'd spent most of the day moving and installing custom-made furniture for *Big Max*, bringing the passenger areas to a higher level of fit and finish than the rest of the ship. To Jayne's point, however, the comfort and cleanliness did put him in a better mood.

"Is it strange that we just accept floating around in space now?" Jayne asked as they moved from *Big Max* to *Poecile Aerie*.

"No stranger than asking a seventeen-year-old boy to run around in the jungles of Vietnam," AJ said.

"You were seventeen when you joined the Army? I didn't think that was legal."

"Lots of us were," AJ said. "My high school signed off on my work to-date, gave me a diploma, and off I went. I figured I was going to be drafted anyway. And besides, at that age, carrying a gun sounded a lot more interesting than more trigonometry."

"That makes sense," Jayne said, picking up a box of parts near the main garage entrance.

"Replacing these parts won't take much work," AJ said. "There isn't much fooling around with these little systems. Either they work or they don't, best I can tell."

"Seating for six and some cargo room," Jayne said. "Feels like it's a good size."

"Agreed," AJ said, opening a side panel. "Have Nit show you how to replace that inertial control panel. It's on the inside toward the front."

"Sure," Jayne agreed, plucking a shoebox-sized part from the box and a couple of tools from a nearby workbench. "Did I overhear Darnell say he only had an hour left on *Big Max*?"

"He's still helping Lisa, though," AJ said, sliding his own part into place. "You've been quiet about going back to DAS. What gives?"

"I feel torn," she said. "This is fun, but I love the academic environment."

"Are you starting to think you can't have both?" AJ asked, his gut twisting as he imagined yet one more time around this particular merry-go-round.

Jayne must have picked up on his reticence because she chuckled. "No, nothing like that. I just don't want to miss out on everything you guys are doing."

"See what kind of flexibility DAS has," AJ said. "You're always welcome out here. Doc, it's your life, you can make it work."

"When we get married, are you going to keep calling me Doc?"

"Don't do that," AJ said. "You redirect when you don't want to think about something."

"I know, I just feel like I've pushed DAS about as far as I can."

"Do they have access to another human with your extensive knowledge of biology and who was instrumental in developing a vaccine that saved humanity from the Korgul, not to mention created an immunology for Xandarj?" AJ asked.

"Well, no ... not when you say it *that* way," Jayne said.

"That's the truth, Doc," AJ said. "And should I call you Amanda? Mandy? I mean your initials are AJ. I feel like that'd get confusing."

Jayne shook her head. "I've never been a *Mandy* and ... you know, call me Doc all you want. If you called me Amanda, it'd just feel weird."

"How's that system coming?" he asked, picking up another part and snapping it into place.

"Wasn't that hard," she said. "As a surgeon, I wish people had nice bolts like that where we could replace parts so easily. It would sure simplify things."

"Then you'd get paid like a mechanic."

"It'd be worth it. Just like when alien medical tech gets discovered back home," she said. "A world without disease would be a wonderful thing."

"Longer life spans will put pressure on a lot of systems," AJ said. "We'll need to produce more food. Housing will grow short. There are a bunch of implications for people not dying."

"I have no moral qualms about it. I believe in the oath I took to first, do no harm. We'll just need to figure out how to feed people," Jayne said. "I need another part."

"Grab anything," AJ said. "Nit can tell you where it goes."

The pair worked on the small craft until forty minutes later when they were left with a stack of old parts.

"Want to see if it'll fire up?" he asked.

"It's too big to fit through the primary hatch," Jayne said. "How are we getting it out without venting the atmosphere?"

"You must have missed it," AJ said. "Lisa got parts for the photonic pressure barriers for the garage doors. We haven't been running them since no one ever goes out that way."

"You don't mind if I drive?" she asked.

"Nope. I'll get the door open," AJ said, picking up tools and old parts and moving them away from the somewhat battered old shuttle-craft. "Lisa, can you read me?"

"Yup. What's up, AJ?"

"Doc and I just got this shuttlecraft ready for a test run," AJ said. "Are we going to run into any trouble with the countermeasures you've got set up?"

"Negative," she said. "Sensors are all passive. Appreciate the heads-up though, because I'd hate to shoot you up with my tungsten launcher. Since you're going out, would you see about capturing that derelict fifteen hundred kilometers off *Poecile Aerie's* starboard bow? The crew was rescued, but the ship is outside the range Mads Bazer gave us for storing stuff."

"Sure," AJ said, started the photonic generator and opened the furthest garage door. "Be a good exercise for Doc and me to figure out how to recover wreckage."

When AJ turned around, he found that Jayne was already holding the coiled length of thin cabling he'd left on one of the work-benches. He'd added loops to the ends and located a handful of manual shackles and magnetic attachments, not sure what he'd be getting into when he tried to haul something.

"This what you're looking for?" she asked.

"Always the smartest girl in your class I'd bet," AJ said. "Do you like being the teacher's pet?"

She opened the back hatch of the shuttlecraft and set the coil into the small cargo compartment. "Only if it comes with perks," she said, lifting her eyebrows.

"So many perks," AJ said, shutting the hatch and sliding into the port side front seat.

"I thought you wanted me to drive," Jayne said, taking the opposite chair.

"I do," AJ said. "You have controls right in front of you. Just pull that stick back."

"Just this stick?" she asked.

"It's the default control set for a lot of small vessels," AJ said. "Stick forward for forward acceleration. Stick back to reduce that or reverse. Tipping to one side or the other causes bank. You can lift or push the entire thing up and down for vertical movement. Oh, and twist to spin on the vertical axis."

"How do you know this?" she asked.

"Kind of my thing."

Jayne nodded, experimentally lifting the stick. "It's not working."

"Sorry, you have to squeeze the stick to let the AI know you're driving."

The shuttle shot up quickly as Jayne lifted the controls a bit too hard, but it stopped short of impacting the ceiling. "Gosh, I barely moved it. Oh, Nit's telling me she's reconfiguring the sensitivity. We messed all that up with our repairs."

"That makes sense," AJ said. "Good to know the proximity sensors are working."

"No kidding," Jayne agreed, lowering the shuttle back toward the deck as she turned it around so the nose oriented on the open garage door. "That door looks smaller than it did earlier today."

AJ nodded. "You'll get it."

She pushed the small craft forward and had to monkey with it a few times to get it through the door but in the end, she made it out.

"Where to?" she asked.

"We have decent fuel. Why don't you fly around a bit and get used to the controls," AJ said.

"How about I fly out toward that wreck Lisa wants us to check out?"

"Sounds like a plan to me," AJ said, surreptitiously working virtual controls so he could see if there were any vessels in the vicinity. Finding none, he relaxed into the aged seat and took in the sights. Having been trapped on the station for several days, he was enjoying the freedom and another chance to view their surroundings.

"It's easier to control out here," Jayne said. "Fewer things to hit."

"You seem to have a knack for it," AJ said. "BB is showing me a connection point on the backside of that wreck. If I could get you to set down right in front of the engines, I could put a shackle on and connect to our cable."

"That ship has to outweigh the shuttle by at least ten times," Jayne said. "Are you sure we can pull it?"

"That's a common misconception," AJ said. "As long as we don't put too much stress on the shuttle's engines or overstretch the cable, we won't have much trouble moving it. It's the opposite side of that dynamic we have to be careful of. If we get too much of a head of steam, we won't have enough power to stop the wreck from busting up *Poecile Aerie.*"

"Basic physics, I suppose," Jayne said. "Looks like it'll just take us ten times as long to get back."

"Now, you're officially a junker," AJ said. "Slow and steady gets the job done, especially with heavy loads."

"I'd say it was peaceful out here if that wreck wasn't a reminder that people are out to get us," Jayne said, slowing her approach. When they arrived at the indicated location, it became obvious that Beverly's initial plan wouldn't work. The tow hook on the vessel was missing and in its place was a gaping hole caused by some sort of explosion.

"Lisa really did a number on these guys," AJ said. "She talks with Seamus for targeting so she can avoid causing too much damage to the critical systems. Probably not how I'd do it. If someone's coming after me, they'll get the sharp end of the stick every time."

"When I was younger, I'd probably have argued that with you," Jayne said.

"What changed?"

"I've been shot at quite a bit more," Jayne said. "I'll set down next to the hole and you can figure out how you want to lash things up."

"Seal your suit. There's no airlock on this ship," AJ said.

Jayne did as he said and set the shuttlecraft onto the back of the much larger ship. Seeing the wreck close up, she could tell it had been designed for intergalactic travel, if not space combat. "Let me know if you need me to move," she said as AJ unloaded, taking the long cable with him.

"Yup."

Having spent a good portion of his life securing cargo, AJ set to the task, first unspooling the cable and then looking for a way to hook up. As he scanned the gaping hole, he realized Lisa's shot had been a through-and-though. It would be a simple matter to drag the cable down through the middle of the ship, out the belly, and connect it topside in a loop. With cable to spare, he secured both ends and added a tow hook with a shackle.

"That was pretty simple," AJ said, turning to inspect his work.

"AJ, we might have a problem," Jayne said.

A virtual window popped up in his periphery and he turned his attention to it. A vessel was headed in their direction and making good time. "I see it," AJ said. "BB, warn Lisa and Darnell."

Beverly appeared in front of him in her Jetson's spacesuit. "They've been warned," she answered. "It's a slight difference, but the heading of the approaching ship suggests their destination is *Poecile Aerie,* not the shuttle craft. The resolution of our sensor equipment, however, isn't fine enough for me to be sure."

"We're pretty exposed," Jayne said.

"How far out are they?" AJ asked.

"With current acceleration, they're thirty minutes out," Beverly answered.

"We need to drop the cable," Jayne said. "We can't make it back with this thing in tow before they get here."

"You're right. Give me a minute," AJ said, pulling up a magnified display of the hull of *Poecile Aerie* and the junk surrounding it. "BB, remember that thing we did with the pistols in jump space?"

"Of course, AJ," Beverly said. "It was horrifying and elegant in equal parts."

"Is that a compliment?"

"To my recollection, I did all of the computations," Beverly said.

"Everyone's a critic," AJ said. "Doc, see this old VEAH arm we took off *Big Max*?"

"Yes?" Jayne said, not following.

"Ask Nit if the two of you could nudge the wreck enough so that it hits that old VEAH arm. The VEAH is large enough to absorb at least five meters per second if we line the ship up right."

"There's no such thing as *absorbing*," Beverly said. "The arm is at rest. A collision would push the arm toward *Poecile Aerie*. I don't have enough data to accurately calculate if the wreck would rebound or join with the VEAH arm."

"That arm wouldn't move very fast," AJ said. "I'd bet a low impact would cause minimal damage. Tell me the plan lacks elegance. Sure, it'll take the wreck a few days to move that far, but that's no big deal."

"Three-point-four days at five meters per second," Beverly said. "The accuracy desired is considerable."

"Think you can handle it, Doc?"

"For the record, we're going to push this wreck toward our home and hope when it crashes it doesn't cause too much damage?" Jayne asked.

"Right. Are you game?"

"And then what do we do?"

"We hustle home so we don't get caught out in the open."

"Why does this feel like such a bad idea?"

"I share your concern, Amanda Jayne," Beverly said. "An object with this much mass, even moving slowly can cause damage."

"Look, worst case is we come out, hook back up and make adjustments," AJ said.

For several minutes, Jayne struggled with the controls, even going so far as to pull the entire wreck around and start over. In the end, however, she got it set on almost the perfect heading.

"You're a crazy man, Albert Jenkins," she said, providing slack so he could disconnect the cable from the wreck that now moved on a collision course with their home.

"Not the first person to say that," AJ said. "BB, any update on that incoming ship's course?"

"It is definitely headed for *Poecile Aerie*," Beverly said. "It would not be difficult for it to change direction and intercept this shuttle. I suggest you move quickly."

"It just doesn't seem like we should be able to travel fifteen hundred kilometers so quickly," Jayne said. "I know we have inertial systems, but ..."

"That's because Earth cars have to overcome atmospheric friction. They only really accelerate for a short period of the trip. We can just keep accelerating out here," AJ said. "BB, with constant acceleration, how much g-force are we pulling to get home in twenty minutes?"

"Roughly one-half of the force of earth's gravity or .5g," Beverly answered.

"What are these engines capable of?" AJ asked.

"That depends on the mass of the shuttle and the occupants. As currently occupied, 1.5g is possible," Beverly answered.

"I'll keep that in mind just in case that ship decides to get curious," Jayne said.

"Amanda, AJ, can you read me?" Darnell's voice came over the ship's small speaker system.

"We're here," AJ said. "What's up?"

"Sorry about the confusion. The incoming ship is my doing," he said. "It's bringing a load of chemical fuel. I got a good price on it and *Big Max* is one of the few old ships left that can still burn it. Petey found a stockpile and we might have bought 'em out."

"How good a price?"

"About a third that of Fantastium," he answered. "Still cost a pretty penny, though."

"Are we back to beans and rice?" AJ asked.

"No, not that bad," Darnell said. "The deal was hard to pass up. I talked it through with Lisa. Sorry, I forgot to loop you in."

"Lisa okay with it?"

"She wasn't thrilled with the cash outlay but in the end, it was hard to argue sixty percent savings," Darnell said.

"Are you done with *Big Max*?" AJ asked.

"I was just getting ready to take her out for a spin," Darnell said. "Would you mind receiving the fuel?"

"How much room do we need and how does it get stored?" AJ asked.

"I'll send you the details."

"Copy that," AJ said. "I was hoping to take a run out to start grabbing wrecks this afternoon. Jayne's getting pretty good in this shuttle. If we could nab even one piece, I'd have a better feeling for things."

"AJ, I've got *Big Max's* galley loaded with food and water," Lisa said, cutting in. "There's no reason we couldn't make a run this afternoon. It's not like we don't take our sleeping quarters along, after all."

"Are you good with that, Doc?" AJ asked.

"Sure, I'm game. I wanted to try out those new linens," Jayne said. "Where are you putting the shuttle?"

"There's a good spot under her belly that's close to the small, forward crew elevator exit," AJ said. "*Big Max's* entire underside has hitch points for securing loads. We might have to juggle things for the return trip, but we'll figure that out when we get there. We could leave the shuttle in the debris field between trips if we wanted."

"Aren't you worried about someone stealing it?" Jayne asked.

"If we turn off all of the electronics, it'll be impossible to distinguish from all the other junk," AJ said. "Leaving it behind wouldn't be my first choice."

"What about Farah?" Jayne asked.

"She showed up twenty minutes ago," Lisa said. "I think she thought I wasn't around because I startled her when she was grabbing some food. I think she's been sneaking in when we're out. I wasn't sure before, but grains were going out faster than I'd been expecting."

"Do you think she's up to no good?" AJ asked.

"I have no idea," Lisa said. "I might have done a little exploring earlier and set up a few cameras, though."

"Probably a good idea," AJ said. "Anything yet?"

"Best I can tell, she's going forward," Beverly said. "She got ahead of my cameras pretty quickly because I didn't know what direction she was going. We'll know more later."

"We need to set cameras up on the back side of *Poecile Aerie*," Darnell said. "Not for her, but if someone wants to approach from that side, we'd have a hard time seeing them."

"Never a shortage of things to do," AJ said as Jayne slowed the shuttle. Instead of docking in the garage, she flew beneath *Big Max* to look at the underside.

"Anywhere you want me in particular?" she asked, rolling the shuttle over so she could land upside down on *Big Max's* belly. When they were within a yard of contacting the ship, the shuttle was pulled firmly against *Big Max*.

"Is that you, Darnell?" AJ asked.

"That's me. I got a notification to engage the magnetic clamps," he said. "Looks like it pulled you in pretty nice."

"Sure did," AJ said, venting atmosphere. "Go ahead and take her out for a shakedown. We'll get ready for that fuel delivery."

"Copy that."

TWENTY

JUNKERS AT LAST

"I hope that's the last fix for this trip," AJ said, slumping into a new bridge chair next to Darnell. Having set out late in the afternoon, they'd run into problem after problem with their newly installed engines and in the eight hours they'd been en route, only one of those hours had been under acceleration.

"If it's any consolation, we're back online," Darnell said. "Did you notice if Lisa was still up?"

"Nope, her and Doc are sacked out in the galley on that new couch," AJ said.

"Yeah, I wondered if that's what happened to my coffee," Darnell said.

"I'm not that tired," AJ said. "Why don't you catch a few hours rest. I'll watch things here for a while."

"You've been up as long as I have," Darnell said.

"Yeah, but if things break, you'll need to wake me up anyway," AJ said.

"You've got a point," Darnell said, standing. "We have four and a half hours until we hit the first group of wrecks. Wake me up in four?"

"I'll get us into the area and shut things down so we can all get some sleep," AJ said. "If you wake Doc, tell her to go to bed without me, would you?"

"Can do," Darnell said, yawning wide and walking from the bridge.

"You know I'm perfectly capable of waking you if issues arise," Beverly said, appearing on the forward bulkhead, which protruded eighteen inches from the curved wall at the front of the bridge. She wore a 1950's-era white sailor's uniform, complete with flared pant legs and a round white hat.

"Am I crazy for trying to start a business with all this crap going on?" AJ asked, ignoring her statement.

"By *crap*, do you mean the bounty hunters?"

"That and what's going on back home," AJ said. "Don't we owe it to humanity to make sure Earth isn't being taken advantage of?"

"You have come to the aid of your people and your country time and time again. While those efforts were noble by any account, they did little by way of providing for your basic needs. A drive to survive is instinctual for all successful species."

AJ smiled. "How about Beltigersk? I guess I've never really understood what was required for your survival back home. Are there Beltigersk carpenters and electricians? Do you have jobs?"

"Due to our size, jobs that improve our physical space are unusual," she said. "Similarly, nourishment is not difficult to acquire. We have survival needs, however, such as the balance of our environment. Mostly, intellectual pursuits have a high priority as for many millennia our physical needs were so limited. It was only when we started to interact with other species that we became concerned with such things."

"I wish I knew how to help Earth," AJ said.

"Do you mind a suggestion?"

"I'm all ears."

"That's a funny idiom," Beverly said, scooting forward so her legs hung off the edge. "Trust the people of Earth."

"I don't understand."

"Right now, bad actors are taking advantage of Earth's transition toward joining the galactic community," she said. "Perhaps you can find a way to offset their actions."

"Never gets boring around here," AJ said, settling back into his chair and stretching to rest his heels on the narrow work surface.

AT TWO HOURS OUT, Beverly woke AJ to flip the direction of the ship's acceleration, so they slowed in relationship to their destination. Two and a half hours after that, she woke him to bring the ship to a stop in relationship to the space junk they were to pick up. And finally, two hours after that, she woke him because he'd requested she do just that.

Using *Big Max's* relatively weak sensors, AJ scanned near-space and found it devoid of anything aside from the two wrecks they'd been targeting. He was focused enough on the task that he didn't hear Jayne's approach. It was the smell of coffee that alerted him to her presence.

"Permission to enter the bridge?" she asked quietly, leaning against the front wall, holding out a covered cup.

"You're a dream," he said, accepting the coffee.

"You didn't come to bed last night," she said. "How much trouble did you have with *Big Max?*"

"We made it here," he said, pointing out at one of the wrecks only visible to the naked eye because of a light he'd managed to point at it. "Do you feel like pulling that shuttle out of position so I can try to latch onto that wreck?"

"Sure, how difficult will that be?" she asked.

"Depends on if *Big Max's* engines keep cutting out at low pressure," he said. "Ideally, you'll stand off several hundred meters, just in case I hit the throttle too hard."

"That's assuming I'm gonna let you take the first crack at it,"

Darnell said, joining them from the opposite side of the bridge. "The two of you could wrangle Object 41-C and bring it back this way while I pluck this other flower like a bee in heat."

"Nothing like a butchered metaphor to kick off the morning," Lisa said, joining them. "Anyone up for breakfast? I was thinking of making eggs."

"This shouldn't take more than forty-five minutes," Darnell said. "Mind if we see about hooking this junk up first?"

"I don't mind," Lisa said. "Just checking the room."

"I'm probably too nervous to eat," Jayne said. "AJ's gonna have me run the shuttle again. I'm still learning the ropes."

"Sounds like it's settled then," Lisa said, claiming a chair.

AJ and Jayne made their way to the elevator at the back of the bridge and rode down quietly. The shuttle was still attached, upside down on *Big Max's* belly. Using thrust boards, they glided out and entered the craft.

"Not sure I'll ever get used to quick changes in what's considered up and down," Jayne said, closing her eyes as she settled into the seat.

"Makes me feel like I've got a hangover," AJ said moving aft to double-check that he still had his grappling line and shackles.

She punched at the controls and started the vital systems. "It's not very far, how about we connect our suits to the atmo ports on the console," she said. "I don't want to keep pressurizing and depressurizing."

"Atmo ports?" AJ asked, working his way back to the front and sliding into his chair.

"Didn't you read the shuttle's operator manual?" she asked, her raised eyebrow indicating she already knew the answer. When AJ didn't answer, she continued by depressing a small, round panel next to her knee, extracting a thin pliable tube, and attaching it to a port over her thigh. "Atmo port. Keeps us charged on O2 so we don't deplete the suit."

With Beverly's help via a flashing outline on the console, AJ mimicked Jayne's actions and connected his suit. "That's handy."

"Hold on," she said, tapping out a sequence on the console. The shuttle shuddered as it detached from beneath *Big Max* and floated free. She directed the small vessel out from beneath the much larger tug.

"Darnell, you're free to start your operations," AJ said, once they were a hundred meters away. "Happy pollinating." His last comment earned him an approving grin from Jayne.

"We're lined up on 41-C," Jayne said. "It's tumbling at less than a single revolution per second."

"Point six hertz," AJ said.

"Do you have a solution?"

"Ideally, we'd have a net. I'll make one for next time," he said. "Let me see how much mass we're looking at. It'll give me an idea of how much force we'll have to use to stop it."

"Thirty-five hundred pounds," she said.

"That's not great," AJ said.

"You have an idea on how to capture it or should we just get it with the net next run?"

"We picked these two objects because they were outliers. Ideally, we need to take care of things while we're here or it'll be a big-time sink next trip," he said. "I've got an idea. It's gonna kinda suck though."

"Suck for whom?"

"Me," AJ said. "I'm going to run over there and use my thruster board to counter the rotation."

"While riding it? Do you have any idea how sick that'll make you?"

"I'm hoping BB will have some solution for that. BB?" AJ said.

BB appeared, wearing a bright blue cowboy hat, a red-fringed leather jacket, and jeans. "So, you want to ride the space junk, eh, cowboy?"

"Can you keep me from throwing up? And if I pass out, I'll need you to control the thruster board," he said.

"You'll need to approach from the dead center," Beverly said. "At sixteen feet across, the tips are moving at thirty-two feet per second.

It would feel like being hit by a car at twenty miles per hour. If you can stay within two feet of the center, that will reduce to four. The impact won't be pleasant, but very survivable."

"Are you seriously considering jumping on that spinning piece of junk?" Jayne asked, shocked.

"I think Beverly just said it's not that big of a deal."

"What she said was, if you do it just right, you'll survive."

"People survive getting hit by cars all the time," AJ said. "Seriously, I think I've got this."

"I don't like it, but go ahead," Jayne said. "At least you won't get ground into the pavement."

AJ chuckled and opened the hatch, floating free of the ship until the atmo port tether yanked him back. "Dang it," he grumbled, releasing the tube.

"Not exactly giving me a lot of confidence here," Jayne said.

"BB, can you control the thrust board independently?" AJ asked.

"I can, although I was thinking that perhaps I could simply set the thrust board in place without you on it and eliminate the object's tumble without directly involving you," she said.

"You didn't think to bring this up before?"

"I believe it was you who told me that you prefer to work through a problem before receiving suggestions," Beverly said.

"Snarky little ..."

"AJ, be nice," Jayne said.

Pulling the board from where it rested against his back, AJ gave it a shove toward Object 41-C. As it glided through space, the board started to spin on a horizontal axis until its periodicity matched that of the object. With ease well beyond AJ's flying capability, Beverly set the board into place and slowed the tumble until it was unmoving in relationship to the shuttle.

"A thrust board won't produce enough force to work with heavier objects," AJ said, catching the board as Beverly brought it back.

"Agreed," Beverly said. "I all but exhausted the board's energy reserves. Of course, I could have brought it back for a recharge, but with larger objects that might require quite a number of cycles."

"We should brainstorm ideas," AJ said. "We'll run into this type of problem from time to time."

"Fourteen of the remaining seventy-one objects are currently tumbling at a speed more than point five hertz," Beverly said. "The net idea you have thrown out would be effective for the smaller objects, but a net sufficient to counteract the more massive objects would potentially break apart upon contact."

"What other ideas do you have?" AJ said, pulling the capture cable from the shuttle.

"This is not an uncommon problem with space junk," Beverly said. "The Vred have a device specifically designed for such a purpose. The pattern compatible with our current contract is three hundred credits. Would you like me to send this to Lisa Jackson?"

AJ growled at the thought of asking for approval, but he needed to play nice. "Sure. That'll work."

"What's all that blue material on the side of 41-C?" Jayne asked as AJ worked to secure the capture cable. The material she was referring to was frozen, some of it flaking off as it came in contact with the cable.

"No idea," AJ said, brushing it from his suit.

"Without full analysis, it appears to be septic fluid common in Cheell vessels. It is only blue when fully saturated with waste," she said.

"Are you serious?" AJ asked, shaking his head as he secured the cable ends to the shuttle.

"It is harmless, AJ," Beverly said. "Although it smells quite pungent. You should brush it from your suit."

"This just keeps getting better and better," he grumped as he got ready to reenter the shuttle. Looking at his front, he only found a few spots where the septic material had contacted his suit. With the back of his gloved hand, he whisked it away.

"Did you just get sprayed with space poo?" Jayne asked as AJ slid into the shuttle.

"Of course I did."

"Are you set for me to head back?" Jayne asked.

"Yup. We're all connected. I'd take it slow," AJ said. "Darnell, how's it going over there?"

"*Big Max* is in position," Darnell answered. "I need you to come back and run out the tie-downs. I don't think those magnetic grapples are sufficient for something this big."

"Copy that. We're inbound."

Settling back in his chair, AJ relaxed as Jayne accelerated toward *Big Max* and its payload. "Any thoughts on where we'll put 41-C?" she asked as they closed in on their destination. "Nit recommended placing it on the starboard side and capturing both Darnell's 19-C and our 41-C with the straps."

"That would work. We could do the same with the shuttle," AJ said. "When we get back to *Poecile Aerie,* I'll weld a permanent docking point on the side of *Big Max* where we can secure the shuttle. I don't love strapping it to wrecks. Too many sharp edges."

"You got lucky. There's a good spot for the shuttle on this load," Jayne said.

"Lucky, huh?" AJ said. "We might define that differently."

Jayne grinned slyly. "I wouldn't count on that." Before AJ could respond, she maneuvered the shuttle to orient her payload.

"Once you get close, I'll get out and help position it," AJ said. "I brought magnetic come-alongs with a hefty load rating."

A few minutes later, Jayne had Object 41-C sitting ten feet off Object 19-C that was already nestled beneath *Big Max* and tentatively held in place by *Big Max's* magnetic grapples. "That's about as good as I can get," Jayne said, taking her hands off the shuttle controls.

"That's more than close enough," AJ said. "I've got lines I'll pull around that'll cinch this up securely. Let me get you free from the load and you can reposition."

"Sounds good," Jayne said.

He unclipped the atmo line from his leg and opened the shuttle door. Looking out into space prompted a rare moment of introspection. His life had changed so much in the past year. Never, in his wildest dream could he have imagined he'd be floating in space, routinely capturing space junk for his big hauler. He wasn't sure if he was more struck by how much had changed or in fact, how little they'd changed.

His distraction came to an end as his feet came to rest on *Big Max's* belly and he opened one of several lockers that held the equipment he'd need to secure the loads. Spooling out a wide strap, he pushed away from *Big Max* and made an inelegant arc over the top of 19-C and the smaller 41-C. With some effort, he adjusted his direction and landed on the opposite side of the junk, once again on *Big Max's* belly. He clipped the end of the strap in place.

Using the strap to guide him back to the top of the pile, he unclipped the 41-C from the shuttle and instinctively patted the side of the vessel. "Go ahead and get re-situated," he said to Jayne. "I'll work on drawing a few more straps over these babies."

The entire process took less than thirty minutes and soon they were both back in the elevator, heading up to *Big Max's* passenger space.

"Now you're an expert junker," AJ said, companionably patting Jayne on the back. "All we have to do is rinse and repeat that process thirty more times and we'll fill our contract. Let me know if you're up for quitting your day job."

The pair stepped off the elevator to the smells of breakfast wafting forward from the galley. "Do you smell that?" Jayne asked.

Greybeard appeared from the bridge, his tail wagging happily. He suddenly whined and slunk back.

"Yeah, smells good. I love it when Lisa cooks," AJ said, looking curiously at Greybeard.

"Not *that*," Jayne said, her face contorting. "I'm getting a feces smell. Ammonia. Oh, AJ, that blue stuff has melted on your suit. You're dripping septic fluid on the deck. That's awful."

"Traitor," AJ said, glancing at Greybeard. "Don't let Lisa clean that up, I'll get it once I'm out of the shower."

"Don't move," Jayne said. "I'll get some towels. We don't want you tracking that through the entire ship. Better yet, take off the suit."

AJ shook his head but acquiesced. With Jayne's help, they placed his suit into a bag for later cleaning. Once the mess was contained, they dropped into their quarters and AJ headed for the shower, taking the bag with him.

"Avoid the blue ice in the future?" Lisa needled when he joined the rest of the crew in the galley.

"Understatement of the universe. How'd the hookup go on this side?" AJ determinedly changed the direction of the conversation.

"Generally, not bad," Darnell said, stabbing at a strip of protein that resembled bacon. "We need better sensors on the underside. I was mostly blind. If not for Petey's ability to project a virtual location on the wreck, I'd have had a tough time."

"I've got a few things we need to manufacture for next time, too," AJ said. "We should see if we can squeeze in another trip today. Objects 14-A through F look like something we could grab in a single run. Lisa, do we have enough credits to get that thruster pack manufactured?"

"It shouldn't be a problem," Lisa said.

"I hate to be a spoilsport," Jayne said. "But I was thinking about going back to DAS in the next couple of days."

"Do you have time for one more trip?" AJ asked hopefully.

"At least one," Jayne said, resting a hand on his arm.

TWENTY-ONE

UNPLEASANTRIES

"AJ, there is a communication from Lefty Johnson," Beverly said, interrupting the idle chitchat between AJ and Jayne as she sailed the shuttle toward Dralli Station. In the last seventy-two hours, they'd successfully captured fourteen of the seventy-two contracted objects. AJ's device that would level out the larger tumbling objects was ready and awaiting pickup. Since Jayne had decided it was time for her to return to DAS, the Vred-designed tech would come in handy.

"What's it say?" AJ asked.

Beverly appeared on the dash of the shuttle wearing jeans and a hooded sweatshirt that was emblazoned with *DAS* across the front. She was holding a stack of books held together by a belt. "They were picked up by Hetra three days ago and are en route to the jump space point near Mars. Lefty also writes that there were minor difficulties with local authorities but no casualties."

"Did he expand on *minor difficulties*?" AJ asked.

"No."

"Can we respond before they reach jump space?"

"There is not time for a message to be delivered. Hetra's vessel will arrive with your three friends in twenty-three days," Beverly said.

"If we really get after things, we might even have our current contract finished before they get here," he said.

"What happens then?" Jayne asked, guiding the shuttle into Mads Bazer's docking bay.

"First, we'll bring Frenchy and Ruiz to you so we can start their therapy," AJ said. "After that, we're going to deal with this bounty thing a bit more aggressively."

"What does *more aggressively* mean?" Jayne asked. A small vibration passed through the shuttle as it settled onto Dralli Station's deck.

"The way I see it, the bounty is a symptom of a bigger problem," AJ said. "Someone wants to shut us up. Kind of dumb if you ask me. By biffing, they've put us on guard and pissed us off."

"And that means?"

"Same thing it always does," AJ said. "We've gotta take the fight to them."

"I was afraid you were going to say that. AJ, I need you to be careful," Jayne said.

"AJ, I believe Amanda Jayne's escort has arrived," Beverly said, pointing out the front window at a trio of large, well-armed Xandarj wearing DAS uniforms. "I've verified their security credentials, as has Nit."

Jayne gave AJ a lingering kiss. They'd agreed not to say their goodbyes outside of the shuttle. "Promise me you'll be safe."

"We'll do our best," AJ said, grinning. "See you in twenty-three days?"

"You've got a date," she said. "I'll get arrangements squared away for Frenchy and Ruiz's therapy. We'll need to get their agreement first, though."

"I can't imagine that'll be a problem."

She gave AJ a quick, final kiss and then opened the shuttle, exiting quickly. Gripping his pistol tightly, AJ watched as she approached the security detail, wary for signs of trouble.

"You can relax, AJ," Beverly said. "Nit is monitoring the communications of the security force. Everything is as it should be. Further,

Nit and I will exchange a secure code every fifteen minutes. If they are attacked and Nit becomes unable to communicate, we will know this very quickly."

Even so, AJ watched with apprehension as Jayne was escorted into Dralli Station, disappearing from view. Sighing with resignation, he exited the shuttle and made his way to the storage locker that held the newly manufactured items that would greatly increase their efficiency at retrieving large space objects.

"AJ, Mads Bazer approaches," Beverly warned as AJ struggled to set the heavy machinery into the back hatch of their shuttle.

"I saw that you were to pick up items today," Mads said from behind him. With a final clunk, AJ slid the machine from the gravity-assisted cart onto the floor of the shuttle. "I take it you have found the capacity to become productive on my junk pile."

AJ bristled at her possessiveness but tried to push the emotions from his face as he turned to greet her. "How's the whiskey business going, Mads?" he asked.

"It is marginally profitable," she answered, noncommittally. "Do you have any Pertaf treasure to report or treasure hunters to register?"

"We both know there's no treasure on the *Poecile Aerie*," AJ said.

"Do we?"

"Lefty Johnson is the only registered treasure hunter," AJ said, shrugging. "We've seen evidence of squatters but so far haven't been able to locate anyone. You're welcome to come out and inspect things anytime you want as long as you give eight hours' notice as is in our contract."

"A whisper in my ear says that you contracted with Xandarj Shipping Consortium," she said. "What is the nature of this?"

"Mads, what are you fishing for?" AJ asked. "We're doing regular old junker business out at your junk pile."

"I did not expect you would so easily repair the Veneri EAH vessel or even this shuttle," she said. "I am starting to become concerned that I undersold this contract."

"The shipping consortium asked us to move old derelict heaps out of the shipping lanes," AJ said. "We're bringing the stuff back and storing it. The margin on the deal is fairly thin, but we're managing. I'm not even sure why I'm telling you this. Why don't you tell me what your real concern is so we don't have to dance around it."

"There is a rumor that you uncovered something in the *Poecile Aerie* wreckage," she said.

"I think you're looking at it," he said. "We found this shuttle and it was in good enough shape to repair. Repairing and using found equipment is completely within our contract."

"You were shrewd in forcing me to specifically identify the treasure of Pertaf," she said. "If I find you had prior knowledge of a large discovery you will profit from, I will be quite angry."

"Let's be clear," AJ said, his face growing red. "If you made a bad deal, that's on you. So far, you've been ecstatic to take the deals I've offered. I'd bet you're making out considerably better on selling my whiskey than you're letting on. Now you accuse me of taking advantage of you? We're not partners, Mads and you need to stay out of my business."

"Ah, there is the real Albert Jenkins," Mads said. "Do not tell me what I must do. I will not be intimidated by one such as you. Heed my warning, Earth man, do not cheat Mads Bazer." Having had her say, she turned and stalked off, leaving AJ flat-footed.

"Crazy old woman," he grumbled, heading back to the storage lockers for his next load.

Twenty minutes later, the shuttle was packed almost full with fresh food, staples, and a variety of other materials not available in their new home. With his work complete, AJ slid into the shuttle and sighed. His conversation with Mads continued to bother him. What kind of rumor could she know about?

"BB, are you picking up any suspicious craft?"

"A difficult question, but with the available public scans, I believe your best exit would have you take a sharp angle down, away from Dralli Station," Beverly answered. "Some craft meet the criteria for higher risk."

AJ lifted from the docking bay and glided through the wide photonic pressure barrier. Once clear of the station, he did exactly as BB advised. Fortunately, no craft followed.

"Mads Bazer is requesting communication," Beverly said after they'd flown about halfway back to *Poecile Aerie*. "I have video available."

"Put her on," AJ said and then looked at the virtual video panel Beverly projected. "You have AJ."

"Albert Jenkins, I wish to apologize for our conversation," Mads said. "I did not seek to create a rift of anger between us."

"Fine. It's forgotten," AJ said, his voice conveying anything but forgiveness.

"I find it difficult to trust others with my possessions," she said.

"Do you have the resources to make money from your junk pile?" AJ asked. "Seems to me like you've made out quite well because of our efforts."

"I would like to believe the benefit is mutual," she said. "I provided you with considerable credits and with those credits you launched an enterprise. That sort of initiative is lost in the current generation of Xandarj who would rather experience a life of sitting as opposed to taking risks with capital and effort. I respect your ingenuity and drive."

"I'm getting misty-eyed, Mads," AJ said, dryly. "Cut to the chase. What do you want?"

"Fine," Mads said. "I dislike pleasant speaking. There is a rumor that an artifact was found on *Poecile Aerie*. The nature of this artifact is unknown, but the rumor suggests it is of considerable value."

"Give me more details. Where'd you hear this rumor?" AJ asked.

"You are not denying this."

"I am. We have not found any artifact of any value that we can determine."

"So, you *have* found an artifact?"

"How private is this conversation?" AJ asked. "How can I trust that you won't sell the information I have?"

"An intriguing answer," Mads said. "Are you looking to sell information?"

"No," AJ said, his face flushing red in anger. "You know, forget it. Nothing here that infringes on our contract, Mads. I've got better things to do. Goodbye."

"Hold on, Albert Jenkins," Mads said. "Are you asking for confidentiality? A secret to be kept, perhaps?"

"Can you keep a secret?"

"Yes."

"Will you?"

"Will you trust me if I say yes?" Mads asked.

"When we had that run-in with the Cheell last year, you looked the other way for profit," AJ said. "I'm not sure I *can* trust you."

"You would punish me for helping you. I find that amusing," Mads said. "I am a better partner than an enemy. You should decide which you would be."

"We found the very well-preserved body of who we think to be one of the Poecile daughters," AJ said. "Her body was preserved in a suspension chamber of some sort."

"How well preserved?" Mads asked. "Were there any data drives on this body?"

"For right now, that's all I have," AJ said.

"If you find information on this body, please allow me to auction it," Mads said. "There is much money surrounding the failure of the Poecile family. If sabotage of *Poecile Aerie* could be proven, there would be significant shifts of power at the highest levels of Pertaf government."

"Can you keep that secret?"

"I will keep your secret, Albert Jenkins," Mads said. "Plan to act on it soon, though. Secrets have a way of revealing themselves. Once they are known, there is little residual value."

"Good chat," AJ said, nodding at Beverly, who closed communications.

"Do you think it was wise to tell her about Faramor?" Beverly asked.

"She knew something," AJ said. "I only gave her a small amount of the truth. I needed to discover how much she really knows."

"And you believe she does not know Faramor is alive?"

"Doesn't seem like it," AJ said. "Besides, this isn't the biggest problem we have. Could you fire off a message to Queenie and let him know we've got a project coming up in twenty-three days or so?"

"Is *project* a euphemism for dangerous task?" Beverly asked.

"Yes," AJ said. "If I know Queenie, he's not going to want to miss out on the action."

"Do you want to provide him with any details?"

"Nah, he doesn't know Ruiz or Frenchy," AJ said. "Besides, he's not a big-picture guy."

"And you think he'll drop everything and come back to Xandarj?"

"I do. Is there any way to send that expedited?" AJ asked.

"Of course," Beverly said. "Both Halfnium and Xandarj are Galactic Empire systems and are therefore connected to the Tok communication infrastructure. Such a short message will cost only a hundred credits and arrive within the hour. Should I send it now?"

"Yup," AJ said. "Jayne still doing okay?"

"Very well, in fact," Beverly said. "Two of the highest-ranking DAS board members interrupted their own days to make in-person apologies. A public display of this nature has only happened one other time in DAS history."

AJ glanced at the communication panel on the shuttle's dash. A low-priority message from Lisa requested that he moor near *Big Max's* aft elevator so supplies could be offloaded.

"Lisa, how soon are we looking to take off after the Object 7 cluster?" he asked.

"I thought that was probably you on approach," Lisa said. "Darnell and I are on board working on a small atmospheric processor issue. We'll have it fixed in twenty minutes. Can you manage bringing the groceries to the galley on your own?"

"Yes, do you need help?"

"Nah, Petey's giving good directions. Did you have a nice chat with Jayne?"

"I did. I also had a weird conversation with Mads about a rumor she heard," AJ said.

"A rumor about what?"

"Probably better to have that conversation in person."

"I see," Lisa said. "Can you remember not to freeze the banana-looking things this time? Those are proteins that taste a lot like pork – that is unless you freeze them. If frozen, they end up tasting like mush."

"Is that what we've been having for breakfast?" AJ asked.

"You have an issue with breakfast?" Lisa asked.

"Quit while you're ahead," Darnell cut in, chuckling.

"No, of course not," AJ said, backpedaling. "I was just thinking I liked that protein and maybe we should keep freezing them."

"You're a bad liar, AJ," Lisa said. "I had to throw the rest out last time. They were inedible."

AJ settled the shuttle onto the side of *Big Max*. The mooring points he'd installed allowed for an easy connection between the shuttle and the larger ship and while it didn't functionally change how *Big Max* sailed, the engineer in AJ didn't like adding mass to one side of the centerline without adding it to the other.

Each trip out to the debris field had brought new stresses on *Big Max* to the forefront. In addition to manufacturing the thruster/stabilizer, they found no shortage of aging parts that needed replacing. Invoking his junker skills, AJ salvaged almost two-thirds of the parts from other, non-functional EAH vessels. That, however, still left them with a sizeable manufacturing bill for new parts. Before unloading the groceries to the galley, AJ set the newly manufactured parts into the engine room for later installation.

To his surprise, when he arrived at the galley, he discovered Farah sitting at the long, stainless steel table, quietly reading on a thin, electric tablet.

"What in the hell?" he asked, trying to mask his startle reflex.

"That is an unfamiliar reference," Farah said, blinking owlishly, her head swiveling to orient on him as was common with Pertaf.

"Does Lisa know you're here?" AJ asked, depressing a button to lift the stack of crates he'd set into what amounted to a dumbwaiter below the galley.

"Lisa Jackson asked me to remain in the galley while she and Darnell Jackson completed their work," Farah said. "Have I done this incorrectly?"

"No," AJ said, recovering. "Why don't you make yourself useful and unpack these while I get the next load?"

"I would like to be useful," she said.

"You better figure out a good explanation as to where you've been hiding the last couple of weeks," AJ said over his shoulder as he sent the dumbwaiter back down. "Before that, though, you stay up here and I'll load from below, okay?"

"I do not know why you need an explanation for my absence. I was moving through my grandfather's vessel," Farah said. "But I will help you unload these supplies. It is a reasonable trade for my consumption."

AJ bit back irritation at her defensiveness and set his mind to unloading the shuttle. On his last load, he ran into Lisa and Darnell, who were enjoying some joke between them as they exited the third 'tween deck.

"Get it all fixed up?" AJ asked.

"I guess," Darnell said. "According to Petey, the unit wasn't likely to cause much trouble, but he felt the routine maintenance was important since it hadn't been done in a century or so. We'll breathe better. A fluid filter was blacked out with gunk."

"Maintenance on old equipment is never a bad idea," AJ said.

"You found our visitor in the galley?" Lisa asked.

"What's she doing here?" AJ asked.

"I figured we'd wait until you got back to ask her. I think she wants to talk with us."

"This should be good," AJ said. "You should know, Mads knows something is going on over here. She said she'd heard a rumor about us finding some artifact. I ended up telling her we found Farah's body."

"You what?" Lisa asked. "Are you seriously expecting Mads to keep that to herself? I bet she's auctioning that to the highest bidder right now."

"She knew something," AJ said. "I had to find out how much."

"I hope that doesn't bite us," Lisa said.

"Me too, although I led her to believe that Farah wasn't still alive," AJ said. "Mads wants us to look for any data devices that might have been with her. She says there's still interest back on Pertaf about what happened to *Poecile Aerie*. She thinks she can sell whatever we find for good money."

"Nothing good about screwing with this girl's life," Lisa said.

"I don't disagree," AJ said.

The small group exited the elevator together and walked down the wide hallway, which, due to Lisa's theme for the day, looked a lot like an alpine forest. Stopping about halfway down, they descended through a hatch, which led into the galley. When they entered, they found Farah seated at the galley table, which now held the bulk of the supplies AJ had sent up the dumb waiter.

"So much for helping unpack," AJ grumped, lifting an eyebrow at Farah.

His slight wasn't lost on the younger Pertaf. "I was not of a position to learn household chores," she said. "I am unfamiliar with how to accomplish the requested task."

AJ blinked, unsure whether he'd actually heard what he'd thought. Just as he was about to answer, Lisa stepped in. "It's not that difficult," she said. "You can help me this time. Generally, the idea is that frozen things go in the freezer, cold things require refrigeration, dry things go in the cupboards and so on."

"I don't recognize most of the items beyond the fruits," Farah said, looking balefully at Lisa.

"That's fine, dear. Maybe we can work on cooking lessons as well," Lisa said, handing her a frozen item. "I bet you can tell where that goes."

Farah nodded and managed to open the freezer on her first try. Knowing better than to get between Lisa and the cupboards, AJ and Darnell picked non-food items from the crates and distributed them to various pantries. In short order, the crates were emptied and stowed. Darnell had started on dinner, much to Farah's continued interest.

"Lisa said you had something you wanted to talk to us about," AJ said when the four of them were finally seated around the table with plates full of a savory pasta dish that resembled spaghetti.

"I do," she said, setting an odd-looking utensil next to her plate. "Perhaps we should eat our meal first."

AJ nodded and dug in. As busy as they'd been, regular meals were uncommon.

"What do you think of the pasta, dear?" Lisa asked, glancing at Farah. "Do Pertaf have something similar?"

"I am not certain," Farah said, pushing a forkful of pasta into her beak-like mouth. "Is it a grain-based carbohydrate of some sort?"

"Ours is," Lisa said. "I modified yours since Pertaf prefers higher protein intake."

"That was quite thoughtful," Farah said.

A message marked *urgent* showed up on the table next to AJ's plate. While the image looked very real, like someone had etched it onto the table, AJ knew it was simply Beverly being cute. The message came from Mads Bazer, which grabbed his attention and caused him to instinctively tap the header.

"Message?" Darnell asked, recognizing AJ's gestures.

"Mads Bazer," AJ said. "Marked urgent."

AJ bit his lip as he read the message and then glanced uncomfortably at his pistol, which sat on the countertop a few yards away. When he started to get up, Farah interrupted him. "Hold on, AJ," she said. "Tell us what she said."

"I think you know what she said."

"I suppose I do," Farah said. "And I really do dislike this next part. You've all been so kind and accommodating."

"What'd the message say, AJ?" Lisa asked.

"There was no missing Poecile heir," AJ said. "It was a story made up by the Pertaf investigators back in the day. They were trying to flush out saboteurs aboard *Poecile Aerie* at the time."

"Please sit, Albert Jenkins," Farah said, holding two sophisticated-looking pistols, one in each hand. "I assure you, this weapon will pierce your armored vac-suit. I would prefer not to use it."

TWENTY-TWO

VALUE OF FRIENDS

"That is *such* a relief," Lisa said, sighing. "I can't believe you were right the entire time, AJ."

AJ held his hands high and shrugged as Farah gave him a confused look. "Is my translator working poorly?" she asked, daring only a slight glance in Lisa's direction. "Do you want to be captured?"

"Oh, no, dear. That's not it at all. It's just that you've been such a mystery and I'll admit, I was so invested in the idea that you were a long-lost orphan with a chance to be reunited with her people. It's a lovely story," Lisa said.

A small burp escaped Farah's beak and she turned to Lisa, weapons following her gaze. "What have you done, Lisa Jackson?"

"Nothing permanent," Lisa said, holding up her hands. "Honestly, I couldn't figure out what AJ was all fired up about – something about a little string that got moved or something? But you gave yourself away with the other bounty hunters you brought aboard *Poecile Aerie*. I'm guessing you didn't see those little cameras we've been installing all over the ship. It was a brilliant, long play on your part. You knew Mads had made a deal with us for rights to this junk heap and that it would only be a matter of time before we all came out to claim whatever we could. You snuck onto the ship, probably from the far end where we couldn't monitor, and pretended you'd been in stasis on *Poecile Aerie* since it was destroyed. You made sure we'd end up *finding* you. After gaining our trust with your sob story, you had plenty of time to gather help so when the time was right, you'd grab us."

Farah's arms drooped. "I'll ... I'll ...," She struggled to lift her arms, and then slumped forward, her face falling into her pasta.

"I'm sure glad your sedative worked," AJ said. "I was starting to regret leaving my pistol on the counter."

"That sold it," Lisa said. "It made her think she was safe."

"What do you want to do with her?" Darnell said, taking Farah's weapons. "And what are we going to do about her friends roaming around *Poecile Aerie?*"

"It's kind of a problem," AJ said. "They've invaded our space and we don't have a great way of defending it while we're gone."

"So, we don't," Darnell said.

"I don't follow."

"Look, we've no reason to set foot back on *Poecile Aerie* while we're finishing this contract for the consortium. I say we drop Farah in the garage, pull the big fuse from the generator and take off," Darnell said.

"Do we have any idea how many friends she brought along?" AJ asked, looking at Lisa.

"Three," Lisa said. "They're well-armed. That's one of the reasons Darnell and I weren't interested in working on the station."

"Do you have a read on where they're at?" AJ asked.

"Let me check," Lisa said, retrieving a tablet. After several minutes she finally answered. "I can't find them."

"I don't like even odds," AJ said. "Especially since we don't know where they are."

"We know where they're not," Darnell said, pulling his pistol and standing. "BB, how well can you see the interior of *Big Max?*"

Greybeard barked, setting his paws on AJ's legs. He didn't need

Beverly's answer to know things were turning south. "Two just entered the aft airlock and are on the way up. The third is outside our sensors," Beverly said.

"Big D, take Lisa and Farah back to your quarters and lock it down," AJ said. "I've got this."

"No way, that's three against one," Darnell said.

"I love you, buddy, but you've got a total of twenty minutes of live fire experience," AJ said. "I got this. Trust me. Besides, I'm taking Greybeard."

"Where?"

AJ snatched his pistol from the counter. It was two short steps to the dumbwaiter cabinet. He jumped up and squeezed inside – just barely. "Dammit, no room for you, Greybeard," AJ said. "You gotta go with Big D."

Not having time to see what Greybeard would do, AJ slapped the dumbwaiter control, his stomach dropping out as it fell much quicker than expected. Dropping thirty feet, the tiny elevator stopped, throwing him off balance and causing him to tumble out onto the floor of the supply room. Scrambling to keep from making excessive noise, AJ steadied a stack of boxes he'd partially knocked over, praying that he hadn't been heard.

Having spent the better part of the last month working on *Big Max*, he'd become familiar with its maintenance corridors and access hatches. "BB, show me where they are," he said, wiggling back behind a pipe chase and pulling himself upward.

Unsurprisingly, the two Pertaf who'd already entered *Big Max* through the aft hatch had been joined by a third in the main corridor. They had started a quiet, room-by-room search. From their movements, AJ deduced they were well trained or possibly that all Pertaf moved with efficiency. Regardless, he needed to improve his odds.

He smiled to himself as he pulled up between two of the sleeping quarters. The bunk rooms were separated by a wide gap where long runs of filtration tubes terminated. With no need for efficiency, such pockets of unused space were common throughout the vessel. With a view from Beverly, he watched as one of Farah's crew worked her way into the room directly adjacent to where he hid.

AJ held his breath as the female Pertaf passed within inches of him. He had no move until he removed the small panel that would otherwise block his weapon. When the woman was finished and turned to climb up out of the room, AJ punched out the grill, flinging it across the hallway space. The Pertaf's response was instantaneous. She spun toward the noise and sprayed automatic fire across the hall in an arc that started with the grill and ended at the entry where AJ's face had been only seconds before.

"They're hidden in the walls!" she called loudly, thinking AJ had fled.

He hadn't. Instead, he moved to another grill and punched it out with the nose of his pistol. He fired his blaster, catching the woman first in the abdomen, then her shoulder, and finally three shots in the wall next to her head.

The Pertaf woman sagged against the wall but fired back, her aim finding him with automatic fire. Recognizing the danger, AJ moved for cover but the close quarters slowed him. Energy bolts found his side just as he slid out of view. Knowing he had little time, he allowed gravity to pull him into a tangle of tubing. He cursed as he felt fittings snap under his weight, but ignored the damage he was causing and wriggled through until he fell beneath the crew quarters.

"How bad, BB?" AJ asked, tentatively feeling his side.

His back against the 'tween deck's smooth floor, AJ pushed with his boots, sliding his body slowly through the ship. With limited room for movement, he knew he'd be in a pinch if one of the invaders found him.

"You've a significant injury in your side," Beverly said.

"Did I at least disable that Pertaf merc?" he asked.

"Her compatriots are tending to her," she said. "She has lost consciousness."

AJ felt the wave of an explosive charge before he heard it. While there was no shrapnel, he knew the blast was close. And though he didn't see the action, he instinctively knew one of the attackers had blown a hole in the side of a bunk room to give chase. "Of course, they brought breaching charges," AJ grumbled.

"A Pertaf has entered the 'tween space," Beverly said. "It is imperative that we move quickly."

"Not enough time," AJ said, painfully struggling to turn. If one advantage, it was that his pursuer didn't have any more room to move than he did.

"You are trapped, human," a male Pertaf called. "I see the blood trail. There is no reason for you to die today."

"If you poke your beak down here, I'll put a hole in it," AJ called back, trying to slide backward.

"I have lowered a video sensor," the Pertaf answered. "I am not required to expose myself to acquire deadly aim. Your death is not desired, but it is acceptable for fulfillment of the bounty."

AJ located the arm of the second Pertaf and the thin-barreled pistol he was holding. Both had been lowered into the space beneath the crew quarters. The gun looked to be aiming directly at him. He considered trying to shoot the pistol out of the Pertaf's hand but figured it would only draw fire and he was a considerably larger target.

"You guys move like a team," AJ said. "Ex-military?"

"I see you trying to escape," the Pertaf answered. "It will not work. Yes, we had special training before resigning from service. You have done well to disable Kenistra. She is very quick."

A gray object, moving quickly between the decks drew AJ's attention. "Darn it, Greybeard!" AJ grumped as the Pertaf soldier's gun turned to address the new danger. AJ swung his pistol up and fired with abandon at his enemy. His heart raced as the pistol swiveled back in his direction. Deciding to trust Greybeard's tenacity, AJ made no effort to find cover in the cramped space but instead continued to lay down fire.

Turned out, AJ's distraction was all that was required. Greybeard raced through the 'tween deck and launched himself into AJ's line of

fire. "Holy crap!" AJ exclaimed, barely able to redirect his fire so it
didn't hit the angry dog.

With many shots sent downfield, the Pertaf's aim was horrible,
even though one of the bolts embedded itself into AJ's shoulder. The
bad news was that the pain was intense, causing AJ to howl in agony.
The good news was that at least the armor on his shoulder pads had
been doubled.

Having lived through combat, AJ knew that momentum in a
battle was critical. Clamping down on the pain, he struggled to move
forward, hoping for a chance to help Greybeard engage the soldier. A
second howl of pain filled the space. At first, AJ wasn't sure if it was
from Greybeard or the Pertaf. Furious growling, the sounds of snapping bone, and the clattering of the soldier's pistol on the deck told
him what he needed to know. One more down, one to go.

New gunfire drew yelps from Greybeard, who dropped to the
deck, unmoving. AJ lurched forward and grabbed the loose skin of his
canine friend's neck and pulled him out of the shooter's line of sight.
A familiar metallic taste filled his mouth, as did a fresh surge of
energy. He knew Beverly had given him an adrenaline boost that
would be short-lived and come with a price.

Greybeard struggled against his grasp, trying to regain consciousness. "BB, tell Seamus to keep him calm. I'll get us out of here."

The dog calmed as AJ slipped his legs over a ledge and pulled
both him and Greybeard behind cover. "Seamus reports that Greybeard has extensive damage along his spine," Beverly said. "It would
be best not to move them further."

Carefully, AJ slid Greybeard into a small alcove and took stock of
his injuries. "Am I good to move?" he asked.

"Yes. I'm able to isolate your pain for now," she said. "There will
be a price for you and Greybeard."

"Can you see the Pertaf?"

"All three are still conscious, but only one appears to be mobile
enough for continued aggression," she said.

"I get that," AJ said, limping over to the hatch that would give him access to the aft elevator. "I'm gonna need your help on this next one. Are you up for it?"

"Of course, AJ," Beverly answered, appearing next to him in drab olive with a camouflage-patterned headband. Her face was grim with determination, but the overall effect caused him to chuckle. She didn't comment, other than to shake her head in irritation.

AJ crouched as the elevator pushed up toward the top deck. Aiming his weapon, he glanced at the virtual display of the remaining Pertaf, creeping up the ladder that would give him access to the same passageway AJ had entered.

"I've got you pinned down," AJ called. "Toss your weapon onto the deck. This doesn't have to go badly."

"Did you forget about the camera on the end of our weapons, human?" the Pertaf asked, poking his pistol up over the lip of the hatch.

"Now, Beverly," AJ said.

Suddenly, the projectors that had been displaying a serene alpine scene on the walls started strobing images of AJ and Greybeard rushing at the hatch from all directions. Synchronizing the strobe, Beverly counteracted the effect for AJ, replacing the chaos with the original scene so he was no longer affected by the visual distraction.

The impact on the Pertaf, however, was considerable. The bounty hunter squawked in confusion, allowing AJ to rush forward and kick the pistol from his hands. The weapon skittered across the deck and Beverly cut the strobe effect. "Nice and slow, bird boy," AJ said, keeping far enough back from the hatch so the Pertaf's friends, should they be close, wouldn't have an easy shot.

"How did you do that?" the soldier asked, slowly crawling out of the crew space and kneeling on the deck.

AJ ignored the question and grabbed the plastic loops from the Pertaf's belt, pulling the feathered arms behind his back and tightened the restraints in place. "Damn but your guns hurt like a mother. Appreciate you bringing cuffs, though," AJ said, sitting heavily next to him on the deck. "How beat up is your team?"

"They will live," he said, dispirited. "Is Treta dead?"

AJ stared at him for a moment, the adrenaline leeching from his system. His shoulders sagged as the physical tole of his injuries started to catch up to him. "If you mean Faramor, I don't think so," AJ said. "Big D, Are you guys okay? I've got a couple of bogies trapped in crew quarters."

"AJ, you're kind of a badass, did you know that?" Lisa answered. "We're fine, but it looks like you could use some help."

"I wouldn't turn it down," AJ said. "Farah's ex-military, so don't give her any latitude."

"We'll be right up," Darnell said.

"Thanks, Big D," AJ said and turned to the captured merc. "Tell your team to put their weapons down. If you make me chase them, I'm not going to be gentle. You copy?"

"What do you intend to do with us now that we're captured? Why would you not simply dispatch us?" he asked.

For a moment, old ghosts came back to bother AJ's conscience. Rationally, he knew he'd always acted with honor as a soldier, but it didn't change the weight he would forever carry. "Because I don't have to," he said simply.

The two soldiers from vastly different backgrounds locked eyes for just a moment as understanding passed between them. "You have my respect," the Pertaf finally answered. He then called out to his team. "Nork, Kenistra, we will surrender with dignity. We are bested and the humans will not cause further injury."

Settling Farah – or Tetra, as her team called her – next to the Pertaf AJ had captured, Darnell and Lisa set about securing Nork and Kenistra.

"Well, that was exciting," Darnell said, joining Lisa and AJ who were in the recreation room opposite the galley, the space having been converted to a temporary brig.

"Greybeard okay?" AJ asked.

"He's resting on your bed," Darnell said. "Petey says he'll be down for better than a week. How are you doing?"

"BB says three days, minimum," AJ said. "I might be up for capturing old wrecks though."

"Not a chance," Lisa said. "Besides, what are we doing with those guys? We can't keep them forever."

"I had a thought about that," AJ said. "What are the odds, given their line of work, that they haven't pissed off local authorities somewhere?"

"What are you thinking?" Lisa asked.

"I'll tell you in a minute," AJ said. "BB, see if Mads Bazer is up for a call."

"You should rest, AJ," Beverly said, appearing in a 1960's era white nurse's dress.

"Soon," AJ said, straightening in front of the virtual video screen that popped up in front of him.

"Last time we talked, you were annoying," Mads said, glaring at the screen. "Are you prepared to act as a good partner should?"

"We're not partners, Mads," AJ said. "But I might have a piece of business for you."

Mads sighed. "How generous."

"Look, your message about Faramor Poecile really helped me. I'd like to repay the favor," AJ said. "I'm sending you some bio-data and pictures on a Pertaf ex-military team. They came out to recover a bounty on us and they might have trouble of their own out there somewhere. If they're wanted, I'd make it worth your while."

"Bounties are bad business," Mads said, tipping her head back as she typed at an unseen keyboard. For several minutes she typed, gestured, sighed, and generally made it known that she was being inconvenienced. Finally, she looked up. "Explain *worth my while.*"

"Fifty-fifty cut," AJ said. "We have them trussed up like pigs at a roast. You just need to come pick 'em up."

"Not interested," she said. "Unsavory business."

"So you've said," AJ said. "Do you have a counter proposal?"

"I'll give you a thousand credits for the lot of them," she said.

"Mads," AJ said, disapprovingly. "You can do better than that."

"You've irritated me," she said, pouting her lips.

"Tell you what, you get someone out here in the next two hours and I'll give 'em to you for twenty percent of whatever their bounty is," AJ said.

"Two thousand," Mads countered. "You owe me for the free information I provided."

"Defeats the idea that it was free, wouldn't you say?" AJ said.

"Nothing is ever free with me, Albert Jenkins. You will accept two thousand," she said, grinning lopsidedly. "I will send a transport to your location."

"Always good doing business with you, Mads," AJ said, tapping the virtual button that closed comms.

"We are worth considerably more than two thousand credits, human," Kenistra said, glowering at him from where she sat.

"I suppose," AJ said.

"Why would you make such a poor deal?" Nork asked, still nursing his splinted arm. Greybeard had broken it with his vicious bite. "We are worth at least forty thousand credits."

"Believe it or not, having that grumpy old Xandarj pick up the phone whenever I call is worth more than that."

"What's a phone?"

TWENTY-THREE
STOWAWAY

"What do you bet they have a vessel on the other side of *Poecile Aerie?*" AJ said, standing next to the hatch of the unused crew quarters they'd converted to a temporary brig. Having turned up the gravity next to the ladder from near .0gs to 3.0gs, it wouldn't be impossible for their captives to escape but it was unlikely. Even so, Greybeard lay next to the hatch, his muzzle resting on his front legs, happy to keep watch.

"I can't get over being disappointed that Farah's not actually the last remaining heir," Lisa said. "And I don't get how Beverly missed it."

"That part isn't much of a mystery," Beverly said, appearing between them. "This group was successful at making minor modifications to historic Pertaf records. It also helped that Faramor is, in fact, a blood relation to the original Poecile family."

"That makes sense," Lisa said, "I wasn't picking at you as much as I was curious."

"Farah, I'll make you a deal," AJ called down. "Tell me where your ship is and I'll notify whoever you want that they can come get it for a small storage and towing fee."

"Why would you do that?" she asked.

"We're not thieves," AJ said. "I'll even send your personal effects along with Mads, assuming they're not weapons."

"Human fingers can't effectively use Pertaf weapons," Farah said.

"That's the deal," AJ said. "We'll likely find it anyway, why waste our time? I'll just add the hourly to your fees."

"Humans are strange," Farah said. "It is lashed just forward of the ruined engines on the portside. There is a security code."

"Big D, want to run us over?" AJ asked. "We have a few hours before Mads arrives. We can get their stuff packed up and send it along with them."

"Can do," Darnell answered. "Tell me you're working on a plan to end all this bounty nonsense."

"I'm working on a plan," AJ said. "Just waiting for Lefty and the boys to arrive."

"I sure hope so, because this is getting old," Darnell grumped, walking toward the bridge.

"Did you just say that flying around in alien space – in a spaceship that can damn near lift a battleship, by the way – is getting old?" AJ called after him.

"You know what I mean," Darnell said, disappearing around the corner.

Big Max lurched as Darnell unmoored and moved to the opposite side of *Poecile Aerie*. Following the line of the massive vessel, he moved aft until he reached the point where the ship's engines were.

"I see their ship," Darnell called back. "Do you want me to try using a grapple and pull it out?"

"Alright, Farah, here's the deal," AJ said. "If you set booby traps or anything of the like, now's the time to fess up. If one of us gets so much as a hangnail retrieving that ship, I'll space the lot of you, no questions asked."

"What of your deal with the angry Xandarj?" Farah asked.

"To the best of my knowledge, she didn't specify dead or alive –

and I didn't ask," AJ said. "Trust me when I say, we take the safety of our family seriously. Last chance, here."

Farah looked at the other female Pertaf and AJ noticed a slight nod, causing Farah's eyes to widen, if only momentarily. "There might be a trap," she said. "I will tell you of it, but you will release me in exchange."

"Not happening," AJ said. "We'll just blow the vessel. No skin off my back. It's your stuff in there. If you don't care that everything gets blown up, I sure as heck don't."

"How do we know you will keep your word and return our possessions?" Kenistra asked.

"Everything but ordnance," AJ said.

"Chits?" she asked.

"I'm not a thief," AJ said. "Your money is your own."

"We will see. The code you have is incorrect." She provided a new one.

"What would that other code have done?" AJ asked.

"A small charge designed to fully incapacitate the first person seeking entry," she said.

"Are there other surprises aboard?" AJ asked.

"Not if you utilize the code I provided.

"Fair enough," he said. "Appreciate the cooperation. Farah, go ahead and climb out of there. I'm taking you with me."

"You're what?" she asked.

"Not a tough concept," AJ said, pulling his pistol out and pointing it into the hatch, but not specifically aiming it. "BB, give Farah a little help with the gravity well on that ladder so she can join us. The rest of you, don't even move. I'll pop her first and then I'll do a bit of *spray and pray* while we turn the gravity back up. You'll never get out."

"This is unnecessarily complex," Kenistra said. "You have the code."

"And I'll be happy to punch it in," AJ said. "I'm just going to make sure Farah is between me and that door. Lisa, do you mind keeping an eye on our guests with Greybeard's help?"

"I can do that," Lisa said.

Kenistra and Farah exchanged meaningful looks but said nothing as Farah climbed the ladder and allowed herself to be led to the aft airlock.

"Now would be a good time to tell me if you have other compatriots hiding back here," AJ said, pushing Farah to the airlock after checking her mask fit.

"You've made it clear you intend to sacrifice me if there is trouble," she said. "There are no more of us."

"You might think about fessing up to whatever caused the look that passed between you and Kenistra," AJ said. "This isn't my first rodeo."

"I don't understand *Rodeo*," she said.

AJ pushed her out into space and allowed her to flail as she drifted away from *Big Max*. "I don't imagine you need to, either," AJ said, sitting on the edge of the airlock so his feet hung over. "It feels like you still think you've got the upper hand. You underestimate me. See, back when I was a young man, I got sent to war. It was ugly – like war should be. The enemy did bad things to us and we responded in kind. I've seen things that can't be unseen. I've done things I wish I hadn't needed to do."

"Why are you telling me this?" she asked, slowly tumbling away from *Big Max*.

"I'm still that young man I was fifty years ago," he said. "Older, arguably wiser, but generally the same person. I take threats to my country, my family, and myself seriously. I don't have trouble getting ugly if that's what it takes. I have a sense that you're not being entirely truthful with me and I want you to know who you're dealing with."

"Our pilot is still aboard. He knows we've been captured," she said. "He probably has our two mega-joule laser weapon aimed at you right now."

AJ jumped back and closed the airlock. Quickly calculating, he imagined that such a weapon, with short highly concentrated bursts, could penetrate *Big Max's* thick skin, but would not be overly effective without a lot of luck.

"I guess we'll space your friends then," AJ said over comms. "Good luck on getting picked up before your O2 runs out."

"Wait," Farah said. "I'll get him to stand down. I was just trying to be honest."

"He exits the ship and turns himself in – no weapons," AJ said. "You seriously brought five people to take us down?"

"You have a considerable bounty," she said. "We preferred to be prepared and split a large payout instead of failing and receiving nothing."

"Sorry to disappoint you," AJ said. "Talk to your pilot now."

"He is coming," Farah said.

"Fine." AJ waited and, sure enough, a few minutes later, a slim male figure sailed out of *Poecile Aerie's* ruined engine bays and landed gently against the hull of *Big Max*, not bothering to help Farah, who was still tumbling away.

"I'm right behind you," Darnell said, surprising AJ. "I'll take him to the brig so he can join his friends."

After transferring the prisoner, AJ pushed away from *Big Max* and used the thruster board to intercept Farah. Together, they glided to a ship hidden in one of *Poecile Aerie's* cavernous breaches.

"Is two mega joules legal in most systems?" AJ asked, helping Farah through the door.

"No, but they're not that hard to disguise," Farah said. "We've been boarded several times but since we keep the important parts packed in crates, it's considered cargo."

"How much is it going to jam you guys up to be turned in?" AJ asked, working to clear the ship while not losing control of Farah.

"That's a good question," Farah said. "I'll probably end up under house arrest for a year and have fines to pay. Kenistra and Nork aren't part of my normal crew. They are mercenaries and they'll have more trouble. Are you going to file a complaint with Dralli or Illiden?"

"Probably not," AJ said. "We prefer to work things out on our own and we just need you out of our hair for a few months."

"Perhaps on a different day, we would not be enemies," Farah said.

"Do you want to show me your personal items?" AJ asked.

"There are five bags in the cargo hold," she said.

"That's helpful."

"On this kind of mission, there is an advantage in being able to quickly adjust," she said.

AJ TOSSED the last of the five Pertaf packs into Mads Bazer's shuttle. Aside from a few fancy blinking lights and no obvious wheels, the craft could have passed for a panel van back on Earth. Out of an abundance of caution, he'd searched each pack, finding a variety of weapons as well as credit chits. True to his word, he kept the weapons and returned the chits, although he suspected Mads Bazer wouldn't have been quite as generous.

"We're agreed. You'll keep these guys locked away until I give the word and then, if Farah does her job, you'll let her go, right?" AJ asked.

"I don't like releasing her, but I will keep my word," Mads answered. "I hope your plans work as you expect. You are risking much."

"I don't disagree," AJ said. "I wish it could be another way. Sorry, it's irritating."

"Even when you are annoying, you bring me good fortune, Albert Jenkins," Mads said, gesturing to a couple of thugs she'd brought along to load the prisoners. "What will you do with their vessel?"

Instead of attempting to fly the bounty hunter's vessel back, AJ and Darnell had used *Big Max* to pull it from its hiding place and drop it in a pile close to the garage.

"Looking for ownership records right now," AJ said. "I'll reach out to whoever owns it and let them know what they need to do to get it out of impound."

"That is an interesting approach," she said. "I'd have thought you would remove the valuable parts and sell them."

"Nope. The general idea is to expend minimum labor to make maximum profit," AJ said.

"Your contract with Xandarj Shipping Consortium seems quite different," she said.

"Ah, different idea entirely," AJ said. "We're getting paid to pick up and store junk. What do you bet someone will decide we've got something of value sitting out here once I post pictures of all the junk we've grabbed? First rule of junking is, you can always use more junk."

"I thought the first rule was, nothing's free," Lisa said.

AJ shrugged. "Maybe the rules don't have a specific order."

"Or maybe, you're full of it."

Darnell chuckled. "She's got you there."

"We'll talk at a future point." Mads Bazer turned and trundled off to climb into the ratty old shuttle.

"What now?" Darnell asked.

"We'll do a quick search of their ship and then I say we head back out and finish our job," AJ said. "I'd hate to get behind on our contract."

"You're unphased by all this, aren't you," Lisa said. "You've been shot and don't tell me that arm doesn't hurt. You *need* to take a couple of days off and let Beverly get you healed back up."

"No rest for the wicked," AJ said. "Besides, I want to have all this done before Lefty and Queenie arrive."

"And what if more bounty hunters show up?" Lisa asked.

"We deal with them," AJ said. "Of course, it'll be a lot easier if we snag that laser. We'll have to decide if we want to put it on *Poecile Aerie* or *Big Max*. They both produce more than enough excess power."

"We don't have a weapon on *Big Max* that we can aim," Darnell said. "It'd be handy to fly in one direction and shoot in another."

"We're also spending a lot of time on *Big Max,*" Lisa said. "That's got my vote, too."

"I'll see what I need to do," AJ said. "Maybe you two could figure out what our next retrieval looks like. Maybe we could get four objects this time, although I'm going to need a pilot to help me when I'm out retrieving those smaller objects."

"I'll be your pilot," Lisa said.

"I suppose I'd best get started then," AJ said. "We've got a long couple of weeks ahead of us."

TWENTY-FOUR

WHAT AILS YOU

"So, you finished that big contract with the shippers?" Jayne asked, pulling the plate of chocolate cake toward her side of the small table so she could take another bite.

"We did. Sorry I couldn't make it last weekend, figured it'd be better to get that cleared off our schedule," AJ said. "How is it that a little café inside of DAS has chocolate cake?"

"Actually, it's one of my contributions and it's a big hit," Jayne said, smiling broadly. "I had to get help from an interesting Tok girl."

"The raccoon-looking aliens?" AJ asked.

"The same. You probably remember how smart they are? Well, anyway, Gordatine – not her full name, mind you – she's an absolute genius with everything related to tech. It took us a little over an hour to get the texture right, but it's a pretty close match. Gordatine says it was easier because our ingredients are simple."

"That's interesting," AJ said, reaching across and taking another bite of the cake, this time assessing the flavor and texture more carefully. While it wasn't exactly right, it also wasn't far enough off that he'd have thought twice about it if she hadn't warned him. "Is that a good use of time, though?"

"At first, I struggled with that too," Jayne said. "But it's amazing how much you learn when you work on a task together, even one as simple as recreating chocolate cake."

"Did you at least work on ice cream?" AJ asked.

"Not yet," Jayne said, smiling. "I was talking with Lisa the other day. I can't believe that Pertaf woman was a bounty hunter. I guess I don't understand why they didn't try to take us earlier. It seemed like a long time for her to wait to spring a trap."

"The setup was her idea and her crew didn't initially come out," AJ said. "She contacted them after we brought her to Dralli Station that one time."

"That was a gutsy move on her part," Jayne said. "You could have done just about anything to her. I can't imagine taking that kind of risk for a payday."

"There's more poverty out here than we've been led to believe," AJ said. "I think Farah knew the risk and was willing to take a shot at the bounty because she really needed the money."

"And yet, with a few barrels of whiskey, you've created a thriving business," she said.

"For a lot of these species, they've become dependent on their governments and have lost track of how to fend for themselves," AJ said. "It's easy when you see big dollar signs that someone's offering for a specific service. It's a lot harder to imagine how to make money without someone footing the bill."

"That's an interesting thesis," Jayne said. "Would you mind discussing your thoughts with some of my DAS fellows at some point in the future? I bet they'd love to argue the nuances of what you're saying."

"I don't know, Doc," he said.

She placed her hand on AJ's arm. "No pressure, just think about it."

"We got word that Frenchy and Ruiz exited wormhole space earlier today," he said.

"Isn't that early?" Jayne asked.

"A few days early," AJ agreed. "They got into jump space more quickly than we'd been led to believe. If you ask me, Lefty told us the wrong date just in case someone was listening in."

"What is it they say about being paranoid?"

"Lefty would tell you it's paranoia that's kept him alive all these years," AJ said. "Is it possible to move up the date of their appointments?"

"To when?"

"Today?"

"Oh ... well ... of course," she said. "There's some planning to do. We're going to record the entire process and make a study of it. There's quite a lot of interest about the therapy here, which is helpful because it gives me access to some really smart people ... aliens ... well, whatever. When will they arrive?"

"Forty-five minutes if you give the go-ahead," AJ said. "They're already at *Poecile Aerie*. Blue Tork said he'd run out an get 'em in a fast shuttle if you gave the go-ahead."

"I feel like there's something you're not telling me," Jayne said.

"Kind of," AJ said, sending a quick message to Blue Tork.

"You don't want me to worry, so you're holding back," she said. "Lisa told me Queenie and Sharg will be here tomorrow. This is more than some sort of old-friends-getting-together thing. You're going to go after the people who have a bounty out on us, aren't you."

"You're not wrong, but I'd feel better if we had this conversation in a more private location," AJ said.

"I understand. Bounty hunters are just going to keep coming," she said. "You do know this therapy will take a few months to have full effect on Frenchy and Ruiz. They're not exactly in fighting shape."

"Don't count those old bastards out," AJ said. "Frenchy took a grenade fragment right to the gut and he's still kicking around. Ruiz got cancer from Agent Orange and sure he's had some tough days, but he's come through harder."

"That wasn't meant to be a commentary on their bravery," Jayne said, holding her hands up defensively. "I was there, remember?"

"Yeah, sorry, Doc," AJ said. "Defending my boys is kind of a knee-jerk reaction."

"I get it," Jayne said. "If they're close, we should walk over to the office so I can let the team know the schedule has moved up."

"I'm a little worried about a big group. They could be a mite bit skittish, meeting aliens and all."

"We've already dealt with that. We'll use the optic redirection projectors that will make them feel like they're walking through what looks like a college campus on spring break. They won't see anyone except for us," Jayne said.

"That was good thinking," AJ said.

"Since they're to be studied, it's important they don't interact with any of those performing the study," Jayne said.

"Except you," AJ said.

"I'm the one performing the procedures," Jayne said. "I'll be studied as well. The opportunity to observe western medicine in action has garnered more interest than the study of a therapy they consider to be somewhat trivial."

"It could be a trivial procedure, but I don't imagine the boys will see it that way," AJ said. "How about you head to the office and get people rolling? I'll meet the boys in Mads' loading bay. I just got word they've arrived. If that doesn't work, we could head to a bar. I'm sure they could both use a drink after their long ride."

"No, no," Jayne said. "I don't need them getting mixed up in a bar. I remember how that turned out last time."

"Give me twenty minutes?" AJ asked.

"I've already sent out an announcement that we're going early," Jayne said. "I'll meet you at the main DAS entrance. This is exciting, AJ. We're going to make history today."

When AJ exited the DAS main entry, he was joined by a pair of burly Xandarj men who wore a uniform marking them as employees of Red Fairs. It was Lisa who'd requested help from Red Fairs and AJ was grateful for her forward-thinking.

Time hadn't been easy on either man, but even from across the bay, AJ could see the pride and dignity with which they carried themselves. It was a big middle finger to both nature and man, neither of which had been able to take them out.

"Damn, you boys get uglier every year," AJ said when he was ten yards away. Frenchy quirked his head and focused on AJ, giving him a pinched glare.

"And you don't look a day over eighteen," Ruiz said, just before his breath was choked by a racking cough.

"Son of a gun, is that really you, Jenkins?" Frenchy asked.

AJ smiled and embraced the man, fighting to keep emotion from becoming overwhelming. He couldn't imagine why he hadn't found time to visit his old friends. "Yeah, it's me all right," AJ said, moving to hug Ruiz since he'd stopped coughing.

"Is it real?" Ruiz asked. "I see aliens all around, but that black fella, Jackson, he said he flew birds back in 'Nam. I seem to remember a fella like that."

"Black fella?" AJ asked, chuckling.

"Don't be an asshole," Ruiz said, slapping AJ's arm.

"Any second thoughts?" AJ asked, glancing at Lefty. Lefty shook his head slightly to indicate that he thought things were on track.

"Hell, I'd swallow a live cobra if it'd get rid of this cough," Ruiz said, working to keep the cough at bay.

"Yeah, wear this damn ostomy bag for a week and then ask me that question again," Frenchy said.

"I'm not sure if the ostomy issue will take more work to fix," AJ said. "I'm not sure if Doc knew about that or not."

"Won't know if we don't get moving," Frenchy said.

AJ led the group back to the DAS main entrance and though the two men had spent limited time around aliens, they did little gawking as they moved along.

"Pretty fancy digs," Ruiz said as they passed through the entrance which required AJ and Lefty to surrender their weapons.

"Why aren't they letting us in?" Frenchy asked, pushing on a door that was still locked.

"Someone is carrying a weapon," AJ said. "Lefty, any more donations to make?"

"Not me," Lefty said and then smiled as both older men pulled multiple pocket knives from hidden locations on their bodies.

"TSA doesn't catch the belt knives," Frenchy said. "They must have good scanners here."

Lefty tried the door, which opened for him this time. Even though the glass had appeared transparent, they were all surprised to find that Jayne stood just inside. Instead of her casual clothing, she wore a white doctor's jacket and had a stethoscope wrapped around her neck.

"Corporals LeBeau and Ruiz, I assume?" Jayne asked, tipping her head back.

"Reporting as ordered, ma'am," Ruiz said, pulling his hand up to a salute and then breaking down in a coughing fit.

"We'll see what we can do about that cough, Corporal," Jayne said, professionally. "Follow me."

When the two didn't move, Lefty prompted them. "You heard the major. Move out."

Frenchy smiled as he looked back at AJ. "Kind of overdoing it a bit, aren't you?"

AJ shrugged and returned the smile.

"Remove your clothing and put on these robes," Jayne said. "If you need help, someone will be in shortly. Don't be disturbed if that someone has extra body hair, as that's common for Xandarj."

"I'll need help," Frenchy said. "I can't move my left arm much higher than my chest."

"In light of your ostomy, we'll be moving you to an outpatient surgery suite once your initial therapy has concluded," Jayne said.

"Outpatient? Won't I need to at least spend the night?" he asked.

"The Galactic Empire has considerable advances in medical techniques," Jayne said. "The procedure to repair your intestine and bowel is relatively straightforward and should be complete within thirty minutes."

Frenchy blinked without saying anything and a single tear rolled down his cheek. He swallowed hard as he accepted the gown from her and entered the door she'd indicated. Ruiz, seeing Frenchy on the move, grabbed his robe and disappeared.

"How long will it take, Doc?"

"Twenty minutes each for therapy and I'll need another thirty minutes with Frenchy. There's a nice bench over there for you and Lefty." She pointed at a wooden park bench AJ hadn't noticed before. "A young Tok might come along and offer you drink service. Go easy on him, he's just curious."

"WHAT DO you suppose is taking so long?" Lefty asked, scanning the grassy courtyard suspiciously again. He and AJ had been sitting quietly for ninety minutes trading only a few passing observations as they waited for Frenchy and Ruiz to emerge from the small medical building.

"Ask me, I might have been more skeptical if they'd gotten done faster," AJ said. "Ruiz wasn't sounding too good and I guess I didn't know Frenchy was so busted up. Take as long as they need, I say."

"Yup," Lefty agreed and leaned against the bench, closing his eyes – at least partially. "Don't suppose anything we have to say about it will help much."

AJ nodded. It was one of the things he liked about being around men of his generation - talking to fill time wasn't required. Movement at the entrance to the short building caught his eye and he nudged Lefty's knee.

"I see it," Lefty said, slowly sitting forward. "Looks like Ruiz. Does he look different to you?"

AJ inspected the older man as he exited the building. "Kind of hard to tell."

"That's what I was thinking."

"Hey, boys," Ruiz said, walking over to meet them.

"How do you feel?" AJ asked, skeptically.

"Like a million bucks!" Ruiz drew in a big breath and blew it out. "I don't know the last time I could get a full breath. Does anyone feel like going for a run? Or a beer. The old lady made me stop drinking, but I could really use a beer."

AJ laughed. "Slow down there, bubba. We still haven't seen Frenchy."

"There he is," Lefty said, standing as Jayne and Frenchy exited the building together. "Seems like he's got a little more pep in his step."

"You got that right, brother," Ruiz said. "I used to run all the time when I was younger. Then the cancer came and I couldn't breathe. It's a horrible way to live."

"How'd it go, Frenchy?" AJ asked.

"I feel pretty good," he admitted, exchanging a concerned look with Jayne.

"You don't sound convincing," AJ said.

"Oh, no, they really did a job on me in there," he said, lifting his arms above his head. "I haven't been able to do that for years."

"Mr. LeBeau ...," Jayne started.

"Friends call me Frenchy," he interrupted.

Jayne nodded with a smile and continued. "Frenchy has expressed some concern regarding relearning to fully utilize the restrooms."

AJ looked over to Frenchy. "Stinky stuff goes in the bowl," AJ said. "Hasn't changed much since you were a kid."

"It has for me."

"Bubba, if that's your biggest concern in life, I promise we'll get you through it," AJ said, clapping the man on the back. "You were in there longer than we expected. Did everything else work out okay?"

Frenchy looked to Jayne. "Would you mind fillin' them in? I'm not real sure what all you did."

"Frenchy and Ruiz both suffered from several conditions that have been addressed in full," Jayne said. "An old injury to Frenchy's

abdomen required considerably more reconstruction than I'd anticipated. In my opinion, it is something of a medical mystery as to how
he is still alive."

"Old shit's just too stubborn to die," Ruiz said. "Spend ten minutes
with him and you know that."

"You were not in significantly better shape, Mr. Ruiz," Jayne said.
"Your lung function was at a critical level and you should have been
on supplemental oxygen."

"Oh, they gave me a tank. Told 'em I didn't need it," he said.

"That was very risky and likely the cause of much of the cardiac
damage we discovered," Jayne said.

"You sound just like my doctor in Mexico," Ruiz said.

"Sounds like a talented physician," Jayne replied. "Nonetheless,
the procedure for eliminating abnormal cell growth worked flaw-
lessly. Mr. Ruiz's cancer will not recur and his body is completely
free of it."

"Is it expensive?" AJ asked.

"No," Jayne said. "Most of the time we spent working on Ruiz was
making modifications to the existing therapy for human biology. Now
there's a team working on adapting the process so it will be compatible with human medical technology. I hate to say it, but I need to go,
because I'm a critical part of that team, given my knowledge of
human medicine."

"Kind of hard to argue with that," AJ said. "Bringing home a cure
for cancer would help a lot of people."

"No, AJ. It's not just cancer," Jayne said. "That's a small part of
what we did today. The same processes we used to adapt the cancer
therapy to Ruiz we then used to address the cardiovascular damage to
both men. We fixed degenerated tissues, nerve receptors ... the list
just goes on and on. AJ, this work will cure disease on Earth as we
know it."

"Fine, I suppose I can spend a few days getting caught up with
the boys. You go do your whole save-the-world thing. We'll talk later,"
AJ said.

Jayne smiled and then grabbed his cheeks, pulling him in for a kiss. The move earned them hoots from Ruiz and Frenchy.

"Ata boy," Lefty said, approvingly.

When they separated, Jayne's cheeks were flushed and she hurried away, embarrassed by the attention.

"That's one fine woman you have there," Ruiz said.

"I feel like I know her," French said.

"I already told you she served," Lefty said. "She was over there with us."

"I definitely would have remembered her," Ruiz said.

"Hey, you're talkin' about my girl," AJ said.

"Damn, I wish my old lady was still around," Ruiz said. "She was one fine woman. I'd give anything to have her back."

"Sorry, man," AJ said. "Now, we've got a bit of a problem we need to discuss, but this probably isn't the right place to do it."

"Is it about those gray, spindly lookin' boys who were shooting at us back home?" Frenchy asked.

"Those weren't boys," AJ said. "Those were Cheell. We aren't sure what their role in all this is. I'd like to take you fellas out for dinner, but we've all got prices on our heads, so we'll be eating in."

"Have any beer?" Ruiz asked.

"Nope, too heavy to bring all this way, and the beer they make around here all tastes like fruit," AJ said.

Lefty waggled his eyebrows. "That's not entirely true."

"You're saying you have a line on decent beer around here?" AJ asked.

"I might have brought a couple of suitcases of my favorite back with me," he said. "I was thinkin' of selling it, but with Queenie comin' in and these boys back from the brink, I figure maybe we've earned a couple of brews."

TWENTY-FIVE

FRAT PARTY

"That was a mighty fine dinner, Mrs. Jackson," Frenchy said, opening his third beer. "I can honestly say I don't recall ever having meatloaf that good."

"Please call me Lisa, Frenchy, and you're quite welcome," Lisa said. "Darnell, would you make a couple of plates and deliver them to our prisoners?"

"Maybe I could help out," Ruiz said. "You know that Hetra isn't such a bad gal. I mean for someone with a beak for a face. I kind of feel like maybe that fella she's runnin' with might be leading her down a bad path."

"Ruiz kind of took a shine to Hetra on the trip out here," Lefty explained, holding a beer out to Ruiz to let him know that no insult was intended.

"I don't see no problem with that," Ruiz said. "What's your plan for those two? I don't think I could get behind you hurtin' them or nothing. Well, maybe Kornat – he's an asshat – but not the girl."

"Nothing like that," AJ said. "So far, they've lived up to their part of the bargain. We just have one more task for them and then we'll call things even."

"Fair enough," Ruiz said, standing up so he could help Darnell.

"When's Queenie supposed to be here? I don't remember the last time I laid eyes on that old reprobate," Frenchy said, waving off a beer offered by Lefty.

"Any time now," Lefty said. "And that's fair warning. If you want more beer, you better get to it. Queenie will be thirsty."

"Did I hear one of you blokes disparagin' old Queenie?" A deep Australian accent echoed through *Big Max's* hallway and into the galley. A moment later, a lanky blonde man effortlessly dropped through the hatch, enjoying the attention he'd garnered. "Well, look at you all. What a good-lookin' group all snuggled up in here."

Frenchy got up and exchanged a hug with the young-looking Australian. "Good to see you ... ah ..."

"What's the problem, mate? Cat got yer tongue?" Queenie asked, grinning broadly as his seven-foot-tall, reptilian-skinned, Vred girlfriend climbed down behind him.

"Uh, er, so ... uh," Frenchy stammered, unable to form any semblance of a sentence.

"Mr. Roland LeBeau," Sharg's voice was a smooth alto. She was careful not to smile and expose her rows of sharp teeth. "McQueen has told me much about both you and Mr. Ruiz. My name is Sharg and I am pleased to make your acquaintance."

"You're ...," Frenchy stammered, looking from Sharg's face and then back to her hand. Finally, he decided it was safest to simply shake it. "A croc ... alien?"

"I am familiar with the similarities between Vred biology and Earth's non-sentient crocodiles," she said. "I assure you that ours is a very peaceful society and I mean you no harm."

"Breathe, Frenchy," AJ said, chuckling as he greeted Queenie and moved to greet Sharg. "Here, let me show you how it's done." Stepping between Frenchy and Sharg, he embraced the tall female Vred. "Darn good to see you, Sharg."

"I too enjoy the moment of our reunion," she replied.

"Hey, Sharg. I don't suppose our boy here has taught you about Earth beer yet, has he?" Lefty said, offering a beer to the large alien.

"He has, Lefty," Sharg said, accepting the beer. "Alcohol does not quickly metabolize in Vred physiology, so I will enjoy a portion of this and share the remaining with my Queenie."

"Whatever works for you," Lefty said, grinning.

"Frenchy, you got fat," Queenie said, sitting at the table. "I thought you were getting a makeover, eh?"

"Better fat than ugly," Frenchy joked.

"Nice one," Queenie said, knocking his beer can into the side of Frenchy's.

"Went to the spa earlier today, the pretty doctor said it would take maybe a month or two for things to really kick in. I'll be honest, though, I haven't felt this good in years," he said.

"I know just how you feel," Queenie said. "Kinda interesting that you did it without a rider. That kind of medicine's got a bit of promise to it, I think. Maybe useful outside this group, no?"

"That's partly why I asked you to join us, Queenie," AJ said.

"Figured it had to be something like that."

"When Darnell and Ruiz get back, I'll tell you what I've been planning."

"Sounds fair enough," Queenie said, popping open another beer. "Not sure I need all the details, though. Just tell me we're savin' the world and all that. I've already joined up, you know that, mate."

"We're coming," Darnell's baritone echoed into the galley just before Ruiz lowered himself through the hatch.

"It's obvious by now, but someone put a price on the heads of everyone in this room. Whoever it is, took out some good men before we figured out what was going on," AJ said.

"Who?" Ruiz asked.

AJ listed those who he knew had been killed.

"That's cold," Ruiz said. "You can probably skip the details in that case. I'm in, no matter what the ask is."

"Same here," Frenchy said. "I might not be in as good a shape as I was at twenty, but you put a gun in my hand and I'll do what needs doing."

"Appreciate you saying that but I figure I at least owe you the broad strokes," AJ said. "Turns out Hetra and Kornat aren't specifically bounty hunters. They're one step up the chain toward management and are responsible for deliveries."

"Hetra said something about you turning the tables on her," Ruiz said. "Said you had her dead to rights and didn't finish the job when most others would have."

"Don't get distracted by the pretty bird girl, Ruiz," Lefty said. "She's on the wrong side of this."

"No, I'm just sayin' maybe she leans our way a bit."

"Or she's playin' you," Lefty pushed.

"Hey, guys, stop," AJ said, recognizing that the combination of a long day and alcohol was causing tempers to flare. "Hetra has a role to play. If she plays nice, we won't cause trouble for her. If she comes after us, we'll deal with it when it happens."

"As long as Ruiz understands that just because his parts are working again doesn't mean we put the team at risk," Lefty said.

"You arrogant prick," Ruiz said, standing up, his face red.

"Lefty, leave it alone," AJ said. "Ruiz has his priorities straight. Nobody's questioning that."

"Better not," Ruiz said.

"Wait 'till he finds out that just about every Xandarj thinks he looks like a male model," Queenie said. "I bet he goes furry within a week."

"Guys, stop," AJ said. "Can we at least talk about this or are you all too damn drunk?"

"AJ, I'd say we should probably table the conversation until breakfast," Darnell said.

AJ nodded. "Anyone up for a Diamondbacks game?"

"You get that out here?" Frenchy asked.

"It's a couple of weeks old," AJ said. "If you know the score, don't tell me."

"I'd watch," Darnell said.

It was AJ's turn to make breakfast. He'd gotten an early start after turning in following the fourth inning of the game. Fortunately, Lefty and Ruiz had decided to leave things alone and AJ thought he'd heard them singing loudly only a few hours before he'd awoken.

"The whole ship smells like a frat party," Lisa said, yawning as she slipped into a chair at the table, accepting a cup of coffee from AJ.

"I don't think there's any beer left," AJ said, wiping down the table. "Otherwise, I'd kick them out."

"Probably good to let them have a free night," she said. "Lot of stress getting out here, especially for how old they are."

"I'm impatient to see them change," AJ said. "I can kind of see the men I used to know."

"They're in there," Lisa said. "I was."

"You know, you didn't really change that much," AJ said. "You kept yourself in good shape."

"That's probably the nicest thing you've ever said to me," Lisa said. "Thank you."

AJ shrugged. "Well, when you were pickin' on me back when I didn't want to give you any ammo."

Lisa's grin was lopsided. "Oh, I know it."

"I'm kind of wondering about something," AJ said.

"You're wondering how I might fit into this big mission you've been thinking about," she said.

"That's creepy the way you know what I'm about to say."

"Didn't take a genius to see what was on your mind."

"Thing is, I need you and Big D to stay back on this one."

"You talked to Darnell about this?"

"No," he admitted. "Wasn't sure how he'd take it."

"Sounds like you're expecting trouble. He won't appreciate being left behind."

"Not happening," Darnell said, entering the galley from the side entrance. "If you're going, I'm going."

AJ shook his head. "Not this time. I've looked at it from every angle. We just don't have room. That transport of Hetra and Kornat's is tiny. I don't want to hurt your feelings, but I need guys who have boots on the ground experience."

"I don't know what you're thinking, but I had plenty of time with boots on the ground and even more in the air with jackasses firing everything they had at me," Darnell said, growing angry. "Besides, Frenchy and Ruiz are fat old men. You can't seriously expect me to believe I couldn't take either of their places."

"I checked Jayne's expectations. When we arrive in the Cheell system, it'll be almost three weeks from now. Then it'll take us three days to get to the planet we're headed to. That's almost an entire month. Ruiz and Frenchy will be damn close to normal fighting shape by then. This isn't a competition, Big D. If there was any component of this that required someone to fly a ship into fire, you'd be top of my list, but this is a ground-pounders mission. It's the right call. Plus, I'm a little worried about leaving Lisa home, unprotected."

"Shit," Darnell said, sitting heavily in a chair. Lisa came up behind him and slipped her hands over his shoulders.

"If this goes wrong, I need someone to look after Doc, too," AJ said.

"That's bull. Amanda Jayne doesn't need anyone looking after her," Darnell said.

"I need you to be okay with this," AJ said.

Darnell nodded. "I get it. At least you're leaving Greybeard, so I don't have to face being replaced by a dog."

AJ's face blanched and he swallowed hard. Lisa slapped Darnell's shoulder and barked out a laugh. "Oh, baby, you got him good there."

Looking between them, AJ felt confused as he asked, "So, you know I'm taking Greybeard, right?"

"I know. Seamus is a cipher expert. You can't afford to leave him behind."

"You're an asshole."

"Still not done being pissed at being left behind," Darnell said.

"I owe you, buddy."

Ruiz slid down the ladder and turned to the room. "Something smells good in here," he said, slapping his stomach. "What's for breakfast?"

Lisa picked up a plastic bag and held it out to him. "If that hallway isn't spotless, there won't be any breakfast," she said. "And don't test me."

"Don't suppose I could have some of that coffee, first, could I?"

"No, but I'll make you a deal," AJ said. "You get that hallway cleaned up and when you're done, you can bring Hetra back with you. We're going to talk about the mission."

Ruiz's face lit up as he pulled the bag from Lisa's hand. "Now, that's something I can get behind."

"He looks better already," Lisa said, once the man was out of the room. "His face is thinner and he looks like he's moving better."

"I hope so," AJ said. "We're gonna need all the help we can get."

TWENTY-SIX

ENEMY WITHIN

"Hit me," Beverly said, leaning forward in her dollhouse-sized chair and tapping on the green velvet table in front of her.

"You have eighteen," AJ said. "Are you sure? You're not cheating are you?"

The trip through jump space from Xandarj to the Cheell solar system had been long and mostly uneventful, aside from a certain amount of bickering amongst the crew of seven squeezed into a transport ship designed for no more than five. AJ had scheduled his watch to coincide with their arrival in the Cheell system and he'd asked Hetra to sit in the co-pilot's seat, even though he'd bound her wrists.

"You hold the deck of cards, Albert Jenkins," Beverly said. "I am just making a good guess as to what is next."

"You get tossed out of Vegas for card counting," he said.

"Then it is good we are not in Las Vegas," Beverly said, tugging on her translucent green-brimmed visor.

AJ flipped the next card. "Four, you bust," he said, grinning. "What about you, Hetra?"

"Why would it matter if someone counted these cards? Isn't it always the same number?"

"There are a limited number of cards that add up to ten," AJ said. "I'm not sure hitting an eighteen is ever called for, though."

"Hit me," Hetra said.

"You have seventeen," AJ said, exasperated.

Hetra smiled and nodded. "It appears humans *are* capable of simple math." AJ sighed and flipped a four onto her pile.

"You've got to be kidding," he said.

"I win, again," she said. "Will you now release my bindings? I will not attempt to warn the Chautin Corporation."

AJ checked the display and noted their transition to the Cheell system would occur in minutes. He gathered the cards and slipped a sleeve around them, stowing them in a pocket next to his chair. "I'm sorry, Hetra, you've been a good sport, but we've got a lot riding on this."

"You will need to trust me once we exit jump space," she said. "If I do not provide correct answers, they will be more suspicious than I already expect them to be."

"Just stick to the story," AJ said. "Faramor Poecile wants her freedom, even if it means lying about capturing us."

"They will have an armed guard," Hetra said, rehashing an old argument.

"Farah told them she only caught *me*," AJ said. "How many guards will they have for one measly human?"

"You shouldn't underestimate how much the Cheell fear you," Hetra answered.

"Ten seconds, AJ," Beverly warned, making a show of folding up her card table and stuffing it into an imaginary slot on the forward bulkhead.

The most disturbing aspect of transition to normal space was the shift of perspective. While in jump space, the background shifted from blurred colors to complete blackness, but never a stable field of stars. The Cheell system was nestled in a populous portion of its galaxy and the stars were more densely packed than Earth's system.

Given the large population of the Cheell system's three inhabited planets, it was no surprise that the area near the jump space transition point was bustling with activity. A pair of armored vessels, both three times larger than their transport, slowly turned in their direction at the same moment an indicator on the communication display flashed.

AJ's heart thumped in his chest as the moment of truth had finally arrived. If Hetra gave them away, they wouldn't have time to make it back into jump space. "Answer it," he said, tapping a button on his display that would allow Hetra to communicate.

"This is Borna Eight Nineteen. We're sailing under Pertaf registration one seven five seven seven four," Hetra said, confidently. "We have no quarantine to declare."

"One moment, Borna Eight Nineteen." A gray-faced, big-eyed Cheell appeared on Hetra's screen. AJ couldn't tell if the Cheell was male or female, only that it seemed mildly interested, at best, in their ship. A few moments later, the Cheell turned its head, checking something off-screen. "What is your destination, Borna Eight Nineteen?"

"Cheell-3," Hetra answered. "I have a late delivery for the Chautin Corporation."

AJ bristled at Hetra's introduction of the word *late*. It wasn't in anything they'd discussed. He watched with concern as the Cheell typed on its keyboard and then looked up. "What was the nature of your delay?"

"Cargo was not properly secured," Hetra answered. "We had to wait for fresh packaging."

"Chautin confirms. Profitable travels." The Cheell's image immediately disappeared from the screen and the pair of armored vessels turned away.

"Nicely done," AJ said, leaning over and clipping the binding at her wrist. Leaning back, he turned to Ruiz, who'd been hunkered down behind his chair, out of the camera's line of sight. "It'll just take us a few days to sail to the planet."

Ruiz, who'd lost eighty pounds of fat and gained twenty of that back in muscle, shrugged. "Hurry up and wait," he said. "Life never changes that much."

AJ reached over his shoulder and scrubbed the freshly grown stubble atop the man's head. "Doesn't change, eh?"

"Reminds me of an old mission where we got stuck sitting in the backs of those trucks for almost thirty hours," he said. "Brass didn't want to let us out because they had intel of enemy movement. Were you in on that?"

"I don't recall it," AJ said.

"Total cluster. Turned out to be villagers trying to skedaddle. We ended up capturing ten old ladies and a couple of kids. I remember just appreciating getting out of the back of that truck."

AJ nodded. "How are you feeling?"

"Aside from cooped up, I'm perfect," he said. "Old me wouldn't be able to walk for weeks after sleeping on the floors like this. I'd forgotten just how nice it is to not wake up sore."

"I hear you there," AJ said.

AJ RESTED his hand on Hetra's shoulder. Three days of travel through the busy solar system had brought them to the fifth planet from Cheell's large, slowly expanding star that, while bigger and whiter than Earth's large sun, produced only slightly more energy. It was well known that the star was in its final phase, but also that it would be hundreds of millions of years before it finally started swallowing the system's planets.

"Once we're clear of your ship, our business is done, and Beverly will transmit the ship's control codes to you," AJ said. "I'd recommend getting out of here as quickly as you can."

"Sweet girl, if you find yourself back in my neighborhood, maybe we could grab a drink," Frenchy said, leaning against the wall next to her seat.

Hetra gave Frenchy an appraising look. "You do not look like the man I once met but you have also not changed," she said. "Are all Earthmen kind of heart even though they pretend to be otherwise? Albert Jenkins seems to be such a man as well."

Frenchy shrugged. Like Ruiz, he'd lost considerable weight and the once fine features of his face had been restored. "Some men fight because they like to fight," he said. "I fight only because it is the right thing to do. I would much prefer a vacation through my ancestors' vineyards with a beautiful woman."

"It is nice to have hope," Hetra said.

"Weapons check, boys," AJ said, joining his veteran squad in the packed hallway.

"I don't get why you're sending her away with our only escape vehicle," Ruiz said. "It's crazy. How are we getting out of here once we finish executing this crazy plan of yours?"

"We'll book a passage," AJ said. "It's not that hard. According to BB, Cheell law doesn't exactly look favorably on the bounty-for-hire business. The guys we're up against are operating outside of the law, so we shouldn't take much flack or have trouble chartering a ride home."

"That patrol seemed pretty chummy with Chautin," Ruiz grumbled.

AJ recognized the man's argumentative nature for what it was – nerves before combat.

"I made contact with Chautin again and am transmitting video of Albert Jenkins in our containment cell," Hetra called back. In fact, the video was from weeks before when he and Jayne had been captured, the only change being timestamps and removing Jayne from the scene.

"Let's hope they accept it," AJ said.

"If they don't, we won't know," Lefty said. "They'll bring us in either way and we'll be pinned down."

"It's not too late to turn back," AJ said. "You see the plan as well as I do at this point. I know it has a bunch of stink on it, but I can't imagine us getting a better shot at these guys."

"I liked it better when I wasn't the one making the plans and could just bitch about what the brass decided," Lefty said, sighing.

"Definitely a different perspective when we're the ones making the calls," AJ said. "The goal needs to be as few casualties as possible."

"No promises," Lefty said. "We have no idea how many guns we'll be up against."

"They've told us to come down," Hetra said. "It's a different drop-off location than I've done before. Are we moving forward?"

Adrenaline dumped into AJ's stomach. There were so many unknowns that he considered calling off the mission right at that moment. The only thing pushing him forward was the knowledge that without decisive action, there'd continue to be a price on the heads of all the people he loved. AJ exchanged a concerned look with Lefty, who gave him an almost imperceptible nod.

"Go ahead, Hetra," AJ said, checking his weapon status. He had a full charge and had dialed the weapon to a low setting that wasn't likely to be lethal for a Cheell wearing armor, but nothing was guaranteed in combat. That Chautin had struck first blood made the risks acceptable.

An hour later, after a bumpy entry into the planet's atmosphere, the transport leveled out. Through the tiny view he had of the transport's front window, AJ could see churning storm clouds that looked ready to release a torrent of rain.

"We're setting down in a hangar ten miles from a small city," Hetra said quietly. "There are eight people and three vehicles. They have a containment chair that it looks like they'll use to transport you."

"Chair?" AJ whispered. Beverly tapped into the ship's video feed and showed the scene to AJ. There was a chair with straps hanging from it and looked like something used to transport Hannibal Lecter.

"Are you ready, Albert Jenkins?" Hetra asked, walking back into the crowded hallway. "Remember, you are drugged and have difficulty walking."

AJ strapped his pistol to Greybeard's back and held his arms in front of him. Hetra placed a pair of cuffs on his wrists and ankles that had been modified so they had no locking mechanism. They would stay closed as long as there wasn't much pressure applied.

"I've got it," he said. "Let's do this."

Hetra pushed open the hatch which allowed cool moist air to swirl into the cabin. It was a relief for the inhabitants to breathe something other than the recycled air of the transport ship. Hetra gave AJ a shove and followed behind him.

He stumbled onto a slotted metal platform that had been pushed up next to the transport. A spray of rain blew in over the transport's hull and struck his back. The water was cold and felt like ice pellets, even though none of it was freezing on the ground.

Under Hetra's direction, he stumbled forward only to be met by a single Cheell who held a scanner that projected a thin grid of green lines when it was shined on AJ's face.

"The prisoner is confirmed," the Cheell said, dispassionately. "Payment is transferred."

Hetra gave AJ a hard shove in the back and sent him sprawling down the stairs and onto the hard pavement. "Crap hole ejecta!" she squawked.

Without wanting to, AJ reached forward to catch his fall and ended up breaking out of his arm cuff, something that was soon recognized by several armed Cheell who stood only twenty feet away.

"It is loose!" one cried out.

Every part of AJ screamed to get up and fight, but he resisted. Instead, he groaned and pretended to ineffectively crawl forward, even as four armed Cheell ran at him.

"That was unprofessional, Hetra Kairn," the Cheell with the scanner said, slowly backpedaling and putting distance between himself and AJ. "It will go in my review of your services."

"The human is disgusting," Hetra called over her shoulder. "Write whatever you want."

"Water," AJ croaked, licking at the pavement.

"Pick him up. Put him in the chair and let the doctor look at him," the Cheell ordered and then turned back to Hetra. "You were paid to transport in good condition!"

"He's alive. You deal with it," she said, stomping back into the transport and squeezing past the men who were ready to move.

"Go!" Lefty whispered to Greybeard just as three of the Cheell pushed weapons onto their backs and bent to help lift AJ into the restraint chair.

Greybeard sprinted from the transport, barely ahead of the four soldiers. Lefty, Queenie, Frenchy, and Ruiz poured through the door and spread out, acquiring targets and firing. Upon hearing the noise, AJ lurched to the right and bowled into two of the guards, pushing the smaller aliens to the ground. In the space of a couple of seconds, Greybeard arrived next to him, giving him access to his weapon.

The initial moments of combat were over even before Hetra had the transport ship lifting from the pavement. Even though they had quickly taken control, Hetra wasted no time, turning the ship around to flee. If this had been the only resistance, the mission would have ended as quickly as it had started, unfortunately, some sort of alarm had been tripped and a squad of armed Cheell poured through a door at the back of the hanger.

"Take cover!" Lefty demanded.

AJ raced across the pavement, searching frantically for the Cheell who'd scanned him. He might have missed the smaller Cheell if not for the device sitting a couple of feet from his prone body. A blaster round tore at AJ's armored side and shot pain into his ribs. He knew better than to stop and inspect the device, instead he dove over the Cheell and wrapped his arm around the alien's neck.

"Tell 'em to stand down," AJ growled against the skull, which had no apparent ears.

Blaster fire ricocheted back and forth across the hanger floor. Even if the Cheell wanted to stop the fighting, the scene was too active for anyone to listen to him.

"I am not important," the Cheell squeaked.

"I'd say the same thing," AJ said, dragging him over to his team, who'd taken up positions behind the parked vehicles. "Lefty, how many are we looking at?"

"Ten, maybe twelve," he said, holding his weapon around the front of the vehicle. He fired without line of sight. "There were eleven, now there's ten." Confidence filled his voice.

"What'd you do?"

"Camera on the gun. Rebel does the aiming," he said. "Surprised your gal doesn't do that for you."

"She's a pacifist," AJ said.

"Make that eight," Queenie said. "And really? Gertie helps me aim, too."

"Aww shit," Ruiz complained, spinning away from where he'd been standing, a patch of blood widening on his abdomen as he fell.

AJ knew Ruiz looked bad, but they were pinned down and even with Queenie and Lefty firing, they couldn't afford to lose a shooter. He jumped over to where Ruiz had positioned himself and lined up on the advancing Cheell.

"I help you aim," Beverly said, projecting a red dot along where his blaster would hit.

"You do," AJ admitted, even though he knew she'd never go for the camera setup Lefty and Rebel used. He fired a quick triplet and was gratified when the Cheell soldier ran back for cover.

"He's hurt real bad," Frenchy called, working on Ruiz.

AJ fired more shots to where the Cheell had holed up and turned to take in the scene. "Get him in that transport van," AJ ordered. "Lefty, Queenie, lay down suppressing fire. We're gonna get a ride outta here."

Lefty and Queenie increased their rate of fire even though they didn't have specific targets. AJ knew they had precious little time before reinforcements would arrive, so he grabbed the small Cheell and dragged him in behind Frenchy and Ruiz.

"No wonder there is a bounty on you," the Cheell complained. "You are murderers!"

AJ aimed his pistol at the Cheell's leg and fired, causing the

Cheell to scream in both horror and pain. "Don't you forget it," AJ growled. "Now start this truck up and get us out of here."

"I, uh, they'll never let you out."

"That's not your most pressing problem now, is it? You get moving or I'm gonna shoot your other leg." AJ said. "Lefty, Queenie, Greybeard, get in now. We're moving!"

The van lurched forward, spun in the hanger, and started onto a gravel road that was a hundred feet wide. The van used gravity repulsion, but with the unevenness of the road, it had little effect.

"Move over, Frenchy," Lefty ordered. "I've got a medkit and Rebel knows how to fix old guys."

"How bad?" Frenchy asked.

"How would I know?" Lefty growled. "Give me a minute."

AJ turned his attention to the Cheell driver. "What were you going to do with me once I was strapped into that chair?"

"You were to be delivered for questioning," he said. "By now, they know this has gone poorly. You have made your plight worse, Albert Jenkins. No one attacks Chautin."

"Worse than you guys trying to kill me all the time?" The Cheell didn't have an answer and kept quiet. "I want to talk to whoever put that contract out on us."

"You are asking the wrong people."

"I don't think so," AJ said. "You're collecting the bounty."

"Chautin is merely a conduit," the Cheell said. "We did not issue this bounty."

"Right, so why did you want to ask me questions?"

"It was a condition of the bounty," the Cheell said, shrugging.

"And after that?"

The Cheell remained silent.

"Look, I'm already deep in this. One more dead Cheell isn't going to change things," AJ said.

"You were to be disposed of."

"Mate, are you seeing all those vehicles?" Queenie asked, pointing out the front window.

AJ looked up. A horde of vehicles barely preceded the dust storm they'd kicked up.

"Nothing to lose, bubba," AJ said, pressing his pistol into the Cheell's neck. "If Chautin didn't issue the bounty, then who did?"

"Am I to believe you won't kill me if I tell you?"

"Think of it in the other direction," AJ said. "I'll absolutely kill you if you don't."

"The bounty was issued by a syndicate of Earth corporations in your medical sector," the Cheell said, slowing the van as the horde descended on them. "They wish to slow the release of medical technology on Earth."

"Well, hell," AJ said. "Why are we always our own worst enemies!?"

TWENTY-SEVEN
NO PLAN SURVIVES

"What's the play here, AJ," Lefty asked. "We're not shooting our way out of this one."

"I might have screwed the pooch," AJ said.

"Get what you came for, mate?" Queenie asked.

AJ nodded as the Cheell pulled to a stop having run out of room to drive. "Give me a copy of that contract," he said. "I need names, dates, everything."

"I am a mid-level functionary. I am unable to see all details," the Cheell said. "Please do not kill me. I speak the truth."

Greybeard barked, placing his paws on the Cheell's leg and pushing on him. Soldiers poured out of the surrounding vehicles but were slow to approach.

Beverly appeared, her rocket pack keeping her aloft between AJ and the Cheell. "Have him access the contract, perhaps Seamus can gain entry. We have little time."

"It feels like a last stand," AJ said.

"Albert Jenkins, time is of the essence! Tell him!"

"Okay!" AJ answered, holding his hands up defensively. "Log in and get me as much of that contract as you can."

"Right now? Here? I don't have my normal systems," the Cheell whined.

"If you want to make it out of here alive, you'll do as I say," AJ growled, pushing his pistol even harder into his neck.

"Yes, okay," he answered. "But you should know, a commander has arrived. He demands you all exit the vehicle, or you will be destroyed."

"Tell him we're coming out," AJ said, "and then get that contract."

The Cheell gulped heavily, but before he could start speaking the van was hit hard from the side, sending the occupants airborne as the vehicle rolled over. Chaos filled the interior. Instead of coming to a stop, the transport continued to move, skidding along the gravel as if being dragged. AJ just managed to catch a glimpse outside and saw the gathered soldiers all firing at once, only they were targeting something above them. In response, a low-sounding blurp preceded a bright flash. Two Chautin vehicles exploded and were tossed into the air.

Suddenly, with the sound of squealing metal, the van was lifted into the air. A bright yellow band appeared outside the window and AJ recognized it as a cargo strap. He realized what was happening and why the metal of the vessel's structure was complaining. "Darnell! Is that you? Stop compressing the straps. You've got us."

"Damn boots on the ground," Darnell answered, angrily. "I've pulled your ass out of so many fires and this is how you want to play it?"

AJ shook his head and looked for Beverly. "Did Seamus get that contract?" he asked.

"Perhaps not in its entirety, the Cheell recognized the intrusion and removed our access. We know the identities of the individuals who funded the bounties. There are two board members of health insurance corporations, two CEOs, and several untitled individuals," she said. "There is more than enough to implicate them."

"Big D, are you going to land this thing so we can come aboard?"

AJ had to shout due to the wind and rain that blew through the door and the gaps in the compressed vessel's cabin. "We've got injured."

"You're lucky, then," Darnell said. "Otherwise, you'd be riding it out down there."

"Will you let me go?" the Cheell asked.

The wind lessened as they approached the ground and when they were only a couple of feet from landing, the yellow strap suddenly retracted and the van fell, violently jarring the inhabitants.

"Not yet, but soon," AJ said, picking himself off the floor. "We're going to need your help to fully communicate just how much we're not going to put up with anyone sending bounty hunters after us."

"I will pass along your message," the Cheell said, hobbling toward the open door. "It does appear that as a group, humans are difficult quarry. At a minimum, a renegotiation of your price will be required to take into consideration the increased risk and associated damage to property."

AJ caught up with him and grabbed his arm, guiding him from the vehicle. "I think maybe a face-to-face might be nice."

"That is impossible," the Cheell said. "Chautin is a reputable business and would never allow for the open discussion of bounties."

"The problem with that thinking is that you can come to my house and crap on my doorstep without any thought to what happens when I come to your house," AJ said, jerking him toward *Big Max's* aft airlock.

"I thought you would free me," the Cheell squeaked.

"Probably still in the cards," AJ said, roughly tossing him through the airlock door as the rain intensified. "Your bosses just tipped their hand. They sent such a big force out to the middle of nowhere for this exchange for two reasons. First, they didn't want to be connected with whatever was going to happen out there. Second, if there was trouble and my friends came after me, we'd be looking at a big fight. High probability we'd just turn and run."

"What's going on, AJ?" Jayne asked, meeting him as he closed the airlock door against the pounding rain.

"Jayne! How in the world ...?" AJ asked.

"I don't understand," the Cheell said, looking warily between Jayne and AJ.

"Darnell told me what was going on and I asked to come," she said. "And we *are* going to talk about you running off on dangerous missions without talking to me first."

AJ closed his eyes and nodded. "It'll need to be later," he said.

"What is a tipped hand?" the Cheell asked, pressing more than he had before.

AJ pushed a button to send the elevator to the top deck and considered the small alien. "I can see it in your little gray face, alien," AJ said. "You already know where this fight is headed and you're scared."

"I assure you I do not."

"What are you talking about, AJ?" Jayne asked.

"Hang on a sec. How is Ruiz?"

"Queenie is treating him," Jayne said. "Back home, it would have been grievous."

"I need him," AJ said, stepping into the long corridor that was the primary access to the bridge as well as the hatches leading down into the crew quarters and galley.

"I'm not sure," Jayne said. "I'll go check."

"Thank you," AJ said, dragging the reluctant Cheell forward and then calling out, "Lefty, can you meet me on the bridge?"

"Coming," Lefty answered, his head popping up through the galley hatch.

"You ready to apologize yet?" Darnell asked, even before AJ made it into the bridge.

"Thanks for bailing my sorry ass out," AJ said. "I didn't want to drag you guys into this mess, but we'll have to get all warm and cuddly about it later."

"You need to get it through that thick skull of yours that we're stronger together," Darnell said.

"I get it. My bad."

"Damn straight," Darnell said.

"What's the plan, Jenkins?" Lefty asked, settling his back against the forward console.

AJ glanced nervously at Lisa. He hated the idea of dragging her and Jayne into combat. She seemed to read his mind. "Don't even think about playing that gender card right now. I've got as much on the line here as any of you," she said with a fire in her eyes.

"We need to take this fight straight to Chautin corporate offices," AJ said. "The whole reason the transfer was out in the middle of crapsville was that they don't want it splashing back on them. I say we bring this show right to 'em."

"You can't do that," the Cheell spoke up.

"Why?"

"There are innocent office workers there and the civilian patrols will not allow it," he said.

AJ frowned. "No innocent at Chautin."

"Police could be a problem," Lefty pointed out.

"BB, can you get an address for Chautin HQ?" AJ asked.

"Yes, they have a campus approximately forty-two miles northwest of our location," she said. "Cheell do have civilian law enforcement that will become alerted. They will have the technical capability to stop *Big Max*."

"They won't," he said, an ironic grin on his face.

"Why?" Lisa asked. "Of course, they will."

"They won't because our little buddy here is going to call his boss' boss and let them know we're coming," AJ said.

"You're going to warn them?"

"When we get a little closer, yeah," AJ said. "I'd bet everything that Chautin can't afford for this whole thing to go public. Remember, we have a legitimate complaint. Chautin has issued a contract on us. Tell me, is that legal, even for Cheell?"

"No, AJ. No civilization would allow contract-for-hire murders," Beverly answered. "You are suggesting that the civilian patrols will overlook your infractions as well."

"We've got an old Earth saying that I feel like the Cheell need a lesson in," he said.

"Here we go," Lisa said.

"Don't pick a fight with a pig, because you'll just end up rolling around in crap and the pig will love it," AJ said. "We tell Chautin we're coming, they're going to want to try to handle it in-house."

"What if they bring that large force we just ran into?" Lisa asked.

"They won't," Lefty and AJ said together.

"You seem pretty sure," Lisa said.

"There are no certainties in combat, only momentum," AJ said. "Chautin showed their hand. It's time for us to show ours. BB, can you pull up a topographic view of the Chautin campus?"

TWENTY-EIGHT

HOME TO ROOST

"We've got a civilian patrol on our tail," Darnell warned.

AJ's hand clamped around the Cheell's arm as he thrust the communicator back in front of his face. They were still five miles from Chautin's campus and had attracted attention he'd hoped to avoid. "You better talk to your boss and let him know that we're bringing this crap storm to his house, no matter what. He better call off those cops."

"I ... he won't ..."

"You're the first Cheell they're gonna hand over to your civilian patrol," AJ said. "They're going to blame this whole thing on you. Trust me. I don't care if they're Cheell or human, all politics works the same way."

The Cheell nodded as he accepted the communicator. He tapped on the side and pressed it to his face.

There were eight tightly packed into *Big Max's* short airlock, including Greybeard and Jayne, who hadn't been willing to stand by with so much riding on the outcome. They'd only left Lisa behind to ship's blaster and Darnell in the pilot's seat. The smell of sweat and tension-filled the confined space, bringing back old memories for the soldiers who gripped their guns, just waiting for that door to open.

"I don't miss this part," Frenchy whispered, gripping his blaster rifle.

"You got this," Ruiz said, clapping his hand on Frenchy's back. "I got your six."

"My boss wishes to speak with you," the Cheell said.

"Tell him to call off that patrol," AJ said. "We'll talk when we land."

"He does not wish you to land."

"AJ, they're getting pretty insistent," Darnell called again.

"Tell him the cops will be right behind us, his choice. We're coming in hot, either way," AJ said. "Darnell, how much time?"

"Thirty seconds," Darnell said. "I've got eyes on the campus."

The Cheell spoke rapidly into the comm device, then closed it suddenly, handing it to AJ.

"Let me guess, he didn't like your answer," AJ said.

"He said the patrol will not enter Chautin campus and you will be taken into custody upon arrival," the Cheell said. "I am no longer an employee of Chautin."

"Did he threaten you with legal problems if you tell anyone what happened?" AJ asked.

"It was more of an offer of a contract on my life," the Cheell said.

"Sounds like maybe you'd be better off helping us," AJ said.

"You shot me."

"Sorry about that," AJ said. "It's not like we didn't get the wound fixed up, though."

The Cheell nodded. "You should land in a different location than you plan. The office you wish to visit is in a different location."

"Where?" AJ asked.

"Cops are buzzing off," Darnell called back. "We're going in."

"Hang on, we've got a location update," AJ said as Beverly projected a map on the wall. The Cheell pointed at the new location, which apparently got communicated back to Darnell.

"Got it. We're starting to take small arms fire. It's gonna get a bit dicey. Lisa, back those guys off on that pedestrian bridge," Darnell said, distracted.

A loud explosion preceded the jostling of the ship as it landed unevenly. *Big Max's* engines whined as Darnell fought to regain level.

"That's about as good as we're gonna get," Darnell said. "Good luck, we'll provide as much cover as we can."

"What was that explosion?" AJ asked, checking out the courtyard image Beverly was providing to his HUD. A virtual blue contrail appeared and marked their desired path and AJ knew it was time to move. "Lefty, go!"

Darnell didn't need to explain the explosion as AJ's eyes raked over a pedestrian walkway that had collapsed, dust still billowing from the rubble. Following Jayne, AJ dragged the reluctant Cheell through the hatch. Sporadic blaster fire pierced the spreading dust cloud and Lefty adjusted their path to take advantage of the cover afforded.

"Contact left," Lefty said as calmly as if he was ordering coffee.

Without hesitation, Queenie, Frenchy, and Ruiz turned and smoothly returned fire from a pair of guards who were dressed in unarmored clothing. The action took only moments and the group moved through without any loss of time.

"What floor?" Lefty asked, noticing the elevator banks and stairwells in the building's atrium. A ding sounded and a flood of Cheell poured from the elevators. If not for Lefty firing into the air, they might have been deluged by the fleeing mob. Instead, Cheell scattered in every direction, turning away from the fire.

AJ shook his captive's arm. "No time to hold back. You're part of this now," he said gruffly.

"Four floors down," the Cheell said.

"Down," AJ ordered.

Lefty nodded and led the group into a stairwell that had considerably fewer Cheell in it than had been exiting the elevators coming from the upper floors.

"How far?" Lefty asked.

"Fourth level," AJ said.

"Copy."

The crowds thinned as they descended, but once they'd turned to the final level, blaster fire sprayed across the stairwell. A couple of rounds knocked Lefty to the side.

"Grab him. They're trying to protect the elevator shaft," Frenchy said, leaping across Lefty's body, his rifle firing on full auto.

Ruiz and Queenie both leaped over Lefty and followed Frenchy, bellowing a wordless battle cry at the top of their lungs.

"Aww shit," AJ said. "Jayne, I'll drag Lefty to you. Help him but keep your head on a swivel."

He shoved the Cheell he'd been babysitting against the wall, forcing him to slide to the ground. He hated losing his hostage, but his team needed support if they were to succeed. He dragged Lefty into the outside corner of the stairwell and then bounded down the rest of the stairs to assess the situation.

The corridor they'd come to was a full-out firefight and Frenchy was already on the ground and no longer shooting. Queenie and Ruiz were pressed against opposite walls and had taken defensive positions behind large planters, both of which were taking a beating from automatic blaster fire and were quickly crumbling away. Queenie's aim was unerring and soon the return fire was limited.

"This fight doesn't have to go this way," AJ called out. "I just want to talk to the guys in charge."

"You are shooting. We will not speak with armed villains," a Cheell called back.

"You put a contract out on our heads," AJ called back. "What did you think we were going to do?"

"This office has nothing to do with such dealings," the man answered. "That is another division."

"Sucks to be you then," AJ called back. "You'd better find someone who can talk or this is gonna get a lot uglier."

"Our forces will overwhelm you soon," the Cheell called back. "I'm nobody. You are naïve to have come here."

AJ swallowed hard. If he came up dry, getting out again was going to be a problem.

"That is Serkanen," a quiet voice said next to him. "He is the top Chautin officer on the contract with the Earth corporations."

AJ glanced to the side and found the Cheell he'd roughed up standing beside him. "Why are you here?" he asked.

The Cheell shrugged. "My fate is now linked to yours."

"Queenie, if you have a shot, take everyone but that guy speaking," AJ said.

"Cake," Queenie answered, popping off a couple more shots and dropping one of the Cheell who stood in front of Serkanen.

"There is no benefit in shooting us!" Serkanen cried out in frustration. Just then, the elevator door opened and Serkanen jumped into it. The powerful Cheell laughed as the door closed. "You have lost now!"

"I hate that guy," Queenie said, standing up.

"Jayne, we need help," AJ said, rushing back to Frenchy. The man was still breathing, but his armor had been pierced and he was bleeding badly.

"AJ, they're rolling in some serious weight out here," Darnell said. "Things are gonna get tough real soon."

"Dammit," AJ said, racing for the stairwell, hoping to outrun the elevator. After only half a flight, he was brushed back by gunfire and had to retreat. "We're pinned down. Darnell, if you can get out, you should take off."

"Not happening. Besides, we can make quite a mess if things turn that direction," Darnell said.

"Bubba, we're in deep down here," AJ said as Ruiz and Queenie flanked him and returned fire.

"Albert Jenkins, you should return," the Cheell called out.

"Got a bit of a firefight here," AJ called back. "Can it wait?"

"No," the Cheell answered. "It is important."

"Of course it is," AJ said. "Hold this?"

"We got it, mate," Queenie said.

AJ raced back and pulled up short as he made it to where Jayne was tending to Frenchy. Standing just outside the elevator door was Serkanen, who was gingerly holding an arm that was bleeding profusely. Greybeard barked loudly and exited the elevator behind him, snapping at the Cheell's backside.

"Well, that's a nasty turn of events, now isn't it?" AJ said. "Call off your soldiers or this is gonna go real badly for you."

"What do you want?" Serkanen asked.

"Call 'em off and we'll talk," AJ said.

EPILOGUE

"Good afternoon, folks, and welcome to Chase Field, home of the Arizona Diamondbacks! It's a beautiful afternoon for game one of this year's World Series."

Static filled the stadium as the announcer was cut off.

"Uh, sorry to interrupt your afternoon, folks." AJ's voice carried over the stadium's loudspeakers. "If I could draw your attention directly above the stadium, you'll see a big silver spaceship and maybe a couple of F-16 fighters escorting us in."

A collective gasp rose from the crowd.

"I see it!" A teen stood up, pointing, followed by dozens of similar declarations.

"No reason to panic, this is a planned part of the World Series festivities," AJ said. "So, sit back, relax and enjoy the show!"

"You will cease all communications or you will be fired upon!" The comm set on *Big Max's* bridge relayed the excited demand. The threat was real, as a pair of F-16s had quickly caught up to the massive, rapidly descending vessel.

"Will you talk to them, Big D? I'm kind of in the middle of something here," AJ said, placing hands over his ears.

"Don't fire," Darnell said over comms. "Our current mass exceeds five thousand tons and there are seventy thousand spectators in the stadium directly below us. Do not fire!"

AJ nodded, mouthing *good* to him.

"Field personnel, please clear off so we can proceed with our planned demonstration," AJ announced over the stadium's speakers.

"They're getting mighty itchy, AJ," Darnell said, warning in his voice.

"Hang tough, Big D," AJ said. "They're not going to shoot us down over seventy thousand people."

The field came into view and Darnell slowed *Big Max* until it stalled thirty yards above second base and rotated, giving the spectators a great view of the large vessel.

"How's that for an entrance?" AJ announced over the public address. "Can I have a big round of applause for our pilot? Go ahead and set her down, Captain, and show the good people of Arizona the wonders of the latest in alien technology. That's right, folks, you heard it here first. This is a freshly purchased, bona fide alien spaceship."

"You know we're going to leave divots, right?" Darnell asked, muting AJ's outgoing.

Duh. AJ mouthed.

"Now that we've landed, I'll ask that you turn your attention to the big screen and we'll play a short public service announcement so we can get on with the game," AJ said.

His face appeared on the big screen as a pre-recorded video started. "Aliens live among us. They're not only friendly, but they've brought along with them the cures for every disease known to mankind. In addition to this public announcement, which is going out over every satellite, we've sent massive volumes of data to every research institution on the planet with all the information required to make you and your loved ones healthy once again. The thing is, this is information your government and the healthcare industry don't want you to know. They've been working hard to keep you in the dark about aliens and their extraordinary technology – but now you know. You need to make sure you tell ..."

The video stopped as power was cut off to the entire stadium.

"That was quick," AJ said, sighing.

"Time to pay the piper," Darnell said, kissing Lisa. He knew it might be the last time he'd be allowed to see her.

"This is the right thing," Lisa said.

As a group, Lisa, Darnell, Frenchy, Ruiz, and AJ made their way back to the elevator and then out onto the field, where they lined up and knelt, placing their hands over their heads.

"DO you know what kind of pandemonium you've caused?" Baird asked. "I suppose you think you're heroes."

Two weeks had passed. AJ had lost track of his friends, having been separated from them immediately after being captured.

"Did you know Earth's major healthcare CEOs had taken contracts out on our lives?" AJ asked.

"No," Baird said. "We suspected it might be the case, but we didn't have anything we could move on."

"I suppose that contract I brought back – proof that backs up what I'm saying – was conveniently lost?" AJ said, confident he was right.

"AJ, the unrest in America is extreme," Baird said. "There's widescale rioting and thousands of people have died. You screwed up."

"Give it a rest, Major," AJ said. "If you guys spent even a few minutes looking at the data we dropped, you'd know you could be saving millions of lives a year."

"And if we did, what about the population?" she asked. "It'd balloon."

"That's the line you're going with?" AJ asked. "Disease is good. It keeps the population down?"

"No," Baird said, shaking her head. "But it's a real problem and you don't have to deal with it because you went rogue."

"You didn't give us much of a choice," AJ said. "You were too worried about foreign relations and making money."

Baird shook her head. "You've made a huge mess. Wouldn't it be nice if we could all live in your black-and-white world? Did you even think about what happens to all those millions of people who will lose their jobs because we don't need hospitals anymore? You didn't give us any time to transition. The world can't handle this kind of change so quickly."

"You underestimate humanity," AJ said.

"You're dangerous, Jenkins," Baird said. "You don't think about who gets hurt when you do whatever you think is the right thing."

A knock at the door interrupted their conversation. "Who's that?" AJ asked.

"I want you to know that I don't agree with what you did," Baird said. "I think you're reckless and self-serving. If it was up to me, you'd be locked away for the rest of your life."

"I lived a good life," AJ said, shrugging. "So, humanity has some adjusting to do. Did you know the world's governments knew about aliens and what their technology could do for us before my wife died of cancer?"

Baird's lips thinned and she didn't respond for a few seconds, not until there was another knock at the door. "I hope I never see you again, Albert Jenkins."

She stood, walked to the door, and pulled it open. She was replaced by a pair of suited men, who visually swept the room and stood inside the door. They were followed by a much older man who, in person, looked different from AJ's recollections.

AJ stood and saluted.

"At ease, Mr. Jenkins. I'm pretty sure you're a civilian and aren't required to salute anymore." The man returned his salute, all the same.

"Thank you, Mr. President," AJ said. "For the record, I didn't vote for you."

"I won't hold that against you," POTUS said, a well-known smile spreading across his face. "Do you know why I'm here?"

"I don't," AJ said. "Although, I could probably guess since we haven't been making a lot of friends lately."

"No, I suspect not," the President answered. "I'm here to offer you a way out."

"Out of ...?"

"This general mess you're in," he said.

"I'm not going to deny what I said in that stadium."

"I wouldn't ask you to," the president said. "Thing is, I need a straight shooter on my team, someone who's seen what's out there, will make an honest assessment, and won't pull any punches."

"Never been much for politics," AJ said, chuckling.

"That's what I need. Did you know my daughter is sick? Not everyone knows that," he said. "I understand your wife was sick before she died."

AJ nodded. "That's true."

"You made claims about what could be done with alien technology," he said. "How people could be healed. Our top scientists are looking at the data and they say it's legitimate. Is it?"

"Did you find Amanda Jayne yet?" AJ asked. "We dropped her in Germany. I figured you guys would have already picked her up."

"We did," he said. "What do you say, Mr. Jenkins, will you join the team? There's a full pardon in it for your entire crew. Jayne included."

"So that's what got Baird all fired up."

"She's not your biggest fan."

"How long of a gig?" AJ asked. "I've got a junk business I'd like to get back to on Xandarj."

"Give me two years," POTUS said. "Together, we'll change the world."

AJ shook his head. "If someone had asked me to shake your hand when you got elected the first time, I'd have told them they were nuts; it would never happen."

"And now?"

"Seems like this might be bigger than all that," AJ said.

"So, that's a yes?"

"That's a yes," AJ said. "When do we get started?"

But of course, that's another story entirely.

ABOUT THE AUTHOR

Jamie McFarlane is happily married, the father of three and lives in Lincoln, Nebraska. He spends his days engaged in a hi-tech career and his nights and weekends writing works of fiction.

Word-of-mouth is crucial for any author to succeed. If you enjoyed this book, please consider leaving a review, even if it's only a line or two; it would make all the difference and would be very much appreciated.

FREE DOWNLOAD

If you'd like to receive automatic email when Jamie's next book is available, please visit http://fickledragon.com. Your email address will never be shared and you can unsubscribe at any time.

For more information
www.fickledragon.com
jamie@fickledragon.com

ACKNOWLEDGMENTS

To my wife, Janet, for polishing myriad rough passages so they are readable and kindly fixing my poor grammatical habits. Also to Diane Greenwood Muir for excellence in editing and word-smithery. I cannot imagine working through these projects without you both.

To my beta readers: Carol Greenwood, Kelli Whyte, and Chuck Rivers for wonderful and thoughtful suggestions. It is a joy to work with this intelligent and considerate group of people. Also, to my advanced reading team, you're a zany, fun group who I look forward to bouncing ideas off.

Finally, to Elias Stern, cover artist extraordinaire.

ALSO BY JAMIE MCFARLANE

Junkyard Pirate Series

Spaceship Troopers Series

Privateer Tales Series

Printed in Great Britain
by Amazon

83688022R00180